Perilous Shores

Traveler's Luck, Volume 1

Eric Gibson

Published by Thrillingspree Books, 2023.

This is a work of fiction. Similarities to real people, places, or events are entirely coincidental.

PERILOUS SHORES

First edition. November 28, 2023.

Copyright © 2023 Eric Gibson.

ISBN: 979-8223734789

Written by Eric Gibson.

Also by Eric Gibson

Traveler's Luck
Perilous Shores
Poison Harbor

Standalone
Apothecary Inc.
Press Heart to Join

Watch for more at https://www.thrillingspree.com.

Chapter One

Uncharted islet in the Antylia Archipelago

Nowen had succumbed to the temptation that he so rarely felt. The urge to participate, to form ties. He just wanted to be left alone to pursue his work, but without support from his superiors, his work had quickly dead-ended. He trailed behind and watched the other mages cautiously. Instructor Darden, a fit man of indeterminate old age, led the group at a brisk pace. He looked more like a scribe than a mage, though Nowen supposed, the two overlapped in the case of a wizard specialized in the calculations of teleport rings. Behind the instructor, walking side-by-side as always, were Gladlow and Meese. The stoic Gladlow would look even less mage-like himself but for his two concessions to tradition. A broad-sleeved, purple, hooded robe, reaching just below the knees of his trousers, and a straight walnut staff, the top half bound in elaborately tooled leather. Both affectations looked quite wizardly. His lack of traditional beard made him look young, and the curly black hair did nothing to compensate.

Their destination had been nearly invisible until the boat was in danger of running aground. A floating plank walkway made for an unsteady dock but allowed a dry landing on the shallow sandbar. Loose sand soon gave way to limestone and a narrow path between waist-high rocks. The way opened into a circular depression without the group slowing down. Nowen saw they crossed an etched magic circle covering the floor of the depression, its sigils partially obscured by blown sand and accumulating guano.

Nowen asked, "Why not jump us to this circle? Is it broken?"

Meese said, "We're keeping a hand on the purse strings." He removed his garish, wide-brimmed hat and mopped his forehead. Though having a build often referred to as stout, he was practically weedy by his people's measure. Meese was of the Dwarrow presumably, by his four-foot-four, however there was no trace in manner or speech. His beard was trimmed in the Human style of bushy and medium length, while his hair was clipped short and styled carefully. His robes and hat were crimson with orange accessories wherever appropriate. Nowen understood that Meese only wore the hat in order to remove it with a flourish and slick his hair down with one hand. He did this when buying time to think, or when passing any woman.

The sandstone path went on for another dozen yards and led to a second clearing, this one more exposed. The circle on the ground was better cared for.

Nowen looked back at the trail and asked, "Did we really just walk through a magic barrier? I didn't feel anything."

Instructor Darden began his spell and nervousness rose before Nowen's first teleport.

Meese said, "We only call it a barrier because the Crown uses the code name *Rampart*. It has no influence inside or outside its border. The only thing it seems to bar is dimensional travel through it."

Gladlow said, "That's not accurate. You can jump through if you can see your target. It's more that spells can't see through it."

Nowen asked, "How did the Institute manage to secure the one piece of land on the map where we can walk across it?"

Meese said, "This piece of land wasn't here when the map was drawn."

Gladlow said, "Hush. It's time."

The three stepped into the circle and the world changed around them.

• • • •

The *CHS Indomitable*

Wellstone studied the roster scrawled on a hanging slate. It was good policy to know who was where, but this time she was looking for something specific. Divers rose in the ranks by a number of methods, not least of which was luck. Regardless of why, the bigger your haul, the better your territory. The giant urchins clustered together occasionally, no one knew why, but it made for quick work. A streak of silver urchins might catapult a diver up the rankings, or a graveyard of shells might be left by the ravenous binging of some oversized species of triggerfish or crustacean. Luck, however, didn't last. Eventually, skill or determination would have to do the rowing, so to speak. Even with all three traits on ample display, no one rose as fast as a diver by the name of Pel. On this voyage, Wellstone had watched a slew of seemingly random events cause havoc with the roster. This wasn't terribly unusual, but everything that occurred, raft reassignment, illness, injury, or lost equipment, seemed to ease the way for one woman.

"Bring her in," Wellstone said without taking her eyes off the leaderboard.

"Aye, chief," Rillan said, waving down his younger counterpart Carlin before she could comment.

Wellstone caught this from the corner of her eye and turned to her subordinates. "What is it?"

Rillan raised his hands as if to protect himself from involvement.

"It's just," Carlin said, "she's number six now. Raft One."

Wellstone waited and Rillan declined to comment.

"Nobody cared that we questioned her before, but now... well, none of them are accusing her of anything. Every squid will blame us if she breaks her streak." Carlin looked between the two of them and sighed. "I'll bring her to the office after galley."

Wellstone thought the girl looked tired, not physically, she was as tireless as your average twenty-year-old Human. She performed her duties in an exemplary manner all the while pursuing her passion for marine research. She normally handled the double career with a sweet-as-honey attitude, even when twisting elbows and smashing stills, but once per month, she was plagued by nightmares. She was on her third sleepless night.

Wellstone asked her first deputy, "Did you do the other thing?"

Rillan shrugged. "We raided Jonn's not-so-secret operation. We ignored the still and tipple to make clear we were looking for other things."

"Anything to report?"

"Nothing much. What were you expecting?"

"From Jonn, nothing much," Wellstone said, "But if any of the others are moving Crown property off the ship, our only chance to find it will be when they're looking for a better hiding place." She walked away leaving her deputies to follow.

Carlin asked, "Who's next?"

"I think... Daine."

Rillan swore under his breath.

Wellstone smiled cruelly. "You shouldn't be encouraging the squids to break rules."

"There's no rule against it. Not really. And he's a free-diver so it doesn't interfere with the harvest."

Wellstone said, "He's supposed to be catching us food."

Carlin asked, "Rule against what?"

"I'm paying a bonus if he can find me a Jova shell." Rillan shrugged. "We're going to make an offering of it for a good birth."

Carlin said, "Jova isn't a goddess of fertility."

"No," Rillan said, "but she's a protector of women. Lissa thinks it can't hurt."

"You know, it's only called a Jova snail because it has a pretty shell, it doesn't actually have anything to do with the goddess."

"It's special enough to carry her name, so..."

Carlin added, "The locals' word for it means 'nasty biting snail.'"

Rillan said, "Well, it's not the strangest thing she's demanded, so just let me row with the current, aye?"

Wellstone let her two deputies prattle on as they wended their way to the lower decks. She rather liked Humans, and these two in particular, but she would never understand the need for so much talk. Humans didn't just talk, they argued. They didn't trade, they haggled. If they didn't have the facts, they could at least share their opinions. At length. She knew why the Human tongue had become the common language throughout most of the known world, they overwhelmed the others with sheer quantity.

There weren't a great number of her people at sea, but she wasn't interested in starting a family for another few decades anyway. She fit in just fine with the mostly Human population of the Crown fleet. From time to time, upon seeing her four-feet-eleven, someone would comment that they thought her kind were smaller. The Dwarrow were known by other peoples for many traits that were either never true, or reflected the antiquated practices of isolationist clans that hardly represented the entirety of the mountain people. Helena Wellstone was, admittedly, born deep underground in the fastness of a cavern stronghold, but hadn't so much as entered a cave or dug a hole since her twenty-eighth birthday. She *crafted* little more than a fine stew and *forged* absolutely nothing at all. Her only incontrovertible racial quality was a certain sturdiness that she would not trade for anything after working a decade aboard the Crown fleet.

"Daine, how fair you this fine afternoon?" Wellstone said while knocking outside the opening. There were no doors on this deck, and she took advantage to step inside. Daine's cabin was double the size of the others, but his duties were doubled as well, serving as he did as unofficial divemaster. Aboard one of the rafts he'd be referred to by the half-mocking title of commodore, but free-divers dropped over the side without the benefit of enchanted charms or a platform to rest on. They held their breath, using weights to speed their way down, and ropes to ease their way up. Their efforts improved the health and morale of everyone aboard ship, but more importantly, saved the Crown a small fortune in supplies. In addition, they hauled and stowed the rafts and did a large share of urchin processing.

"Helena," said Daine with a big smile. "Closing in on the next bonus. We're on our way out if you'd like to walk and talk." He grabbed up a bag of weights and started to slip past her, but the two deputies filed into the room. Rillan gave him a friendly nod and began looking through crates and net bags. Carlin flanked him and tried to look stern. Daine didn't seem worried. Though tall and strong, the young woman was nonetheless a head shorter than him and the bright pink head-wrap holding back her springy locks did little to intimidate. They all observed Rillan as he moved the panel hiding the still and gave the closet a perfunctory search. He did little more than rattle a few flasks of the seaweed liquor the sailors called treenail. Daine watched this with amusement. "If you tell me what you're lookin' for, I can surely help you find it."

Rillan said, "There doesn't seem to be anything amiss. We'll let you be on your way."

Daine said, "We've got our eye on some tasty looking runner fish—"

"After I take a wee peek in the bag."

Grabbing Carlin's tunic in his free hand, Daine threw the lass into Rillan, causing the two to go down in a tangle of arms and legs. He hauled back the bag of weights and looked at the sword Wellstone had drawn. He absolutely towered over her, but she could imagine him trying to calculate his chances. She stood relaxed and waited for him to decide. He dropped the weights in Carlin's lap, eliciting a feeble protest. Rillan dusted himself off and without taking his eyes off the big sailor, snatched up one of the flasks and downed a healthy portion. Daine gave a half-shrug. That was fair.

"A few copper ones, chief," Carlin said, dropping four copper lumps on the floor and continuing to dig through the bag.

Daine said, "Those were found on the sea bed. The lads give 'em to turn in."

Wellstone sheathed her sword as she stepped forward. "It doesn't matter where they come from, failing to hand in lanterns guarantees the lash."

"They get passed around a few times, but they always make their way to the purser's. You know that's how it's always worked..."

She narrowed her eyes. "Doesn't seem like enough to get you so bothered. Rillan?"

Rillan began thoroughly searching the man, but sailors wore little, and squids even less. Rillan shook his head at her.

Daine said, "I feared for my bonus. I'll lose half my pay—"

Wellstone said, "That's a lovely shirt, Daine. I don't think I've seen you wear it... or any shirt really."

"Kasandra presented me with it," Daine said, looking over at Rillan, "the bosun's mate?"

Rillan nodded in appreciation.

"She was making fun, but what kind of fool turns down a gift from a woman like that?"

Wellstone gently took his hand and pushed the roll of his sleeve up to his elbow, exposing a leather strap. He didn't resist as she turned his arm over, revealing the breathing charm buckled to his forearm.

Any vestige of camaraderie was gone from her voice. "You'll see her again when her master garrotes you to the mast."

Carlin unstrapped the Tesco's Breather and handed it to her chief. Wellstone held it towards the criminal and asked quietly, "How did you get this? The only ones not accounted for—"

"Helena, you have to believe me—"

"The diver from earlier today," Wellstone said, snapping her fingers at Carlin.

"Steppa, from Raft Six. The longboat was called out to search, but they found nothing."

Wellstone said, "Rillan, order the longboat out again. Take the squid search team this time. They're looking for a weighted corpse somewhere outside his dive sector. Ask the quartermaster to hold all of Raft Six for questioning."

"I think the girl's ready," Rillan said, trying to look earnest.

Wellstone was in no mood for his nonsense, but Carlin spoke up. "I want this one." Wellstone eyed her for any trace of reticence. She had to be fearless to free-dive over the side of the *Indomitable*, without pay no less, but she had never once volunteered to set foot on a smaller boat.

Wellstone said, "Go." Carlin hurried out. A longboat crew was always at the ready. They'd be on their way in moments. Wellstone placed the breather in a pocket and took a couple of flasks from the still. Tossing one to Daine, she opened the other and took a long pull.

"A last drink for the condemned?" He twisted the cork out but didn't drink.

She said, "It was likely a murderer who sold you that. If they have him to execute..."

"I... honestly don't know what I was going to do with it—"
Wellstone asked, "Who sold it?"

"Mickel," Daine said. Then he finally drank. "One of my divers. He couldn't be the killer, but I don't know where he got it. He'll talk to me though." He pleaded, "Will you speak for me?"

She almost shouted her words. "I'll tell the godsdamned truth. But I'll not ask for your death. Let's find Mickel."

They made their way in silence. Daine had lied and another dive wasn't scheduled for hours. The free-divers would be in the secure hold cleaning urchins. The aft of the hold was practically a vault. The precious metals would remain below, while the shells and viscera were hauled up to be dumped before the *Indomitable* moved to new territory. The creatures' gonads thickened the ever changing chowder, and the lantern-shaped mouth structures thickened the Crown's coffers. The three wove through the orlop deck, seemingly past a hundred women and men, performing as many different tasks. Wellstone reached for the ladder and the deck jerked out from under her, accompanied by the deafening roar of shattered timbers and shearing iron. Her first thought was they had run aground, but the ship was at anchor and often took two hours to set sail. Seawater poured sideways from the hatch below and when she gained her feet, she realized the ship was listing to port. The floor she stood on was now the joint between the deck and the port bulkhead. Most everything heavy was secured, but the valley they stood in was rapidly filled with sliding ropes, tools, and sailors. The press of bodies split as mobs tried to scramble to the fore and aft hatches. Whichever choice she made, they would be at the back of the crowd. The water reached a depth that made it impossible for Wellstone to stand. She tried to clamber up the deck but slid back into the valley. Daine was pushing into the crowd, the regular crew and artisans only able to resist his strength with sheer numbers. The waterline passed over the lower deck hatch but the swirling torrent could be felt strongly. She thought the water was rising more slowly, but it would fill the deck in minutes. She turned in time to raise her arm against a glancing blow from a plank of wood.

"I'll be having that charm, Helena." Rillan swung again, smashing her arm back into her face and sending her under. She surfaced expecting a killing strike, but Daine had an arm wrapped around Rillan's throat from behind. His other arm held Rillan's knife wielding hand out away from them. The deputy's face was already purple as he clawed at the sailor's arm.

"I had the same idea," Daine said. "Go. Break into the purser's office and bring as many breathers as you can."

Wellstone stopped treading water and let herself sink. She fished the leather band out of her pocket and strapped it around her throat. She had trained with the breathers but knew she wouldn't be able to force herself to take that first breath until her lungs screamed for air. She swam close enough to the hatch to grab the railing and pulled herself through the lessening current to the underside of the hatch. She was able to pull herself along the rafters to reach the aft before she felt the rising panic. She pushed out every bit of air she could and nearly blacked out before taking a painful, desperate gulp. She thrashed for a moment as her mind tried to convince her body it wasn't drowning. The last bubbles rose from her mouth and she swam down through the open door of the office. She made her way to the security cabinet and jammed her thick sword into the gap near the lock. She heard talk that the cabinet was protected or cursed but had never been able to find out the truth. This operation was so cheap, they probably spread rumors rather than pay a mage to hex it. She gave the blade a savage twist. The cabinet burst outward in a blinding flash of short-lived sparks and boiling water.

She jerked awake in a slowly swirling cloud of burned parchment and leather. She scrabbled around the remains of the cabinet only to find dozens of melted charms, some fused into lumps of three or more. Her tears were swept away underwater but she still sobbed in frustration. A scorched wooden box on the floor of the cabinet had somewhat protected its contents from the fury of the fire-trap she had triggered. If only she had been so lucky. She could feel intense pain rising on her face and hands. She opened the box and grabbed the small tangle of broken straps and loose charms. One of the quartermaster's lads would have spent the return voyage repairing the buckles. It was Wellstone's hope that they would still function if the charm itself was undamaged. She stuffed them in a pocket and swam for the door. It was nearly pitch black, but the disorientation she felt when the ship first listed was gone. With its corridors filled with water, she couldn't tell if the ship was sideways or upside down, but it didn't matter. She knew every inch of her home and made her way quickly to the deck above. She was much too late. She tried not to look at the faces of the crew she swam around and under. Being surrounded by the dead made her long to draw her sword, but she had left it behind. She unbuckled the scabbard and let it sink. As she neared the hatch to the weather deck, the ship seemed to lurch upward with a loud groan. She gave up carefully skimming past her dead shipmates and clawed her way to the hatch using anything in reach. She burst from the hatch and took a second to reorient herself in the blue light. The vessel was resting to port. The ship hadn't risen upward but moved sideways along the sea bottom. She swam up to clear the bulwark and came face to face with the nightmare of every sailor. She froze and continued to drift upward as enormous reptilian eyes followed her. It seemed to decide she wasn't worth killing, or perhaps it could see she wasn't carrying anything now belonging to it. It shoved the ship's keel, moving it another dozen yards along the sea bed and into ever deeper water. As she rose, Wellstone could no longer make out details, but the monster was massive enough to move a ship six times its size. She began swimming but couldn't bear to surface and leave herself completely blind to what was moving beneath her. She was content to move away from the deeps. The sea grew warm, but she felt it might just be the salt on her burns.

· · · ·

Raft One, starboard line.

Pel swam along the sea bed to the giant ink-black urchin and thrust her weighted spear. Just before contact she planted her right foot in the sand and spun to the side avoiding a foot-long spine fired like a crossbow bolt from near the point of impact. She felt the delicate shell crack but waited and checked her surroundings. A mile outside the reefs, shallower waters let the sun shine bright. She was secretly terrified of the depths she was forced to hunt while earning a spot on the more desirable diving platforms. She had recently begun toying with the idea of coming back next year and working her way to the end of the line again but knew it was impossible. She'd soon be suspected of smuggling and blacklisted. Though she should be able to avoid any other penalty, she would certainly be banned from diving again. The three-foot urchin appeared to shrink in size as every spine receded a few inches. She used her spear to turn the creature over and examine the pentagonal mouth. There was a great deal of blackened corrosion, but it seemed healthy. That was the trick with the black ones, you wanted them big enough to have grown a good sized lantern, but the oldest ones, likely from repeated injury or just wear, had more corrosion than silver when harvested. The greens were much hardier. The bigger they were, the larger the copper lantern. The greens's roe was edible too, though she hadn't developed the taste for it. As tempting as it was to process it on the spot, it was against the rules. She didn't want to attract any more sea life than necessary. Adding it to the other three, she wrapped them in a bundle of loose netting, and towed it back to the raft.

Pel wasn't one to envy others, but Hara was possibly the fastest swimmer aboard ship. She was six feet tall and born to the water. Whenever the girl climbed back on the raft, she stretched her arms up and arched her back, and Pel thought the same thing every time: that girl has to be more than Human. When Pel climbed aboard she always got a wink from Jepps, but stopped being annoyed days ago. She wasn't sure the old man realized what he was doing. It was practically a twitch whenever he saw tits. With all the scar tissue, maybe that eyelid was the only body part still responding to the fairer sex. This time, "Commodore" Jepps was distracted by Hara's outburst.

"We have to raise the yellow." The usually unflappable Hara was digging through the first locker anchored to the aft.

"Yer messing about. I'll not be able to find a thing now," Jepps said. There was zero chance anything Hara did to the chests would make them less organized. Jepps didn't seem worried, and Becker sat on the edge of the raft with his legs in the water, probably on a half-hour rest. He was a strict rule follower, but Pel was beginning to think he was timing his rests so that they were on the raft together. He wore as little as any of the male divers, with the exception of six steel bands, one on each wrist and ankle, and above each elbow. She thought they might mark him as being from one of the semi-local tribes, but there was no hint of accent to prove it. She could do worse than the rugged youth, for example with any of the other four divers in her crew. If there was trouble, it was best they get it sorted before any of them came back to make things worse.

"Hara love, what's happened?" Pel asked. It sounded motherly and forced, but the girl didn't seem to hear. She gently turned the girl around. "Hara, what's wrong?"

"They don't believe me. I saw a thing in the water. Like a man," Hara said. She didn't seem frantic, but the girl wasn't meeting her eyes.

Becker said, "I told her it was one of the Lizards—"

"I've met the *people* on dives before. I think they're beautiful. This thing looked like a reef eel, but pale."

Pel said, "Eels can get enormous—"

"Can they get arms and legs?" Hara visibly tamped down her frustration. "It wasn't an eel, it was an eel *man.*"

"Commodore, raise the warning flag," Pel said.

Jepps took over digging through the lockers and dropping random items on the deck.

Becker said, "I believe you saw what you saw, but an eel-man is hardly the most frightful thing in these waters." He sounded confident but Pel noticed he had taken his feet out of the water.

Pel asked, "Hara, what else did you notice? Tell us everything."

Hara told them she stayed in her assigned territory of the port bow. This put her close to the reefs, but the creature was seen on her opposite side, meaning it swam directly through their dive sectors. She first noticed what she thought was a close grouping of three sharks, nothing to be worried about, but certainly worth keeping an eye on. The reef sharks of the region were not aggressive and there was no danger if the rules regarding fishing were upheld. When the sharks moved near, she gathered her net bag close and prepared to return to the raft. In the event of an attack, the urchins she harvested would make an effective deterrent to most creatures. She only got one clear look at the thing swimming between two sharks. Up until that moment, it had kept itself hidden, and it took a long look at her as well with its unblinking eyes. She didn't remember it holding anything but had a vague impression that it wore something on a sling around its chest.

Soon two more divers arrived only moments apart. After another round of explanations was complete, Rowan and Nesh seemed to be in agreement. Pel wasn't surprised. Rowan was the best of the best and Nesh was the closest thing to an apprentice that the divers had. Nesh did some of Rowan's work, and the other reciprocated by teaching the younger man all of his bad habits.

Rowan was the senior diver on raft one, and though it granted no actual authority, he felt perfectly comfortable giving orders. He and Pel had similar backgrounds, though more than a decade apart. Both were soldiers whose war was over. Each had a tendency to step into leadership gaps, but his experience and confidence had her backing down more often than not. She thought they would be good friends, as he reminded her so much of those she had served with. They were not friends, but it no longer bothered her. She understood he just didn't want to be reminded of the past.

Rowan said, "You lot did the right thing, it's best everyone stay alert. We'll need to harvest what we can in case they pull us in." With that, he and Nesh dove in and disappeared. They would swim along their shared border and separate further out.

Becker hadn't moved and Hara was making a pretense of examining her spear. Pel said, "He's probably right, we don't want to fall behind and lose our spots." This was especially true for her. A fortune in bribes, and no small effort on her part, had put her on raft one. It would ruin everything if she wasn't still near the top of the ranks when the ship rounded the cape in two days. She glanced at the sheer cliff walls beyond the reef. There was no slipping ashore before then. She looked at the younger divers and added, "Still, I wouldn't mind some company. Hara, you want to partner for a little while?"

Hara threw her arms around the other woman and squeezed tight.

"Becker?"

"Thank the gods. Let's go."

Pel said, "Beck, you're fore, so we'll strip your territory on both sides and keep each other in sight." She turned to Jepps who was leaning on the winch.

"Have the others repeated the signal?" Pel asked.

Gesturing over his shoulder, Jepps said, "Masha on two and what's-his-name on three are showing the flag. I don't think it's gone on. The *Indomitable* won't acknowledge for some time yet. The longboat is out, but it's nothin' to do with us."

Pel took his spyglass. She was always surprised at his ability to read the flags this far away. She couldn't find the ship through the glass, so peeked out at the horizon to locate it. Not only was the ship not visible, the horizon wasn't where it was supposed to be. She used the telescope to find the furthest raft... just in time to see it snap out of sight under a rising wave. It didn't float, it was like it was pulled under.

"Everyone in the water! Something's happened to the ship, we're losing the rafts! Grab something and move!" When she reached for her own dry bag, she managed to snare what she hoped was the medical satchel and snatched up her spear on the run to the edge. She dove in and swam hard for the bottom, letting her breath out in a single rush of air. She waited until she touched down before letting the water enter her lungs and activate the Tesco's. It was painful and terrifying every time, but she forced the calm to come and looked upward. Becker was halfway to her carrying something large and she saw Hara just as she dove in. Viewed from below, the raft shot up and forward. She was watching it pass out of view when the pain struck her. A torrent of scalding water swept her away and for several painful moments, she was unaware of her surroundings or her companions. The heat receded as the swirling currents calmed and she uncurled herself from her fetal ball. The sea felt bathwater warm, and a great deal of sand was clouding her view, but she was able to swim towards Becker. She had lost everything but the one bag she had instinctively wrapped herself around. The rest was already lost to the drifting sand. The young man was unconscious and slowly being pulled to the bottom by the entire locker he had ripped from the deck. He roused as she helped him extricate his hand from the leather handle. He seemed dazed but understood that he was to wait there. The breathers allowed speech, but it was imperfect and could be hard to understand from more than a few feet away. The divers learned to rely on lip reading and hand gestures to reinforce their communication.

Hara was found drifting nearby, barely able to remain conscious. Pel got her companions swimming toward the reefs. She walked along the bottom with the locker until they were getting too far ahead, and left it behind to catch up. Without reasoning it out, she felt they were safer gripping the ocean floor. She had a notion that the heat must be from a fire on the surface, though it was all clear above. The waters shallowed as they entered the protected region near the cliffs and she risked swimming to the surface. There was nothing to be seen through the choppy waves around the reefs, but in the air, just above the water was a plume of cloud. Pel returned to scouting the cliff perimeter but kept her distance from the crashing water until she felt a change in temperature. The water was back to normal for the dept, but she felt a current of genuinely cool water and imagined she detected a change in the taste or smell or whatever one used with their sinuses filled with seawater. She led the other divers up the almost undetectable current to a cleft where fresh water had cut through the limestone cliffs. Becker was all but towing Hara along as she kicked feebly. A miniature beach had formed in the half-submerged cave and they all dragged themselves onto the sand, coughing up water and taking in lungfuls of air. Pel dry-heaved a few times, the nausea a sure sign she had spent too long on the breather. Hara couldn't stop coughing and her breathing was labored. Out of the water, it was clear Hara and Becker were more badly burned than she. Though Pel was feeling some soreness, Becker's brown skin was turning bright red, and Hara's was forming large blisters.

"Hara, can you speak?" Pel asked as she rummaged in the bag. She had managed to save nothing but what looked to be Nesh's dry bag. There was nothing to help the girl.

"I can breathe better, but it hurts." Hara's voice was weak and raspy.

"Your lungs are scalded, sweetheart. What kept you?" Pel's frustration made it impossible to remain calm.

"Jepps had to save the raft," Hara said. "He said we were going to need it." She touched the knife she always wore on her thigh. It reached from hip to knee, and she had it whenever she dived. Pel knew the young woman had spent two seasons diving for food to supplement the *Indomitable's* supplies before being noticed and offered a raft. The girl tried to say something else, but her voice failed.

Pel said, "You cut the raft loose. I'm betting you saved the raft and Jepps. Don't talk anymore, I'm going to find the healing bag." She handed Nesh's flasks to Becker. "Make her drink water, then start her on the treenail. Water it down if you have to. If that stream is fresh, both of you drink as much as you can."

Already exhausted, the nausea not receded, Pel waded back into the sea. Returning to the locker, she searched it but found nothing of immediate use. Bundling a few things together for her return, she swam in widening circles and found the bag of potions and salves within half an hour. Using the locker as a landmark, she took her bearing and retraced her route. Nearing the security of the reefs, she began to hear strange noises and see hundreds of shapes swimming in the distance. She thought they were real, but it was by far the longest she had used a Tesco's Breather. She swam on the surface, her head pounding and ears ringing, and went under only long enough to make it through the rocks to the little beach. She found Becker sitting apart, head on knees. She found Hara beyond her help.

Chapter Two

Southern jungle, Isle of Arux-Troth.

"Darden will pay for this. I swear he will," Meese said aloud. He did so every hundred yards or so. The rest of his breath was saved for cursing and smashing undergrowth. The long abandoned trail was probably more difficult to walk than the dark of the surrounding jungle. Sunlight reaching the ground had allowed the growth of grasses and brush to hamper their movement. Fast growing trees had toppled in the loose sand and lay across the path at semi-regular intervals.

"Instructor Darden performed an illegal teleport into Crown territory... when you *blackmailed* him!" Nowen said, voice rising out of his control, "Why are we not in one of the hells right now?"

Gladlow said, "He didn't have the address." Nowen recognized this as one of Gladlow's jokes. They tended to simply be the truth spoken at the worst time. The truth it was. They were sent to the original tower, the first of three, precisely because it contained the only magic circle to which Darden knew the unique runes. He was part of the initial group of mages who, along with an army of laborers, had established a bridgehead on the isle the natives called Arux-Troth. When the tower was abandoned in favor of a basecamp further inland, Darden abandoned the mission in favor of academic pursuits. He was now an instructor of obscure maths and comely grad students.

"That cheap bastard owed me for an entire unpaid summer of work. I only reminded the Senior Professor of Practice of his obligations. And of the deputy vice-chancellor's daughter." Meese continued whacking at brush with his staff for a moment. "His title should be Endowed Professor." He turned to grin back at his companions and caught sight of Nowen. Even severely overburdened with his abundance of gear, the man was tightrope-walking a fallen log that Meese had found to be a substantial obstacle. "You're loving this you Elven wanker."

"You've never sounded more like your ancestors," said Gladlow from the rear.

"Maybe I meant he wanks Elves."

"Makes sense."

What Nowen had initially liked about the two mages was their ability to work together. They had been nearly inseparable through all of their schooling, and it showed in every interaction. Even when their magic disciplines diverged, they continued to live together. Times like this, Nowen felt like an outsider at a family reunion.

He said, "I'm not loving this. We're following a termite eaten map that was obsolete thirty years ago." He had imagined a more academic sort of trip, getting the chance to see the island secrets uncovered by generations of Institute researchers. Instead, they had camped in a sandstone hovel previously stripped of any useful supplies. They had been walking since just before dawn and Nowen had seen enough of the night to know he didn't want to spend the next outside. "It will be very dark, very soon down here in the basin. How sure are you that the original base camp is still habitable?"

Gladlow said, "It's still listed as a supply cache. I'll be satisfied if it has a roof."

The roof was all that was left of the old building on the edge of dense jungle between two rocky hills. The trio stepped out of the weeds onto the bend of a wider path running from the west and turning northward. The route matched the old map and still saw enough traffic to keep the trail sandy and free of growth. The building itself had once been a sturdy structure built from local materials. Much of the front and sides had fallen away leaving a skeletal framework of rough timbers. Peering inside revealed there was also no back wall. Gladlow gestured to Meese and the area lit up with torchlight when the Dwarrow mage removed the cap from the end of his staff. The wood swirled with flames and the yellow fire poured upward out of the metal cup as he removed it, but he didn't flinch at the flames licking his hand.

The ceiling was low and the sloping dirt floor was soft and streaked with patches of grass where sunlight had reached in through missing sections of wall. A well traveled path swerved left around a precarious jumble of rotten furniture and bunks reaching the rafters.

Meese began, "I'll take—"

"Bashton?" a voice called in a loud whisper, "is that you?"

The three men looked to each other in surprise. Meese said, "Hello?" There was no reply.

Gladlow set his pack down and waved Meese left while he crept right. Nowen was left standing in the middle of the room.

Before the two flanked the wall of rubbish, the voice whispered, "I only have two hands! Hold this so I can get a proper look."

Nowen's ears pricked up and he turned in a small circle. "Lads, the voice isn't coming from back there."

"Where is it coming from?" Gladlow growled.

"Everywhere." Nowen shrugged at their frustrated looks. They continued more quickly, Meese waving his torch-staff and Gladlow with his right fist cocked back as if he would throw a punch. Nowen continued to sweep his eyes to the rear, instinctively keeping companions at his back. He was taking off his pack and drawing a dagger when Meese's roar spun him round. The mage was sunk halfway into the earth, left arm trapped and the other using his staff to keep himself above ground. Gladlow was instantly there pulling on his friend, to no avail. His pack seemed to be snagged on ragged boards. Nowen looked at his long knife and ran to help.

"I'm bloody stuck. I'm bloody stuck!" Meese suddenly froze. "It's clawing my leg—push me through! No, no, no, it's biting me!" He turned his head and screamed in Gladlow's face, "I said push, halfwit!"

Meese let go of his staff and thrust his arm up over his head, Gladlow threw all of his weight down on his friend's shoulders, and Nowen arrived to stomp on the protruding pack. Meese dropped into the dark in a tumble of debris. The remaining two leaned close over the hole.

Meese began screaming incoherently, but Gladlow recognized the words and managed to drag the Elf back from the hole before a puff of flame and smoke shot upward, accompanied by the rumble of a roaring furnace. They rose to their feet and saw where fire glowed through several thins spots around the room. The flames died and it was quiet for several heartbeats.

Nowen yelled out as searing pain gripped him from behind. He saw pale flesh as an arm pulled his head to the side. A glint of red flashed from Gladlow's ring as he thrust his fist toward him. A gesture and a word sent two white, incandescent hornets toward Nowen's chest. One swerved past his ear and the lower slipped through his armpit. The force separated the creature from Nowen's back and the thing discarded him to charge the other wizard. It was a naked man, starved and pale, his skin stretched over a bony skeleton. Gladlow met its charge with a staff across the skull that would have laid out a person, but the creature slashed him with black claws and he fell instantly. He remained unmoving on the ground as the creature bent towards him. It had completely disregarded Nowen and he launched himself at the thing, sinking his dagger into its back. It stood up straight as Nowen let himself drop, hanging all of his weight on the blade and opening a bloodless slice. The ghoul threw him off and turned. Its face showed surprise even while so distorted with evil. Its head was stove in and leaking clear fluid. Nowen raised his dagger but stumbled back as the creature was engulfed in flame. Meese blew on his hand and dusted himself off as the thing dropped to its knees and fell to the side, smoldering.

Nowen leaned forward. "It's still mumbling something. It's saying—"

Meese stomped on it three times. "What was it saying?"

"Bashton."

The trio sat in a makeshift barricade with a small fire. They didn't need the warmth, but it seemed to help with the insects and their flagging morale. Gladlow had been unable to move for a brief time but the effects passed quickly. They had each sustained a minor wound, with Meese's bite winning when they compared injuries. It was agreed to save their most valuable healing concoctions for real emergencies and settled for rubbing an herbal salve into their wounds to stave off infection and speed natural healing. They ate quickly and slept fitfully. The morning seemed to arrive late, but they'd had nothing better to do before daybreak than prepare their spells, and themselves, for a new day. They searched the ruins in the light of dawn.

"That is the creepiest thing I've ever seen," Gladlow said. The other two just nodded. They were standing before a nightmare rendition of a Tidings tree. Gnarled branches were randomly shoved into the ground and the pile of scrap wood at the back of the structure. From it were hung baubles and tokens presumably from the creature's victims. Worse were the thing's own incomprehensible creations of twig and sinew. And bones. Every second ornament was a bone hung from a branch.

Meese said, "I'll check the tunnels. They're less terrifying."

Gladlow shrugged and began taking down anything of interest.

They regrouped at the remains of their campfire and laid everything on a cloth. A small platinum earring was the only modern jewelry, everything else was polished stone of one sort or another. The blue ones with inclusions like waves crashing might be valuable. In addition, there was a corroded sword Meese recovered from underground and a bone tube. Nowen cast a quick spell and poked around the items, disappointed. His eyes were drawn to Meese's staff which Meese knew would only show him a wisp of enchantment from the flame illusion permanently adorning it. Gladlow had two active enchantments on his person, but Nowen would assume they were both protective in nature. Nowen had observed him cast one, but combat magic wasn't his specialty. Gladlow's ring would be the only source of substantial power, and to Nowen's eyes, it would shine small but bright.

Meese said, "So, I see you had a probing spell cocked and at the ready. Anything more useful against..." he pretended to think, "the hungry undead? No? How about Locate Beer? Do you know that one?"

Gladlow intervened before Nowen took the bait. He pointed to the carved bone. "What's that?"

"I think it was the first thing hung by that creature," Nowen said as he pulled the end from the tube and extracted a roll of papers. He went quiet and sat back as he perused them.

"I guess he'll just read those to himself then. Let me tell you about the tunnels." Meese outlined his theory that mudslides had rendered the building unusable. Stacks of bags and crates had been buried under earth years ago, explaining the low ceiling. The ghoul had dug through rotten crates and under tables leaving a semi-stable tunnel. Meese thought the sword looked like Orcish steel to him, which seemed a bit out of place, but not valuable.

It was past time to move out and Gladlow decided on west. The second tower should be that direction and the naturalists and researchers studying Lizard culture were the most likely to know something of the information he sought. Nowen explained the contents of the scroll tube as they walked. It contained notes and even a crude map scribbled on torn out journal pages. It seemed to be from the earliest Crown survey ship sent to plan the urchin harvests. One of the scout crews discovered an undersea cave with an unusual number of urchins including a rare white, or platinum urchin. They had harvested all but the white and falsified their records. They returned a week later to collect it in secret, but there were already more of the creatures including a second platinum. There was something special about that cave.

"The poachers were named Shek and Bashton," Nowen said. "It's disappointing, isn't it? From the very beginning, the harvest was rotten with cheating and greed."

Meese said, "It's disappointing we were nearly killed by a ghoul named Shek."

• • • •

Western Reef

Wellstone swam slowly, conserving her strength. She felt it was only luck she had made it to the relative cover of the reefs. Groups of monstrous eel-people swam among prowling sharks collecting the bodies of sailors and divers. She had seen one of the bodies up close and it appeared to have been boiled alive. The sharks fed at their leisure, while the eels tied down the limbs of each corpse and towed them away with a line around their neck. For a while the water was cloudier than usual but the course sand had settled out by the time she had found a place among the corals to surface for air and rest.

She had skimmed along the bottom, freezing whenever she saw movement, but the eels were busy with their work near the surface and the sharks paid her no mind. One fast-moving group would have seen her for certain, but she hid beneath a coral shelf waiting for them to pass. It was some time later she began to pay the price for that tactic. She must have come in contact with one of the innumerable varieties of stinging anemones inhabiting the reef. She had previously shed most of the clothing slowing her down, and now a ring of flesh on her upper arm had gone pale surrounded by welts of darkening red. She could feel more of the excruciating effect on her shoulder and back.

Wellstone realized she was staring at an object in the distance as she treaded water. It was between her and the cliffs, but further west. If it was the longboat, as she hoped to all the gods it was, she could never catch up by swimming. Still, it was a more tempting goal than the sheer sandstone cliffs and the only sign of survivors she had yet seen. She would have to be careful how she approached, in case she wasn't the only thing following.

Weaving through the maze of shallow reefs, Wellstone made her way towards the craft. She stayed submerged, only peeking above the water when backtracking disoriented her, or no way presented itself other than up and over the corals. As far as she could tell, the longboat hadn't moved, but when she last looked, she thought she saw a figure standing in what she could now confirm was the *Indomitable's* pinnace. It was long, sleek, and decked over, unlike the smaller jolly-boats aboard the massive ship. She saw no sail, and couldn't guess their reason for remaining stationary for so long. It became clear when she closed the distance and saw the five eel-men circling the boat in the lagoon between the reefs and cliffs. Several oars floating on the surface and the size of the eels' passel of bodies told the story. Most of the corpses were dressed in the squids' preference of minimal to almost naked, but a few wore the loose clothing of sailors and the cheap calfskin shoes available for purchase from the purser's office. Even with their focus on harassing her crew mates, if she attempted to swim up from below, her approach would be noticed. They were much faster than her in the water, she was unarmed, and there were five of them. They had every advantage, though luckily this was one of the few groups she had seen without one to four sharks present. If she swam any closer, or left the cover of the barrier reef, she would be the next body added to the heap.

It took only a few moments for one of the eel creatures to notice the new corpse drifting into the open. Wellstone kept still and breathed as shallowly as she was able. She assumed the fire-trap burned her face as much as her hands and the anemone sting was an alarming mass of blisters surrounding bloodless white flesh. It was an effective disguise if she could keep her nerve. As she hoped, the ease of their day's harvest had made the creatures complacent. One of them broke off and swam towards her alone. She watched it with half-lidded eyes and prayed it wouldn't circle around behind. It came straight to her, but despite its lack of alarm, it wasn't completely careless. It half-heartedly jabbed at her with its spear but she grabbed the shaft and pulled with all her strength, guiding the tip past her as she yanked the two of them closer together. She reached for the knife on its harness but the creature was startled into using its natural weapons. Its teeth sank into her left shoulder. If she hadn't flinched back, it would have been devastating, but it only managed to clamp the first few inches of its jaws onto her. As she reached her hands to dislodge it, she realized she had succeeded in snatching the knife, and turned the move into a savage cut across its thick neck. She had seen their swimming skill and expected a stronger opponent, but it seemed their tails did most of the work. With its teeth in her shoulder and its arms unable to match her strength, it died quickly in a cloud of blood. Grabbing up the spear and kicking off from the sea floor, she swam straight for the two eel-men darting toward her. The others had spread out, one to watch the boat, the other to guard their harvest. Wellstone dolphin kicked her feet in unison to maintain her speed and hoped her bluff would work. With her captured spear held straight ahead and the spreading blood in her wake, the two creatures were unsettled enough not to attack their first pass. When they split around her, she shot past and swam hard for her true target. The longboat was only a few lengths away when the eels realized she was nearing escape and closed ranks to cut her off. She maintained her course and one of the creatures positioned itself between her and the vessel. It waited to meet her charge, both of them knowing the other three would be on her in seconds. A flash of silver reached down from the surface materializing as a harpoon in the monster's back. It was pulled, thrashing, towards the surface. Two divers plunged into the water and swam to join her. She turned in time to see the eels stop short of her. Seemingly before they realized how easy it would be to dispatch her and be away, several more splashes made Wellstone look back. Three more crew were in the water, though she could see they were sailors and not likely to be equipped with breathers. However, the threat worked and the surviving creatures retreated with their slaughter. Even so burdened, they were much too fast to pursue.

Wellstone knelt on the deck, heaving water from her lungs and bile from her stomach. She was aware of questions being voiced, as well as reassurances about her injuries. Somewhat ironically, she thought, they explained the greatest danger to her was dehydration. She could only look at the dead eel-man still bleeding on the deck. Her vision went dark and the last thing she could remember thinking was that it looked so much smaller out of the water.

• • • •

Southern Cliffs

"We should be looking for survivors," Becker said again. He had repeated some version of this every few minutes as they climbed. Nothing Pel said seemed to sink in. She was beginning to fear he was in a more fragile state than she initially thought. All the more reason to find a safe place to rest. The climb would be easy under better circumstances. The limestone precipice looked daunting but was stable and covered in plenty of handholds and ledges carved from the trickling waterfall.

"Our best bet is to head where other survivors will, and that's to the beaches." Pel leaned out from the wall and tried to estimate how far they had climbed. She guessed half-way.

"The beach we anchored by a couple of days ago is just to the west. We could swim around the cliffs in a couple of hours," he said. To Pel, his voice sounded dazed, but he seemed strangely agitated.

"Over to your right. Let's stop for a rest." She pulled herself up and sat next to him on the ledge. "The heights don't seem to bother you. Wish I could say the same."

"This is nothing compared to a swaying mast," Becker said. "The longboat is to the west. Jepps said as much. We could swim there in a couple of hours."

"Becker, we should keep dry for a while." She stopped his protests by opening his water flask and reminding him to drink. "I know the isle is dangerous, but the ocean is obviously more so right now. It feels like... I think this is better."

Becker handed her the bottle, but she only took a small sip. He asked, "What did you see? What could destroy a ship so quickly?"

"I don't know," she said, looking at his burns. They weren't severe, but they covered every inch of him. He couldn't seem to quench his thirst.

"What were you about to say? What does it feel like?"

"I was going to say it feels like a harvest," she said quietly. "During the war, sorcerers would lay waste to our villages, then send the scavengers in. Goblins or kobolds would swarm over the area, until nothing was left. It wasn't warfare, it was just how they fed their armies." She added his flask to their few belongings and slung them over her shoulder. They wordlessly continued their climb.

The climb grew easier, but they continued to pick their way carefully. Pel had time to consider what her goal actually was. She had just lost her diving wages, along with all of her possessions. There was a generous purse waiting for her at the Institute, if she could complete her mission to collect the mages' research and smuggle it back for them. But smuggle it aboard what? The climb ended, not by clambering over the edge onto solid ground, but in a wet morass of detritus collected at the end of the creek before it dribbled down the cliff. The footing was treacherous in the tangle of rotten branches and algae, but slipping only meant getting muddy. They were just entering the split in the limestone rocks, with jungle trees overhanging, when Becker screamed. She had kept him ahead of her as they climbed, but it hadn't yet occurred to her that he was left to lead them into new territory. He seemed to be stuck and covered in sea foam. She stumbled forward to help him up, but something slammed across her chest, spinning her around and sending her to her knees. She turned in time to avoid the next strike as a thick rope of water and foam whipped forward and slapped the muddy water where she had been. An amorphous mass of gelatinous water clung to Becker's chest, a tendril wrapped around his back, another around his thigh. Pel drew Hara's blade and met an attacking limb. She felt the blade bite something like flesh, but the tendril was reabsorbed only for another to take its place.

"You have to smash it!" Becker yelled as he struggled to protect his face and neck.

Pel grabbed up the most substantial branch she could see and swung it with all her might at Becker's chest. The rotten log disintegrated in her hand, but the blow sent liquid from the creature's body spraying in all directions. Becker was knocked backwards against the rocks bordering the stream and the creature plopped down at his feet. It continued to bludgeon them with a single snakelike arm while the young man kicked at it wildly and Pel lifted another weapon. Becker pulled his knees up to his chest as Pel tumbled forward holding an enormous flake of limestone. She landed on top of it with a loud crack of stone on stone. Fluid and inclusions that looked like foam at the shoreline drained away leaving a clear membrane as the thing's only remains. They each grabbed fist-sized stones as they hurried away from the rocks and waded out of the small creek. Becker knelt on the ground while Pel took in their surroundings. They were on the sandy border between thick jungle and limestone cliffs. She knew the border of the isle's basin formed a natural path around the rim. It could be followed west to search for the likely landing place for the longship or east to the series of wizard towers secretly placed by the Magical Research and Preservation Institute. She was ignoring the abrasions from fumbling with the rock but noticed an increased stinging across her forearm.

"Beck, I'm going to treat it like a bluebottle sting," Pel tried to sound confident as she smeared one of the pots of salve onto his chest. She knew the main ingredient was brown kelp, but it smelled of yeast and cloves. "How do you feel?"

"Partially digested." He gave a bright smile but his breathing was labored. "That was a spume-jelly. They're really rare."

"The little shits are more rare now." She poured a small bottle into the last of the treenail liquor and swirled it around. "Drink this. I was going to wait until you could sleep, but it will help with the pain and swelling."

"Ugh. It tastes like liquorice."

"Coltsfoot, I think. You're going to have trouble keeping your eyes open, so we better march."

"Pel, shouldn't we make a shelter? There can't be much daylight left."

Pel sighed. "I'm going to ask you to trust me. I know a place just to the east. We might find help before nightfall."

"Know a place? How?"

"If we survive the night, we'll talk in the morning."

Pel stayed alert and pushed the exhausted Becker to keep up. She skipped the smaller path that should lead to her pickup spot on a little beach and opted for the well worn trail a mile further to the only shelter in the area. This was all from her memory of the map she was shown. There were no more incidents and she led them right to the wizard tower just before night dropped into the basin. The structure was called a tower either by tradition or as a joke. It was a smooth sandstone cylinder, slightly wider at the bottom, and about as tall as your average cottage. There was no one home.

· · · ·

Arux-Troth Basin, southern perimeter

"How about this one?"

"And risk him blinding one of us every time he gets startled? Let me teach him Burning—"

"No. Just... no." Gladlow rolled his spellbook up and stowed it in the large waterproof tube he used to protect his papers and scrolls. His travel book was just a stack of parchment, stitched at the spine, with no covers. His real books were stashed in a secure locker at the Institute library, one of the benefits for members of the organization.

From the trail ahead, Nowen called back over his shoulder. "I did have a spell ready, you know, but the undead don't sleep."

Meese said in a fake whisper, "How does he have such incredible hearing?"

"Nowen, tonight I'll teach you the hornet spell," Gladlow said.

"That's not necessary—"

"I insist. It's not very powerful, but it's damn near foolproof."

Nowen stopped in the path with crossed arms and waited for them to catch up. "I'm no fool unless you count coming with you on this expedition. We were supposed to observe the senior researchers. Master wizards, with guards and... and porters. I should be learning clairvoyance from Master Whitecloud, not how to kill dead people... more."

"I didn't mean it like that," Gladlow said, "Just that it never fails. What would have happened if old Shek had grabbed me instead?"

"Nowen would have put you to sleep so you died painlessly." At their looks, Meese held up his hands and backed away.

Nowen said, "I know you, Gladlow. How much will this spell cost me?"

"Nothing. It strengthens the group."

Nowen looked skeptical but uncrossed his arms.

Gladlow continued, "I can respect your not wanting to be in my debt. Let's honor tradition and trade. We'll return each other's book when you finish copying the spell." He stuck out his hand and Nowen shook it.

Meese said, "Glorious. Now that we're invincible, how much further are we walking today?"

Gladlow said, "See how the rock face is getting shorter? Soon it opens on a beach. The tower should be on the path down."

Nowen said, "We just show up and they'll let us join the expedition?"

"They were expecting us before our excursion was canceled, and they've asked for more workers. They'll be thrilled to see us. Let's get to the tower and get something besides jerky to eat." Gladlow walked two steps up the path and stopped.

A meagerly dressed woman stood on the path, waiting politely. She wore a knife longer than her short-pants and a jerkin that only covered her chest. Gladlow was so entranced he failed to notice her sunburn or salt-matted hair. He realized he was staring and that it was probably too late to say something charming.

Meese punched Nowen on the arm. "Are those ears decorative?" He stepped forward and swept his hat from his head. "Madam?"

She said, "There's no one at the tower. We spent the night on the roof and waited as long as we could."

Nowen prompted, "We?"

She whistled over her shoulder and a young-adult man crept out of the trees behind her. He looked badly sunburned and half covered in mud. He wore more jewelry than clothes, only a loincloth and satchel. She said, "We're survivors of the *Indomitable*. I'm Pel, this is Becker."

After a brief discussion, everyone agreed that the two should accompany the mages west. If nothing else, it was the direction of the only fresh water anyone had seen. Gladlow walked in front while Meese and Nowen tried to get more information out of the castaways.

"The ship must have gone down quick if you only made it out with your underwear," Meese said.

"They are divers, obviously," Nowen said, "So, Miss Pel—"

"I know they're divers. That's a Tesco's on her wrist."

"You recognize it?" Pel asked through a bite of jerky. The piece of dried beef in her hand must have begun as an entire steak.

"I even know Walther Tesco," Meese said. "He's a bit of a knob."

Nowen snorted. "He's one of the most successful mages to graduate from the Institute's college. He is *brilliant*."

"Brilliant at being a mouthy prick."

"And you know him?" Nowen asked.

"To say hello to, though I avoid it—"

"Because he's a prick," Pel finished for him. She shook the strap on her wrist. "Anyone using one of these things suspects it."

Meese grinned and said, "If the Crown ever needs a suppository that lets them see in the dark, they have him on retainer."

As they were laughing Nowen rolled his eyes to the other survivor but didn't make the biting comment he had planned. "Mister Becker?" There was no response from the man. He just plodded along in a daze. Nowen reached out a hand but didn't want to touch his tender looking skin. He settled for standing in Becker's path and waiting for him to stop. "How are you feeling?"

"Sorry," Becker said, sounding perfectly normal. "I'm a bit fuzzy from the medicine."

"How are you feeling?" Nowen repeated.

"Parboiled," he said but his lips were too cracked to fully smile. "Bit of a headache, to be honest."

"This isn't sunburn." Nowen looked behind the young man's ears and then the palms of his hands. "You're burned everywhere. What in two hells..."

Everyone had stopped. Pel said, "There was a wave and we abandoned the raft. We were in perhaps sixty feet of water. I was at the bottom, he was in the middle, and our companion Hara had just dived in... and the sea boiled. I've given him most of the water, but nothing quenches his thirst."

Meese asked, "And Hara?"

Pel shook her head. Becker acted as if he didn't hear.

While the Elf dug through his massive backpack, Gladlow saw Meese trying to catch his eye. He was probably about to protest the use of such a valuable resource on someone who could stand and walk. Normally Gladlow would agree, but the kid's burns looked nasty. He gave a surreptitious shake of the head, but the Pel woman was watching him. Neither of the survivors had reason to distrust the vial of liquid, it likely looked very much like the ones hoarded by their ship's purser. Becker drank it down.

Nowen said, "That will make you hungry, but don't eat until it overpowers your thirst." He handed his own water to the man before turning to Pel. He looked her up and down while she met his gaze with a raised eyebrow. "You look to be in much better shape." An involuntary grunt from Gladlow elicited a snort from Meese. Nowen continued, "We should go to Uljar-Molik. The researchers living there can tell us when the next meeting is."

"The Lizard village?" Meese said, "No, thank you. We'll wait in the tower and signal for retrieval. These two want to go home."

"Apparently my ears *are* superior to yours," Nowen said, with extreme sarcasm, "because I heard her say no one was *there*. We can't open the door."

"He can."

Everyone turned to look at Gladlow, who shrugged with one shoulder.

Nowen narrowed his eyes. Without taking them from Gladlow, he asked Meese, "He has the password?"

Meese grinned. "You could say that." He tapped the side of his nose and winked.

Nowen looked defeated. He addressed Gladlow directly this time. "Of course, you have a proscribed spell. How?"

He shrugged again, so Pel asked, "What spell?"

"An opening command I picked up..." Gladlow trailed off realizing these were the first words he had spoken to her. By the gods, had he just been staring with his mouth open the entire time?

Nowen wore his stern look. "Not from any of the instructors, you didn't."

"My boy here dueled for it," Meese said proudly.

"That could get you—" Nowen started.

"It was more of a wager..." Gladlow explained to Pel. She was arching one eyebrow again. "It's, umm, a large expenditure of power for such a small outcome but it's because... no matter." Gladlow turned to Meese and said, "I have to agree with Nowen."

"You do?" No one looked more surprised than Nowen.

"I can open the door," Gladlow admitted, "but I can't foil whatever protections might be in place."

Meese said, "No one even knows they're here, why would they put anything nasty on the door?"

"Because they can. Some of these people conjure elementals to do their laundry. If we can't find the expedition party, we should find one of their colleagues in the village."

"Fine," Meese said, "Where's the village?"
It was Nowen's turn to shrug.

Chapter Three

Western coast

Villago was the *Indomitable's* third mate, commander of the rescue squad, and certainly the highest ranking survivor. Wellstone's rank had always been more nebulous. The position of constable was unique to the harvest ships. Her responsibility was to protect Crown property, but in reality, she policed a village worth of rowdy divers as they lived their lives aboard the massive vessel. Her authority didn't extend to the others, however, her reports could destroy careers, and the resulting deference put her unofficial rank somewhere just below the mates in the eyes of the *Indomitable's* crew. She had intended to act only as advisor to Villago, but the man seemed unwilling to make unpopular decisions.

Wellstone had convinced the majority that spending a couple of days gathering supplies and performing repairs was paramount to surviving what promised to be a three week journey. Villago had agreed to put off a vote until fresh water was found. With the sail in tatters, the longboat was driven by eight oars. They couldn't just tighten their belts and chew shoe leather. They needed food as well. Villago led a party inland consisting of himself, two crew, Carlin, and Wellstone. Two guards were left on the boat with four injured. The two squids were spear-fishing and a final pair of crew were crafting replacements for several lost oars. Fifteen survivors from 211 sailors.

"Nothing has changed since yesterday," Wellstone said. She was tiring of repeating the same arguments. "Unless you plan to weave a sail out of palm fronds and iguanas?"

Villago held up the three-pound reptile. It was a salty blue fading to drab green. He had killed it with a thrown knife, but no one had managed the feat again. He said, "There's enough of these wily bastards to feed us but we're armed with fishing spears and harpoons. It'll likely be dried fish for the trip home."

Wellstone slapped a bug and looked around to make sure the others were out of earshot. "Will the crew stay long enough to dry fish?" The other two pairs were within sight but spaced some distance away as they picked their way through thorny underbrush. The thick jungle canopy could be seen ahead. Maybe the ground cover would thin out a bit under the trees.

"It's an even split. Half would leave this instant—"

"With, what, four days water for a twenty day voyage?"

"—the other half when we find water."

"Madness," Wellstone sighed, "I told you what I saw."

Villago said, "No one doubts you. But they're sailors and you won't convince them that this island is safer than the open sea."

Wellstone just gave him a pained look.

"I know, even after everything they've seen. When we return, they'll vote, and we're rowing for home."

The air cooled slightly in the shade of the jungle. The limestone outcroppings dropped out of sight as the land sloped almost imperceptibly downward and the trees grew larger. They were entering the great basin, reported to be riddled with rivers and tributaries. Wellstone was confident they would find a water source before long. She was still considering the difficulties of removing one of the water puncheons from the boat, carrying it to the source, and hauling it back 500 pounds heavier. Added to what they had, they'd need to fetch two.

"Chief, take a look at this," Carlin called from nearby.

The girl was standing at the edge of an almost-clearing. The undergrowth was more sparse and the trees trunks ahead were enormous. She waited patiently for her five companions to gather. She pointed out into the jungle, then raised her arm upward. The canopy was particularly dense, but through the gloom, huge shapes materialized in the trees above. A pair of sturdy log huts were suspended 20 feet above the ground, each encircling an enormous hardwood tree. A rope bridge stretched between the front decks of the two structures.

"Did the Lizards build them?" Wellstone asked.

Carlin said, "Maybe. I don't think they live in trees though. Maybe it's a lookout?"

"No," Villago said, craning his neck, "I think you can probably see farther from down here."

"Everyone stick together, you two watch our rear." Waving the sailors back, Wellstone led the way. As they got closer, she could see something at the base of one of the trees. She could just make out a wooden railing sticking up from the ground when a voice calling out made her freeze in her tracks.

"There's a spider boy hiding in the bushes." It sounded like a little girl above them, but there was no movement from the treehouses. Just colorful birds high above.

Carlin called out, "Hello sweetie, are your parents home?"

Wellstone gave her an exasperated look and the other woman shrugged. There was no answer. Wellstone took a step forward and felt something sticking to her foot. She looked down to see the jungle floor ahead was a sea of white webbing almost obscured by the dead leaves and detritus stuck to it. She shouted, "Weapons up!" and the jungle exploded around them as black shapes charged from every direction. She stood stunned at the dog-sized arachnid impaled on her spear. Its spasming body dragged her flimsy weapon down as another of the beasts leapt at her. Carlin swatted it out of the air, in a panic, wielding the fishing spear like a staff. It was an effective enough defense to buy Wellstone the time she needed to extricate her weapon. When she pulled on the spear, the dead body was only dragged towards her. She gritted her teeth, stomped her bare foot on the spider's abdomen, and yanked the shaft free. Several thick threads of silk draped across her and the others, but she thwarted the urge to flail at them.

"Look out!" Villago shouted.

Wellstone turned in time to see a horror drop to the ground in the middle of their circle. It screeched in rage from a partly Human face and a second wave of spiders charged the group. Carlin screamed in response and clubbed it with the broken shaft of her spear. The creature launched a mass of webs at the girl before leaping at Wellstone. She rolled away and rose instantly to her feet, but felt the web lines constrict on her legs. There would be no more dodging. The thing flashed past and scuttled through the group, unhampered by the webs now tying the group tighter together by the moment.

Wellstone tried to keep it from circling behind her but was becoming more tangled. "Villago, the iron!" She watched him clip the line to his harpoon but hesitate to throw his weapon away. The remaining spiders were circling, waiting until their prey was immobilized. The monster stopped in front of her and she got her first clear look at the thing. It was a small man, roughly her size, but with a bulging belly and four stick limbs. His body was covered in bristling black hairs. The face was the least Human thing about him, his two eyes spider-like, and his mouth framed by dripping articulated fangs. Instead of another charge, it fired more webs at her while she struggled to place her spear between them. Villago finally took his shot, the barb of his weapon sinking into the creature's back. It fled on all fours, screeching until it ran out of line. Villago and every sailor within reach hauled on the rope, dragging the thing struggling and clawing the ground, within reach of their spears. The surviving spiders vanished into the jungle as their master's ichor soaked into the earth.

• • • •

It took most of an hour to cut themselves free and for Carlin to tend their wounds. She called out many times to the unknown watcher, trying to coax her out or thank her for the warning that certainly saved their lives. There was no response.

Carlin finished salving and bandaging Dalla's bites and sat back on her heels.

"I feel sick, am I poisoned?" The woman's voice was calm but her shaking hands told a different story.

"Dalla, you'll be fine," the other sailor, Ben, said. "Look, I was bitten too. Your blood's just high after the brawl." He hauled Dalla to her feet. "Try standing up straight. Walk around a bit."

Carlin hadn't been impressed with the two of them. Ben spent most of the trek staring at her ass, and Dalla groaned about her duties continuously. She had to admit they were good in a fight though. Sending them to cover the rear had been the best decision the Chief could have made. Ben didn't let a single enemy pass, and Dalla was absolutely fearless. Until the fight was over.

Carlin said, "They're not venomous, see here?" She lifted a spider's fangs with her little finger. Her attitude had changed completely once the critters stopped moving. She couldn't seem to keep her hands to herself. "I think they're giant tree spiders, a kind of tarantula."

"Well, it hurts like three hells," Dalla said looking over her shoulder in disgust.

"No doubt. Actually, all spiders are venomous, but not to us. Tarantulas, at least." She moved to their former master and flipped the ragged body over with a foot. "This thing is another matter." Using a twig this time, she lifted its fang and pressed an empty salve bottle against it. Clear fluid flowed openly from it. She cautiously milked the other fang as well.

Ben leaned in. "There's no saying what a bite from that would do."

Carlin said instantly, "Paralysis. The question is whether you would remain conscious or not."

"Hmm. You did good in the fight, but I could probably show you a thing or two if you like."

Dalla said, "I'd be happy to help. Besides, I owe her."

Carlin felt a hand on her waist and turned to Ben. Both of his hands were visible as he leaned on his spear.

He said, "Let's, the three of us, have a drink when we get back to camp."

"I need to check in with the Chief." Carlin gathered her things and retreated. Sometimes she liked the attention, but it was incessant. Brown skin was hardly rare in the tropics, but most of the crew were from the north and she seemed to hold endless fascination for them. Helena said she was too pretty to be inconspicuous anywhere, and too genial to be taken seriously, but the Chief was like that. The nicest compliments were offered as terrible character flaws. Helena Wellstone had been her superior and mentor for two years, and she was worried about what the Chief would say about her showing during the attack. She remembered screaming quite a lot. Though she did well in martial lessons, her training seemed to drop through the bowsprit when faced with actual combat.

"Carlin, what do you make of this?" Wellstone was standing on a four-by-four deck with railings on two sides. It was just lying on the ground, not attached to anything. "Did it fall from the house?"

Carlin lifted one side a few inches causing Wellstone to grab the railing to steady herself. "I don't see a way up, do you?" She looked upward. "I think it's a conveyor."

Villago said, "It's still being constructed? There's no rope and tackle."

Wellstone cursed under her breath. "It's the damn mages, isn't it? They're still sneaking onto the island."

Carlin shrugged, "It's always been assumed they do. As long as they don't interfere with the urchin beds, nobody looks into it." She pointed to a spot above them where the deck ended. "A mage could just levitate the platform straight up. The question is, how do *we* get up there?"

Wellstone said, "We don't. We map it and leave it be. No need to set off a trap and melt our skin off."

"Wait a minute," Villago said, "there could be supplies up there—"

"And information." Carlin nodded at her leader earnestly.

"Damnit."

The only rope they had was two harpoon lines they spliced together, and it was meant for dragging canvas drogues, not being climbed by people. It took another half-hour to get a throw line over a branch and prepare Wellstone for the ride up. She stood in a loop tied to one end while a pair of sailors hauled down on the other. Arming herself with Dalla's cutlass, she was hoisted twenty feet into the air, then simply stepped off onto the treehouse porch. Carlin was impressed by the Chief's bravery.

She yelled upward, "What do you see?" and saw the woman flinch hard at the sound of her voice. Helena leaned over the edge and glared at her. Carlin moved back to keep her in sight as she moved to the first door.

"The door is open. It's all webbed up inside. Stinks. It's a nest." Carlin could see she was hacking at something. Wellstone slammed the door and said, "It's a total loss."

"If it's just webs, there could be—"

"Total loss!" Wellstone was already picking her way across the bridge. She could be heard rattling the door handle.

"Is it locked?"

"It's loose. It just spins." She pounded on the door and called out, "If you're in there, open the door." She looked down at Carlin and called through the door again. "Listen... dear heart, you can come with us. You'll be safe, I promise." Nothing. She stuffed the cutlass in the back of her belt, climbed onto the railing, and grabbed the low-hanging roof. She hauled herself up and positioned herself over a tiny window on the side of the building.

"Chief? You're thirty feet up..."

Wellstone grabbed the edge at her feet and swung down to hang over the edge of the roof. Scooting sideways to line herself up with the opening, she let go and caught the window ledge on the way down.

Villago said, "That's the craziest thing I've ever seen. What the hells is she going to do now? She can't fit through there."

Holding on with one hand, she tossed the cutlass in first before following with one arm, head, and waist. Her hips wedged the gap briefly, but she just turned her bottom to the diagonal, and disappeared inside.

Ben said in awe, "She's like a rat crawlin' through the scupper."

"Douse that talk, mister," Villago said without looking round.

"What did I say?"

Carlin had pity on him. Most of the sailors didn't encounter Wellstone's folk often. "Nasty people call them rats, Ben."

"I didn't mean anything—"

A black shape flew from the window and tumbled across the ground. A dead tree spider rolled to a stop with its legs curled upward. The door opened and Wellstone stepped outside to drop a sack over the edge before going back inside.

• • • •

Southern Jungle, basin perimeter trail

It was decided, after Pel's suggestion, to return to the creek she had come from and follow it upstream looking for signs of the natives. They would have time to spend a couple of hours looking before having to make a final decision about where to camp for the night. Meese kept everyone talking while he evaluated their situation. The first problem was Gladlow. The lad was acting love-struck after two minutes near the Pel girl. She was certainly easy to look at, if you like women who can push you around, and who didn't, really? But he hadn't seen his friend like this before. Usually, he was slightly less interested in women than Meese thought was healthy, subsisting mainly on underclass-mates throwing themselves in his path. Gladlow looked like your average man on the street, meaning compared to most mages, he looked rather hale and hearty. Meese thought he would look right at home washing cows and raking onions, or whatever farm-boys did. Pel had her eye on Gladlow too, though Meese had a feeling it wasn't requited passion, not yet, but an effort to keep the biggest threat in sight. That wouldn't do.

"Pel, you have some experience with swords?" He said while untying a bundle from his pack.

She altered her pace so they were walking side by side. "I do." She sounded wary. "How did you know?"

"I didn't grow out of stone a full-fledged wizard," Meese said, bringing his considerable charm to bear, "I was a blade-smith a lifetime before you were born. Now, I didn't make swords, but I sold them for my master, and I could spot who was buying one to hang on their hip and who was replacing one lost in battle."

"And which of the two was more expensive?" She asked.

"I think we both know the answer to that. Have a look." He handed her the bundle. She took it hesitantly, but in her excitement, she stopped in the trail to unwrap it.

Pel was quiet, staring at the old weapon.

"It's seen better days, but there's no damage." Meese didn't think it was disappointment that made her go quiet, but he suddenly couldn't read anything from her face. She looked to him like one of those ancient beauties carved in marble, certainly lovely, but a different era's ideal woman.

She said under her breath, "As well break his blade ere his spite."

The others had gathered round. Becker asked, "Is that from a poem?"

"No," Gladlow said, "It's what King Eawold said of the first Orc warlord. He was commenting on his cruelty, but the king actually said it while complementing their weapons."

"What does it mean?"

"The only thing stronger than their weapons was their hatred of man."

Pel looked surprised at Gladlow's comment. "That's right. They were the first of the beast races to forge their own weapons and armor. They were rumored to be unbreakable."

Meese quickly changed the subject back to the present, "Well, that was due to them being relatively soft. This one's a bit better, and it's also only a decade or so old. If you'd like to carry it a while, I'm happy to be rid of the weight."

Pel just nodded while she gave it a thorough examination. It was a bit shorter than a broadsword, with a single edge and no guard on its long grip. "It's heavy." She held it straight out and the muscles of her arm flexed, but it was perfectly still. "It's much better balanced than it looks. Thank you, Meese."

After that, he could feel Pel was more relaxed. There was a lightness to her step while she searched along the path for stones serviceable for cleaning and sharpening her new toy. Meese was beginning to understand what Gladlow had seen so quickly. There was something about her. Meese shrugged his shoulders in surrender. That boy was about to have his heart destroyed. Meese needed to have a serious talk with him, but it would have to wait. In the meantime, he could do his friend another small service.

"Becker, my lad, how are you feeling?"

"Tired, but good. Thank you. All of you," Becker said seriously. "I've meant to ask, but shouldn't we be looking for the other survivors?"

Meese said, "First things first. I'm hoping for a guide or at least a map. We need to let our superiors know we're here, as well as everything we can find out about the shipwreck. Now that your head is clearer, why don't you tell me everything you can remember?"

Becker remembered very little from their escape onward. Hara had been upset at something she saw. She was digging through the lockers looking for the signal flags. He remembered someone saying the longboat was away, which usually meant a missing diver. He remembered the wave rising and deciding to take the entire locker. Becker and Hara had helped shift it and knew it was loose. The speed with which it dragged him to the bottom may have spared him Hara's fate. Meese realized his mistake. He had only meant to reveal what there was between the two castaways. Becker's memories were all colored by what Hara was doing or saying at the time. The young man's eyes were wide and his breathing quick and shallow.

"Calm down, calm yourself."

Becker slowed his breathing. "She stayed to cut the raft loose. I didn't realize until just now... Jepps didn't have a breather. She might have saved his life. I can't believe she's gone. We..."

"She was your girl." Meese wiped a hand over his face. "I'm sorry lad, I didn't mean to make you go back there."

"I've been in love with her since last season, but we were new."

Pel suddenly appeared and wrapped her arms around him. "I'm so sorry Beck, I didn't know."

He said, "She didn't want to tell anyone. You know how much attention she got from the men on board, always returning gifts and turning down advances. It was easier to have a reputation for not being interested. Everyone had to try once, but then most left her alone."

Pel asked, "So, how did you manage the impossible?"

He actually smiled. "I don't know. I really don't."

Pel unstrapped her knife and handed it to him. It was practically a shortsword. Meese assumed it must have been Hara's. Becker took it wordlessly. Meese left them to walk together at the rear. He hurried past Nowen, who was reading while he walked, useless git, to join Gladlow a few yards ahead.

"I have good news and bad news..."

Gladlow kept his eyes ahead and on the treeline. He took the point position very seriously. "Give me the good news, and keep the bad to yourself, thank you."

"Have it your way. Pel doesn't seem to have a man..."

Gladlow looked around wildly before leaning over and rasping, "What in three hells are you up to?"

Meese shrugged innocently and said, "Just scouting the trail ahead. It's all clear."

"We've known each other for less than four hours and she hasn't said a word to me."

Meese shrugged again.

Gladlow glared at him. "She's been through a lot and she doesn't need me, or *you*, intruding."

"Of course."

Gladlow waited a ten-count before muttering, "Oh gods. What's the bad news?"

"She's possibly a Reformist—"

"Horseshit!" Gladlow shook his head.

"Maybe she's just repeating what she heard, but nobody else says 'beast races.' She's a nice girl, just be careful what you say to her."

"Meese, there's no way she's one of them."

"You've known each other for less than four hours and she hasn't said a word to you."

"Fuck."

• • • •

Western Jungle, river bend

Wellstone watched the Goblin camp for a few more minutes before sliding backwards on her belly far enough to stand and return to camp. Carlin greeted her anxiously.

"Chief, how many are there?"

"Eight."

Villago said, "Then, it's over. We harvest what we can on the way back and we shove off at daylight."

"We don't have *water.*" Wellstone was frustrated by his sanguinity. "It's *suicide* to launch without resupply."

"You just said we can't get to the water unseen," said the third mate. He was becoming a bit exasperated himself. "We can launch, circle the island for a river, and go ashore just long enough to restock." Wellstone started to protest but he cut her off. "Stop for a minute. We're outnumbered, injured, and armed with fishing gear."

Dalla said, "They're just Goblins. Maybe we can chase them off?"

Wellstone said, "Maybe a few, if we kill most of them. Listen—"

Villago said, "What are the chances that we all come back alive if we keep—"

"Villago! Please. Will you let me give my report?" Wellstone opened the research notes they found in the treehouse and flattened out the sketched map. It was for tracking some sort of bird, but they identified the beach where the longboat landed, the treehouses, and the river they had just reached. "On the map here, near the river. This has to be a village, right? It has the same symbols as the treehouses, but more of them."

Carlin added, "It's on a river delta, which is where anyone would put a village..."

Villago said, "You want to ask the primitives for help? The Lizards?"

"No. The Goblins are here." She pointed to the map next to the river. "I couldn't hear them over the water nearby, but they have no supplies. They don't plan to be there long. They don't even have a watch set up. They're sitting around picking their noses and telling dirty jokes."

Ben asked, "Do you think we can sneak up on them? The river noise would work for us."

"No chance, even with the water. Have you seen the ears on those things? They'll hear if you *think* too loudly." Wellstone was relieved to have everyone's attention. Even Villago was focused. "I propose we watch until morning. They're waiting on something. When it happens, we attack from behind."

Carlin asked, "Even then, we're not armed very well."

"Neither are they. At least not when we get close. They seem to be strictly archers. I think they're in place to provide support for a raiding party. The only other weapons they have are clubs and flint knives."

Villago said, "I suppose it's possible, if their weapons are primitive, and we have surprise on our side."

"Well, their bows aren't primitive. Neither are their clothes. It's strange, I didn't see any metal."

Carlin said, "There isn't any metal on the island except from the urchins. The Lizards use bronze for their tools and weapons. What do you mean about their clothes?"

"They were normal clothes like you would see around the port. I would swear they look like sailors."

Dalla said, "Goblins with good clothes and good bows sounds like—"

"I know. It must be a Hobgoblin raiding party they're waiting on." Wellstone sighed. "It's true, Goblins go feral pretty quickly without their masters to wrangle them."

Villago said, "I don't like this."

Wellstone nodded. "It makes circling the island too dangerous. There's no outrunning Hobgoblin pirates if we're seen." She took a deep breath and made her final push. "The Hobgoblins and Lizards will keep each other busy, and the Goblins will have their backs turned. We'll have a clear path to the water and new bows for hunting game."

Chapter Four

Southern Jungle, borders of Uljar-Molik

Pel had resigned herself to the loss of both her wages and likely the payment she would have received for smuggling the parcel back to port. She had spotted what she thought was the path down to the tiny beach where she was to pick up the package, whatever it was. She thought it best to leave it hidden until her situation improved. For the time being, there was little to be done but follow the three mages. They were strange, but she found herself liking them as a group. Meese and Nowen bickered like brothers and looked to the quiet Gladlow to mediate. She suspected they were only friends through him. She read Meese as a troublemaker, and a charming one. Nowen would rather read about people in a book than interact with them. Gladlow didn't seem to like her much, but that was all right. He was doing the right thing despite her and Becker hampering his mission. She could respect that.

"I can break trail for a while," she said as she trotted up beside him. "I'll take a watch shift tonight too, if that's alright with you."

"Please do," he said, surprising her. She had been prepared for some sort of rebuff. "Meese won't be quiet walking point and Nowen can't stay awake on watch. You're already as useful as both of them put together."

She laughed, making him smile in return. She admitted to herself she may have misjudged him, but it was strange when he didn't say anything else or move back with the group. He just continued walking. She had often been called dour or unfriendly herself and was always surprised by the accusation. They walked in silence for perhaps a mile.

Gladlow drank and offered his flask, but she just smiled and tapped her own. He said, "So. Pel. Have you been diving long?"

"This was my first season."

"Do you like it?"

"I did."

"Right. Sorry." He pinched the bridge of his nose for a second like he had a headache.

Damnit. She had wanted to get him talking, then she shut him up the second he asked a question. Maybe there was something to her reputation.

"So, Gladlow... what exactly is your mission here? If you're allowed to say."

"Mission?" He looked at her in surprise. "Honestly, we're not supposed to be here at all. The authorities and our own superiors agree on that." She thought he was going silent again, but he was just gathering his thoughts. "What do you know about the Institute?"

"Well, wizards grouped together to do research and have a school... and they stick their noses wherever they want, generally pissing off the Crown."

It was his turn to laugh. "So, you know it intimately."

"I never really understood how it's different from a guild."

"It's like a guild *for* the guilds. It started during the war as a counter to the negative effects conflict has on advancement."

Pel said, "Advancements, like weaponry?"

"Exactly. And tactics, construction, farming. Everything. War is like a smith's hammer beating on civilization. It can indeed strengthen and refine certain aspects, but war diverts all development along a single path. Imagine what it does to magic."

"It becomes just another weapon."

"Yes. If not killing directly, then used for interrogation or espionage. Spells of healing and resurrection have become the sole domain of the gods and their priests, not because civilization can't develop them, but because war directs *all* efforts into *war* efforts."

Pel was finding herself completely caught up in his passion. "How does the Institute stop it?"

Gladlow looked a little embarrassed when he said, "Money. And they don't stop it. The Institute makes sure that the other paths to progress that war suppresses are still explored. Mostly by funding any project or study that a mage of good standing wants to put their efforts into."

"Why are the three of *you* here?"

Gladlow found that hilarious and waved away her apology when she realized what she said.

"I was supposed to join an expedition. I called in debts, then ran up new ones, threatened, bribed, and begged to be included. I trained and prepared for most of the year. Two weeks ago my sanction was withdrawn. I couldn't find out why. I assumed, maybe hastily, that it was political. I... came anyway." He gave an unapologetic shrug.

"And your friends?"

"Nowen threatened to tell on me if I didn't bring him along. Meese didn't even ask, he just made our travel arrangements."

"This expedition—"

Gladlow held out a hand to stop her. "What is that?"

It took her a moment to see what he was pointing at. In the jungle, just off the path, a creature stood watching them. Its shape was difficult to discern at first as it blended almost flawlessly into the undergrowth. Their staring made it nervous and as it darted into the trees, its movement revealed it to be a bipedal reptile, something like a monitor lizard. Pel flinched when four more, previously unseen, followed it.

"Nowen!" Gladlow called. When the elf caught up to them, Gladlow asked, "The Lizards. Do they wear pants?"

"Pants?" Nowen looked baffled by the question.

"Do they wear clothes?"

"The Uljar-Molik wear more than others of their kind. Mostly decorative wraps and belts. Their status is displayed in a complex—"

"So, yes then?" Gladlow raised his hand out in front of him at eye level and asked, "What's this tall, looks like a lizard, and wears only the scales it was born in?"

Pel reached out, touching his outstretched hand. She pushed it down level with his chest.

Nowen said, "That must be an adolescent. They don't wear clothes, or have any possessions, until their—"

Pel interrupted him this time, making Gladlow smile, as she hoped it would. "Would an adolescent range far from the village?"

Nowen crossed his arms and said, "No."

She examined the path and the edge of the jungle while everyone looked on. "I think they cross here, probably to make their way down to the beach. I think we'll find a path to the village that way."

The way was not clear at first, and even Pel was beginning to doubt, but it widened as it merged with a well-worn trail. They caught glimpses of the Lizards as they paced them at a distance from either side. When the jungle simply ended, the creatures darted into the open and ran across a field of mixed grains and grasses.

Becker asked in awe, "Did they plant this?" It was a jarring sight, appearing as it did from the wild jungle.

"It's likely wild grains they've tended over generations," Nowen said. "Those are crops though." He pointed ahead to where the grassland ended in a muddy marsh. A raised path cut through the center and on either side were meandering rows of giant spear-head shaped leaves rising out of watery paddies. Slightly uphill and still some distance away, spiked palisades stretched across the immediate horizon. Lizard silhouettes could be seen standing on squat structures at regular intervals.

Meese said, "They have a town wall, almost."

The adolescent Lizards were running around a rock lying amongst the strange crop. The rock rose and uncurled. A giant Lizard stood and stretched with audible cracking sounds. It must have been eight feet tall, but when it was done stretching, its stooped height was closer to seven. It was a dusty grey with the vibrant green of youth almost obliterated by time.

"Nowen, you're up," Meese said with a nasty smile.

"Uhm, right." Nowen pulled his hand from one of his many pouches, throwing a dusting of something into the air with a word and a flick of his hand. Nothing happened, but Nowen seemed satisfied. He dusted his hands and wiped them on his yellow robe, leaving a soot mark. He stepped forward while thumbing through the book he had been studying all day. The big Lizard was taking swipes at the little ones and hissing at them, but it stopped to listen to Nowen's greeting. It was full of hissing consonants with his own name thrown in. The big Lizard responded in kind.

"His name is Trolsht." Nowen went back to flipping through his book. He said something else but got no response other than a hand raised slightly and dropped back to his side. It gave the impression of a shrug. Nowen went back to flipping through his book.

Meese said, "I think this is going well."

Pel leaned over to Gladlow and asked under her breath, "Was that magic?"

"Not very flashy, was it? For a while, he can understand their language."

"What's the book for?"

"The spell doesn't help him speak it."

It took time, but Nowen was able to communicate their desire to speak with the non-reptile persons visiting the Uljar-Molik. Nowen finally snapped his book shut and turned to the group who had long since sprawled on the ground to wait under Trolsht's shade tree. The big reptile moved slowly and steadily, breaking small shoots from his plants and sticking them in the mud to form new rows. The young Lizards had bored of dashing past the interlopers, seemingly daring each other to get closer. It was the only kind of play Pel observed, but they suffered from the same excess of energy that plagued Human children.

Nowen said, "So. Trolsht is not the one we should be talking to unless anyone has questions about sweet-root."

Meese asked, "Are they worshipping you as a god yet?"

Nowen ignored him. "He confirmed that there is a smooth, pink individual who frequents the village, but he doesn't know anything else. I asked if the person was named Whitecloud, and he said it was possible."

Pel asked, "Who is Whitecloud?"

"She's the only researcher to be effectively adopted into the tribe. She's supposed to have a hut in the village," Nowen said. He seemed to be waiting for that to sink in.

Gladlow said, "She was a priest doing studies on converting the tribes-folk to her religion—"

"She's not just a priest, but a skilled mage as well," Nowen corrected.

Gladlow relented. "She is pretty amazing, but when you have seven centuries to work with, multiple careers aren't that impressive."

Meese said, "I'm buying a bawdy house when I'm three hundred."

Pel asked, "Centuries?"

Nowen said, "She's an Elf."

Becker said, "This Trolsht isn't certain whether a centuries old Elf lives in his village?"

"He's very old."

Gladlow asked, "Can we look for her?"

Nowen sat down. "Not until the hunting party comes back. The village is blockaded and every person is on guard while they're away. They'll be back a few hours before nightfall to start preserving meat. If they were lucky, there'll be a feast tonight, and I think we'll be able to trade for supplies."

"Speaking of trades." Gladlow dug his case out and unrolled his spellbook.

"Gladlow, I don't think it's necessary—"

"What was the one stipulation for coming with us?"

"Was there only one?" Nowen rolled his eyes but began digging through his pack. "You have the final say on security matters."

Gladlow said, "I say it's time."

Meese gestured to Pel and Becker. "Let's find something else to do for a couple of hours."

Pel followed him some distance away. "What are they trading?"

"The most intimate of intimates," Meese said, waggling his eyebrows. "We don't want to disturb the lovebirds."

Pel gave him the raised eyebrow.

"Spellbooks," He said, grinning. "It requires a lot of trust, which Gladlow is about to, hilariously, betray."

Becker asked, "Betray how?" He settled down in the sun and closed his eyes.

"Gladlow worded the arrangement so that they trade spell books until Nowen is finished copying one spell."

Pel said, "That sounds fair..." She sat and began working a chunk of sandstone along the edge of the Orc blade.

Meese chuckled, "I guarantee Gladlow can copy two or three before Nowen finishes."

"Is he some kind of genius?"

"The Institute isn't short on geniuses, but no, not really." Meese settled down in a comfortable spot. "Gladlow... applies himself. He's a good student, but he only advanced past me because I took some time off to... not study." He shrugged in embarrassment.

Pel asked, "So, you're all still in school?"

"No, none of us *have* to attend, but when you want to learn something new, you have to pay or work for an instructor. Or else spend unending hours in the library. Gladlow does all three. See, I chose a discipline to focus on, everyone does after a few years. Except Gladlow. He spends every copper on spell research. He scribes scrolls to pay for more instructors, to learn new spells, which he scribes to scrolls and trades for more rare spells."

Pel said, "You said he won a spell dueling?"

"How's he going to impress you if I tell all his stories? Let me tell you how I came upon that blade."

· · · ·

Gladlow only copied two of his friends's illusion enchantments, and nothing earth-shattering. It was the principal of the thing. One was obviously an early acquisition, likely from his first mentor. The other allowed the coding of messages, but could easily be used to forge documents. That was a little more shady than Gladlow had learned to expect from Nowen. His friend had only been a full mage for two years and hadn't advanced quickly. He intended to focus on divination magic but he spent as much time researching historical and cultural texts as he did casting. Elves and their lifespans. They always thought they'd get around to it.

Gladlow left Nowen to study his new armament. Honestly, it was mostly for Gladlow's own peace of mind. This was not the situation he thought he was bringing his friends into. He wandered over to the others and sat nearby. Becker was snoring, but Pel gave him a friendly smile before returning to her sword repairs. She had unwound the old leather and was whittling thin shavings from the wooden hilt. Meese was telling her about the time their favorite innkeeper hired them to exterminate a rat infestation, then refused to pay them except with a line of credit. He was telling it wrong, but no one was listening anyway. Gladlow pulled his hood up to shade his eyes and watched Pel work. He woke to the sound of drums and gongs.

Nowen said, "This is Ssorsh and Rossh. They have to stay with us at all times." He waved to the two seven-foot Lizards standing nearby. They were identical in every way, right down to their vibrant green extremities and blueish underbellies. One carried a spear, the other an elaborately carved war-club.

Gladlow stood and brushed himself off. "Which is which?"

Nowen looked at them and shrugged.

The five, along with their two escorts, were let into the village. The barrier around the settlement was made up of an elaborately spiked palisade of jungle hardwood. There was no actual gate. Each interlocking section stood on its own and had to be lifted and moved by a mob of villagers to gain entry.

Nowen pointed to three squat, permanent structures, one on either end of the wall and one in the middle. "I've seen drawings in the library. Uljar-Molik is laid out as a perfect triangle. They have an unexplained affinity for threes."

Becker asked, "Is Uljar-Molik the name of the village or the tribe?"

"One and the same. They differentiate between people and things, of course, but the village and tribe are thought of as a single entity."

Ssorsh and Rossh led them in through a gap made in the palisade, but as soon as the gap was closed, they just stood and waited patiently.

Meese said, "So, no tour then."

No one seemed eager to move, so Gladlow headed toward the center where the most activity seemed to be. A large group was setting up what looked to be hide tents, but he realized what they were just before Pel said "They're meat smokers. That one over there already has fish drying."

Gladlow was surprised, but he hadn't paid much attention to the literature on the Lizards. He hadn't thought there was much chance of contact, considering it was absolutely forbidden without official sanction. "I didn't know they preserved food."

Nowen said, "I don't think tribes outside of the local islands ever have. Or grow crops, or raise livestock."

"What sort of livestock?"

"Crocodiles and giant larvae."

Meese said, "Ask them not to show us the dairy."

They moved past groups processing large hog-like creatures Gladlow wasn't familiar with. They must be what was brought back from the hunt. Most of the buildings were clustered around the center of the village, and no two were alike. Something noisy was happening in a small square off to the side. For a moment it appeared several villagers were playing dice as they squatted on the ground in a group, but he soon realized it must be a method of bartering. Accompanied by the hissing chatter of the crowd, recognizable items passed to and fro, including bronze blades and jewelry, as well as more mundane items like rolls of twine or wooden plates.

Pel pointed and said, "Urchin lanterns. Lots of coppers and a few silver."

So many of the copper lanterns changed hands that they were very nearly used as coins. The most mysterious items were little pouches and packets of various sizes and colors that moved in and out of the trades, seemingly at random. While Gladlow observed, a Lizard reached over into a different pair's trade, grabbed a handful of the brightly colored packets, and dropped a large shell in their place before adding some of them to his own barter.

Becker said, "I... expected us to draw more attention."

Gladlow nodded. "It is a little strange..."

"Oh, they're watching us very carefully." Pel indicated a group right in the middle of the action. "Especially the one over there with the blue scar on his mouth."

Gladlow watched and could see she was right. He wasn't trading anything himself but seemed to be involved somehow. When a trader addressed him, he went to their patch of ground and moved some items around. So, an arbitrator of some sort. Gladlow began to get caught up in it, watching items move back and forth, switched for others, and always the little packets moving around.

Gladlow blurted out, "There's no profit."

Meese asked, "What's that, now?"

"I've been watching a few of those items move around from trade to trade. Copper lanterns—"

"Sern," Nowen said. "They're calling them sern." He opened his book to write notes.

"If the coppers are one, the silvers are worth six, and the little packets are worth half a copper. And no one is making a profit." Gladlow shook his head. "All of the trades are perfectly even."

Meese said, "That feels wrong somehow." There were several nods from the others. "Let's see how they handle a lad from Lower Furbish."

Gladlow swiped at him, but in a flash, Meese was squatting in front of a Lizard sitting with a stack of goods. Blue Scar gave up all pretense of nonchalance and stared intently as Meese extracted a dagger from his robes with a flourish, unsheathed it partially, and laid it at his feet.

Gladlow arrived behind him too late to stop it, but said anyway, "Do you think trading one of our weapons—"

"My hands are my weapons." He made a spell's elaborate hand motion, ending with a rude gesture.

"You mean you're shit at throwing daggers. Go ahead and trade both of them."

Meese's trading partner held a clawed hand over the blade and looked at him for permission. Meese made a generous shooing motion toward it. The Lizard picked up and drew the dagger only briefly before laying it down and scratching a line in the dirt between them. He then laid four silver sern and two copper on his side of the line.

Meese looked up at Gladlow with a confused look, "That's a lot of silver..."

Pel said from over his other shoulder, "That looks like more than twice what it's worth on the mainland."

"I was just fooling around, I wasn't trying to rob them blind. Nowen, will they be insulted if I back out?"

Nowen flipped through his phrasebook. "I have no idea, but they are pretty hard to insult."

Gladlow said, "Well, every other trade has been even, this one must be too."

Pel said, "They want the steel."

She was right, of course. Everywhere they looked there was high quality bronze crafting on display, but no iron to be seen. Gladlow walked over to another barter that had ceased in order to watch the big trade. He held his hand over the items and looked at the owner. The Lizard looked to Blue Scar who said something and imitated the gesture Meese had made. The other repeated it, shooing the items to Gladlow. These people adapted quickly. He gathered up a dozen of the random looking bags and packets, trying to make sure he got at least one of each, and swapped them for a silver sern from Meese's trade. No one reacted so he patted his friend on the shoulder and said, "You can take your dagger back, or wipe out the line and accept the deal." Meese did the latter and the dagger disappeared. He gathered the loot into his arms and turned back to the group. He was grinning hugely.

"You think you made off like a pirate, don't you?" Nowen sounded disapproving. "We aren't supposed to be doing anything that affects their culture."

Gladlow said, "I think we have a bigger problem. No one is trading food. How do we get supplies?" No one had any ideas. "Nowen, our friend with the scar seems to be important, ask him about Whitecloud."

Gladlow joined everyone in examining what turned out to be spice packets. "Are they medicines, do you think?"

Becker said, "The big ones are just sea salt."

Pel held up a tiny black packet to Gladlow and said, "I don't recognize this one, but it reminds me of something."

She held it so he had to lean in close to smell it. He was surprised by the pleasantness of it. "It smells like a library."

"That's it. Old books." She raised her eyebrow at him questioningly, and he realized he was grinning like a fool.

Nowen arrived to say, "I think Ssorsh and Rossh are going to lead us to Whitecloud's hut."

They all followed the two to the northern corner of the village. They stopped by one of the small cylindrical earthen buildings. It was rubbed smooth, with a thatched roof and vents cut around the top. Ssorsh and Rossh took up posts to either side of the hide serving as a door. Gladlow stuck his head in and looked around. There was only enough light to see shapes, so he muttered the first word of power he ever learned and tapped an object hanging overhead. It was a lantern, but it didn't ignite. The entire body of it shone a bright white. The room was lit in stark tones, illuminating a bed, table, and makeshift shelves with a few crates and boxes. Nothing else.

Gladlow shoved the hide out of the way and exited. "Nowen. Did you ask them to take us to Whitecloud, or to her hut?"

Nowen shrugged. "I'm... not sure. Both, maybe."

Gladlow pinched the bridge of his nose. "Throw your language spell, get out your book, and ask the twins about the last time anyone has seen an outsider of any sort in the village. If they can't help, ask them who can. Find out who will sell us some food. You can understand them better than they can understand you, so just get them talking."

Nowen crossed his arms and asked, "Anything else?"

"If we're going to have to camp in the jungle, I'd like to know now." Gladlow turned to the others. "We'll give it tonight, then in the morning we'll head back and I'll crack open the tower."

Over the next two hours, they learned the lay of the village and little else. Their young guards believed no outsiders had been in the village for at least twenty days, but it could be many more. An older female and her ward—or apprentice, Nowen wasn't certain—could apparently speak some common, but neither were available. Food wasn't traded, ever, but on a brighter note, just being let into the village made them junior citizens of a sort, and the position very generously came with meals. As for camping, the palisade wouldn't even be opened again until daybreak and the hut didn't belong to Whitecloud. It had been built specifically for outsiders, as only children sleep indoors.

The smokers would be tended throughout the night, but the feast was ready quickly and the villagers were already tucking in. Fires were lit in the three central hearths, seemingly for the sole purpose of roasting the so-called sweet-root. The Lizards ate everything else raw but didn't seem to mind when the outsiders roasted other victuals on the provided sticks. There was pork from what Becker dubbed the devilpigs, fish, slabs of white meat, and sweet-root. The five of them sat on carved log benches laid in a semi-circle near the hearth. Gladlow watched Meese spread his newly acquired spices on a handkerchief and set about trying every food and spice combination available. Gladlow grabbed up the bag of salt and made a show of offering it to Nowen and Becker before making his way toward the other end. Becker ate the least of all of them, his depression coming and going throughout the day. Gladlow sat down next to Pel and held out the salt. They ate quietly for a while, each getting up from time to time, each time sitting back down next to the other.

Gladlow asked, "Were you tired of seafood?"

Pel smiled and licked her fingers. She looked a little dazed when she said, "Pardon?"

"I was just wondering when you last had fresh meat?"

"More than a year, and nothing this good." She grinned. "Thanks for the salt, I didn't think anything could make it better."

He couldn't think of anything else to say, so he took a big bite of the white meat on a stick he was carrying.

She said, "I should at least try something else. Trade?"

He wordlessly swapped sticks with her and ate slowly. He felt he would burst soon, but she had barely slowed.

"Is it bird, or fish?"

He said, "I assume it's the crocodile Nowen mentioned."

She stopped for a second before talking through a mouthful, "It's damned good. I'll never look at them the same."

The feast was winding down, with most of the villagers scattered about, bellies swollen. Some tore off morsels and tossed them to snapping youngsters, the smallest of which were only waist high. An older specimen roasted a last sweet-root and half dozed while he nibbled. An elaborately sashed and belted individual arrived with a basket. Their skin was painted in blue whorls and something glittering. Lizards wandered over and pulled whitish objects from the basket and handed them to others. No one seemed to get one for themselves, and Gladlow could see no reason for who was chosen to receive. A few swallowed them in one gulp, others passed them on to someone else. One even tore it up and fed it to a little one. It wasn't until a Lizard pulled one from the basket and walked toward him that Gladlow saw what it was.

He said under his breath, "Oh, no."

The villager set a grub the size of a large fingerling potato on the bench between them and made the shooing motion they had learned earlier. Gladlow thought he recognized the individual from the trade.

To Gladlow's shallowly disguised horror, Pel picked up the thrashing grub in one hand and said, "I'm game if you are."

He pulled the last bite of pork off with his teeth and handed her the skewer. She ran it through one end and out the other and rolled it over the fire while Gladlow tried to look unconcerned. Their friends had gathered to watch and offered no sympathy, but plenty of nasty smiles. He saw Meese whisper something to Nowen and knew the bastard was laying a bet. He felt light-headed as Pel checked the crispy white skin for temperature before biting off half and handing him the other. He looked her right in the eye and ate his portion.

She said through a mouthful, "I didn't want to let on until you had eaten yours, but that's terrible."

"It tastes like eggs and potting soil."

"It tastes like coconut and gravy."

"Why is it greasy?"

She laughed but said, "Don't talk about it! I wish I hadn't eaten so much pork."

Gladlow worked the last bits out of his teeth and swallowed again. He noticed the Lizard was still standing nearby. He gave a seated bow and said, "Yes. Thank you. Such an honor."

Pel was red faced from holding in laughter and gave a little bow too. The Lizard bowed back, and Gladlow had to hold his laughter as well. "Great, we just taught him to bow. That's not even a thing we do."

"We taught *her* to bow."

"Her? How can you tell?"

Pel said, "Well, the females are a little slimmer, they have different jewelry, prettier eyes, and they were the only ones eating the grubs."

Chapter Five

Meese stepped around limp bodies as he made his way back from the piss trench. Unbothered by insects, comfortable in the warm night air, and tightly packed with comestibles, most of the reptiles just dropped where they were and went to sleep. There were a good number on the watch towers, but the last people up and around were the folks gathering the children from every corner and marching them to the largest, and only, stone building he had seen in the village. Meese spent a few moments watching the lines of kids, only behaving now because of the late hour and abundance of food. Even if they were green, they reminded him of the orphanage. Seeing the older ones holding the hands of the little ones made him feel maudlin. That and the pint of port he had won off of Nowen. He had trusted Gladlow not to embarrass himself in front of the lady. He then told Nowen to leave the hut to Becker as the lad needed to rest. Nowen rarely slept anyway, usually just sitting in meditation like an eccentric, as he was doing now. Meese had then given Becker his pack to rest his head on by the dying fire and gave him a couple of swigs of port for good measure. Pel and Gladlow were still talking by the fire, hip to hip. There was nothing more he could do, but settle himself down, and send his best wishes to the both of them.

He jerked awake to the sound of two dozen crocodile bellows. Completely disoriented, he scrambled to his feet and jammed his hat back on his head. Gladlow was shaking Nowen awake and Pel was doing the same to Becker. He felt a bit bleary but was recovering much faster than most of the Lizards around him. They were sluggish and had trouble standing up. The bellowing was coming from the guards up on the towers as they alerted the village. Meese trotted over to his friends as the sounds of weapons clashing rose in the distance. He said, "We should head toward the creche and help guard the little ones."

Gladlow nodded. "Nowen, how many times can you cast the hornet spell?"

"Three." Nowen already had his dagger drawn. He looked determined, but terrified.

"Three stingers..." He pulled the ruby ring from his finger and handed it to the Elf. "That will make it half a dozen."

"Do I need to know how—"

"Just put it on and you'll manifest an extra projectile for every casting. Spread them out, one for each target. Becker, you're with Nowen. Watch our rear." While he spoke he fished out another ring, this one featuring a split geode the size of a berry, and fit it over his index finger. He saw Meese eyeing it. "On loan from the practice yard." They both knew that was code for borrowed without leaving a note. Gladlow turned to Pel and Meese cringed inside. His friend was either about to blurt out his feelings or tell her to stay behind. Don't say anything stupid, boy.

Gladlow asked, "May I?" He was holding one hand ready to cast and held a small boiled-leather emblem in the other. She nodded. There was a slight shift in the light as the spell encased her, but there was nothing else to prove its existence. Gladlow trotted off toward the sounds of frenzied battle, leaving them all to follow.

Pel asked, "What does it do?"

"Best to pretend it does nothing, and don't get hit." He glanced over at her and asked, "Have you fought with mages before?"

"Not closely, no."

"Let me in front until I get off one spell, then move as you will. If you pull back, I'll assume you're prepared for another. Don't get too far away, and don't—this goes for everyone! Don't stand in front of Meese."

Pel pointed and said, "That way, between the lodges. We'll wait for it there."

Meese was relieved Gladlow listened to her. It was a superior spot to make a stand and provided some cover to their flanks. That was the stone creche building on one side and about thirty feet on the other, a longhouse of mud and timbers. Gladlow stood just inside the entrance of the alleyway with Pel to his right and a step behind. Meese took up the same position on the left. They only had to wait seconds before a mob surged into view. They couldn't make out the shadowy enemy yet, but the Lizard silhouettes were easily recognized. They fought like pack animals, all offense, but coordinated enough to isolate and overwhelm. The enemy moved with precision, in formations of eight. One of these groups made it through the villager's line of defense nearly unscathed. They moved toward the buildings but veered when they saw the five standing in the alley. As they entered the light from braziers outside of the creche building, Meese made out seven soldiers armed with shield, short spear, and leather armor. The open faced leather helms and skirts of leather strips did nothing to hide their race. Short reddish fur covered every inch of exposed skin.

Pel said, "Hobgoblins."

Her voice made Meese look her way and see she was barely contained. She was leaning forward and he could imagine her muscles vibrating. If she moved too early, Gladlow would never do whatever he was planning, but she held. Gladlow presented the back of his hand to the enemy, forearm upright, and just as they narrowed their formation to charge into the space between the buildings, Gladlow turned his palm outward with the slightest pushing motion.

"*Akoule-vronte etu seni-mou.*"

A clap of thunder at ground level made every combatant for a hundred yards duck their heads. Those immediately in front of the mage were pelted by debris as the percussion wave slammed into them, knocking four of them backward. Two rolled and regained their footing, now several yards away. Another pair lay unmoving. The three who leaned into their shields were able to hold their ground but were bloodied nonetheless. With their ranks broken, they each charged individually, and one was cut down before anyone realized Pel had moved.

Meese had begun his spell just a couple of breaths after his friend and waited until the enemy was moving to release it. A horizontal arc of blue flame rolled outward from his hand, engulfing the two nearest Hobgoblins. Pel had disregarded Gladlow's last warning and charged through the spell's boundary, but Meese mentally extinguished a few feet letting her pass un-singed. Don't stand in front of Meese, my ass, he thought. He saw Gladlow moving to get a clear view of the final two soldiers and moved to imitate him. Pel was already between them and the enemy and there was little he could do. Gladlow fondled his geode ring and waited for an opening. The main battle pushed closer and another squad could break through any moment.

The two Hobgoblins had moved closer together as they advanced, but Pel seemed to be charging the one on the left, leaving herself open to attack from his companion. Though her first swing looked wide, it was a feint barely brushing his shield but forcing him to raise it. She continued the swing as she moved right, dodging the other's spear thrust, and letting her blade's momentum carry it just over his shield and across his temple as he stepped into the blade, dying instantly. Likely to prevent her dodging, the last soldier swung his spear in a vicious slash, but she rushed forward and blocked, guiding her blade along the shaft into his hand. The spear landed at his feet along with several fingers. He howled in rage and swung his shield again and again, but she absorbed the blows against her shoulder and thrust her sword around it until he fell to his knees. She pushed the Orc blade through his heart and turned to check her companions, rolling her shoulder experimentally.

Meese and Gladlow looked at each other blankly.

Gladlow turned to her and called out, "New plan, we stay back and keep you from being mobbed. Everyone? Don't stand in front of Pel."

• • • •

Western Jungle, river bend

When the alarm sounded, the goblin archers moved forward to the edge of the treeline, Wellstone and the others following at a distance. A chorus of voices rose along with the reptile bellowing. It sounded something like the rhythmic chant of sailors pulling the hawser when the winch was down for repairs. The bellowing and the heave-ho chant was sufficient to distract the Goblins as Wellstone's crew descended on them. With only bows at the ready, the enemy was overwhelmed quickly. Half the goblins broke and ran, a larger number than anticipated, and Wellstone made an effort to drive them through the gap purposefully left for them. She wanted them to head for the jungle, not out into the open. The remaining four tried to fight close quarters, three with actual clubs and one using his bow as one. Wellstone's personal fight spilled briefly into the open, but she dispatched her opponent quickly and dragged him into the bushes. As she walked backward dragging the corpse, she could see the mob of Hobgoblins pulling the palisade section outward. She didn't think she was noticed, so she ducked back to take stock. A retreating Goblin had dropped his bow, but one who stayed to fight broke his across Villago's shins. They were left with four bows and a pile of arrows.

Villago was sitting and rubbing his lower extremities. "That was more of a success than we'd a right to hope for. Let's move."

Carlin came back from spying through the trees. "I want to know why they were here setting up an ambush."

"Let the Lizards worry about themselves," Ben said.

Dalla looked unsure but not enough to argue.

Wellstone explained, "The archers were here to provide cover for their masters' escape. Those Hobgoblins will come out of the breach in a few minutes hauling their loot, and the villagers giving chase would have been riddled with arrows. This isn't war, it's banditry."

Villago said, "We suspected pirates. If they get away with their loot, they'll have no need to bother us."

Even Ben seemed uncomfortable by that. Most sailors wouldn't like the idea of letting pirates go unmolested to later murder you for your ship.

Villago knew he was losing the argument and tried a different tactic. "The villagers would have been slaughtered in the open. Now it will be a fair fight."

Carlin said, "We can do better than that." She turned to Wellstone pleadingly. "Chief..."

Wellstone said, "This was such a well thought out ambush... it would be a shame to waste it."

They each picked up bows and took up positions behind the trees. The sailors looked nervously at Villago, but he silently relented.

Ben said, "Thank the gods," and handed Villago his bow. "I've never used one before."

Wellstone suspected she and Villago were the only skilled archers, but Carlin and Dalla spent a few moments bonding over how they hunted with their fathers as children. It seems they had similar upbringings on opposite ends of the known world. Ben was given the task of keeping watch and Wellstone instructed the women to just fire as quickly as they could, into the largest group.

They didn't have to wait long before six pairs of Hobgoblins carrying litters of baskets and bundles double-marched into the clearing. Wellstone was pleased by the position the Goblins had chosen. To get to the tree line, the looters were moving right across the archers's line of sight and only slightly toward them. The pair in front dropped the handles of the litter when arrows embedded themselves in the lead Hobgoblin's shoulder and thigh, a basket of sweet-root, and the ground twenty yards past. Both Hobgoblins, and the two immediately behind them, pulled the shields strapped to their backs and held them in the vague direction of the tree line. Wellstone cursed under her breath. She was positive hers had hit the basket. She chose a new target towards the middle and took her time. Her shaft thunked into the bandit's side, eliciting a howl and a similar reaction as the first volley. The litter dropped to the ground and several Hobgoblins raised their shields and tried to locate the source of the arrows. She knew there was no hiding from these creatures at night, so she let loose at a pair that made a dash for the jungle. Encumbered as they were, they weren't a terribly difficult target. It seemed not only did all four archers choose the same target, but they had all shaken the cobwebs off. Four arrows hit the front litter bearer in the shoulder, hip, neck, and calf. He fell dead with litter, loot, and partner landing on top of him. After a couple more volleys, the field was chaos. Lizards poured from the gap in their wall, Hobgoblins in chainmail appeared from the jungle opposite, and half of the previous litter bearers were running or limping for the jungle with a shield raised to the treeline and holding a single sack or basket. The remaining six were trotting towards the four archers with shields raised.

Wellstone shouted, "The nearest! Aim for his legs!"

It wasn't an effective strategy, though the soldiers slowed their pace slightly as they tried to run as well as present a smaller target. All the archers together only managed to take down one of them. They would reach them in seconds.

Villago said, "We have to run. If we get separated, meet at the tree—what is that?"

A swirl of sand rose from the ground halfway between them and the advancing enemy. It grew and swirled into a small funnel cloud lifting sand and grass ten feet in the air. The soldiers, along with most of the battlefield were obscured from their ambush spot as the mini cyclone pulled more sand and debris into the air. Wellstone stepped from around her tree as the little storm moved away from her. She couldn't see what happened to the advancing soldiers, but a shield was briefly lifted into the air to be thrown a few yards away. The cloud didn't increase in size but it changed course and headed in the direction of the Hobgoblins' escape route. She could then see Lizards clashing with the armored Hobgoblins. The cloud moved further and she saw a jet of flame roar across the field while two fairy lights, one red, one white, danced around and over each other as they streaked past the Lizards to slam into their opponents. The battle lasted another twenty-count and went quiet. The enemies that could retreat had done so. The only creatures standing in the field were the Lizards, already recovering their property, and a young man jogging in her direction. He stopped ten feet away and a white light appeared in his hand. He was somewhere around six feet tall, with very dark brown eyes and curly black hair. He raised a hand in a friendly greeting.

• • • •

Carlin gazed around in complete awe. The village of Uljar-Molik was legendary, at least amongst those who were even aware of its existence. She, like a few others on the harvest ships, had taken their positions, perhaps naively, to travel and study. Carlin's love was the ocean and its variety of life, but a chance to meet the Lizards in their own environment was a dream she didn't wish to wake from. Meeting new people, not that Lizards weren't people, but people more like her, was exciting as well, though she was leery of mages even if both were damned charming. She was probably just tired of sailors. It was a bit before her time when the Crown had a falling out with mages in general. At present, the Crown made a point of doing nearly everything without them. Even the breathers developed by Tesco, an individual who was obviously and incongruously a mage himself, was an effort to cut wizards out of the process. Every ship once had mages on the crew responsible for all sorts of useful tasks, not the least of which was an underwater breathing enchantment that was much more pleasant than the experience of drowning that a Tesco's offered. The Crown's artificers now had control over the production of the breathing charms, eliminating the need to further involve magicians. The Crown went a step further, some would say too far, several years ago. Spells and potions aiding in underwater activities were officially outlawed, the penalty being the same for unauthorized possession of a Tesco's. Execution. It was well known that members of the Institute refused to curb their teachings after a certain level of expertise was obtained, but as long as they weren't caught providing illegal services to enemies of the Crown, meaning smugglers, it was swept under the rug. The two wizards led their group deeper into the village. They in turn were following a pair of Lizards that had come to fetch them after the fighting was over. Looking at the aftermath, it seemed the conflict Carlin participated in was just the smallest bit of the whole. Villago and the two sailors were uncomfortable and hadn't said a word.

"Mister Gladlow, would you care to explain your presence in proscribed Crown territory?" Wellstone asked. Carlin felt mortified, but she had also learned to keep quiet when the Chief was fishing for a reaction.

Gladlow turned, and walking backward, said, "Constable Wellstone, had I known the Crown no longer disavowed their use of the Rampart barrier, and that the isle of Arux-Troth was therefore under Crown blockade, or that the contested nature of both the isle's status and that of the royal contracts held by the Institute for Magical Research and Preservation, had been resolved... I'm sorry, what was the question?"

Carlin saw the smile Wellstone wore. It meant she had learned what she wanted. The Chief always told her she liked the cocky ones.

"I'm not aware of any policy changes, Mister Gladlow," Wellstone said.

Carlin said, "I'd like to be the first to thank you for your assistance back there."

Gladlow said over his shoulder, "That's not necessary, Miss Carlin, you likely did as much to help the village as we did." He turned towards Wellstone again. "Curses, did I just admit to poaching the Crown's Hobgoblins?"

The one called Meese, which had to be a nickname of some sort, turned his young friend around and gave him a shove. Something was going on between him and the Chief. Meese had removed his hat and given Wellstone a single nod. There was no further greeting and they hadn't even acknowledged each other since. It was strange. Carlin thought that if she spent years without seeing another Human, she'd kiss the first one she met on the mouth. It made her realize, as she had many times before, that she knew little about Dwarrow, and even less about the Chief.

A large group of villagers awaited their arrival. An Elven mage in yellow robes stood chatting with them. An extremely large villager walked through the crowd, which parted around him. He wore a fur collar and stood close to eight feet tall. An open wound looked as if it would make a great addition to the collection of scars covering his torso. He stopped in front of Meese and unceremoniously dropped a massive bronze axe at his feet. He turned to walk away and Meese looked to his friends for explanation.

He whispered, "What in all the hells am I supposed to do with that?"

A small Lizard, perhaps five feet tall, stopped the larger one and spoke for a moment. The big warrior didn't turn around, but an attendant ran back for the axe and returned it. The attendant ran to Meese and placed another weapon at his feet. Meese picked it up and showed it to his friends. It looked to Carlin like a disappointing, skinny sword. The battle axe had been beautifully ornate and she would have loved a closer look.

The villager who had interrupted the exchange stepped forward and looked to the Elf.

The mage said, "This is Voorsh. She ran ahead to give the village warning of the attack. Her master will arrive soon."

Meese rattled his new sword in its sheath and said, "You sort of ruined his exit, but thanks."

"I did break his display..." Voorsh spoke clearly, but in a strange, clipped fashion. "His meaning was to give your... doing to Uljar-Molik with a... to make more strong... your village."

"And it wouldn't make us stronger if I couldn't lift it."

"Yes."

Meese asked, "Why me?"

Voorsh looked to Nowen expectantly.

Nowen said, "I told them it was your idea to guard the children."

Meese looked utterly embarrassed and didn't say anything else.

"As it turns out, the attack on the creche was a feint, while the forces attacking from the west raided the food stores."

Voorsh said, "Yes. Even this was... made less." She gestured to Wellstone's group.

Gladlow said, "Constable Wellstone tells us they need supplies, water, and food, for their boat. We'd be happy to trade."

Voorsh waved this away in a very Human gesture. "We will fill with food, with water. You may lead us there at day."

Carlin noticed a stricken look on Gladlow's face, but couldn't imagine what it was. Wellstone noticed it too.

She said, "You're welcome to join us Mister Gladlow."

His face turned to stone, but he replied, "I'm glad you have room for two more."

"It's Carlin, isn't it?" A woman was walking toward her with an intimidating sword carried bare in her hand. She stuck the blade in the sand and left it standing there as she ran forward and embraced her. Carlin felt her bones creek with the strength of the hug. She wrapped her arms around the woman before it even struck her who it was. She only realized when she was held at arm's length and looked at the other's tear-streaked face.

"Pel?" She realized she was crying too. "Did anyone else...?"

"Only Becker. He was scratched up tonight, but they're taking care of him." Pel almost couldn't ask, "Is this everyone?"

"There's fifteen of us—"

"The longboat crew. Jepps said... he disappeared with the raft. He may be alive."

Wellstone said, "If it looks clear, we'll scout the coast and look for signals."

"Constable. I'm glad you made it."

Wellstone seemed to soften a bit. "You as well."

Meese said to Voorsh, "I, for one, won't be sleeping tonight. Do your people drink?"

The group settled around a relit fire. Most of the villagers had simply gone back to sleep. They had an admirable ability to avoid unnecessary worry. Voorsh had brought a cask of alcohol, strong, but still tasting of fruit juices. Carlin rather liked it but drank carefully. The Chief rather loved it and had already refilled her flask.

Voorsh said, "My people use it to make pain less—"

"Mine too!" Meese crowed to the sky.

Carlin thought she heard a snort from Wellstone.

Voorsh continued, "Corigain likes it much... we trade."

Gladlow sat forward. "You know Master Corigain. Is he here?"

"No. He made a... village in the trees with his wife."

Gladlow nodded. "I knew he was on the island, but he's studying migratory birds or some such."

Voorsh copied his nod. "Lizard-birds. He calls Opteryx. They look like us, they look like parrot birds."

Carlin said, "Oh, no. In the trees? That way?" She pointed the way her group had arrived.

"Correct."

Gladlow asked, "What is it?"

Ben had fallen asleep, so Villago and Dalla helped her tell the story. Wellstone kept quiet.

Gladlow examined the journal and map they had brought from the tree house. "Do you mind if I show this to Nowen?"

Wellstone said, "I suppose you can keep it. I don't see any harm."

Pel asked, "You didn't find any trace of them?"

"One of the huts was webbed up inside with the remains of a dozen meals, but I didn't see anything large enough to be a person. We didn't find much of use. They must have packed for a journey."

Gladlow said, "And Whitecloud hasn't been seen in at least thirty days."

"You're thinking they all went together."

Gladlow looked at Meese. "It would explain why I was canceled. The whole expedition is gone too."

Pel said, "You never told me about the expedition."

Gladlow glanced at Wellstone. "I'm not sure I should be disclosing Institute research—"

Meese made a rude noise and said, "Disclose away! The Institute doesn't do secrets, and you were going to tell her anyway. As a matter of fact, all this talk of journeys and expeditions puts me in mind of a nice game of Traveler."

"What, are we ten years old?"

"It's a time honored tradition to bring luck on the road."

"We aren't traveling together anymore."

Meese said earnestly, "Exactly. Their journey and ours can use all the luck we can scrape together."

"Fine. The expedition—"

"Wait! We have to make the bargain."

"I'm not spitting in my hand."

Meese looked disappointed. "Fine. We've all bled together in the crucible of—"

"So drunk."

Meese glared. "An agreement of truth telling—"

"Unless embellishing a story..."

"Of, course. But no lying, *real* lying, especially if you choose Query." Meese put his hand out. Gladlow added his with a roll of his eyes. Pel next.

Carlin said, "It's not played in the south, but I've heard of it." She put her hand in. Followed by Dalla.

Voorsh shyly put her hand in. She likely had no idea what they were talking about.

Villago kept his seat but said, "It'll be dawn before this many turns, but I'll not tempt fortune. I swear."

Carlin said, "Chief?"

"Don't mind me," Wellstone said and leaned back with her eyes closed.

Everyone settled back and Meese said, "Well?"

"So. The expedition—"

"No, do it good. From the beginning."

"How far—"

"All the way. Sixty-five years ago..."

"Meese..."

"I won't cry." He made get-on-with-it motions at Gladlow.

. . . .

Gladlow had been toying with the idea of using a lesser illusion to embellish his turn, but with the subject matter at hand, it seemed too flashy. He began with one of the traditional ways to start a story.

PERILOUS SHORES

"This is the part you know. Sixty-five years ago, the world shook. No building bigger than a nomad's tent was left standing on the whole continent. Every church and castle fell. We'll never understand the loss of life." He looked to his friend and continued, "From a thousand-thousand tragedies, the worst was the loss of the Dwarrow strongholds. Impenetrable for thousands of years, and half were gone in moments. Half a race of people gone." Gladlow took a drink and everyone followed suit. "It's one of the great mysteries the Institute has dedicated itself to uncovering. Theories abound, but nothing fits. No clouds of ash, so no volcano, but rocks were reported falling everywhere. Perhaps they were comets, and a large one caused a quake. But none of the mysterious rocks left a crater as a falling star does. It was decided that it was a sort of hysteria, people finding rocks and claiming they weren't there before. People bought them, sold them, and made forgeries." Gladlow took a breath. "This is the part you don't know. A man named Corvin began to study the rocks. He started collecting them as a young man and continued even after he graduated and dedicated himself to the Institute. He became not only a skilled mage, but an expert on rocks and soil. He became an adventurer, his exploits supported and boasted by the Institute. He found similarities in the fallen stones and learned to detect fakes. He theorized that they didn't fall from the heavens, but somewhere in the world. They all came from the same location, but he was never able to calculate where. Too many had been moved around, bought and sold. Then a decade ago, it happened again, but much smaller. No quake, but a great wave. Rocks fell from the sky, and he was ready for it. He catalogued them, measured them. He could deduce how far they had been thrown by their makeup, size, and the soil they landed in. His next expedition discovered Arux-Troth. The event that caused the great Quakes, scooped the rock out of this basin and threw it hundreds of miles in every direction. The smaller event originated here as well. The discovery of the island led to many expeditions and studies. The Institute discovered the urchins, new medicines, a culture unique among their kind, and Corvin kept searching. Until five years ago. A party of eight exploring the interior of the island died, except one man. One of Corvin's pupils returned raving about Corvin going mad and killing them all. The Crown took him for questioning and he was never seen again. It was the last excuse they needed to end all contact with the island. Nine months ago, something was found believed to be a clue to the fate of the Corvin party."

Carlin asked, "Do you know what was found?"

"No, but it wasn't definitive. They've been arguing for months. Meese said the Institute doesn't do secrets, but things have changed. The Institute believes our royal contracts are still lawful. The Crown claims otherwise. We keep to the interior and they keep to the urchin beds."

Pel asked, "Why did you want so badly to be on the expedition?"

Meese said, "Corvin is his personal hero. He's been obsessed since he was a sprat. No more questions. Gladlow, you get to choose. Who will it be?"

"It's your game. You choose for me."

Meese made a big show of thinking. "Pel, Story or Query?"

"Oh. I'm not very good at stories, but I'll try. What would you like to hear?"

"Well, after tonight's display of martial prowess, can I assume you were a soldier?"

"I chose Story," she said sweetly.

"Of course, of course. What I'm getting at is, you must know more about the Verencian Legion than the rest of us. Stories you've heard from comrades?"

Gladlow gritted his teeth. Meese was going on about the Reformists again. They modeled themselves after the legendary

Legion and he was testing her. He was about to put a stop to it when Pel replied.

"I know something of the Legion, and it comes from the same disaster Gladlow spoke of."

• • • •

Pel saw real anger flash across Gladlow's face, but now he seemed embarrassed by it. She decided there was little to lose by honoring the game.

She cleared her throat shyly. "Something that most people don't know, is that Verencian isn't a real word. They called themselves the Veren Sea Guard. Then, decades later, on the march, they were called the Legion. Veren Sea. Verencian?" Her throat was already dry and scratchy, so she took a large drink. "After the Quakes, it was chaos. Everyone was trying to put the world back together, but many tried to give themselves bigger pieces than before. The three sorcerers rose to power and carved up the East. The army of Bausta was the first of its kind. He swayed the Orcs, before only fighting amongst themselves, to march against his enemies alongside the Humans that served him. Rumor spread that they were unstoppable. There were no real fortifications still standing after the Quakes. Towns were destroyed one by one and word continued to spread. Soon people just moved out of the way. Famine was taking a greater toll than the interlopers. One town decided not to flee. The port town of Veren had recovered better than most, and they could see the struggle happening around them. They transformed their entire town into a fortification. They tore down their new houses to build archer's platforms in the shallows where the enemy siege engines couldn't reach. Every boat and dock was repurposed to provide barrack space on the water. The place where their town once stood was made difficult to cross by flooding areas and filling them with traps. The Veren Straight became a gauntlet that Bausta's forces had to brave to reach the mainland. For years, whenever they broke through, they faced forces that spent their days training and waiting for them. The Guard grew stronger. They recruited refugees from destroyed towns and became the training grounds from which the best fighters came." Pel looked around. Those still awake in the hour before dawn, were listening intently. "When the Sorceress came, it all changed again. Their fortifications were destroyed, but the Verens had become the strongest army in the world. They went on the move and kept moving for years to come. They became the Legion that most have heard of. But before that, they were the best of us. I prefer to remember them that way."

Meese was looking drunk and smug, most everyone else was just drunk. Voorsh had been called away. Carlin had fallen asleep just moments ago. Villago announced he was going to search for the pisser.

Meese put his hat over his eyes and said, "Well done you." He was snoring in moments.

Pel stood and Gladlow rose in response. She said, "We should claim the hut before someone else thinks of it." She heard how it might sound, but as soon as it was out, she left it there.

"You get some rest. I'm supposed to talk to this Keeshka person." He hesitated for an instant. "I'll be there to see you off." Then he left without more.

Pel knew it was madness, but the thought of leaving in a few hours made her heart ache. She wandered toward the hut, looking forward to not feeling anything. Nowen was there, sitting outside.

Chapter Six

Communicating with Keeshka was a chore even with Voorsh translating. She was a shriveled and ancient Lizard with two milky eyes. Voorsh told him the villagers would be honored to carry her everywhere, but she refused. Every few days, she walked to one of her gathering spots to collect herbs and such. A whole retinue of young warriors and attendants accompanied her at a snail's pace. To Gladlow, she insisted on speaking common, which was not nearly as good as Voorsh's. When he didn't understand, she made bigger and bigger gestures to get it through his thick skull. It was the first impatience or frustration he had witnessed from these people. Eventually, Voorsh just translated everything she said to him no matter the language. He learned little, but before he was dismissed, Keeshka passed him a waterproof cylinder similar to his spellbook case and said Whitecloud asked her to give it to him. Dawn had passed and he sat tinkering with the scroll case. He had determined it was arcane locked, but his opening incantation was damn near as draining as the percussion spell. He decided to wait until he showed it to everyone. He headed for the center of the village to look for his friends. Nowen would probably like to examine it too, as the writing covering it was ancient Elvish. Gladlow looked up from the tube and saw Pel and Nowen standing together. She was loading a pack for the journey and Nowen had a possessive hand on her waist. Gladlow stopped suddenly, wishing he could retreat, but they had already seen him. Nowen's hand dropped and it was like nothing had happened. He was saying something, but Gladlow couldn't look away from Pel's eyes. She left, breaking the spell.

"Where did you get this?" Nowen had the scroll tube, slowly turning it in his hands. "Gladlow?"

"What?"

Nowen shook the tube in front of his face.

"Whitecloud left it for me. It's locked."

"If it's for you, why is it in Elvish?" He went back to turning it slowly as he read. "There are a few letters written to look like Elvish, but they're just common. Oh. It spells 'raincloud.'"

The case clicked and Nowen began pulling papers out. Gladlow grabbed his hand and extracted the tube, eliciting a yelp.

Instead of finding a quiet place to read, he sat down on one of the benches around the hearth. The villagers were gathering empty pots and baskets of food. One of the sailors greeted Gladlow, but though he knew he appeared lost in his reading, he wasn't seeing the page. He became aware of Wellstone sitting across from him, but she wasn't saying anything, just watching him. He looked at the materials in his hand. Two pamphlets looked like his own spellbook, but thinner, and a two-page letter. One of the booklets was research notes written in tiny script, the other was an unfamiliar enchantment and copious notes on pronunciation and gesturing. It seemed even a certain posture was needed, or perhaps a tail? He finally read the letter:

No other researchers on the island arrived for our regularly scheduled meeting. Master Bessemer and I traveled together. The Corvin hunters usually leave word or send a representative, but none of the four were present. The truly alarming absence was the flora and fauna scholars, Betta and Corigain, who have never missed a chance to socialize. Cori called these regular get-togethers "staff" meetings on account of all the wizards. I hope they're just lost following the talking lizard-bird-things they've been watching.

We've decided to look for Wulfric's party first. One, there's four of them. Two, they are only perhaps missing, so perhaps easier to find. Their camp is along the trail north of the Signal Tower. Betta and Cori's tree fort is just west of the village. I've asked Keeshka to give this message to the first mage to come along. If you aren't from the Institute, I suppose I should tell you to follow the trail east to get to the Signal Tower. You'll find it on a path to the beach. Younger tribe members often follow us around so the trails are well stomped. We aren't the only things walking the trails. We've found unidentified footprints but mostly confined to the beaches.

P.S. There may be additional supplies at the Tower. Wulfric was meant to change the password for some time, but I know he lets Vossy pick them. It's been "Salmonberry Scone" for months. Help yourself if you can get in.

Whoever you are, may your gods be generous, Whitecloud.

The second page was a recovery contract with the two booklets listed. It said:

To whomsoever may come into possession of these papers, I hope life brings you prosperity. In that vein, I offer a 100 gold reward for the delivery of our research into the care of the Magical Research and Preservation Institute.

"Something interesting?" Wellstone asked. When he didn't answer, she stood and held out her hand. "I can honestly say it was a pleasure meeting you Mister Gladlow. I hope my report doesn't bring you hardship."

"Yes. It was a pleasure." He said distractedly. "However, I think I'll accompany you to the beach."

· · · ·

"We're walking them to the boat? Or are you leaving with them?" Meese said. He was joking, but Gladlow didn't react, even to look annoyed.

He only said, "There's something wrong."

"I can tell. Do you want to talk about it?" The lad's silence was a clear answer.

Meese put his hand on his friend's arm. "Chin up. Maybe you and Pel can arrange a way to contact each other when we're done here."

"That won't be necessary." Gladlow handed him Whitecloud's letter.

Meese was reading when Nowen arrived with Voorsh and asked, "They're saying you're going with them? Voorsh is taking me to Keeshka, but if you need me—"

"I need Voorsh." Gladlow turned to the young Lizard. "There may be greater danger than anticipated. I think more weapons and fewer jugs..."

Voorsh replied, "It is not needed to carry less. I will ask Sessek to bring hunters. I am needed?"

"To translate."

Nowen said, "I think I have a better grasp of the language now—"

"We need to ask some questions we should have been asking last night. Will you come with us?"

Voorsh said, "Yes."

Meese could see his friend's worry, but couldn't understand it. "Gladlow, the letter is disappointing, but it only confirms what we already knew..."

"She wrote it as if they weren't coming back—"

"She's been a priest for a couple of hundred years, they don't make them more dramatic."

Gladlow sighed. "Listen to me. Wulfric is missing and Bessemer has gone to look for him. They may be the only ones on the island that can use the teleport circles."

"Balls. You're thinking we should get on that boat."

"I'm thinking we should move quickly." Gladlow turned to Voorsh. "At the river, we'll set up an enchantment to carry the water while your people fill the pots. We'll be able to move faster. Go speak with Sessek." Gladlow called after her, "Thank you." He then turned to Meese but appeared to change his mind and addressed Nowen instead. "Bring me Wellstone."

Their little army was on the move, and it did look like an army. Sessek turned out to be the name of the one they had called Blue Scar. Their hierarchy seemed complicated to Meese, but he was a hunt leader which was a big deal. Gladlow asked him and Voorsh to stay close.

Gladlow made sure everything was moving briskly before asking, "Constable Wellstone, would you describe to Voorsh everything you saw after the *Indomitable* went down?"

She just continued to walk with no response. Meese was about to say something when Gladlow waved him down and continued. "Dalla has spoken of it. She believes you—"

"I don't know if I want to talk about it." This was the first sign of vulnerability Meese had seen from her.

Carlin was there to put a hand on her shoulder. "You've told us enough, we can answer questions for you."

"I didn't join the game last night because I was afraid someone would ask. It's gotten worse every minute since you pulled me onto the boat. I sleep less every night."

Gladlow said, "If it helps, we can continue the game now. You know, since we've all bled together in the crucible or something."

She had tears in her eyes when she looked over at him. Meese thought they flickered to him for the briefest moment. She told everything. Carlin sobbed when she learned of Rillan's attempted murder. Wellstone told of the great beast briefly, and the eel-men at length. While she spoke of their harvesting of corpses, there was no sound but Voorsh translating under her breath in their hissing language. By the time Wellstone finished, she was fully composed. Meese had a thought that he could know her for decades more and never see her that vulnerable again.

Voorsh said, "You have seen Boazoch." Every villager in earshot turned to her when she said the name. "I am sorry for the honor. In the past, the one bringing tribute was killed. We do not know why he spares us. We think he enjoys speaking to us?"

Gladlow asked, "What does he look like? Have you seen him?"

Voorsh said, "Yes. Eyes like mine. Hard shell."

Gladlow said, "A shell. Boiling water. Boazoch is a dragon turtle. Meese, what do you know about them?"

Meese said, "There are so few of them, and their territories are so large, that no one knows anything." He shrugged. "It's a dragon."

"Voorsh, your people pay him tribute? Could you tell us about it?"

She said, "Yes. It is allowed. We give gifts of food. Pretty stones. We carve figures. When the sea is coolest, the tribute floats on wood and dried vines. It is made like a beast of the water. One pushes it to sea each day until he comes. The one stays to speak with him. He might kill the one, or demand more. Often he speaks to the one, sometimes for moments, sometimes the day."

Wellstone asked, "The one. Who is chosen?"

"In the past, a person of less use would go. Someone ill or... bad birth? But once a beautiful one brought the tribute, expecting to die. They were the first to be spared. Now the healthiest goes. Sometimes we compete for the honor."

Gladlow said, "I have a question for the group. Would it be possible for Crown ships to anchor off this island for four months of the year, for decades, without paying tribute?"

Wellstone said, "I've never heard of anything like this. No one would board a ship knowing that thing was out there."

Voorsh began speaking to Sessek at length. She then said, "Sessek has seen. Boazoch has spoken to him." After conferring with him for another moment, she said, "He was told his coloring was pleasant, nicer than the others. Boazoch was speaking of a tribe on the other island. They are different than us. Live different. They do not have our blue. He was told that Boazoch is given bright metal..." She gestured to Nowen.

He said, "Silver?"

"Yes, and the other."

"Platinum."

"The others give all white metal to him. But we keep ours for making. He likes the things we make. He likes that we give him much."

Carlin said, "I saw something once. Not in the water, I mean I saw paperwork. Chief, remember that bailiff sent by the Crown? He made me carry his ledgers and follow him around all day? He kept brushing the back of his hand across my breasts whenever he took one from me or handed it back. You called him a filthy little—"

"The ledgers?"

"The urchin lanterns were tallied from the whole season's harvest. It looked accurate. The silver paid for the ship and wages, while the copper was listed as profit. The platinum wasn't there at all, and I know we found three on that trip."

Wellstone said, "That's worth somewhat less than seven hundred gold." She continued to muse aloud. "Though it would be more than he got from any other source. Maybe it's enough."

Gladlow said, "I can't imagine the Crown making a business mistake like failing to pay the toll. What happened to the tribute?"

Carlin asked, "You think he sank the ship over seven hundred gold?"

No one answered. Meese knew plenty of people who would do worse for less.

Gladlow asked, "Voorsh, what about these eel-men? Have you had dealings with them?"

"No." She seemed to realize her answer wasn't satisfactory. "We have never seen such as them."

"They sound like Siyokoy," Nowen said, "but they're on the wrong side of the world. I've only seen sketches."

Gladlow asked, "Are they servants of Boazoch? Or were they just taking advantage of the attack?"

Wellstone said, "That beast sank the ship and boiled the ocean to kill off anyone in the water. These Siyokoy things must have moved in immediately after to gather... It was coordinated, it had to be."

Becker had been listening quietly, but said, "Pel agreed with you. She said at the time it felt like a harvest."

Meese saw Pel just ahead, but he couldn't tell if she was listening. They reached the river without incident and Gladlow took the time to cast directly from his spellbook. The porter spell was useful but was completely unnecessary. It could only carry a sixth of what they needed, leaving the villagers to carry the rest, which they did without breaking a sweat, or whatever reptiles do instead of sweat. Over the years, Meese had nearly broken Gladlow of his long-time habit of using magic to soothe his anger. It was his way of controlling himself when he felt out of control. Deep down, in recent years very deep, Gladlow had a startling temper. Meese hoped this time he was just being overly helpful.

They passed the tree fort, but the sailors didn't see any new activity. The mages agreed to search more thoroughly should they return. The rest of the journey went without incident, but Meese grew more worried. Gladlow insisted on re-casting the porter every hour, maintaining a hovering stack of water pots bobbing behind. Worse, he took to activating his light at every opportunity, a sure sign of agitation. Neither of these took any real energy, but Meese didn't know how much his friend could have left. He didn't seem to have taken any time to rest. As they walked up the shallow incline and exited the jungle canopy, Wellstone and Villago took the lead to avoid panicking the crew with a mob of fifty Lizards. As Meese topped the rise, his stomach dropped. There was a double handful of sailors unloading a large boat sunk in the shallows.

· · · ·

Pel stood on a small rise, keeping watch on the water while the army of villagers pulled the boat onto the shore. Every last thing had been unloaded and scattered across the sand. It seemed the crew planned to stay and repair the boat. She overheard Villago pointing out where a barricade would need to be built. She wondered how she would make herself useful, maybe hunting, but likely guard duty and the inevitable killing when the attacks came. She stayed there on watch while the gigantic water barrels were removed from the ship and placed up on the rise to be filled by the villagers. They then went into the tree line to cut poles and haul them to the Humans' new camp.

Every second she was aware of Gladlow. Without ever looking, she tracked his movements around the beach. He threw himself bodily at the work to be done. She didn't know him well, but she knew it meant he wasn't staying. Midday, the point of no return, was soon to arrive if the others planned to make it back to the village before nightfall. She knew when he was climbing the rise behind her, had wondered how this would go. Was he the kind of man to beg her, or worse, 'forgive' her? Anger rose at the past men who had assumed a claim on her. Anger? Somehow she knew it wouldn't be that. She didn't believe, but still feared, he was a man to walk away without a word. Or perhaps she had hoped he was.

"Pel."

The sound of his voice made her think she might be the one to beg, but she calmed her face and turned. It would be over soon. Only, he wasn't alone. Meese and Wellstone flanked him, the two Dwarrow who never spoke a word to each other.

"I have a proposal for the three of you," Gladlow said, but she felt he was only addressing her. "I intend to collect the papers and personal items of the missing researchers and return them to the Institute. The rewards will be substantial, and I propose equal shares if you all will accompany me. To start, Whitecloud's package contained a letter of recovery worth a hundred gold."

Wellstone asked, "Just us? What about those two?" She gestured down the hill where Nowen looked annoyed and Carlin looked anxious. "Or Villago?"

Gladlow said, "I choose you three, you'll have to decide on the others. Or vote."

Pel asked Wellstone, "Are you agreeing?"

She said, "Miss Pel, it's difficult to admit, but I never had any intention of getting back on that boat."

Pel looked to Meese, but he just gave her a shrug. Did she have to ask?

Meese asked Gladlow, "Why do we have to decide? Won't you be the leader?"

"Maybe I can only have three deaths on my conscience. As for leading, feel free to vote on that too. I abstain."

Wellstone said, "Villago will stay with the ship, probably Ben and Dalla too, but I don't vouch for them. Carlin is another matter, " she mused aloud, "I'm tempted to leave her somewhere safer, but she'd follow me anyway. Any objections?"

Pel saw head shakes all around.

Meese said, "Nowen is useless, but he's a coward. Any objections?" No one laughed. "Fine, he can carry the loot."

Pel turned away, formulating her excuse, the importance of protecting the ship, and how she was needed there. She said, "I'll come."

Gladlow asked, "And Becker?"

"No. He stays."

They took the time to explain to Villago. They promised to send help if there was any to be found. He seemed determined this time to wait until he was sure they could make it home. There was some talk of gathering a tribute themselves to buy safe passage, but repairing and protecting the vessel was enough to worry about for the time being. Becker seemed relieved to be back with the crew but embraced Pel and thanked her. He removed his steel bands and wouldn't let her refuse to take them. When the Lizards headed home, Pel followed with the others.

The hunters ranged ahead as before, but this time joined by Sessek. There was tension in the group, but it could be attributed to the worsened situation. Even Meese was subdued. Voorsh was following Gladlow closely and seemed to make an effort to start a conversation.

"My people make good work for Humans on the beach."

Gladlow looked round at her and agreed, "Yes. Very kind. It put them weeks ahead on fortifying. We can return the favor if—"

She said, "No, no. It was done with... glad." She was quiet for a moment before she said, "Whitecloud, others, are respectful. Dealings, of our peoples, good."

Gladlow said, "That's good. We'll be staying at Corigain's treehouse tonight, but I would like to come to the village to trade in the morning, if we're still welcome."

She said, "Yes, yes. Welcome. I do make myself useful."

"Umm, yes you do. You've been—"

"Gladlow!" Wellstone said, "Are you thick? She wants you to invite her."

Voorsh said, "Correct."

"Oh. It's dangerous..."

"I have weapons for my travels."

Gladlow asked, "What is it you do?"

"Explain?"

"What is your purpose... to your village?"

"I hunt, not food, knowing."

"Knowledge?"

"Knowledge.

"You're a researcher? Are you coming to study us?"

Voorsh said, "Yes. And everything."

Gladlow asked, "Would you give us a few minutes to talk?"

"Yes." She dropped back to walk with some of her fellow Lizards.

"Wellstone?"

"I think we couldn't ask for a better guide than a local girl."

"Meese?"

"She can help Nowen with his phrasebook. And his personality."

"Pell?"

She started. She was listening but didn't expect him to ask her opinion. "I... think even the younger ones looked to be good in a fight, and the more people on watch the better."

Nowen said, "I think that—"

"Irrelevant!" Meese hooted. "You've already been outvoted."

"I wasn't objecting—"

Meese said, "Carlin, what do you think?"

"She's adorable. I have a thousand questions..."

Gladlow said, "I suppose she's in."

Voorsh said from directly behind him, "Equal shares?"

• • • •

Jungle Treehouse, Corigain's office

Wellstone surveyed their room for the night. Having broken into it previously, it wasn't that interesting, but then again she hadn't been looking at the office of a tree-dwelling wizard with an eye towards bedding down with three other ladies. Truth be told, it was more spacious than her accommodations had been for years and much nicer than in years previous to that.

Gladlow shoved the desks and chairs to the walls while fussing and making apologies. "You're sure you don't want to take the bedroom? It's bigger—"

"And comes with complementary spider eggs," Wellstone said from a surprisingly comfortable chair. Pel stood patiently out of the way, while Carlin and Voorsh tried to examine the contents of the drawers and cabinets with only the dim light from the door.

"Right. We'll have it cleaned out in a moment." Gladlow stood there for a moment. "I fixed the door so it won't lock you out. You can just use the bar. It's interesting, I think the shaft of the door handle was cut on purpose when they left. There's a minor arcana, a utility spell that would rejoin the two pieces, so it's a sort of magical puzzle lock."

Wellstone said, "Clever."

"A little. I'm not sure of its purpose when the owner could have easily put up traps, wards, and locks that would slow me down."

"So, it was meant for mages to use, but those less powerful than himself."

Gladlow looked surprised at her insight. "I had a thought like that this morning. Would you read Whitecloud's note and give me your impressions?" He held out the scroll tube.

She uncapped it and unrolled the letter. "It will be awfully dark when we close that door."

Gladlow walked to where Pel was standing, chose a small carved figure of a devil-pig from a shelf, and placed it on the desk. The piggy was soon shining with a harsh white light. He thought better of it and recast his spell, changing the color to a better approximation of firelight. It was much nicer. Showoff.

Wellstone put her bare feet on the desk and read the page. "I think I see what you're thinking. Here, Whitecloud acknowledges the receiver may not be from the Institute."

"Right, and the case was sealed magically, but the password is carved on the outside in common, hidden in old Elvish."

"Who reads old Elvish? Don't say it. Besides old Elves?"

Gladlow grinned, "Mages. Of course, anyone who can read common could probably find it, but it's obvious to someone who's copied a few spells."

Carlin asked, "Magic is just old Elvish?"

"I'll save the lecture on the nature of magic for another time, but spells allow even dissimilar minds to focus power in similar ways. Every intelligent race known has access to powerful magic, but their spells, their systems, can be very different. Elves are one of the oldest races and have some of the most well developed spells. They tend to be a bit easier and a lot more reliable."

Wellstone said, "Be sure to let us know when you're available for that lecture." She almost felt bad at his embarrassment, but Pel was smiling for the first time. "So, both of these powerful mages seemed to feel there was a strong possibility that the people finding their research might not even be from their own Institute."

"Right, all the while hoping someday it would at least end up in the hands of other mages. What do you make of that?"

Wellstone said, "It smacks of a will. Or a suicide note."

Pel spoke up, making Wellstone realize she hadn't spoken a word in hours. "It doesn't have to mean they thought they would die, only that they might not come back."

Gladlow said, "You're right. The thought that keeps these people awake at night isn't dying, it's having their funding cut." They stood there smiling at each other until just after it was awkward. "Well, it might mean there's something here to find. I'll help look in the morning. Do you, any of you, need anything?"

Wellstone asked, "Do I just throw the light out the window when we're ready to sleep, or...?"

"Sure. But it only lasts an hour."

"So, you plan to come to our bedroom every hour to relight the pig?"

Gladlow rolled his eyes upward and exited.

A voice from outside yelled, "Hey!"

Gladlow dropped Meese's staff in an umbrella stand by the door and pulled the metal cap, uncovering the flame. "Anything else? Slippers? Warm milk?"

"That will be all." She jumped up and barred the door before digging through her pack-basket and pulling a large bottle free. "If I could toast the ones we've lost without weeping, I would. Instead, here's to the sailors on the edge of the sea, to the folk in the village... and the fools in the tree!" Taking a long pull, she held it out to Pel, who waved it away. "You can't refuse after a rhyme like that." Wellstone wiggled the bottle until the other woman took it and sat down. Pel drank and passed it to Carlin. Voorsh was there waiting when she lowered the bottle.

Carlin made a face. "Whiskey is so nasty without something to mix." She saw the little Lizard with her hands out and asked Wellstone, "Should she be drinking?"

Voorsh said, "Equal shares," and took the bottle. Her big eyes were watering when she handed it to Wellstone.

Carlin said, "Speaking of equal—"

"No," Wellstone said, "I took the bottle from the boat before we made our pact." She used her basket as a pillow and sent the bottle back around.

Pel said, "So, you stole supplies from those poor sailors on the edge of the sea..." Wellstone noticed she didn't refuse another drink.

"Well, it being contraband, as Constable, confiscating it was my duty."

"And drinking it?"

"I'm off duty at the moment." Wellstone cut her laugh short. "I suppose I'm off duty for good."

Carlin said, "I only had that job because of you. I'll have to start over completely."

Wellstone said, "You can follow me to a new post. I think you'll enjoy helping me guard the fish warehouses."

Pel asked, "I don't suppose there's any sort of pay for survivors?"

"A bit, for the sailors. A calculation of lost wages will be given to them, or surviving kin. I'm afraid you're out of luck, though. Squids are hired by the purser, and the office went down with the ship."

"Perfect."

"As my final act as an officer of the Crown, allow me to offer a generous compensation. Take an extra swig and we'll call it even."

Pel did just that. "Am I horrible for moaning about my luck? I know I should feel more for the people who died, but it's just too big..."

Carlin said, "I only cried when I realized I lost my things. My town has a tradition when young people go away for the first time. Everyone gives you something for your travels. Close family gives you small things to make you remember home, and your neighbors give you something useful. The biggest ship in the fleet went down, and I cried because I lost Mama Bahti's boots." She took a drink through fresh tears.

Wellstone said, "Those were fine boots. I'd gladly wear out two pairs of lesser boots walking to get me some of those."

Pel said, "Talk of boots might make me cry too. My feet have been bare for days. I thought rocks and branches would be the worst, but the sand is rubbing me raw."

Voorsh said from where she lay on her side, "Sand rubs everything, but nice for sleeping."

Wellstone said, "I have to admit the truth of that. My ass bone is cutting a groove in the floor." She shifted painfully. "We need a volunteer to collect our equal share of the blankets."

Smiling slyly, Carlin tried to rise, but Voorsh beat her to the door.

• • • •

Gladlow rushed to open the door. "Oh. Voorsh. What—"

The little Lizard poked a claw at his chest and said, "The females are not..." She hissed something at Nowen. He shrugged and shook his head.

She tried again, "The ground is hard." She punctuated each word with a belligerent finger.

Gladlow said, "Right. We got most of the webs—"

"And desiccated remains..." added Meese.

"—and desiccated remains. We were just dividing up the bedding..." He gestured vaguely behind him.

Voorsh looked at the other two mages, both sitting back on the bed, Meese with a book and his own small flask of Uljar-Molik rum. Gladlow suspected Voorsh's pose with hand on hip was something she picked up from her new mammal friends.

Gladlow said, "Right. Up lads." Nowen sat down in the one chair and closed his eyes again.

Voorsh left with an enormous bundle she made of the mattress, blankets, and the rest of the rum. She left the pillows, but only because she couldn't carry them.

Gladlow held the door. "Can I carry something? You'll need a hand free to cross—"

Voorsh said, "Do not teach me to walk a bridge."

He watched her cross and turned back to the others. "What in the hells was that? I'd swear she smelled of whiskey."

Meese said, "Face it, lads. We're outnumbered now." He hopped off the bed and motioned Gladlow outside. "Let's check the perimeter." He closed the door behind them and sat to one side of the door. The only light was what little escaped from the huts. Gladlow heard him unstopper another flask. He leaned over the railing, but couldn't see the ground. The night was deafening with the sound of insects and, hopefully, frogs.

"Sit down lad, before you fall over."

Gladlow thought he meant fall over the edge but falling unconscious on the deck was a possibility too. He hadn't slept for two days. He sat on the opposite side of the door and took the flask thrust into his chest. He drank and drifted, the noise lulling him but making it impossible to fall asleep.

"I wanted to say something about Pel..."

"Meese, leave it alone. Leave her alone. Your matchmaking rubbish can only hurt at this point."

"I agree. Her past—"

"She's not Reformist. It's not possible."

"I know, I know, I was wrong. I was just looking out for you and I made a mistake. The Reformists stole most of their rhetoric from the propaganda the Verencian Legion used in the war. I remember it well, and it made me nervous for you."

"She was just as concerned as we were about the villagers. The less Human looking someone is, the more they're hated. Maybe she has a relative or someone she picked up a phrase or two from—"

"Gladlow, she's not Reformist. She's Legion."

Gladlow made a rude sound and snatched the flask away. "I think you've had enough."

"You saw her fight..."

"But I've never seen a Legionary fight, at least not with a sword. I saw a sixty year old man attack a fishmonger with a herring. She's decades too young."

"Not necessarily. The Legion slowly shrank as their... recruiting practices changed. They were active until the third sorcerer was killed."

"Child soldiers. How much of that is true?"

"All of it, and worse. My point is, the survivors of the last army would be her age now."

Gladlow took a long drink. "There are a lot of fine swordsmen in the world without abduction and torture." He jabbed the flask to his friend triumphantly. "And I heard they'd be covered in scars. She's..."

"You were going to say *perfect*."

"Shut up."

"That does poke a hole in my map. I would have thought there would be marks, and with how little she's wearing, and how carefully you've looked—"

Gladlow bumped the bottom of the flask as his friend was drinking.

"What, are you ten?" He mumbled as he brushed rum out of his beard.

"So, she's damn good with a sword..."

Meese sighed. "Gladlow, she's *damned* good with a sword. We don't know how good, because Hobgoblin soldiers apparently aren't much of a challenge. Can I repeat your point about her age?" He took an uninterrupted drink. "It's not that though, it's the technique that convinced me. You're right about most of the Legionaries, the ones who didn't kill themselves with drink, just... killed themselves. But a few kept fighting, mostly mercenary work or banditry. There was a customer of Mister Brewbester, Ezz he was called. He was a trainer for the militia. This one time a group of bandits, just grain thieves really, had just hit the town, and every able-bodied man went after them. I stayed close to Ezz and a few of his trainees when everyone split up. They were the only people I knew there. Ezz went right to the bandits, but they laid an ambush. They were just half-starved vagrants, and not armed well, but there was a lot more of them than reported. Anyway, I had watched him training lads and lasses plenty of times when I was picking up or dropping off. It was all stances and repeated movements, all very structured, yes?

Well, I never believed the rumors of him being Legion until I saw him in a real fight. Never taking a stance, constantly moving, and his opponents just seemed to walk into his swings. Every move Pel made last night made me remember Ezz. Hells lad, you know a lot more about fighting than I do, but I would bet my life that those two had the same training."

Gladlow felt tears in his eyes at the thought of a childhood like that for her, but maybe they were for his own upbringing that briefly mirrored it.

Meese heard his friend's breathing roughen. "Lad, I'm not worried for your safety. I'm convinced she's a good and trustworthy girl. But, maybe, you should be careful how you proceed. For her sake."

"There's not likely to be much proceeding, but I take your point." Gladlow stood and pulled Meese to his feet. "It's time for sleep. Tomorrow, there's new purpose to find. We're all starting from the beginning."

• • • •

Wellstone made a show of thinking a moment before answering. "The worst was working the sewers. Always some thief thinking they'll make their brilliant escape through the sewers. Once, I was chasing a fool and took a wrong turn in the tunnels. We ran into a *different* thief escaping from *his* robbery. So, I suppose the first thief was right, at least." That one generated more laughter than it deserved, except from Voorsh who had passed out under a desk on her blanket nest.

Carlin said, "My worst was back home. I was a coffiner, while I studied at the temple. Preparing bodies, preparing coffins, over and over. I didn't mind it so much until my brother died. I started having nightmares."

Wellstone thought the girl was too drunk to cry, but she didn't want to test it. She said, "I know sweetie. Pel. Worst job."

Pel said, "That is a long list..."

Carlin said, "If you had to go back to a past job, the very last one you would do again."

"I was a private guard in an upscale tavern for a while. In disguise so I could watch for trouble without making the patrons nervous. I dressed nice, talked to people, drank—"

"You obviously don't understand the game..." Wellstone said.

"Just a minute. My ass was bruised from the constant grabbing, and my knuckles were worse from punching the grabbers. One man—this is a true story—I broke his hand on his second offense. The next night, he grabs me with his good hand. He must have never looked at my face."

Carlin asked, "What did you break that time?"

"His two friends. I told them he was their problem from now on."

Wellstone raised the bottle to that one. It was damn near empty and she hadn't gotten to the questions she wanted to ask. "How did you manage to get on the squid crew so quickly? Most everyone starts as a free diver for a couple of seasons."

Pel shrugged and said, "I did well in the trials. I've always been a strong swimmer, and everything else was simple."

"And where did they start you again?" Wellstone knew she'd had too much to drink if she couldn't be more subtle than that. Pel was smiling at her. She knew what she was being asked.

"At the bottom, Constable."

"You certainly didn't stay there..."

"Not for long."

Carlin said, "No one has ever gotten to raft One that quickly. How did you do it, Pel?"

"A lot of hard work and a lot of under-the-table deals."

Wellstone stopped with the bottle halfway to her mouth. The other woman beckoned and she handed it over.

Pel said, "It's all rigged to make the divers compete, with the real draw being the possibility of moving to a raft further out. Make quota three days in a row and on the next three your harvest is compared to the divers on the next raft. If you beat the lowest producer by a single urchin, you take their spot."

Carlin said, "Right. So it's possible to move up once a week."

"Barely possible. The further along the chain, the more potential urchins. So a string of luck can get you bumped, and so can divers ahead of you dying, disappearing, or dropping back."

Wellstone knew the system intimately but wanted to keep her talking. She asked, "Dropping back from injuries?"

Pel said, "Yes, or just fatigue. Also, instead of reporting their total, they can sell urchins to those up the chain who need to hit a certain number. They make more than the bonuses for their current raft and drop back to the middle."

Carlin said, "That's why so many stay in the middle and never seem to move up."

"Right. The really clever ones can calculate who will pay a fortune for a single urchin just to keep their spot. The bigger bonuses at the end often get paid to the middle."

Wellstone, "So how did you manage it?"

Pel said, "I found people willing to drop back in return for a big payout. They only lose one spot, so why not sell most of their haul and start over with a lower quota next week."

Carlin asked, "How could you afford to do that?"

"Well, I'm a good diver and rarely needed all of them to hit my target number. I resold the rest so I didn't go broke. It was more about clearing a path."

Wellstone said, "I can see how bright a girl you are, just by your explaining it so well with this much whiskey in you... but you had to have help."

"I estimate fifteen others helped, if you don't include any of the divers I made deals with. It gets tricky when you near the end of the line. Those divers are in it not only to get to the top but start closer to it in the following year. Their rank means more to them than profits."

Wellstone pushed again, "You thought of all of this yourself?"

"No, I could barely keep it straight on the ship. I just followed orders. Before you ask, I need a favor. I'm telling you this because I don't think it matters, at least not to me. I'll even help you with a report if it gets your job back. But I want to tell Gladlow first."

"Why is that?"

"Just... a token of respect or... he's supposed to be the leader, isn't he?"

Wellstone narrowed her eyes and pretended to think, but honestly, she was drunk, interrogating a drunk, and was having a little trouble following. Pel was looking at her earnestly and she was feeling very affectionate to these ladies. "You tell the dauntless Mister Gladlow tomorrow and then help us write a report to the Crown?"

"Anonymously."

They shook hands and Wellstone retrieved Meese's staff. She laid it on the floor between them, watching the flame lick across the wood without heat. She said, "Sleep well, ladies," and covered the flame.

Carlin asked, "What do you think the boys are talking about?"

• • • •

"Oh, that reeks." Nowen sat in his chair with a finger under his nose. "Meese, you're disgusting."

"You can make yourself sick holding back the winds." Meese drummed on his stomach.

"I think it's too late. You may have only days to live."

"I couldn't hammer the splitting wedge in front of the ladies, could I?"

"We were walking in the jungle for hours and you couldn't find an opportunity? I'm trying to meditate."

"How do you expect to improve if you can't ignore a little back-belch? Gladlow. *Gladlow.* How are you able to sleep through all the robe-ripping?"

"Superior concentration."

. . . .

"Pel. *Pel,*" Carlin whispered in the dark.

"Yes?"

"Are you sleeping?"

"Yes." Pel lay for a long moment before asking, "What do you need?"

"Which of the boys is your favorite?"

"How much did you drink?"

"A lot. Meese is the handsomest and Nowen is the, sort of, prettiest, but watching Gladlow work today, well, he's winning me over. Who do you think is the best looking?"

Pel groaned. "Carlin, I don't care. Go to sleep."

"If there was a knock on the door right now, and you answered it, who would you want it to be? Answer and I'll go to sleep. Promise."

From the dark, Wellstone said, "Mention boys again and I'll tell one of them about the chowder incident. And you won't know which one I told."

Carlin said, "Sleep well, everyone."

Pel fell asleep looking towards the door.

Chapter Seven

The trek to the village wasn't long, but it looked to Pel like most of the group was feeling their evening catch up. They tried to drink the river dry and there was no talk of breakfast. Nowen apparently didn't partake on this occasion and Gladlow looked better than he did the day before. Everyone else slogged along behind them quietly. Gladlow did seem gruffer than usual as Nowen seemed to be annoying him. Pel sincerely hoped she hadn't driven a wedge between them, but Nowen at least hadn't noticed anything wrong. It did bring up another thing she needed to take care of. She pulled Wellstone far to the rear.

"Wellstone, I need your advice."

"Drink less."

"About Nowen."

Wellstone rubbed her face vigorously and said, "What do you need?"

"I need to tell him I don't... I need him to back off, but—"

"Break his wrist."

"No, it's my fault. He doesn't seem to hear me though, when I say—"

"That's because he's incredibly immature, selfish, and lazy. Other than that, he seems like a good lad. Be firm and don't give him any slack. If he doesn't listen, break his wrist."

Pel sighed and admitted, "He's a bit whiney."

"We shouldn't be too hard on him. By the look of him, I'd say he's younger than me, maybe sixties. That's something like thirteen in Humans."

Pel stopped dead in the trail with her hands over her mouth. No sound came out, but her mind was screaming.

Wellstone noticed she had left her behind. "What is it? What did I say... Oh no. You already...?" She started laughing so loudly that everyone looked back at them. "Sorry, sorry. I shouldn't have put it like that. Trust me, even a weedy academic like him has been plowing the fields for decades. Come on. It's alright."

Pel resumed walking and everyone went back to their slog.

Wellstone said, "Listen. Elves are strange about that stuff. On one hand, they try to appear less interested than Humans—though, seriously, who isn't? On the other hand, they're obsessed with fertility. They have temples filled with ritualized wrestling, year round. Even if he didn't have a sweetheart forty years ago, he would have slipped it to a few masked priestesses just in service to his people."

Pel breathed deeply. "I don't know what to say to him."

"You've never had to tell someone to shove off?"

"Not without breaking their wrist."

The visit to the village didn't take long, Gladlow seemed determined to keep everyone moving. They took the time to barter and Voorsh brought dried fish and fruit from the storehouse to dump into everyone's packs and baskets. She was impressive in her full raiment as a lore-hunter, a term proudly coined by Nowen. Her natural blue markings were highlighted with painted patterns and she wore a harness of leather bags and tubes. The weapons she spoke of were a crocodile scute buckler strapped to her left wrist with two bronze blades protruding from the front edge, and a small war club cast from copper with the appearance of a single sickle-shaped claw. Wellstone seemed content with her looted Goblin bow and neither she nor Meese responded when anyone suggested she use his newly gifted sword. He had it strapped horizontally across the top of his pack, but otherwise, he and the other two mages looked the same as when she met them on the road, Gladlow with his oak and leather staff, Nowen with a long dagger, and Meese with his iron capped staff.

Wellstone approached her and said, "Pel, it's your turn to give a little advice. Carlin has some training, but it's mostly unarmed, dealing with drunks and pickpockets. Frankly, she's rubbish in a sword fight. What should we buy her?"

Pel thought for a moment. "A small blade is reliable, but being able to keep more distance would be best. I think one of the mid-sized war clubs the Lizards like and a shield. I'm happy to work with her."

"Brilliant. She uses every weapon as a club anyway. Do you need anything? We're pooling our trinkets."

"Ask about the Hobgoblin gear. I could use some of the armor, and I doubt the Lizards need it."

Wellstone said, "I thought of that. There was almost nothing left behind. Voorsh said they collected every body during their retreat. They fought hard for them. There're a couple of shields and no blades."

"They didn't want to arm the villagers with steel and iron."

"Exactly. That explains why the ones outside were in chain and the raiders wore leather."

Pel gave her Becker's bracelets. "See if you can get one of those shields for Carlin, they're well made, and a stout blade for me, less than twenty inches. Get a few javelins for the group, we can use them for hunting or fishing." She didn't bother asking for clothes. The Lizards didn't need them any more than armor. Their rather fine leatherwork was confined to belts and pouches.

They were soon on their way with more than enough day left to reach the mages' signal tower. The group marched, in the same order as that morning, along the main trail at the southern rim of the basin. Pel moved to the front where Gladlow and Nowen led the way.

"I'm just saying," Nowen was saying, "my time is better spent studying other things than the armor spell—"

Pel interrupted, "Gladlow. Can I have a moment?"

He looked over and said, "Yes. Please."

At least he seemed to have some of his good humor back. Pel tried to dismiss Nowen with a flick of her head, but he saw it as an invitation to run his hand across her bare stomach as he turned. She reacted reflexively.

"Ow! What in hells..." He stopped in the trail holding his wrist and was left behind.

Pel cursed under her breath. Now she was pissed off, Gladlow would be all tensed up, and she still had a conversation with Nowen to look forward to. She should have stayed with the boat. "I was hired to pick up a package and smuggle it back to the mainland."

Gladlow said, "That's why you were heading east and knew about the tower." He didn't sound surprised.

"You knew?"

"No, I didn't suspect a thing. I thought you were looking for your raft captain and found the tower on the way down to the beach. Why are you telling me now?"

Pel liked Gladlow when he was acting himself and she felt herself calming down in response. She felt a resolve to make this arrangement work. "After our pact, the reward belongs to all of us. I have to assume it was the Institute that hired me anyway. It's a research package, right?"

"Possibly. It seems like a great deal of trouble when they can teleport. You haven't picked it up yet?"

"No."

"Do you know what it is?"

"No, but we're nearing the area. I wanted to give you the choice of going now or getting settled at the tower first."

Gladlow gave it some thought and said, "I think... now. There's enough day left, and it saves us hours of backtracking in the morning. Would you tell me about the assignment?"

Pel told him as much of the story as time allowed, and answered his questions as best she could, but where Wellstone had wanted to know everyone involved, he was most interested in how the parcel was to be smuggled. Instructions were to shove the package inside a giant urchin and mark it by cutting off a patch of spines. A series of crew would get the package through the searches and into her berth.

"Do you have a reason why you think it was the Institute that hired you?"

"Well, the man told me about the tower. I was afraid of being stranded, and he said that, as a last resort, I could ask them for help. I had the impression that it was the mages in the tower that were leaving the package, that's why it was nearby. Now that I think of it, I just assumed."

Gladlow said, "It very well could have been. The signal tower was the regular meeting place for all of the current Institute researchers. I just think the plan to get you the top diving spot just so you could swim out and pick up a package seems... overblown?"

Pel said, "I thought that too. A lot of money and effort."

"That's the reason in *favor* of it being the Institute. What makes me skeptical is the number of people involved. That's not like them at all."

She said, "It was clever but elaborate. They could have just paid Jepps to retrieve it when everyone was away from the raft. The Commodores could be paid for just about anything."

Gladlow said, "Maybe that's it. They couldn't use someone whose loyalty could be so easily bought. Why would someone think *you* were trustworthy?"

She raised her eyebrow and it started him laughing.

"Sorry, you know what I mean. Why did you think you were offered the job?"

"They wanted someone who could make it through the trials, and then follow their instructions. I had done work for the same facilitator twice before. He recommended me. That's all I know."

The group tightened ranks and made their way down the path cautiously. Pel led the way with Gladlow, each carefully watching the rocks on their side of the path. It dropped steeply and opened onto a small beach with less than thirty yards of sand stretching between the rock outcroppings on either side.

Pel said, "It looks clear, but careful near the water."

The group spread out, some dropping to the ground while others stayed alert on the perimeter. Pel began searching the rocks on the west side and Gladlow followed behind. She immediately found it. A mark was etched into the limestone that was only visible from a few feet away. It looked to be the stylized image of a bird. Gladlow watched over her shoulder as she shifted a large rock underneath it and retrieved a small sandstone sculpture of a crocodile.

Gladlow said, "Well, that's... adorable."

Pel was about to say something when she noticed Carlin and Wellstone standing in the quiet surf. They were shielding their eyes and pointing out over the water. "We better see what they're doing."

Wellstone saw them arrive and said, "There, about a hundred yards out."

Pel didn't see it at first, as she was thinking they meant something under the surface. "It looks like a post sticking out of the water."

Carlin said, "Or a mast."

After much debate, it was agreed that they would inspect it. Another wrecked ship wasn't a coincidence. Pel volunteered immediately, followed by Carlin and Voorsh.

Carlin said, "I'm trained with the breathers, and Voorsh doesn't need one. Can I borrow yours, Chief?"

Voorsh added, "I hold my breath very long."

Wellstone sighed and handed hers over. "It's probably a good time to check these." She pulled out the bundle of damaged charms taken from the purser's office. "I think it's mostly a matter of broken straps, but we'll test them while you have a look. Don't take any chances and come right back."

Gladlow said, "Have Nowen see if the enchantment has failed on any of them." He looked to the other women. "Are they hard to use?"

Carlin grinned and teased, "You really want to go, don't you?"

He shrugged, "I think there's value in each member of the group learning additional—damnit, yes! I want to go."

Pel dangled one of the charms in front of him. "This was Hara's. Now it's yours." She adjusted the buckle for a thicker neck than her friend's, and helped him put it on." He then received a barrage of advice.

Carlin said, "You'll want to leave the robe or you'll get tangled."

As he pulled the robe over his head Pel said, "Remember that you're not drowning. It's a little harder to breathe, but the unpleasant part is over once your lungs fill with water."

"Take your shirt and boots off too, they'll weigh you down." Carlin had disrobed, leaving a similar outfit to Pel's, with short pants and halter.

"If that breather comes off underwater, it won't feel any different. You'll black out in as little as half a minute and die soon after."

"Those pants with drag in the water. Lose 'em."

He undid his belt before their laughter stopped him. "Seriously, ladies?"

Pel brought the bundle of javelins and took one, leaving her Orc blade lying across her pack-basket in the sand. Her new bronze knife was strapped to her leg in a makeshift sheath. Carlin and Voorsh each equipped themselves with nothing but the short spears. Gladlow left his hands free. As soon as the water reached Pel's neck, she dropped down and breathed deeply. Carlin gave a valiant effort to appear unfazed and only hesitated for a few moments to get her nerve up. Pel saw she did seem to have some experience. Voorsh was circling the group like a predator, looking completely at ease in the water, propelling herself effortlessly with her tail. It was impossible for Pel not to be envious of her grace and speed. Gladlow was still holding his breath, but blinking and looking around. He seemed to be studying the effect the Tesco's had on eyesight. They did little more than remove the discomfort of having eyes open underwater. Vision was better than without the charms, but everything remained a blur at any real distance. Pel moved close and put a hand on his shoulder so that he didn't have to struggle to remain submerged.

Her voice was muffled but clear at this distance. "Whenever you're ready, push the air from your lungs..."

He immediately turned his head upward and released a burst of bubbles. Before she could coax him further, he looked her in the eyes and gulped in the water. His eyes went wide and his hand grasped hers against his shoulder, but the muscles of his stomach soon relaxed as he breathed experimentally. A stream of tiny bubbles continued to issue from his grin. Of course, Pel thought, he never missed a chance to show off. She flicked her head towards the hand he was still holding, expecting him to jerk his free, but he just remained as he was, waiting for her to pull away. A squeak nearby made them look at Carlin and retrieve their hands. She was floating nearby, staring at them, knees tucked up and both hands over her mouth. She watched them carefully the entire swim to the sunken wreck.

Pel marveled at the vessel, completely intact other than sitting under fifty feet of water. She had never seen construction quite like it. Primitive in form, nearly flat-bottomed, but constructed with incredible skill. The planks were hand hewn and joined without visible nails. Double ended and sleek, it was thirty feet long with a deck entirely dominated by rowing benches. It would have been fast with a full crew. The mast was nearly an afterthought, with no trace of sails remaining.

Gladlow said, "The oars are missing." He seemed surprised at the rumble of his own voice. Whatever the cause, water or charm, the voice always deepened, but his already low tones were rendered almost unintelligible.

Pel nodded and they moved above the deck after Voorsh made a full circle around the boat. She went to the surface once and dived down to meet them. She couldn't speak without losing her air, but she made a gesture with her fist that Pel didn't comprehend. She looked to the others, who both shrugged. They would need to work on that.

Pel said, "Not just the oars, everything is missing." She swam to the opposite end where the galley had a small aftcastle rising a few feet from the deck. Steps down led to a low door to aft across from the dark opening to the cargo hold. "Gladlow, could you provide some light?" He touched her javelin and the entire shaft shone with white light. It was a strange effect but made the area around her spring to life. The deeper the water, the more color was lost until everything became a monotone blue-grey. Her new light added the color back to the world. She would have loved to have a light like that when diving for urchins or just sightseeing. There wasn't much to see in the hold, however. It was low and cramped, but she could see it had been completely stripped. She turned to see Carlin and Gladlow pulling on the door.

Carlin said, "It won't move. Look here." She pointed to gouges in the wood where considerable effort had been made to open the stout door. Pel could see there was no visible lock.

Gladlow asked, "Should I open it?"

Pel nodded but swam up the stairs. Carlin followed suit. Unlike most of his spells, he didn't make any gestures or fondle any mysterious substances. He simply focused on the door briefly and barked a harsh-sounding word, making the women jump. The door looked unchanged, but Gladlow swung it open and floated to one side. Pel thrust her glowing shaft through the doorway revealing a minuscule cabin. The current occupant had been dead for some time, maybe months. It looked to be a male Hobgoblin, but even with the door sealed, a host of sea life had feasted on the remains. The corpse's chainmail and sword were massively rusted in the seawater, but a small chest of valuables fit under Gladlow's arm. As they rose from the stairwell, they were met by Voorsh. She was gesturing with a downward pat of her hand. She then swam slowly along the surface of the deck, belly scraping the boards, and beckoning to them. All three Humans followed her, keeping low, to the edge of the deck. They peaked over just as she did. Pel saw nothing. Voorsh seemed panicked and darted to the other side and over the edge. Pel swam hard to follow, but Gladlow kicked off a rowing bench and shot past briefly, launching a glowing projectile. The hornet shaped light passed through the water with no visible disturbance and disappeared over the starboard wale. Pel cleared it just in time to see Voorsh run her javelin through a thrashing monstrosity of exposed muscles and organs. It was almost instantly still, so Pel held her glowing spear out and rotated slowly looking for more enemies. There were none to be found.

Chapter Eight

Meese stood in his soaking wet pants and stared at the thing. The thing that had been in the water he had voluntarily been in. The water he had involuntarily breathed. Meese had a carefully cultivated reputation for burning things. Hells, he forwent the use of many nifty spells just to avoid muddying his theme, at least publicly. Never before had he wanted so badly to set fire to a thing. He stood with the others in a loose circle around the carcass Gladlow had helped pull out of the water.

Wellstone said, "It's an eel-man but there's something wrong with it."

Meese thought, something? Everything is wrong with it. At first glance, it seemed to have no flesh, just veins and organs in the loose shape of a man.

Carlin poked at it with a javelin, lifting a limb and dropping it. "Its flesh is translucent, but it was invisible in the water. Look how fast it's drying up."

Pel asked, "Are you sure it's the same creature? I only saw them from a distance."

Wellstone said, "I'm sure. I watched them work. But this is... do you think it's a bad birth?"

Gladlow asked, "Voorsh, can you tell us what happened?"

"Yes. It watched us. When I came to warn, it moved closer. It fled. Gladlow's light hurt it, made it bump into ship and slow. I killed it. Ugly, ugly."

Meese said, "I agree. Succinctly put, Miss Voorsh. I propose an experiment, bear with me, to determine, hear me out, it's flammability."

Carlin continued poking the thing while everyone but Nowen had already backed away.

He said, "I'm positive now, the eel-men are Siyokoy. I don't know what they're doing here though. Or what's happened to this one."

She said, "I'd like to examine it further. I wish I had my journals."

Nowen asked, "You lost them on the *Indomitable*?"

"Yes. All my sketches and reports... just gone. I have a good memory though." Meese thought she might be the most perpetually cheerful person he'd ever known, and he'd had similar accusations leveled against his own person.

Nowen dug around in his enormous pack and handed her a scroll case. She opened it reverently and examined the blank booklet and writing implements. He had already gone back to examining the corpse, but she spun him around and crushed him against her. He looked to Meese in bewilderment. Meese did his best to give him a look that conveyed, 'If you had ever done a single nice thing for anyone in your unending adolescence, you might have received a sweltering hug from a bosomy, bright beauty before this moment.' He could see that, like so many times before, his message wasn't received. He went to have a look in the little treasure chest diverting the others' attention. After fishing out masses of wet mush, probably former maps and such, Gladlow emptied the rest onto the sand. There were a fair number of tarnished silver coins, a few pieces of polished blue stone favored by the Lizards, and a pair of small gourds with stoppers. Gladlow shook one of the primitive bottles and tossed it to Meese. He scraped the tallow from around the little stopper and popped it free.

"Fascinating," he said as he studied the aroma. He put the stopper back and spread the waxy substance carefully to reseal it. "The Hobgoblins have entirely subverted the natural order by making alcohol directly from piss. Genius."

The group was in good spirits for the last hour of their trek, passing the odd little crocodile statue back and forth as they discussed the sunken galley or the nastiness of the eel-man. The crocodilian icon gave up no secrets to Nowen's detection or Wellstone's inspection. She did determine that there were no marks from carving, though that material could easily be sanded smooth. The vomit conjuring corpse was a wellspring of conversational refreshment and a topic no one seemed to abandon for long. Meese trailed behind Pel and Gladlow in the front. He was happy to see that a good deal of the tension from earlier seemed to have evaporated. Gladlow had only put on his boots, stuffing his robe and shirt in his pack and slinging it over one shoulder along with his staff. Meese suspected it was a sort of chivalry, rather than a ploy to show off his willowy and utterly sunless frame. It would be mildly awkward to get fully dressed while leaving your lass to stand watch in her swim briefs. They chatted quietly like old friends while keeping watch on their zones.

"That ship was a sight to see," Pel said, "I didn't know Hobgoblins were capable of that sort of craftsmanship."

Gladlow said, "They're not. Well, none of the clans left today. Their war machines were legendary though."

"So, they bought it? Who still builds ships like that?"

"That was an Orc galley. Not very old either. There is no chance they came into possession of it peacefully."

Pel asked, "Do the Hobgoblins and Orcs fight?"

"Now? Constantly. The clans on the mainland hate each other enough to ignore Human villages. Mostly. The Hobgoblins don't want to risk having to fight a second force, and the Orcs like to save up their ire to wipe out one enemy at a time. It's like they've reached an agreement to put aside their differences until they're done killing each other." He grinned at her.

"I know more than I care to about Hobgoblins, but I've refused to listen to talk about the conflicts for some time. It... makes it difficult to get out of bed. You've studied this?"

Gladlow nodded. "It's part of my field. The study of ancient magic, specifically the spells and rituals developed by other races. The Orcs are difficult enough to study, but the Hobgoblins are a mess."

"What do you mean?"

Gladlow looked at her for a moment. "I'm sorry. I start to spout essays when the subject comes up. Natural hazard of having to constantly justify my work to a bunch of wrinkled old magicians."

She smiled and said, "I like it when you assume I'll understand what you're saying. How are they different?"

"Right. The Hobgoblins have changed since the wars, because of the wars really. They used to be nomadic and... certainly not peaceful. At all. But war wasn't so all encompassing. The sorcerers swayed them so easily. Entire clans gave up every shred of cultural identity and became armies, seemingly overnight. It was as if they found addiction in new weapons, military structure, war. After a couple of generations, even after the sorcerers were dead, there was nothing left but those things." He went quiet for a time.

Pel prompted, "And the Orcs?"

"Hmm? Sterner stuff. Change comes to them slowly. Their race is as old as the Elves, and they're alike in that way. Only a few clans got involved in the war, two of them on *our* side. That was its own mess." He shrugged. "Survivors just went right back to their way of life. No treaties, not even a scrap of goodwill until another decade passed." He looked embarrassed. "Next time, I'm asking the questions."

"We'll see."

The path down was a gently sloping series of small dunes collected between a large gap in the rock wall of the basin. Some jungle still clung to life on either side, but the ocean was clearly visible ahead. They found the signal tower on the left, carefully positioned so a lantern placed on top would be visible from the ocean, but the rest obscured by palms and undergrowth. Calling it a tower was probably some sort of joke. It was a squat cylinder no taller than a cottage and made of sandstone. The door was just a seam in the curved wall.

Gladlow looked around once, stood close to the door, and said, "Salmonberry scone." He pushed on the stone to no effect. He set down his pack and began digging through it.

Wellstone put her hand on the door and enunciated carefully, "Sal-mon-burry-scaan!" She snatched the note out of Gladlow's hand and read it herself while he tried the password twice more.

He said, "Alright. Everyone should stand back. We were practically invited, but there's no need for all of us to be incinerated."

"Wait," Wellstone put a hand on his arm. "Why does it say 'front door?' Is there a back door?"

"No, just the hatch on top. It could be a different—"

Wellstone was already pushing him against the wall. "Lean here big man, and put your hands here." Meese watched in delight as she climbed Gladlow like a ladder, finally stepping a sandy, bare foot on his head to grab the edge of the flat roof and pull herself up effortlessly.

Her voice came from above, "Salmonberry scone."

Gladlow was brushing his head and smiling at Pel. "The utter indignity of it."

Carlin suddenly sounded panicked, "Something is wro—"

The world went silent. Meese heard only the high pitched whine of utterly unnatural silence. Most everyone was shaking their heads or rubbing their ears, but the three mages looked at each other before turning to check their surroundings. In the failing light, sand poured from more than a dozen forms rising from the ground amongst and around the group. Meese was slammed in the shoulder and knocked sideways. A rotting Hobgoblin had emerged from the sand at the base of the tower, flailing and grasping its arms mindlessly. The smell was overpowering and Meese's panicked mind tried to resort to his best defenses, to no avail. The corpse stepped toward him to swing again and an arrow appeared in the top of its head, snapping Meese out of his fugue. He swung his staff, crushing the thing's face and sending it to the ground. He looked around to see others engaged in similar struggles. It seemed several had appeared underfoot, while the rest rose in a perfect ring encompassing the group. They lumbered slowly forward and between them, Meese could see skeletal hands digging their way out of the closest dune. His mind had cleared somewhat and he prepared his single spell not requiring words of power. He looked around desperately for something to use. Carlin had immediately dropped her shield on the ground in favor of wielding her war club with both hands. Meese pointed at the shield, and doubling the power he used on the practice field, flicked his wrist towards the advancing undead. In a burst of sand, the shield launched ungracefully in a straight line from the ground to a second undead Hobgoblin's midsection, never changing the awkward angle it had rested in. The impact folded the corpse in half, spilling rotten entrails and splintering the wood and leather shield. Through the gap he had just made, Meese could see the mob of skeletons rising from the sand. The trap was well laid. The slow moving corpses had attacked from underfoot and the faster skeletons would descend on them while they still engaged the first enemy. There was no surviving the coming rush. He cast about once more for objects to throw, launching the largest remaining piece of the shield, his last dagger, and finally, the stone crocodile discarded in the sand. The statuette exploded the ribcage of a rotting Lizard. He raised his staff, prepared himself, and jumped out of his skin when something pulled at his backpack. He turned to see Wellstone as she drew his sword. Their eyes locked and he felt his heart sink for a moment, but she winked as she dashed off. He didn't know what this would mean, but he was grateful she hadn't heard him scream.

· · · ·

Wellstone's arrows were depleted quickly and nearby enemies were engaged with her companions. As she cast about for a good target, she saw the Elf running toward the gap and gesturing. He ignored the undead on either side and would quickly be pummeled to mush. Unable to shout in the deafening silence, she rolled from the roof and tumbled a second time when she hit the ground, popping up next to her kinsman. She saw no recourse but to acknowledge him, honestly wishing there was a way to spare his feelings. A wink certainly wasn't proper etiquette, but they had both spent a great deal of time with Humans, and she hoped they had rubbed off on him half as much as he let on. The sword was a bit long for her, but it certainly gave her good reach. Nowen stayed to cast a second time, continuing to ignore his surroundings. Carlin hammered the corpse on his right and Wellstone engaged the left just as its haymaker swing connected with the young Elf. She prevented its second blow, nearly severing its arm. She dodged an attack, ending the rotten thing with her saber through an eye socket. She could now see the effect of Nowen's trick. Ten yards away, the closest skeletons had sunk into the sand, having to wade through it while the ones behind piled against them. It only bought a few heartbeats, but Wellstone would waste none of it. She joined Voorsh in putting down the few previously killed corpses having the audacity to rise again. Their last death was quick and final. The little Lizard was fast and brutal, her strategy nonexistent. She punched with the clawed buckler, then swiped with her copper taloned club. One-two, one-two, until the enemy stilled. The last cadavers would be taken by Gladlow and Pel. They had been further accosted by a small group of undead arriving from around the tower but looked like they would be finished in time to meet the skeletal charge. She spared them one final look. Where the fuck had Gladlow's spear come from? It was a short weapon with a foot-long blade. He didn't wield it with Pel's speed and grace, but he was no novice. The gore he was splattered with attested to that. Wellstone knew what she would ask for his next round of Traveler. Hoping they would play again, she braced herself for the charge.

• • • •

When the silence fell, Gladlow cursed himself and didn't stop. He had let everyone down, lulled into a feeling of safety by the large group and their previous victories. He had let himself be distracted by feeling cheated, then foolish, then overwhelmingly sad for what could have been. This day had started with hope and an inner calm, a determination not to let petty feelings change who he wanted to be. The tragedy was, this had made his discipline slip. He hadn't cast his own armor, let alone one for her. The foulest curses continued to fall from his lips and vanish into the terrible quiet. Pel's first swing released him from his bleak reverie. His beloved spells were there in his mind, waiting, but were utterly useless. Gladlow pulled the leather lacing on his staff, unraveling the stitch binding two halves of a small wooden sheath. He let it fall away from the iron blade, put the magic out of his mind, and dredged up the first lessons of his youth. He fought like a madman, letting the anger and hate spill from his mouth. As the corpses fell, he could see the second wave coming. A mass of bones and rusted blades that they could never survive. The last silent curse he shouted had a name, one he hesitated to speak even in his reports and essays, but it reminded him of something from the second lessons of his youth. He moved so he was in Pel's view and helped destroy one of the two corpses she was engaged with. He used the brief respite to move close and pull the blade from the sheath on her thigh. Thrusting the spear into the downed cadaver, he left it standing and prepared his mind for what was to come. Something at the line between spell and prayer, something that had tempted him for years in the way one is tempted, when looking over a cliff, to jump. He carved a symbol into his left forearm, an unblinking eye. Tossing the blade near Pel's feet, he pressed his right palm over the wound and transferred the bloody sigil to his left eye. There was no need to push power into the casting, it would simply take what it needed. Searing pain took the vision from his left eye and he tasted copper. Gladlow cupped his hands as blood poured from his mouth. The undead waded from the sand, and they were met with an arc of blood, droplets of red spattering across dry bones. Wherever they hit, small puffs of steam rose, and the skeletons fell thrashing on the ground. Their cohorts stepped over them to be met by another spray of blood. Gladlow felt the second half of his vision fading around the edges but continued to fling his lifeblood onto the undead. The flow stopped and Gladlow spat the last of it onto the skull of the monstrosity preparing to run him through. He blacked out before the rusty blade struck.

• • • •

With each heartbeat, the outcome of the battle had shifted in Pel's mind, the paths opening and closing before her, each leading to the deaths of several of these others, many ending with her own. She had seen what each was capable of, could estimate the number of foes they could eliminate, distract, or occupy briefly. The situation became incrementally less dire as the skeletons slowed in Nowen's trap, granting the reprieve to eliminate one enemy and brace for the second. Wellstone's sudden addition to the field increased their chances slightly more. She wielded the borrowed saber with awe inspiring precision. Pel was ready to face whatever came, determined to do her part, and trusting, for the first in a long time, that others would do theirs. Her hope crumbled as Gladlow took her knife and left his spear. He was bruised and bloody, fighting with a rare abandon that had little use for dodge and parry, but potentially creating the space she would need to end the battle. It mattered little. There was nothing more fickle than victory. Pel grabbed up the bronze blade on the run. She had left it sheathed, with little need for it fighting weaponless corpses, but now that it was bare in her hand, the weight of it felt good. It shifted her balance and broadened her tactics. Seeing Gladlow rush ahead let her choose her final strategy. The greatest chance for the most survivors was if she didn't include herself among them. The undead were utterly mindless, and a mad attack into their midst would give the advantage to her companions for a brief moment. Each breath she took after would give them another. She would give as many as it took. She launched into a full run but slowed in shock as blood sprayed from her friend onto the skeletons in the front line. They fell to the ground writhing silently, but her mind imagined shrieks of pain. The skeletons behind fell atop them as they too succumbed to shudders of agony. She renewed her attack, and though she'd lost the thread of the battle, she knew that, as remote as it might be, the possibility of victory lived on. Gladlow fell as a blade pierced his belly and three unholy things hacked at his still body. She hit them like a boulder rolling downhill and only slowed when there was nowhere else to put her feet. She rotated and attacked in every direction, ignoring those who were beginning to rise as their suffering subsided. She concentrated the last of her energy on engaging as many enemies as she could keep occupied. She was struck and retaliated viciously. Still, she could hear nothing, but caught glimpses from the corners of her vision as the others fought their own battles. A dull blade opened her back from shoulder to hip, the pain pulling a silent scream from her that felt like glass in her throat. She swung wildly and bones shattered under the Orc blade. The skeleton fell scattered across the ground. She barely parried the next strike with the bronze dagger, and she knew her strength was fading. Her next opponent fell, the same as the last, its bones almost crumbling at her strike. She could see pitting left on the surface as the blood evaporated, and knowing she fought weakened opponents renewed her determination. Just another breath. Just one more.

• • • •

Nowen shook the sand from his hair and stumbled to his feet. He didn't even look back at the horde, terrified that it was already too late to break away. Pumping his legs downhill towards the water, jumping over bodies, and slipping past the last flailing corpses occupied by his companions, he dashed for the invisible, silent line of the sound-suppressing enchantment. He didn't know its limits, or the exact range of his own newest spell, but where they overlapped was where he would make his stand. He tried to shout again and again as he ran, hoping to detect the barrier the instant he crossed, but it was unnecessary. He broke through a wall of sound, almost overwhelming his senses with the intensity of sudden noise. He stopped and spun, the power words already spilling from his lips, the ocean sounds of water and distant birds returning to their natural place in the background of his consciousness. Gladlow's ruby ring was loose on Nowen's smaller hand but flashed with power when he made the arcane sign, adding a pale companion to his own strobing red hornet. His desire was to remove opponents, but he heeded his friend's instruction and sent each attacker to a different target. He chose those not engaged, trusting in the fighters' ability to fight, and hoped that he was easing their burden. He cast into the chaos again, and once more. Shame and despair fell over him, but there was nothing more he could do. He might use a minor arcana again, but he couldn't think of a way to make them useful in the roiling combat. He had studied, not with the near obsession of Gladlow, but he put in his time. He had. Even now he didn't feel the fatigue, the fog that descended after a third real spell. He raised his hand and there was power remaining, further away, deeper, but he could reach it. Two red hornets streaked towards new targets as the ring flashed, adding a third of purest white.

• • • •

Meese was afraid to look at his arm, choosing to keep his left hand tucked in his belt to immobilize it while he tried to assist Carlin with the wounded. She, like him, was badly hurt but with injuries confined to an extremity. Her leg had a ten-inch wound of unknown depth, but she had wrapped it tightly before limping to Gladlow. The utter silence still prevailed, but there wasn't much communication necessary. She placed a folded bundle of cloth on the unconscious Gladlow's abdomen and bound it tightly. He was deathly pale from blood loss, but his pulse was slow and steady. They left him lying in the sand and moved to Pel, her injuries more numerous. Carlin carefully examined each one, choosing to bind some and leaving the others. Meese was most worried about her head wound. They were always terrifying due to the amount of blood, and this one was no exception. Staunching the flow, Carlin checked her pulse again. She looked at Meese and pursed her lips. She gestured for him to check. It felt a bit weak and uneven to him. Lastly was Voorsh. She lay tightly curled and they were afraid to force her to straighten. She was breathing, but it was shallow and fast, blood foaming from her mouth onto the sand. Carlin seemed unsatisfied with her attempts to check heartbeat, but Meese had no wisdom to impart on Lizard anatomy. Meese started in alarm when the sound of the world returned. Night was falling on them rapidly and the noise of the nearby jungle was already at a fever pitch. He jabbed his staff in the ground and released the torchlight.

Nowen, having just arrived from down the hill, was digging through his pack. "I have two tonics left. Who is in the most danger?"

Meese shook his head and turned to Carlin, but jumped to his feet when he saw the person approaching. The woman stopped on a dune slightly above them and casually stood with hands behind her back. She was raven haired with a medium build obscured by chainmail. She had no weapon, helmet, or shield. Her blue and black robes were finely made, and a large silver pendant adorned her chest in the shape of a skull with a tongue lolling from its mouth.

She looked around at the carnage and said, "You weren't our intended, but are obviously deserving of an—"

Meese cut her off with a thirty-foot jet of flame. Disappointingly, her image disappeared as the illusion flickered away. A skeleton in rotting rags was left standing there, burning to cinders. "We were having a private conversation." He turned to Carlin. "Who can survive without aid?"

She looked panicked. "I don't know. They could all three die in the next few minutes. Please don't make me choose."

Meese said, "Maybe we should combine the two draughts and give them each a third..."

Nowen shouted in disgust, "This isn't a gods-damned cauldron party. That might not work for *any* of them."

"Carlin, I'll choose the last, but I need your help. Which of them is in the most danger? Just one."

She said, "Probably Voorsh. In a Human, I'd say it's a punctured lung—"

Meese said, "Nowen, give one to Voorsh. Carlin give the other to Pel." He walked to the door of the tower and said, "There has to be more inside, but I can't climb to the hatch..."

Wellstone surveyed the tower and chose a palm nearby. She effortlessly climbed higher than the level of the roof and threw herself towards it, grabbing the edge and hauling herself up. He heard her speak the password again and realized, that even with their night vision, she wouldn't be able to read in the dark. He grabbed up his staff and threw it to the roof. He heard it clatter and a few seconds later the light disappeared. They were left standing in the twilight, most of the illumination coming from the direction of the water.

Carlin yelled, "Meese, help over here."

Pel was awake but otherwise not in visibly better condition. Her injuries must have been even worse than they thought. She was looking around wildly and trying to stand. Carlin tried to calm her, but she wouldn't stop moving.

Meese said, "Let her go, she'll do more damage struggling. Nowen?"

"I think Voorsh will be fine. She only woke for a second, but her breathing sounds normal-ish?" He added a shrug.

Pel calmed when she crawled to Gladlow and lay back with an arm over her eyes. She had yet to say a word.

Meese went to him and, thankfully, there was no change. He said, "There will be supplies inside."

Nowen said, "Why didn't you give the last one to Gladlow so he could open the damned door?"

"If there *isn't* anything inside, Gladlow would never forgive me."

"Why?"

"Can anyone be so perpetually and willfully *thick*?" He gestured with his good arm at the two wounded next to each other in the sand, but could tell by Nowen's gormless expression that there was no comprehension.

Nowen threw up his hands and stomped over to the tower. After a quick survey of the foliage, he chose a tree and wrapped his arms and legs around it. He froze at the sound of grating stone. The sandstone door of the tower swung open, spilling Meese's torchlight onto a rectangle of sand.

Wellstone stepped out brandishing a waxen rind of cheese. Meese let himself make eye contact, but couldn't bring himself to ask how she managed the password.

She grinned, sucked a small bit from the edge of her thumb, and said, "Camboldamere Blue."

They moved everyone inside the circular room, most of the lifting being done by Nowen and Wellstone, but requiring Meese and Carlin to clumsily assist in moving the larger Gladlow. Four double-stacked beds occupied the wall opposite the door, with a ladder between them granting access to the upper bunks as well as the roof hatch. Gladlow and Pel were laid on the bottom two, while Voorsh crawled weakly under the room's single table.

Carlin said, "I wish we hadn't moved him." She had her back turned while she rifled through a cabinet, but sounded like she was crying. "I don't know how he has any blood left."

Meese stayed calm and started a methodical search. He started by lighting sconces on either side of the room. They used the same spell as his staff but consisted of a metal cylinder that could be rotated to expose the heatless flame. He was not above stealing the design for himself. He searched the four lockers, two on either side of the ladder access. "They're empty." He slammed the last lid down. "Carlin. Anything?"

She swiped the back of her hand across her eyes and said, "Books, papers, ink."

He looked to Nowen who was perusing the contents of the table, but could see there were nothing but empty cups left from a meal. Meese felt heartbroken. "There's nothing here."

"I don't think that's true." Wellstone had been standing out of the way in the center of the room. "It isn't round. The right side of the room is less curved."

Meese was embarrassed that he hadn't noticed but decided to blame it on the searing pain in his arm. He would have figured it out eventually. He watched as she strode confidently to the wall sconce on the right and twisted it upside down. Nothing happened. She turned it all the way around and it came off in her hand.

"That was... disappointing." She examined the large base of the sconce, but it looked as if it was made to be removed and used like a candle.

Meese dragged a chair over to the wall, but she jumped onto it before he could. She pressed her eye to the hole, trying to arrange the light to see inside. She reached her hand in but could only shove her arm in partway.

She said, "We'll need hands more slender and delicate than mine. Carlin. Bring Nowen over here." There was that wink again. "Nowen, there's a protrusion to the left, see if you can reach it."

The Elf could only reach a fraction further. He said, "I can feel it... but pushing does nothing. It's cone shaped. Ugh. I can't grab it."

Meese felt hope rising. "I know this." Clambering onto the chair was difficult with his bad arm. He made sure he could see the target, made a fist with his right hand, and said the word. Flickering with ghostly, green flame, a translucent copy of his hand appeared and wiggled its fingers in perfect time with the original. It slid through the opening and as he pantomimed grabbing a circular object and giving it a sharp pull, there was a grating sound, and a rectangular hatch opened in the wall.

Wellstone had a small armload of its contents before anyone else had moved. She dropped them on the table and said, "There are a couple of bottles here. But I think they're too large for potions. Gin, maybe?"

Meese was looking at what she had left behind in the stone cabinet. There were a few books and scrolls that she had chosen to ignore. He was turning when he saw the inside of the cabinet door. An elaborate glyph was scrawled in the center with no attempt to hide it. He swung the door open all the way and brought his light closer.

Nowen said, "I recognize the smell of these cloths. They have a minor enchantment for bandaging wounds. There are a lot of them, but they're not meant for this kind of injury."

Meese said, "Come look at this, but nobody touch."

They each examined it, but the two mages were at a loss. Nowen said, "This is thaumaturgical script. I could read it magically, but I suspect it will activate when I touch it."

Wellstone asked, "Thaumaturgical. What does that mean?"

"I assume it's the work of Whitecloud."

"The Elf priestess you were looking for. It was hidden for novice mages to find along with more research notes and emergency bandages. It has to be beneficial, yes? Nowen, touch it."

Carlin said, "Wait, we can't waste it. It may only work once. I thought maybe I could read it, but it's been so long. It looks like the glyphs used to contain protection spells. There was one on the floor of the family mausoleum. I was told it would only activate if undead crossed it. These symbols here mean its effects will go in every direction. I can't remember anything else."

They settled on a plan to hedge their bets. They gathered everyone close to the little cabinet, and propped Gladlow in a chair, tipping him back against the wall.

Carlin said, "Wait. Meese, let me see your arm."

Even with no medical training, Meese could see how utterly ruined it was. A rusted falchion had parted flesh and snapped the bone midway between shoulder and elbow. He let them strip him to the waist and he was soaked in blood, the red of his robes doing a fine job of hiding it.

Carlin said, "We should straighten it. You'll thank us later."

Meese felt ashamed for enjoying the look of concern on Wellstone's face, but he kept his own blank. At Carlin's instruction, Wellstone put a foot in his armpit and grabbed his wrist in both hands. Carlin would quickly line up the bone. Meese was left face to face with Wellstone. He looked at her and thought, you want to see control? Get a good look.

Meese woke on the floor just as they were slapping Gladlow's limp hand onto the glyph. Nothing happened even when trying it six or seven more times. Finally, Wellstone touched it herself. The entire room lit with countless motes of light, drifting down like colorless sparks. Each blinked out of existence when they struck a solid surface, but those contacting the living flared for the tiniest instant and were gone.

Wellstone said, "I'm going to be fuming if that was protection from undead."

Chapter Nine

Gladlow woke in complete confusion. There was very little light in an unfamiliar room. It was too warm, he was nude under a rough sheet, and there was, if he was any judge, a delightfully voluptuous woman sleeping face down across his chest. He reached out for a clue and recognized the soft, tiny ringlets cropped close to her scalp.

"Carlin." He shook her gently, but she just slid herself to the side and nestled in the crook of his arm. "*Carlin*. You have to wake up."

Someone pulled the woman off him and said, "Carlin, love, get in my bed."

Carlin stood without opening her eyes and said, "No."

"Climb in bed with Nowen then."

Pel brought some sort of lantern with the smallest sliver of flame showing. She shoved Gladlow over and sat up in bed next to him.

He said, "My arm is asleep..."

She rolled over him and shoved him to the outside. He secured his sheet and hung his hand over the edge, working his fingers.

She spoke in low tones. "You've been asleep for two days. We've poured enough fish broth in you to feed a village."

"Did everyone..."

"Everyone is alive and bored. You and I slept the longest." She seemed to be casting about for something to say. "Your eye is almost normal. I was afraid it might be blinded."

"No harm done." He could see that was the wrong thing to say. "Sorry, I know how close I came. I lost a lot of blood?"

"Lost it? You threw most of it away. Idiot." She grabbed up his left arm and pulled the bandage loose. He didn't struggle. She asked, "What is this?"

He looked down in confusion at the mark he had made. It no longer looked like the lidless eye. More cuts had been made so that it looked like a frowning face. Meese. He told her most of the truth when he said, "An old spell. Primitive. It uses a symbol instead of a word. I think it might predate spoken lang—"

"Where did it come from?"

He sighed. "Want to talk about our childhoods? You promised I could ask the questions next time."

"I didn't. What exactly does it do? Have you used it before?"

"No, and I won't be using it again." He tried to leave it at that, but her eyes were boring into his skull. "It didn't work the way it was supposed to, anyway. I wasn't sure it would work on the dead at all."

"What was it supposed to do?"

"Paralyze with pain for a thirty count, or so."

She mused aloud, "You got the pain part, but it affected them like holy water. Maybe more pain, less harm. They were back up in seconds."

"You've fought the undead before?"

She answered quietly without thinking, "Many times." She tried to regain control of the questioning. "You?"

"Only once before."

"Old Shek." She smiled at his look. "Meese told me all about it. Does your version also end with you slumped on the ground?"

"All my best stories do. Meese's sixtieth. The time I fought Elenoria Brookwood. My eleventh year..."

"What happened on your eleventh year?" She asked expectantly.

"I went away with my first master and grew five inches. I came home and walked into a door-jam."

She convulsed while trying to be quiet. She asked too loudly, "Miss Brookwood?"

"Kick in the plums."

Voorsh interrupted their laughter by hissing, "Sleeping is not funny."

Pel whispered, "Sorry, sweetie."

Laughing released something and Gladlow felt a crushing worry as he remembered moments from the battle. "I can't believe everyone lived."

Pel said, "I can. Of course, I didn't believe we would at first but... I've never been so..." She started to cry softly.

He tried to put his hand on hers, but it landed on bare thigh in the dark, so he gave it a there-there sort of pat and pulled back. She grabbed his hand in both of hers and squeezed tightly for a moment before releasing him.

She asked, "How do you feel?"

"Weak as a mouse. No one else is hurt?"

"Oh, everyone was hurt worse than they let on, but some sort of healing magic was left for us. It gave us a good three week's lead on a full recovery."

Gladlow said, "That would be Whitecloud's doing. I'm glad everyone is alright."

Pel said, "Physically, yes. But there are some problems. Meese set fire to the evil priest that set the trap—you'll have to ask him, I wasn't conscious for it. It's safe in here, but we're going a little batty. I can use some help."

"What can I do?"

She said quietly, "Voorsh hates being inside, but we should probably stay here a while longer. I've been letting her sit on the roof and keep watch, but not alone. Mostly, Nowen sits up there reading books we found here. He's probably the only one who doesn't want to leave."

"I thought you said you need help? It sounds like you've got it under control."

"Carlin is having nightmares. It's bad. She says something is calling to her, making demands, offering bargains. She said it happened at the battle, but since then, only when she sleeps. It's worse when she's alone, so she's been in someone or other's lap since the first night."

Gladlow said, "Ah, things become more clear but... what was she wearing?"

"Not much."

"Oh, I hadn't... I *did* notice, but I meant where did she get it? For that matter... is that...?" Pel was wearing a loose, sleeveless tunic in fine purple.

She smoothed it down. "Your robe. Between the rotting entrails and our own blood, it was one of the only pieces of clothing to make it out alive. I claimed the top half and she used a strip to make her crossed scarf-brassiere thing. I'm sorry we destroyed it, was it important to you?"

"I can only hope I myself find such noble purpose. Wear it well." He took a moment to just enjoy her smiling at him. "These dreams. Do you think it might be a calling? Or is she just having nightmares?"

Pel sighed and leaned her head back. "I don't know. I've known true clerics, but none of them have described anything so... blatant. Have you experienced something like it?" Her eyes flicked down to his arm.

Gladlow admitted, "Something like it, but no bargaining." He always seemed unable to avoid answering her. The best he could do was leave out details that might change the way she looked at him. He sat up in bed to bring himself to her level, grunting like an old man. "I was being raised to fight, but I was small. That spear was my childhood weapon." He looked at her for a reaction, but she was showing only intense interest. "I never advanced beyond it. My mother's people had a sect of magic-users, somewhere between priest and mage, using a blend of what I believe to be divine power as well as subjective spellcraft." He heard the lecturing cadence in his voice and tamped it down. She didn't look like she wanted to leave, in fact, she seemed content just watching his lips as he spoke. "This... cult recruited from the warrior rejects, and I was, apparently, a promising acolyte. I tried to listen for the calling, but I didn't really believe the things they told me. See, I found that the magic came whether or not I believed or called out for aid. As long as the words and movements were perfect, I felt only personal power, my own limits. I ran away and served my first master, my mother made it right with her people. They didn't feel any loss." He took a moment remembering, surprised at the ache still remaining. "For my first two years of study, from time to time, I experienced what I believe to be a calling. An obstacle would be placed in front of me and I would feel a choice. Do it my own way or the other way. It felt like a lure and I rejected it every time. Eventually, it went away. I can't explain it any better than that."

Pel leaned into his shoulder and said, "I think it might help her to hear that. That she can choose."

"I'll talk to her. You've gotten a little attached to her, haven't you?"

Pel nodded. "To everyone, I suppose. I can't remember the last time I was given a choice and chose to stay. Carlin feels like a sibling I should look out for. She's only a little younger than us, but she doesn't seem... so carved in stone? Dwarrow and Elves don't change quickly enough to notice, even you and I..."

"You and I?"

"Know who we are. Even Voorsh has her purpose carved in stone." She looked over at him in embarrassment. "I don't know what I'm saying. I'm probably not being fair to Carlin. She doesn't need my protection or advice, she's a grown woman and she's brilliant. She's taken good care of us, and she does more healing without magic than I thought possible."

"I'll be sure to thank her."

Pel said, "You should. She took especially good care of you. She has a real talent for it. She peeks though."

"What's that now?"

"She peeks. When she was bathing you, or changing your bandages, she would just have a good, long look. She's not even ashamed of herself. She told all of the girls to have a look."

He honestly couldn't tell if she was winding him up.

She saw his look and smiled. "Don't worry, no one took her up on it. Except Voorsh."

He thought about that and shrugged.

She asked, "Do you need to sleep? It's still a couple of hours to daylight."

"I'll be a mess if I don't get a full forty-eight hours, but I'll risk it. You?"

"I'd rather stay here and talk."

No one had ever said anything nicer than that. He asked, "So, who's left to gossip about?"

She looked very serious. "Gladlow, I need you to tell me something. No talking around it, or saying it's not your place. Will you be honest with me?"

"Ask me anything."

"Promise."

"I'll be honest."

"Gladlow. What in nine hells is going on with Meese and Wellstone?" She leaned in and stared into his eyes.

He had a sinking feeling. "What happened?"

She raised her hands dramatically and dropped them in her lap. "Nothing. They never said a word to each other, or even looked at each other—which, how can two people be that good at not seeing each other? It's eerie. I thought it must be an upper-class, lower-class situation. Or a rival clan situation? They've both evaded every question, and Carlin asks *a lot*. Now Wellstone talks to him and he's in a deep depression."

"Oh, no."

"What is it?"

"It's not my place to say..." He couldn't keep a straight face.

"*Gladlow.* What is it?"

"Courting."

Pel's face went slack and she cocked her head.

He said, "I truly don't know much more than that."

"Courting? For marriage? I don't understand. At all."

"Maybe not courting, though that has to start like this as well. They may not even like each other. Their word translates to 'the courtesies.' I don't know the rules. I'm not sure Meese does either." He sighed and shook his head. "It doesn't feel right talking about this—"

"You promised."

"You've known Wellstone longer than me, will she like us talking about their private matters?"

"You *promised*," she said, smiling because they both knew he would tell her everything. She relented a bit. "Just tell me about Meese. Why wouldn't he know the rules?"

He smiled and rubbed his hands together. "Fine. Alright. Remember Traveler, that night in the village? I talked about the Dwarrow strongholds collapsing during the Quakes. In most clans, the strongest, most impenetrable chamber was used for the king and his family. And their treasure of course. In a few strongholds, the most protected chamber was used for the children. A few of these chambers survived and were dug from the rubble. There are endless stories about those weeks, a good deal of it tragic beyond belief. The outcome was hundreds of orphans from multiple clans. Many were taken in by other clans, of course, but you have to remember that no stronghold made it through unscathed. There was as much hardship for them as for the Humans out in the open. So creches were established, paid for by the recovered treasure rooms, and run by people who needed work. Humans mostly, but Elves and Dwarrow too. Over the years, as children could be identified, they were claimed by a clan or given their rightful share of unclaimed funds when they came of age."

"What did they do with it?"

"Some started businesses or bought them outright. Most paid a sort of dowry to join a clan. Meese was one of the youngest survivors, too young to speak, and was never identified. Because of the chaos in the beginning, he doesn't even know which stronghold he was recovered from. By the time he was fifteen or so, it was clear that he and the others would never be claimed. A school was set up with instructors to teach them the history and culture of their people. When he was seventeen, he was assigned an apprenticeship to a smith, that's old for a Human apprentice, but an early start for Dwarrow. It didn't go well."

Pel said, "He spoke rather fondly of it to me."

Gladlow smiled and said, "He loved it, and he loved Mister Brewbester. He was Human, but he offered to give his name to Meese like he was a son. Anyway, Meese was an ass and more than a little insulted that they chose a good, old-fashioned, Dwarrow-like trade to occupy him. So, when he turned fifty, he was considered an adult by his people and entitled to his share of the recovered monies. Most of which was long gone."

Pel said, "Of course it was."

Gladlow said, "But what was left, supplemented by many donors, including the Institute, was placed into a bursary to pay for whatever training or education *he* wanted."

"And he chose to become a mage?"

"Yes. A very un-Dwarrow-like trade."

Pel said, "So, most of what he learned about his own people was from instructors—"

"Many of which were, as well meaning as they were, Humans and Elves."

Pel was nodding. "So, what do you know about the courtesies?"

"How many Dwarrow have you met?"

"Ever? A few dozen. I've only worked with a handful."

"How many of them were women?"

She looked surprised at her own answer. "I've seen them, but Wellstone is the only one I've ever known."

Gladlow said, "I've heard all kinds of numbers, some people saying as rare as one in twenty. I've never heard better than one in six."

"So, she's his only chance?"

"No, it's nothing like that. It's their culture. I think the women are so treasured that the men are supposed to behave a certain way. He's supposed to prove he can let her be until a proper introduction is made, or some such. It's supposed to go like that for a long time, any suitors deciding they aren't interested will start treating her like they treat anyone. The women do the same. They have normal friendships and work together and all of that."

"There's no going back?"

"I don't think so. I think they can sort of start over, but that's the stuff of romantic legend."

Pel asked, "What happens if they decide they *do* want to be together?"

"I have no idea. Maybe any Human who asks that is long dead before they can find out. I just know that for one of them to act this soon is the harshest possible rejection. If she moved first, he's the one feeling worthless. Has he spoken to her?"

Pel shook her head. "No, he's still acting like she doesn't exist. Does that mean he isn't giving up?"

Carlin leaned over from the top bunk. "That is *the* most romantic thing I've ever heard."

· · · ·

Pel stood quietly listening to the arguments around the table. It was time for them to leave the tower and she was surprised at the pang of disappointment she felt. There was no denying that every one of them had needed the reprieve, but in their doldrums, they had begun grating on each other. Nowen was peevish, and she was beginning to think it wasn't the talk she had with him. He had seemed more annoyed that she was interrupting his reading. Meese was so glum he had completely stopped knocking the wind out of Nowen's sails while Gladlow seemed to mostly ignore him. Pel was beginning to recognize that as a bad sign, but didn't want to make things worse. Carlin was starting to lose sleep from her nightmares, but she hid it well most of the time. She had become affectionate with everyone, but no one more than Gladlow. It was fairly innocent, but she enjoyed how it flustered him a bit too much for Pel's liking. She caught Carlin looking at her from time to time when Gladlow was untangling himself. She had the distinct impression the show was somehow for her, but it just made her a little annoyed and maybe a little sad. With Voorsh climbing the walls, and Wellstone's overly relaxed attitude, the morning briefing intended to apprise Gladlow of the dotty theories they had all arrived at in their downtime was going exactly as one might expect.

"You didn't let her speak?" Gladlow said while pinching the bridge of his nose.

Meese was standing with arms crossed. "The only reason for her to show herself was to get information from us—"

"Well now we know nothing about her—"

"We had our hands full... of your entrails."

Wellstone said, "That's not exactly true. About knowing nothing. The colors and the skull meant she was Umbra."

Nowen asked, "Umbra Sedulous? Their symbol is a scroll—"

"No, their real symbol is a skull with a scroll for a tongue. When the Crown tamed them and cleaned up their organization, they were forbidden to wear the skull. Only the clerics wear it now."

Nowen looked at Meese with rare respect. "You were right about them."

Wellstone asked, "Meese, what do you know?"

Gladlow spoke instead. "Meese has been ranting for years that Umbra is a death cult. They used to recruit from the orphanages around Furbish. But their methods changed, what, twenty-five years ago?"

Meese nodded.

Gladlow said, "I think the question is, what do you know about the Crown's official church, Constable Wellstone?"

"Not much." She crossed he arms defensively at his look. "I didn't know they were capable of something like this. They aren't what you think, at least I thought they weren't." She shook her head to clear it. "They were a sort of death cult, but not a malicious one—"

Nowen said, "So, a benevolent death cult."

"They had two missions. The bulk of the organization was focused on an accounting. Their god—"

"Which god?"

"I don't god-damned remember Nowen. Their name means 'to do their labors unseen', or quietly or some such. Their services are private—"

"I can't imagine why."

Meese said, "Shut up, Nowen."

Wellstone continued. "An accounting of the dead. Who died and why. As you can imagine, their ranks swelled after the Quakes. There's nothing like an unending labor to invigorate the zealots. Their clerics, the elite, were dedicated to nothing but the elimination and recording of rogue undead."

Gladlow shrugged. "Huh. A benevolent death cult."

Pel said, "Wait. *Rogue* undead?"

"I know," Wellstone said, "I always thought that was strange phrasing. Not so much now."

"Why would the Crown involve themselves with a death cult?"

Gladlow said, "Magic. In the early days of the monarchy, they could hire mages freely, or coerce for that matter. The Institute consolidated most of the best by allowing them to work freely. The Crown could only influence the ones more interested in other kinds of power. The Church provides a wizard substitute. Is that why they tried to kill us?"

Meese said, "They were trying to kill Corigain and the other researchers. She said as much."

"So, she doesn't know where they are either. Was she trying to prevent them from interfering in her schemes? Or was it the researchers' work she was concerned with? Was she afraid they might find something?"

Pel said, "We think it might be something they already found."

Nowen placed a bundle on the table and unfolded the rags. The crocodile figurine was broken in two, exposing a green-blue interior.

Meese said, "It was somehow damaged in the fight."

Gladlow left the empty shell of the tail end and picked up the figure by the head. Protruding from the sandstone was a thin conical shell spiraling to a dull tip. "This isn't shell. What's it carved from?"

Wellstone looked at Meese. "We don't know. It feels like jade, but we couldn't even scratch it with a steel knife."

"Nowen?"

Nowen looked perturbed, "It's either mildly enchanted or actually created by magic." He gave an angry shrug. "I don't know what sort."

Gladlow asked, "So, what does it do?"

Nowen stood staring at the table and didn't answer.

"Nowen?" Gladlow sighed. "You didn't bring the gem, did you?"

"You mean I didn't *steal* the gem? No, I didn't."

Gladlow pinched the bridge of his nose and breathed deeply.

Before anyone could ask, Meese explained. "A lapis stone is needed for a particular divination spell."

Gladlow said, "I was allotted time—"

Nowen shouted, "Your expedition was *canceled*. That means—"

"*Nowen*. It doesn't matter whether I took the gem on holiday, or played shooters with it in the fucking common room..." Gladlow visibly calmed himself. He shrugged. "It doesn't matter."

"We were supposed to be with instructors, I didn't think we'd need one of our own."

"It doesn't matter," Gladlow said again. Brandishing the statuette, he said, "So, we're confident we can't easily damage it."

Meese and Nowen looked at each other. Meese said, "Nearly confident." He caught the object when it was tossed to him.

"See if you can get it out of there." Gladlow picked up the tail half and looked inside. What's this?" He was holding a strip of thin yellow foil.

"It's gold."

Gladlow said, "Corigain wrapped it in gold and hid it inside solid rock..."

"It would prevent anyone detecting magic from it—"

"Or using spells to locate it," Gladlow said gravely.

Meese and Nowen looked at each other again. Meese said, "This one's my fault, lad. I thought they were only trying to avoid inspections. Gods, it's been sitting in our damned living room for days."

Nowen said, "Salvage all the foil, we can seal it back up."

The two mages went off to a quiet corner to make a great deal of noise.

Gladlow leaned over his old map pinned to the table. He was still in a good amount of pain. Several locations had been added, including the village, treehouse, and western beach. "Something occurred to me this morning. There's no teleport circle in this tower."

Pel asked, "Can we leave if we find it?"

Gladlow looked so sad that she wished she hadn't asked. He said, "I'm sorry. I'm a good six years away from that sort of thing."

Meese called from across the room, "He'll do it in four."

Wellstone said, "I'll need a hobby."

"I meant they were supposed to have made one. It's quite a chore. I think it means they chose another location."

Pel said, "Another tower?"

"Exactly. Voorsh, have you seen another building like this one?"

"No, no."

"Can you show us on the map how far you've ranged? The places you've been?"

She looked down at the map and did a perfect imitation of Gladlow's usual one-shoulder shrug.

Carlin asked, "Sweetheart, have you seen a map before?"

"No, no."

Gladlow gave some papers and a lead stylus to Voorsh and left Carlin to give her lessons. Wellstone and Pel followed him up to the roof where he laid down on his back and stared up through the gaps in the canopy. Pel sat with legs crossed and Wellstone paced slow laps along the edge.

He asked, "Pel, what do you think we should do?"

"Why me?"

Wellstone answered for him, "Carlin will follow me, and the boys will follow Gladlow. Voorsh will go where it's interesting. You're only responsible for yourself."

Gladlow said, "That's not true anymore, is it? I was only asking her opinion."

"Sorry."

Pel said, "It's... I know what you meant." There was some truth in what both of them said. Normally she would at least entertain the idea of the dangerous but direct approach. Now her nerve was tested by the thought of anyone getting hurt again.

Gladlow said, "Imagine you were with six trained soldiers that follow orders, but you don't like very much." She could hear he was smiling. "What would your goals be?"

"Eliminate the threat. This Umbra sect made an assassination attempt. Its failure makes them less dangerous than they were before we knew they existed. For a time at least. Find them before they become a threat again."

"Wellstone? Talk it through."

She stopped and stood quietly collecting her thoughts. "Clear an obstacle. A sea monster, eel-men, and the undead have all served to prevent anyone from leaving this island. We only know of one person responsible for at least a part of it. I agree with Pel. And you, oh intrepid explorer?"

"Only one thing has changed. If we continue to look for the researchers, we might find Umbra instead. We can't let them have the advantage again."

Pel asked, "Do you think we're a match for them? I've never come closer to dying."

Gladlow sat up. "There was some luck involved. That trap was set for a small group of mages with possibly a few guides and laborers. Even with Whitecloud and a few of their own tricks, I think they might have been overwhelmed. We brought more weapons to bear than Umbra expected."

Pel said, "You three still used magic. Wouldn't these wizards also have some spells that would have worked?"

"Not as likely. Meese was using a spell so simple it doesn't need words. He likes it because it's... satisfying. Many don't favor it, including me, because it's inefficient and relies too heavily on your surroundings. And Nowen's was minor arcana, just a utility spell used for landscaping."

Pel asked, "What's landscaping?"

Wellstone said, "It's like gardening. It's an Elf thing."

Gladlow asked, "Have you heard about the beauty of the Elven cities? Somebody has to trim all those hedges and wash all those windows. City Elves work until they come of age, then school, then whatever." He stood up painfully and started down the ladder. "That gold foil gave me an idea. I need to do a little reading."

Wellstone had resumed her laps, but now she balanced on the edge with arms stretched out to either side.

Pel couldn't pass up the opportunity. "Gladlow and I talked last night—"

"Not about what you want to talk about."

"I don't know what that means, Helena."

Wellstone spun in place and continued her stroll backward. "Have it your way."

"So, you were listening when we talked about Meese?"

Wellstone sighed and said, "That was a surprise. I've met plenty of the orphans, they're part of every clan now, but I've never heard of one who decided not to join a clan one way or the other."

"It sounds like he was rejected first."

"That's fair. It explains the name. At first, I thought he may have been cast out, but he didn't have his family and clan names stripped, he never had them to begin with. Meese is a child's name, probably what the other babes called him."

Pel didn't know how to ask, so she just blurted it. "Is he not suitable... ?"

Wellstone sneered at her. "You have it all figured out. You realize he's the one snubbing me?" She stopped her pacing and stood with arms folded. "I thought he must be *playing* at it. I should have taken him more seriously, but he isn't exactly dripping with seriousness."

She kicked a twig, sending it spinning off the roof. "Men are so fucking fragile."

Pel asked, "Will you explain it to me? I want to understand."

"Gladlow was right about a few things, but he doesn't understand why. One in four babes is a girl, exactly, always, in every clan. One in four are boys, who, and this does vary, aren't particularly interested in women... or men for that matter. So this potentially leaves two men to compete for every woman. Triads are common, but usually kept private... that doesn't matter. Anyway, it can get messy."

Pel said, "I can't even imagine."

"Some backwards clans make their women dress as men. Or sequester the women away so they're never seen. One of the dead clans *assigned* women to the most powerful men. Those are all rarities. Most clans are just exceedingly polite. In a hole in the ground with a hundred other people, there's no room for grudges. So, people get near each other and observe without interfering. They watch how someone treats their family and friends. How they lead and follow. They make their decision, make it known, and then abide by it."

Pel asked, "So, what happened with Meese?"

"I'm not from any of those clans. When I was a child, the words *valley clan* used to be a bit of an insult. My home was more of a gorge, anyway. The stronghold was used for emergencies and official offices, that sort of thing. *No one* mocked us after the Quakes..." She paused for that moment nearly everyone had when the disasters were mentioned. "Anyway, we could swing our arms without elbowing someone in the eye. We still observe the courtesies, but they tend to be... sped up. Not so written in stone."

"And you thought—"

"I thought that someone so obviously comfortable with Humans would be more like me. I gave him a grave, and personal insult, that is only made worse by apologizing. Maybe I'm the one who's been unduly influenced by Humans." Wellstone went to the hatch and climbed down.

Pel said, "I'm sorry. I wish I could do something to help."

Wellstone's head popped up with a sweet smile. "You can take some advice. Next time the two of you feel the urge to stay up all night talking and giggling... just do some hand stuff and go to sleep."

Chapter Ten

Southern Basin, perimeter trail

"Who poured sand in your crack, Nowen?" Wellstone asked. The fussy mage in the immaculate yellow robes was beginning to stand out in the group. Gladlow had nearly reached the level of undress the women had endured, having his fancy wizard raiment divided up amongst them as he recovered. He was left with pants, boots, and a sash with all of his magic gewgaws. The leather stitching from his sheath was now holding his struggling breeches together, and he carried his iron boar spear openly. Meese's clothes were so soaked in blood, he had burned his robes but kept his shirt despite the stains. His parti-colored vest seemed to be where he kept his own talismans. He was content as long as his hat continued to survive. Wellstone had to admit she was in favor of the hat. She'd be looking for something of her own if they ever made it back to port.

"What did you need?" Nowen said, making absolutely clear he was being disturbed.

"I was simply inquiring as to your wellbeing, my stouthearted compatriot."

"And why would you feel that was necessary?"

Wellstone smiled and continued walking along beside him. "I've noticed that you often read while we travel, and while this is not the time to lecture you on the danger or stupidity of this habit, no matter how dangerous and stupid it may be, I have also noticed that normally, from time to time, you turn the page."

Nowen snapped his book shut and walked for a few moments before replying. "I admit I'm in a huff, but Gladlow condescending to me... rankles. I certainly don't want to lead, so he's entitled to a certain latitude." He looked at her for the first time to make his point. "In turn, I'm entitled to a few moments to be in a huff."

"Of course, I respect your privacy. Is this about the gem business?"

"That was my mistake, but it's nothing compared to coming on this expedition..."

Wellstone asked, "It isn't Carlin, is it? I think we have quite enough of that nonsense..."

Nowen seemed genuinely confused. "What about her?"

"As we speak, Gladlow is wearing her like a backpack. Carlin is just a flirt. I haven't seen any evidence of her going beyond that." She said it as a warning but she suspected it was too subtle for him to detect.

"You're implying I'm jealous? Hardly." She thought for a moment he was done, but he seemed to open up a bit. "That last part is a surprise, though. She's lovely."

"I think the phrase is spoiled for choice. She's twenty and been surrounded by sailors for four years. I think she's just happy to be around men she can *trust*." Again he didn't seem aware of her implication.

"Well, she's safe there. In the beginning, I had my doubts about Gladlow's interest in women. I've come to suspect he just doesn't want the distraction."

"That's your explanation for his advancement?"

Nowen sounded respectful for the first time when he said, "I've never seen his kind of dedication. He's not even that bright. I mean he *is*, but nothing like some of the people at the school. He puts some people off, but I do too. Meese is the only person he chooses over his studies. He drops whatever he's doing and they're off. Usually to make some money. Gladlow always needs money. That doesn't leave time for girls."

"So, he knocks them back and you mop up."

"Well, it's not always like that but, unlike him, I don't feel the need to avoid *every* distraction."

"Why the huff?"

Nowen sighed dramatically. "He's always implying I don't carry my weight."

"That's usually Meese..."

"Meese is an oaf who doesn't take anything seriously. Gladlow hands out *assignments*."

Wellstone said, "So this is about the locater spell..."

"Developing to the point where one can cast greater spells is a momentous thing for a mage. It's like breaking a barrier you've been pounding on, sometimes for years. It finally happens to me, and what do I get? Schoolwork."

"When he found out you broke this barrier, he gave you a more advanced spell to use..."

"He has less interest in divination than any other discipline. He'd rather I take it."

Wellstone said, "Right, right. So the scroll he gave you wasn't valuable. Was it one of his copies?"

"No, and it wasn't cheap. He would have had to trade for it. He spent every copper on this little holiday."

"I see. He collected a valuable spell, which by everyone's account, he hoards like a dragon, from a discipline he isn't interested in, not making copies to sell, and carried it around until you progressed enough to add it to your little diary there. That's what real people call a present."

They were quiet for a long time before Nowen gave a peace offering, the greatest gift he could bestow upon his lessers. He showed interest in another's opinion. "Wellstone, I understand why Carlin hangs all over Gladlow. They're the same age, same race, at least some level of attraction there, as well as friendship. Why has *Voorsh* started doing it?"

At that moment the little Lizard was walking with one hand grasping Gladlow's belt. Not exactly a horsey ride, but she was probably working up to it.

She said, "I think you'll have to ask her." But Nowen was already scribbling notes.

They were under new protocols handed down from Gladlow, starting with armor spells for everyone. Each mage was responsible for himself and his assigned partner each day, Voorsh being the odd one out, as her natural armor was of a similar quality. It was a large expenditure of resources, but Gladlow maintained that their survival at the tower was as much due to the group's surprising ability to mete out non-mystical punishment as anything else. He intended to relegate the mages to more of a support role. She seriously doubted he was including himself in that plan. He discussed a few other spells, such as a temporary weapon enchantment, however, they were short-lived and he'd be unable to cast anything else while maintaining one. Gladlow admitted that most of his spells were chosen for personal strategies, and he would need to change tactics to be more help to the group.

The immediate plan was simple. They would travel to the edge of Voorsh's stomping grounds and stay in one of her tribe's maintained hunting camps for the night. In the morning, they would head into the unknown, occasionally allowing Nowen to use his new spell to locate the mystery woman's skull pendant. Specifically, the nearest pendant of that type within a fifth of a mile. It was hardly a foolproof plan, but in their explorations, they were hoping to locate the researchers' alleged third tower. Voorsh had taken ownership of the map and carried it in a tube over her shoulder. It hadn't taken her long to grasp the skill, the same concepts being used by her own people in a more ephemeral manner. They didn't make maps out of anything longer lasting than stick drawings in the sand.

Voorsh led them first along the path the mages had taken from the east, this time taking the northern leg. It was easy and open for most of the journey. Voorsh found a sheltered section of the trail still showing sign of the skeletal army's march. It had come from the north, but every other area had long since been obscured. Wellstone guessed weeks but admitted she was unsure. Nowen's locator detected nothing. It was hard to decide when to use it. If he wasted his power, he would have little to offer in a fight. They carried on north for a time, but soon veered east into the jungle as limestone formations began to overtake the trees. They reached the series of caves with hours of daylight left, but they would likely be roughing it from here on, so they stopped to make camp. Most of the caves were interconnected, but their destination was an isolated cavern with only one entrance. The Uljar-Molik had stretched a thin net across the eighteen-foot opening, less as a deterrent, and more as proof that nothing over a foot in size had entered since their last visit. Inside were stored a smaller version of their palisade walls. The group worked together to move the pieces in front of small boulders set there for that purpose. The result was an eighteen-foot row of spears pointed outward, with only a narrow gap to pass through. They went as a group to gather wood and water, only splitting so Wellstone and Voorsh could hunt. Pel accompanied them but promised to hang back.

· · · ·

Eastern Cavern, Uljar-Molik hunting camp

Gladlow sat on a split log bench watching Meese prepare the fire pit. The cavern roof was domed ten feet high and chipped relatively smooth by the tribe, except for a gaping crack running the length of the fifty-foot room. Voorsh said that a good fire could be made inside, but too big and the smoke wouldn't escape quickly. It had a comfortable sandy floor and a smaller room connected to the rear.

Markings and pictograms covered the walls of the lesser chamber and Nowen was determined to copy them all. Carlin sat in the middle of the bench, stitching the end of her suede boat shoe with one of Voorsh's handmade bone needles.

Gladlow asked, "Carlin, how's your leg—"

She pretended she was ignoring him but swung her bare leg onto his lap and completed another stitch.

He scraped his nails on the bottom of her foot making her jerk it away with a yelp. "Healed nicely, I see."

"Why are you looking at my legs, Gladlow?"

"Did you sleep better last night?"

She laid her work down and leaned back on her hands to look over at him. "I slept. Nowen only lays down every few days, so I need a new bunkmate..." She didn't seem to have the energy to flirt and slumped down. "I know it's silly and annoying to everyone. I feel the same way... when I'm awake. As soon as I fall asleep, I'm paralyzed, and terrified, and trying to wake up before it asks me to choose."

"Choose what?"

She said, "I heard you talking to Pel. Do you think this is the same thing you felt at school?"

"I don't know. What is it asking you to choose?"

She shook her head but answered. "It's always something different, and there's only the *feeling* of choice."

"Tell me about the first."

"The first time, I was awake. It began at the tower, before the attack. That's how I know it's not all in my imagination. We won, but everyone was hurt. I thought you, three of you, would die." She shook her head to clear it. "It started with a feeling I can't describe well. Like the world changing size. When the fighting stopped I knew I should make a choice, but I didn't know what choice. It went away when Meese was talking to me. We gave the two healing potions to Voorsh and Pel." She was watching him for a reaction.

Gladlow said, "I didn't know that. It must have been hard. When did you feel it next?"

"Every time since, I've fallen asleep before it comes. I always see you casting a spell that goes wrong. You have gills but still drown, you release a hundred glowing, blue lights and your body catches fire. I always see Pel losing a battle. She's dragged into the dark, or buried under creatures clawing at her. The Chief falls, Meese burns, Nowen turns into a monster, Voorsh is left behind to die." She was quiet for a few moments. Her voice suddenly became angry. "I'm not offered a choice to stop these things. It's as if I'm being shown how helpless I am so I'll choose him."

"Him?"

"That's the first time I've said that."

Gladlow turned towards her. "That's the part that sounds familiar to me, 'So I'll choose him.' I had a feeling of obstacles. They could be moved easily with his power or on my own with great effort." He put a hand on her back. "Pel wanted me to tell you that I was able to choose. That I said no."

Carlin was shaking her head again. "I feel I'll eventually lose. How can you fight something like that? A... god?"

"It isn't a fight. Whatever wants your service, is *asking*."

"Why would an all powerful being want me, and why would it bother asking?"

Gladlow said, "It's believed that a deity taking away a mortal's will would see every other god turned against them. For whatever reason, we have free will." He wrapped his arm around and dragged her into a crushing hug. "I don't know what is being offered to you, and I don't know whether you should say yes or no. There are lots of ways to power, and I don't believe any of them are truly easy. Maybe you just ate some undercooked sweet-root. I do know," he leaned back to look at her face, "my magic doesn't *go* wrong, and I'd appreciate your discretion about the incident at the tower..."

They sat smiling at each other for a moment, and he should have seen it coming, but for the life of him, he didn't. She kissed him. Then she leaned back appraisingly as if deciding whether or not to do it again. She left to see what Nowen was doing. Gladlow was left to berate himself for not feeling what he was supposed to.

Meese said, "Interesting strategy."

"What are you on about?"

"Treating her like your little sister until she's driven to prove otherwise..." Meese's innocent tone showed he was trying to get a rise out of him. "I should be taking notes."

Gladlow was still looking towards the smaller chamber when he said, "If she meant anything by it, she wouldn't have done it in front of you."

"Lad, we've gotten so used to being crammed in small spaces, one person watching is privacy."

Meese's jokes usually made him feel better, but Gladlow's nerves were raw. "You think I have a strategy against Carlin?"

Meese sighed. "No, boy. That was the joke. The idea that you have tact is laughable."

"As if you're any better."

"Carlin has been lavishing you with attention because she thinks it will make Pel notice you. And because she genuinely adores you. Just now, she had a moment where she considered keeping you for herself, but that probably isn't a troll she's ready to bait." Meese looked very smug.

Gladlow was clenching his jaw but forced himself to relax. "I think I knew that. I hate it. I hate all of it, and I'm done. I hate the horseshit with you and Wellstone, and I'm done with that too. Either you follow the old ways and respect her decisions, or you see it with the same disdain as learning smithing from a Human or your language from an Elf."

"Listen here—"

"I'm disappointed in us. I'm going to keep us safe. I need your help keeping us together. We can do better."

. . . .

"Hail the providers. We have returned." Wellstone dropped a large squirming sack on the ground. Voorsh did the same while Pel carried a firkin they had salvaged from the tower. It once contained a nice port wine. The little barrel must have weighed sixty pounds full of water. Meese thought she looked less tired than the other two.

He asked, "So what have you brought us?" This was going to be harder than he thought. Years of self conditioning was hard enough, but he couldn't imagine what it would be like breaking the courtesies if he had actually been raised into it. Mostly he felt foolish and braced himself for whatever derision was coming to him.

Wellstone looked him in the eye and said, "Kinsman, you're going to *hate* this." She opened the sack with a flourish and a pincered grey monstrosity thrashed to get free of the bag. Its shelled body was over a foot long, not including the multitude of clattering legs and massive claws.

Pel said, "Some sort of land crabs were congregating on the stream banks. Voorsh says they're good to eat."

"No, no," Voorsh corrected, "I said they can be eaten, not that they are good." She apparently had doubts about her clarity. "They are not."

Meese said, "Land-crabs. They look like water-spiders to me. Could someone please deal with this one before I lose a digit?"

While Voorsh started killing the creatures and neatly stacking them, Wellstone said, "I thought we might just throw them on the fire, but... I've never seen anyone build a fire like that. Can I help?"

Meese surveyed his preparations. She was referring to the short ring of posts sticking out of the sand. "That's not firewood." A fire snapped into existence surrounding a nearby pile of stones. With nothing to burn, it created no smoke. He revealed a thick leather bundle and laid it over the stakes.

Pel asked, "Is that the leather from Carlin's shield?"

"Just the inside layer—"

Wellstone asked, "So, not the part that cut a dead man in half?"

"No." Meese shrugged. "What? I washed it." Actually, he had also gone through the trouble of wetting it and lashing it to a barrel to give it a passable bowl shape. Tied to the stakes, it created a cauldron large enough to hold gallons of water. The fire disappeared, his spectral hand moved hot rocks to the water, and the fire sprung back to life. Repeat. Soon the water was lightly steaming. The fire was much too large and generated an obnoxious amount of heat for the summer cave, but was only lit every other minute.

Wellstone took immediate liberties by digging through his pack and testing his spices. She chose the peppery one and the last of the salted fish, which was more salt than fish, throwing them in the pot.

Meese asked, "Voorsh, would you like yours cooked, or will that ruin it?"

Voorsh shrugged and said, "It cannot hurt." Meese thought she was sounding more like them every day as she picked up particular phrases. Even the ever present hissing of her speech was almost undetectable, except when she was excited.

Night was falling and the revolting crustaceans were turning a much more appetizing orange color. Pel and Gladlow returned from outside the cavern, her having guarded him as he placed a ward from his spellbook. They dropped the purpose-made boards into place, barring the last opening of the palisade.

He said, "Clanging bells means something bigger than those crabs is forty feet from the entrance."

Meese said, "It's not a stone tower, but I've certainly stayed in worse places."

Wellstone said, "You and me both."

She was squatting near him with her arms wrapped around her knees. She looked very small. Usually, she spread out to fill whatever space she could claim, an arm hanging over your bunk or legs stretched out so you had to step over. It was hard to know what lessons to carry with you, but one had never failed. He had learned from the only father he ever knew that sometimes there was only one piece of security you could offer. He pulled the gifted sword from his pack and drove the scabbard into the sand within her reach. He had sharpened the blade and polished the guard and knuckle-bow.

He said, "If I could, I'd take the tip down for you. It's nearly perfect otherwise. You didn't seem to have any trouble, but a little more weight on the—"

"It's perfect, Meese. I'll take care of it."

"Good, you can sharpen your own sword from now on." He saw she was going to protest and said, "Wellstone, it's not a gift. It should never have been given to me but to the group. Besides, equal shares. You can give me the next faerie wand a grateful citizen flings at you."

She had her face buried, only her eyes showing above her arms. "You must call me Helena."

• • • •

Gladlow thought the meal was a delightful surprise, due mostly to Voorsh's underselling of the crabs. She had never cooked them, her people eating them on the go while hunting better meat. He could see her brain working. If she had been Nowen, she'd be scribbling in a notebook right then. Nowen was the only one seemingly unimpressed. He was anxious to get back to the small chamber. He was using his language enchantment to read the pictograms, but it was time consuming. He had recruited Carlin to copy sections down to give him more time before the spell expired. Gladlow warned him to keep something in reserve, he didn't want to be caught with nothing left to cast. That went over about as well as one would expect, with Nowen leaving in a huff.

Voorsh had gone to sleep soon after nightfall, as she often did whenever there was no drink or Traveler. Carlin and Nowen were in the other room with Meese's torch. Gladlow kept a gold light shining from one of the large stones near the fire as the two Dwarrow sat together for the first time, not near but not far from each other. They were pretending to discuss the map, but what could be that amusing? Gladlow went to the place Pel had claimed near the far wall, where the roof sloped down to a few feet above the floor. There was just enough room to lean comfortably against the wall. She was sitting with the Orc blade across her lap, sanding small imperfections from the surface. He didn't see that it made any difference, but he sometimes did his meditations and diction exercises even when he wasn't preparing spells. He made sure she smiled a welcome before sitting down next to her.

"I spoke with Carlin. I don't know if it helped, but she knows we care about her."

"I couldn't get her to talk about it. Do you think it's a calling like yours?"

Gladlow crossed his arms. "I do. More importantly, she does. It's strange, but a person might have their prayers answered the very first time, or serve faithfully their entire lives and never be acknowledged. She probably never gave it a thought, and now she's being hounded. I believe there are rules, even if we don't know them all. She can weather it."

Pel said, "I'm sure she appreciated it."

"I'm sure too. She kissed me."

Her sanding didn't miss a stroke. "Why are you telling me this?"

"Because I'd prefer she didn't do it again."

She stopped and looked at him. "Why? Carlin is—"

"Confused. She's frightened to be alone. I'm not the answer. Pel? I don't want her." He left that in the air a moment. He had let Carlin tease, hoping Pel would react, and had told himself that wasn't what he was doing. Even after deciding not to lie, he was here, talking around a thing instead of saying it. Maybe that was alright. It could be his own version of the courtesies. He knew better than most how powerful words could be. "I thought you could help. It was probably nothing, and I'll speak to her if she pursues it. But, if you could help me keep a little distance, it would give us the chance to let it go without being embarrassed."

Pel jumped to her feet and gathered up his bedroll and pack, bringing them back and dumping them carelessly next to hers. She sat down and said, "We're probably going to wake up with her draped across both of us, but it's the best I can do. You're on your own with Voorsh."

Chapter Eleven

Pel slept with her back against Gladlow's, hearing him breathe and feeling his heartbeat. She woke suddenly, alone. His bedroll was still a couple of feet away, empty. He stood nearby, face lit with flickering light, a glowing sphere of ice in his hand, vapor crawling across his fingers. The clang of bells echoed in the cavern. She was on her feet, sword in hand as everyone gathered.

Gladlow said, "Meese, a small one please."

Pel didn't turn to look, keeping her eyes on the darkness beyond the palisade. A small glowing coal shot just over the wall and struck something twenty feet past. It flared for an instant, lighting the corridor. A mass of silhouettes were shuffling forward.

"Don't damage the barricade." Gladlow was obviously reminding Meese. Before the sparks died, he threw the ball of ice over, connected with a creature, and sent it to the ground with a crunch and a puff of steam. It looked something like a Lizard, but wrong. Wellstone jumped up on a bench and readied her bow for a target to show itself.

A hollow voice echoed through the cavern, "The flesh of your sons and daughters will join your own in judgment." The figures pressed the barricade, many impaling themselves on the jutting spears. Still, their slender arms reached and flailed at the barrier. They were the slow undead, but they had never been Human. Reptilian like the Uljar-Molik, but all similarities stopped there. Their visual organs were tiny, unlike the Lizard's large, limpid eyes. Their coloring, whether natural or due to undeath, was an almost uniform whitish grey.

Pel kept to the side, slashing and stabbing over the wood, Carlin and Voorsh thrust javelins through the gaps, again and again. Wellstone fired arrows into the roiling mass, Meese threw another mote of fire, and Gladlow more lightning. Nowen was pulling his trick with the sand again, but it had little effect as the creatures piled against the barricade. Light from small fires bounced from the ceiling and illuminated a figure. Two men stood slightly above the masses and slowly moved forward as if carried. One shouted, "He utterly destroys all places, submit yourselves to his embrace, or die in your sins." The other raised a bow and fired an arrow straight into Gladlow's chest. Pel screamed, but it died in utter shock as the shaft smashed against something unseen and spun away in several pieces.

Gladlow pointed. "Nowen, take him!" Two red hornets streaked overhead, weaving around and over each other to strike the man and send him dropping out of sight. The palisade was holding, though it was beginning to strain and creak. They continued to launch arrows and embers over the wall, continued to stab and slash. Gladlow and Nowen ran forward to add spear and dagger. Something changed. The reptilian corpses near the center began to move away or press to the sides. A beast, massive, but too low to see clearly through the barrier, slammed into the wood beams. It was too wide to fit into the entry gap and embedded the spikes on either side into its flesh. As it pulled away, the palisade was dragged backward and began to come apart.

Gladlow said, "Pull back to the center."

It rammed again, several braces splintering or jumping over the boulders. As it pulled back, gaps formed and were filled by the dead clawing their way in.

"Meese. Burn it down."

Pel had only seen this spell once for a split second as she passed. Now she stood at the mage's side as he sent a rolling arc of blue and violet flames through the palisade. The jumble of wood and bodies burst into flame. The beast thrashed and splintered the burning timbers, sending sparks into the air as it backed away.

Pel shouted, "It won't hold. Clear the way!"

Its next charge did break through and brought the monstrosity into the center of the chamber. It was an undead crocodile, eyeless and tattered, sixteen feet long. Pel looked to the gap as two figures strode through, parting ways at the entrance. Neither were Human, but undead things, pale and gaunt. One dressed in scale armor with a longsword and bow, the other in the trappings of the Umbra sect, flanged mace raised high.

The undead cleric called out, "Come die, and have your names counted in the book of the—"

Flames engulfed him, making him writhe. He charged the mage but was met by Pel's blade. She shuffled back and took in her surroundings before fully engaging the thing. Gladlow and Voorsh were cut off by the great beast. Wellstone had her blade drawn with Carlin by her side. And Meese was unleashing more fire at the horde pushing through the flames. Smoke filled the ceiling and Pel could already feel it in the back of her throat. She saw Nowen looking around the chamber, possibly panicked. She turned and launched an attack at her opponent, but shouted to Nowen, "The warrior, Nowen. Take him out!" She let the others fade into the background as she dodged a swing and slashed her blade across the cleric's thigh. Her blade struck a good blow but barely cut his dead flesh. She retreated a step and set herself. She decided to take a risk to end this quickly.

The undead thing raised its arms wide and said, "All of the dead, great and small—"

She slashed while feinting towards his mace and dodged the resulting swing. She let the mace graze her, trusting in her friend's magic, and brought her blade across the thing's neck. Even bare, the flesh of its throat only parted, the blade failing to sever its head from its body. Her intangible armor protected her from his weapon, but she was wracked by pain in her left arm. The creature's empty hand had brushed her, filling her limb with the pain of an infected wound, but multiplied tenfold. She threw herself backward to regroup. The thing was a wight. She was unable to slay this horror on her own. She would occupy the cursed thing until her companions could come to her aid. It was baring its unholy teeth and mouthing words silently. She drew her bronze blade into her aching hand and said, "I'll gladly die today if all I've managed is to shut you up."

· · · ·

Meese couldn't see any more movement behind the flames, which was just as well. Smoke was filling the chamber rapidly and only the living needed to breathe. He turned in time to see Nowen cast his last projectile at the longsword wielding undead. He shouted to the Elf, "Nowen, smother these flames." Meese froze and blinked his eyes rapidly at the pair fighting the crocodile. Gladlow was in the middle of casting and Voorsh was *expanding*. She grew until her head hit the ceiling, then coughing out smoke, the ten-foot-tall Lizard lunged at the crocodile as if she'd done it a hundred times. Maybe she had. Waving her hand through its jaws, they snapped shut on empty air, and she grabbed the end of its snout in one hand. She rolled over its back, bringing its head back with her. The two giant reptiles thrashed on the ground while Gladlow jabbed at it opportunistically with the boar spear. Meese saw Wellstone and Carlin trying to deal with the warrior, but the blade barely nicked it and Carlin was able to do nothing more than dodge. Meese had enough strength remaining to cast a lesser and a greater spell. Unleashing the flames once more, he shaped them to pass the women without harm. The creature staggered in pain but barely slowed. Meese wanted badly to launch the last of his power at the hated thing, but he took the boy's lead, knowing he should do so more often. He called out, "Carlin, Helena, run to me!" and began his last spell. They bolted towards him and Helena blocked its swing at Carlin, but the creature scraped Helena with its hand. She kept running, but he could see the agony on her face. "Helena, I have to touch your sword." She slashed it towards him but stopped the blade within reach. He laid his hand across the metal and completed the connection with a ringing tone. The light reflecting on the blade gave a wobble and he grabbed Carlin's hand and pulled her away. Meese felt an almost overwhelming despair at his loss of power. He looked around helplessly at the struggles around him. Nowen was shifting the sand to smother the flames, preventing the smoke from worsening. There were a few moving corpses in the tangle, but they would keep for a moment. "Carlin, help Nowen with those undead." Voorsh and Gladlow were occupying their opponent, but unable to kill it. Voorsh was preventing it from bringing its jaws to bear but was counting on someone else to do the damage. He knew Gladlow was maintaining her size and would be unable to cast anything else with a lasting effect. Meese was doing the same with Helena's sword but could do nothing more than throw embers anyway. Gladlow was desperately trying to finish the beast with his spear, but that would need time they didn't have. Meese had lost track during the fighting but thought Gladlow should have something left. Pel and Helena were each too evenly matched in swordplay with their opponents and would be worn down quickly by the creatures' touch and the smoke.

Meese threw an ember at the undead warrior, but it and Helena were moving too quickly. At least he might still hit the creature by aiming over her head. He yelled, "Gladlow, do you have anything left?"

"Just tell me what to do!"

Meese wanted to scream at *him* to choose. Wasting time was unacceptable, so he went with cold-blooded strategy. "Take the warrior." A white hornet slammed into the dead thing. Meese was worried that it might distract Helena, but he had nothing to worry about. She used the opportunity to lance a brutal thrust through its midsection. For the first time, it seemed to weaken. Helena recovered while only receiving a weak blow herself. He spared a glance, and Pel looked the same as before, working her way slowly backward, trying not to get pinned.

"Gladlow—" he started but another glowing light weaved around Helena to hit the warrior. Meese added his ember and Helena lunged, throwing out caution, and finished the thing with her blade piercing the base of its throat. She howled when it clutched at her and brought them down to the ground, but she twisted the blade savagely until it grew still.

· · · ·

With nothing left to cast, Gladlow felt strangely focused. Having so many options removed was freeing. After a particularly successful thrust, he left the spear protruding from the thing's side and looked for an opening to time his leap. Voorsh was clamping the beast's mouth with her left hand, making it impossible for her to bring the buckler's spikes to bear. Her right was being used to hang onto the thrashing creature, her copper club long since shrinking to size as it fell away. She was holding its head back as best she could to expose its underside to her companion. The next time the croc slammed its body down, Gladlow wrapped his arms around its head, clamping his hands on the edge of its mouth near the end. Voorsh let go and slammed her dual blades into the thing's side, immediately doing more damage than any of Gladlow's spear thrusts. The creature, less restrained, slammed itself down with renewed vigor. Gladlow managed to remain on top, but the breath was knocked out of him by the force of the landing. His vision blurred on the edges and he saw the flaw in his plan. If he lost concentration, his spell would end, along with his life and Voorsh's soon after. Voorsh gripped its eye socket and pulled back hard, driving the buckler into its back and sides over and over. Gladlow only had to hang on and trust his companions. His whole world shrank to the fabric of the spell and his hands on the creature, gripping so hard his fingers sank into the rotting flesh. For once in a long time, he felt absolutely certain he could succeed. Gladlow never lost focus. In school, when others completed a lesson and moved on, he went back to the basics of the craft. He had struggled early on but learned a valuable lesson by having to focus on the little things. That's all being a mage was. It was memory and imagination. It was pronunciation and penmanship. It was concentration.

Gladlow felt the time run out. The fabric of the spell unraveled and collapsed. He still hung on, but without Voorsh's strength and weight, it wouldn't be long. The beast's thrashing did seem weaker, but his body was still thrown over the side. He still kept his grip, but the creature battered him against the ground. If it had been anything other than soft sand, he would have broken. When he was finally thrown off, he scrambled backward to avoid those snapping jaws, but the rotting giant was still. Voorsh was covered head to tail in rotting gore, shaking entrails from Gladlow's spear. Wellstone was withdrawing her blade from the monster's side and Meese clambered from its back with a gory blade of his own. Gladlow was trying to get his breath back and clear his head, but he couldn't look away from that sword. Why was Meese carrying a sword? Pel's sword. He climbed to his feet, working his hands to uncurl them from their claw-like state. The cave was still and hazy with smoke. He knew people were talking to him, but he didn't hear. Carlin was kneeling by Pel and he feared the worst. He started breathing again when he saw that Carlin was bandaging the injured woman's arm. He stood near and looked down at her. His thoughts were fractured. She looks... breathing... but a person doesn't bandage... is she breathing?

"Carlin?"

She was crying but calm. "She's alive, but I don't understand what's wrong. Mostly minor injuries, but her chest is badly bruised. Maybe she's bleeding inside."

Wellstone said from behind, "The thing's touch. My arm is still hurting terribly, but it's started to go numb."

Carlin said, "Do we have any healing—sorry, I know we don't."

Gladlow gestured at the pale corpse. "What are these things? There's no blood, no rot. Wellstone? Tell me about fighting it."

She blew air through her lips and stared into space for a moment. "Very Human swordplay. It reacted to feints like anyone does. It was tough. Like trying to slice rawhide." She smiled at Meese. "Until your trick with the blade... is that permanent? Because—"

"Wellstone."

"After that, there was nothing special at all, except the touch. Like fighting a person."

Carlin said, "A person. What did the touch feel like?"

"Well, it hurts of course. I don't know how to describe it. It felt like dying."

"How does it feel now?"

"Better. A bit numb."

"How do *you* feel? Sick or dizzy?"

Wellstone shook her head. "I feel good. A bit tired, come to think of it. My blood is usually still boiling right now, but I could nap."

Carlin said, "I think it was a wight. I remembered wight was the ancient word for person. Mama told me about them. I don't think there's anything we can do." Carlin looked at Gladlow. "I didn't mean it like that. I don't think we need to do anything. I think she'll recover." She hugged him. "If they kill you with their touch, you become one of them. But she's alive."

"We have the bandages. They're a mix of herbals and a minor enchantment. Use one on every cut and scrape." He knelt beside her. "Give me a belt."

· · · ·

Wellstone leaned over, hands on knees, and heaved once, hard. She didn't vomit, but her mouth watered heavily and she let it drop to the sand. She reached her arms up and stretched her back. "I never thought it was possible to improve on the smell of a rotting corpse. These fellows have cracked it."

Voorsh was waiting for her help moving another cadaver. She said, "Shessa-Molik smell bad always. Living is worse. Angry is most worse."

Carlin's interest was piqued. "Did you know them?"

"Yes-no."

Wellstone said, "Understood," and went to pick up another pair of spindly arms.

"Many look the same, smell the same." She grabbed the feet and had to waddle to avoid stepping on the dragging tail. "No names, only smells."

Meese dusted his hands and said, "Their leader, Rotting-Clam-Farts isn't going to blame us for this, is he?"

Voorsh said, "She is the one we burned first with the wights."

"Gods blind me, I'm sorry Voorsh..."

"Do not be sorry for me. Her tribe is dead."

Wellstone asked, "This is *all* of them?"

Voorsh said, "I think yes."

They were all more subdued after that, working as Gladlow did, quietly, though less desperately. They worked first by the glow of Meese's bonfire, then in the light of dawn, stacking alternate layers of broken palisade and corpses.

As they finished, the fire burned without Meese's help, greasy black smoke billowing upward. Gladlow spoke for the first time in hours. "Voorsh, I think we have to leave the croc where it is."

She said, "Yes, yes. My people will clean the cave."

"You could just..." Meese said to Gladlow, making a shrinking motion with his hands and waggling his eyebrows. It made

Wellstone smile, but the younger mage was incapable of good humor at the moment. She thought he looked ready to fall over, but he was still almost maniacally moving.

They followed him back into the cave as he said over his shoulder, "I don't think it's the time to waste energy."

Wellstone saw what he had been doing when she thought he was taking a rest break. He had roped the dead crocodile's mouth shut and staked it to the ground. Obviously, he was talking about not wasting *magical* energy. She had to admit she understood his reluctance to leave the sleeping Pel in a room with it. When dead didn't always mean dead.

Gladlow checked for her breathing and looked around for something else to do. "Where is Nowen?"

Wellstone heard an edge to his voice. She said, "He unburied the wood and bodies then went to rest." All three mages had rested enough to cast a couple of spells each but would need real sleep to recover any more.

Carlin said, "You know how he is, he usually just meditates instead of sleeping. He's in the back chamber."

Gladlow headed that way without another word. Wellstone said, "Meese, he's going in there to start a fight, you should stop him."

Meese said, "Nowen will yell at him, 'You can't treat me like a child' and Gladlow will say, 'I expect more from you' and they'll stay out of each other's way for a couple of days. It's the natural order."

Wellstone knew something Meese didn't, and she had seen Gladlow's tension build and patience evaporate. Now wasn't the time, but she someday needed to talk to Meese about the lessons Gladlow was learning from him. Dwarrow self-control had translated into bottled Human feelings, and those fermented and bubbled until the container broke. The boy was about to pop.

"Meese, go watch the door and keep that fire going strong. I'll relieve you after a quick nap."

Meese was too tired to argue and left with a half-hearted wave.

"Carlin, sit with Pel. Sleep if you can." The girl nodded and walked away.

Wellstone crept to the small cave entrance and checked the light. It was all coming from the room, so she didn't have to worry about shadows. The sand and her exhausted bare feet were incapable of making sound, though her cracking joints might give her away. She covered her mouth to keep from snorting. She was getting a bit punchy herself.

Gladlow said, "Right back at it. Anything worthwhile?"

"To me, absolutely. No combat applications, if that's what you mean."

"No, I meant worth your time and energy. What else would I mean? You've spent a great deal of it."

"This is what I'm here for Gladlow."

"What are the rest of us here for?"

"Why don't you tell me?"

Wellstone peeked around the corner to see Gladlow jab his finger at the other man.

Gladlow said, "Not to escort you through your own, private expedition. We're not your guards and porters, Nowen."

"I'm not here to fight. I didn't train to fight. But that's all you want from me! Why is that? Do you just like to be better at something?" His voice sounded frantic. Wellstone felt stupid for not realizing Nowen might be more bottled up than Gladlow. They had all been through a lot.

Gladlow's voice was dangerously quiet. "None of us came here to fight. But we all have to. I thought I made a good compromise with you, Nowen. I gave you my spell and my ring so you could fight from the back and never miss. If that's so much to ask, I'll have my ring back."

Nowen stood frozen, and Gladlow silently waited.

Nowen finally broke. "I lost it. You already knew that didn't you?"

Gladlow shouted at him, "I gave you a fucking locator spell. Was that not worth your attention either? You—"

"You think I didn't try that first? It was too far away. I must have left it at the tower. I'm sorry. But I didn't need it. You saw me cast two without it—"

"With it, you would have three!"

Nowen screamed, "So what? Are you simple?" His voice changed as he tried to sound more reasonable. "Two more damned bugs wouldn't have changed the tide of that nightmare."

Wellstone gave up all pretense of hiding and stood openly in the doorway. Maybe her presence might calm things. Gladlow looked controlled, but Nowen looked genuinely frightened of him.

Gladlow said, "Two. You only cast twice? Should I be relieved you spared a third of your spells to protect..." he trailed off into silence.

"Gladlow, let's stop shouting at each other. It wasn't like that. We all thought we were safe. I didn't know any of this would happen." He had his hands out protectively, and Gladlow's silence was completely unnerving him. "Gladlow, listen. I'm sorry about the ring. It was just a mistake. Listen, I know this isn't what you're angry about..."

Gladlow's face showed real anger for the first time, but he kept his voice level. "What are you talking about?"

"Pel and I... no, listen. I'm saying I'm not in your way. You can have—"

Wellstone stepped between them saying, "That's enough." At the same time, she reached as high as she could and gave them both a small shove in the chest. Nowen stumbled away but Gladlow didn't move. She looked up at his face and put her other hand on his chest, patting him gently. She knew his heart pounding was telling him to run or fight. He did neither.

"You think I'm jealous. While she could die?" He spoke like it was a revelation. "You've always thought so little of me. Your first word to me was *savage*. Do you remember?"

"I apologized. We're friends."

"You never stopped thinking it. You had a magic ring on your hand, completely unique in the world, but because *I* made it, it was worthless."

"I'm sorry—"

"It doesn't matter. This is my expedition. You begged to come. I don't lead because you let me. I lead because it's mine, and all of you choose to follow. From now on, the only concern you have about me and her? If anything gets through *me*, or gets through *her*, you're dead. You did well in the fight. You did what was asked of you. You'll do better next time because you'll give us *half*."

Chapter Twelve

Pel's eyes were open before she was truly awake. She was staring at a rock ceiling and listening to a voice.

"I thought a thought and thought I ought, share the thought I thought I ought. Thank you very much for this. There's a fairy lass to kiss. Have a merry glass of piss. Responding with alacrity, the fairly—"

"Gladlow?"

His face appeared over her. It was smudged and he recently had a bloody nose. His curly black hair was sticking to his forehead and he was smiling as big as she had ever seen.

She cleared her throat. "Shut up." She had a moment of panic when she couldn't reach out her hand, but Gladlow was already unstrapping her. "What—"

"It was just a precaution," he said. The straps weren't tight, she could have slipped out if she wasn't so weak.

"No. What were you reciting? It's terrible." She was pushing herself up, but nothing seemed to be happening.

Gladlow pulled her into a sitting position and she crossed her legs with difficulty. He said, "Speech exercises. I know they're annoying. Meese has forbidden me when he's awake."

She blinked her eyes and looked around. She felt dazed. "I would like to forbid you as well if that's alright?"

"Agreed."

"Precaution against what?"

His smile continued but with a hint of insincerity. "Another wight."

She understood and was a little impressed. "Wights. You knew what they were."

"No. Carlin learned about them when she was little. I never thought of how dangerous a mortuary could be..." His face became deathly serious. "Are you in any danger?"

She tried a smile to reassure him but was sure it came out sickly. "If I've lived this long, I'll be fine soon."

He sat on the ground in front of her, knees almost touching, and passed her a water flask. "When did you first learn about them?"

"Also when I was little, but more as I grew."

Gladlow asked, "You've fought them before?"

She chose that time to take a long drink from the flask but found herself answering with a nod. She braced herself for one of the questions she normally avoided, but he surprised her.

"Can you tell me what you know about them?"

She said, "They're twice as difficult to kill as when they lived. Their touch hurts you and prevents healing until the effects wear off. It makes clerics less effective on the battlefield. What makes them really dangerous is their control of lesser undead. The mindless corpses suddenly flock like birds and can be used strategically." She took another sip of water. "They can be accidental, I suppose feral is as good a word as any, or they can be raised with purpose like these."

Gladlow said, "Rogue or sanctioned by the church."

She nodded. "Would you help me over to the wall?"

He helped her stand and waited a moment to make sure she wouldn't go down the second he stepped away. He grabbed up both of their bedrolls and packs to make a moderately comfortable seat where she could lean her back against the wall. He said, "I'm sorry we left you to fight alone."

She could see it was something that had been bothering him. "The best strategy was for me to occupy him until you lot could kill him." She thought about it and realized she hadn't felt alone at all. "Your magic armor is spoiling me."

That certainly pleased him, he was back to smiling in an instant. "It's not the greatest defense..."

"Well, I've never been more comfortable. Not right now, obviously." She was weak, but there was only one place that truly hurt. She peeked under her tunic and felt around her chest and ribs. He looked worried, so she tried to make light of it. "A wild swing caught me right in the chest. Now they match."

He shook his head and started to say, "They always..." His mouth snapped shut.

She raised one eyebrow as high as it would go.

"Carlin did *not* offer a peek..." He grinned and shrugged. "But she described them in great detail."

Laughing hurt. "Idiot."

She wasn't awake long that time. She awoke next to the sounds of chopping. Gladlow was using the Orc blade to dismember the giant crocodile. She watched the grisly work with a smile on her face. The beast was gone later and she smelled smoke from a fire outside the entrance. Carlin woke her to eat a few bites of rabbit meat, drink broth, and go outside. She dozed lightly as Carlin changed a bandage. Pel could swear the flesh of her arm was stitched like cloth. She couldn't remember it ever feeling so good to go back to sleep.

Wellstone was smiling at her. "Pel, did you hear a word I've said?"

"Sorry."

"I thought you were awake. Well, I'm not repeating all of that. Come on, it's time to go. Walk and eat."

Her bedroll and basket were already being carried by Gladlow and Carlin. He handed Pel her sword. Meese was back to having a blade strapped to his pack, this time the wight's longsword. Carlin carried its longbow and the other's mace. She hung her war club on the inside of a new palisade. The group had rebuilt it. Instead of a spiked barricade across the inside entrance, it was further forward and shaped like an arrowhead pointing outward. Large boulders must have been moved by magic, both to brace the structure and provide good cover to defenders. It was perhaps too tailored to the specific battle they had fought, but it was a definite improvement over the old. She found herself feeling proud of these people who would leave this borrowed place, this place that had saved their lives, better than they found it. It was a new concept for her, like the letter Whitecloud had left. Leaving something behind in the hopes it would be useful to people who came after. Even if you would never know who they were. She decided not to ask about the palisade, preferring the idea that it was all Gladlow. He was walking up ahead, the group keeping her to the middle. She could accept that. She would pull her weight when she was back to full strength.

"Carlin, can you tell me where we're going?"

The girl whispered back, "New campsite, but we're going *quietly*."

Pel looked at Wellstone who rolled her eyes. The group was quieter, but only compared to the usual chatting and clattering. Gladlow always walked like he was trying to destroy everything underfoot, and even when they were walking on loose sand, Meese's pack produced unidentifiable clinking and rattling. Now Carlin had added a loose quiver of seven arrows sliding to and fro. This was opposed to Wellstone and Voorsh who were always breathing on your neck before you heard them coming, and even Nowen, whose huge pack was apparently only filled with books and papers.

Carlin couldn't be silent for long. "Voorsh and the Chief tracked those things for quite a ways. The dead leave a trail even I could track. It led up into what's called karst terrain. It's all holes and caves and rocks where the jungle thins out. Voorsh says it's too dangerous to go far in without ropes and such, but that just means the dead couldn't have come far either. We're camping rough tonight, no fire or anything, up on higher ground with lots of ways out. I remembered wights don't come out in the day. We search at dawn. If we don't find anything in a few hours, we use the rest of the day to put as much distance between us as we can."

Pel said, "It's a good plan. It's true they don't like sunlight, but I don't think anyone knows if it hurts them or not." She went back to watching those ahead of her and concentrating on not making noise with her footsteps.

Carlin said, "You can walk up front with Gladlow if you want, but he's forbidden to talk." She started snickering. Pel heard a snort and looked round at Wellstone.

She said, "It's true. He can't *whisper*. Either nothing comes out or it sounds like someone calling from down a well."

Carlin said, "He tried to go with them to scout, but they sent him back."

Wellstone added, "There won't be any playing Traveler tonight."

The three of them received a glare from Gladlow, but it only made it harder not to laugh.

It was a long, miserable night, all of them feeling more exposed than any time they could remember. They crowded into a sheltered area, relatively flat, with enough outcroppings and ridges to provide decent escape options. It would take hundreds of undead to surround them and that hadn't been seen since the wars. With no light and little talking, it was just an exercise in listening to creepy sounds for endless hours. Nowen wanted to look every time he heard something, but had to be reminded that if he could see them, they could see him. Luckily, *they* were just nocturnal rodents of some sort and a multitude of insects.

They were back on the march before dawn had fully arrived, and no one complained of the early start. They searched and backtracked for two hours before they found what they were looking for. The terrain had evened out as the rock gave way to jungle, creating a green path running parallel to the larger basin path they were avoiding. It was rougher, with slightly higher elevation, and showed signs of large numbers of feet passing through. When they lost the trail again, it likely leading further up into the rocks, Gladlow gave Nowen the signal to try the locator. Nowen performed the spell, concentrating for a moment, and shook his head.

Gladlow said aloud, "Damnation," and shrugged. "I say we cut back west to the big trail."

"Maybe we should see what that's all about," Carlin said. She was shading her eyes and looking up ahead over the canopy. "That's a lot of scavenger birds. I think they're vultures."

Pel said, "Scavengers don't usually go near the undead."

Meese said, "To the scavengers we go!"

Gladlow asked, "How far is it, do you think?"

"Another two miles in the direction we're already going," said Wellstone.

"Carlin, do you think it's worth checking?"

"They don't usually circle like that if they've found anything, but then why are there so many?"

"Alright. Last stop, then we move our asses back into the jungle to climb a tree for the night. Or similar."

The trail grew easier, so Pel was convinced it wasn't too much of a waste even if they learned nothing. She was most wary of walking into a previous massacre by their quarry. Individuals killed by the undead had some unknown potential to rise themselves and they already knew a village was slain to create the last horde they encountered. She still felt they were executing the best plan left for them, even if it was thin.

Soon they were unable to see more than a glimpse of the birds as they came closer to being beneath them. Eventually, they heard the grunts of vultures on the ground. Four of the birds were tearing at a carcass and hissed in anger and alarm at the interlopers driving them away.

Pel said, "That's a Hobgoblin."

Gladlow said, "Everyone stays within sight, but spread out and see if there's anything else. Wellstone, what do you think happened to it?"

Pel stayed close as Wellstone leaned over the corpse, holding her nose. "It hasn't been dead long, a few days maybe. It's hard to say how he was killed, scavengers will often start with the wounds. They've just found this one though, probably by luck. It's not what brought all of those others here." She stepped back to take a breath. "He's been stripped."

"You're right. They took everything. Hobgoblins don't really do that to their own. Just valuables and equipment."

Wellstone said, "Goblins do. I'd say whoever his companions were, there was nothing but Goblins left.

Gladlow waved Nowen back and bid him use the spell again.

"Are you sure? That's two armors and two locates, I'll only be able to do a little more."

"We'll have to rest before long, we'll give you time to recover."

Nowen performed the spell and seemed surprised at its success. "There. I don't know how far away, but it's that direction."

It seemed the dead Hobgoblin was at the head of a trail leading up through sandstone outcroppings. It wouldn't have been a logical place to explore from the look of it alone. The path broke out into the open and a wooden wall came into view. It was made of sharpened logs set in the ground and plastered over with cob. A building rose a full story above the perimeter, perhaps a hundred yards away, with a shutterless window and a thatched roof. There was a gate almost straight ahead. It stood slightly ajar but was held shut by a rotting log. In the sky above the compound, easily a hundred vultures wheeled about. Periodically, several birds would circle low before dropping out of sight behind the wall, only to rise flapping into the air moments later. The sounds of wings and the scavengers' plaintive hissing repeated over and over.

Everyone set their extra burdens out of sight off the trail. Gladlow sent Voorsh in one direction and Nowen the other, to run and look around the ends of the wall, while Wellstone crept to the gate. Pel and Meese stayed close to Gladlow, and the three followed Wellstone at a distance. She was unable to see anything through the small opening of the gate, and everyone finally gathered around it. The two runners reported nothing but more walls and no gates. Gladlow carefully stepped on one end of the log and jumped up, grabbing two of the sharpened timbers poking up out of the cob wall, and dragged himself upward to look between them, all without making noise that could be heard over the scavengers' ruckus. After a moment he dropped down with a confused look on his face. He bent down and signaled Wellstone onto his shoulders. Straddling the back of his head, she was able to look comfortably into the courtyard. Pel pulled herself up and peeked. A scattered group of eight armored figures stood motionless, facing random directions. Four were armed with maces and four with bows. Five bloated corpses and no less than ten dead vultures lay on the dusty ground. As she watched, several scavenger birds landed to feast on the rotting carcasses. As one, the eight figures charged the birds. Maces and bows thudded into the ground or whistled through the air, not one striking a target, but serving to force the scavengers to return to the sky. The eight guardians became still and dropped their arms to their sides once again. One froze facing Pel, its grinning skull staring at her with empty eye sockets. The pinprick red glow she knew was there was not visible in the bright sun.

"Did they not notice us?" Wellstone asked. They were all gathered back near the trail.

Pel said, "I don't think they care. They're mindlessly literal. It looks like their master left orders to protect the courtyard."

Meese asked, "Isn't it strange that no one has cleaned up the bodies?"

"It is. The undead are one thing, but openly rotting corpses is a sign there's nobody home."

Gladlow said, "We'll alert everyone by fighting them. If we think there're no people, I'm tempted to be loud and flush everything out into the open where we can retreat if we have to."

Carlin said, "Anything that doesn't like sunlight will be separated..."

"It's not a terrible plan," Pel said slowly, "but we can't assume the building will empty out. Wights aren't stupid like the rest. They might keep some troops in reserve to protect them."

Gladlow said, "Alright, we go about it just like the village. Stay behind me until you hear the boom—"

"And don't get in front of Meese," Pel said, smiling.

"Exactly. One casting each should thin them out a bit, but then he and I will conserve our energy and try to occupy a few of them."

Wellstone said, "If you can, take the ones with bows. They can still club you to death, but it will take longer. Same to you Carlin. Pel, Voorsh, and I will take the maces.

"Nowen," Gladlow said, "when we enter, try to get up on the wall and keep watch. Don't get distracted by the fight, if we're getting flanked, we want to know as soon as possible."

The plan worked well. Gladlow's explosion damaged a good number, scattering several more. Meese finished two with a jet of roaring fire, and the women trotted in and engaged the rest. It was chaos for a moment, but with the numbers suddenly even it was a matter of the lesser fighters holding out until the skilled ones freed themselves from their partners. No undead reinforcements made themselves known, and their group was left with relatively minor bruises and cuts.

"This isn't real armor," Pel said, lifting a leg bone with a wooden greave strapped on. All of the armor was carefully painted boards with surcoats draped over them. The maces were bone with small iron flanges.

Wellstone said, "They were kept looking presentable. So, they were likely visible all the time." She moved to the Hobgoblin bodies, nearly unaccosted by anything bigger than insects, they were badly bloated. "Hard to tell with fuzzy corpses, but they look pretty green to me. I'd say they've been dead no more than five days. Ugh." She had to step back again. "Their weapons and armor are intact, though no one is going to wear that leather again... Spears and clubs, no shields." She used her sword to slash a bag one of the corpses had collapsed across. "Grain. The body has... leaked into it. Maggots—" She gave one dry heave and waved everyone away even though no one was moving closer. She walked away dusting her hands.

Pel suspected Wellstone was done with her assessment, so she added, "It looks like all of the dead vultures were killed by arrows. At least until they ran out. Not bright enough to salvage their ammunition without a command. Carlin, you should collect the unbroken shafts. I can show you how to make repairs. Vultures and turkeys make the best fletching." Carlin looked a bit green herself but went about the task stoically. The freshly dead held no disgust for her, but the truly rotten she wasn't so fond of. Pel joined Gladlow in examining the building, slowly walking forward. The upper room sat atop a much larger construction of timber and smoothed cob. There was another wall of the same style, only waist-high, surrounding the ground floor. A ten-foot gap, with no gate, was centered on the wall. As they approached, over and through the barrier could be seen more bodies on the ground of the sheltered inner courtyard.

Gladlow said almost to himself, "What are we looking at here?"

Pel said, "I'll bring Wellstone."

"Bring Meese too."

Everyone came to pick their way through the field of the dead. Some were formerly priests of the Umbra sect, others were their rotting corpses or skeletal soldiers. Some were in rows as if on the march. Many were paired or grouped, priest to undead, locked in struggle seemingly against one another. All were blackened by an intense flame showing no source or fuel.

Carlin said, "There are forty-eight bodies here in the courtyard."

"How can you tell?" Nowen asked quietly.

"I counted heads."

Pel turned a body over, it was more intact than most. "This was a wight. That makes two, I think. A little less than half of the bodies were living when... this happened."

Pel followed Gladlow to his friend who was standing at one end of the courtyard.

Meese said, "I don't know what could have done this. I've never seen anything like it."

"Are we talking about a dragon flying past—"

"No, no, nothing like that. This was magic. A tightly controlled fire spell, but big. I didn't know priests could do something like this."

Gladlow said, "So a fireball was set off—"

"No," Meese said, sounding a bit impatient, "look at the groups. Each one burned, with the ground beneath baked by the heat, but between the groups the earth is normal."

"Multiple fireballs?"

Meese shook his head. "Still doesn't fit. Besides, people turn from a blast. Victims who die immediately will have their feet pointed to the epicenter. I think this happened all at once. An intense fire was shaped to cover every combatant on the field." He pointed up. "Without lighting the thatch."

Pel said, "Wellstone agrees. She said everyone burned in the middle of what they were doing, and what they were doing was killing each other."

Gladlow said, "Gather everyone up, we're looking inside."

A walkway decked with rough wooden planks surrounded the structure on three sides. A large door stood open at the front of the building. On the dusty ground, just before the wooden deck, there were the remains of a large burn pile. Judging by the ashes, it was agreed to have been books and scrolls. Pel kept pace with Gladlow as they stepped through the door. The room was dim but clearly lit by deck prisms set in the ceiling, just like on the *Indomitable*. The first time she had seen them Pel was sure they were magic, but they were just shaped glass that shone sunlight into the space below. Pews partially filled the room, and a semicircle of stools and small tables surrounded a round stone altar with a wooden x situated behind it. Draped in blue vestments, an effigy of a warrior was suspended from it. An ancient helmet and gauntlets were affixed along with other pieces of armor. Only the helmet and armored gloves were real, the rest just bone carvings representing pauldrons and greaves. On approach, an offering plate could be seen atop the stone.

"No one takes anything unless we agree," Gladlow said, "Getting your ass cursed by a death god isn't worth... umm... four gold, twenty silver."

Carlin said, "Look at the carvings on the altar." Pel could see they were of bones and papers, skeletons and scrolls.

An open room at the back was a mess, but no immediate danger. A hallway lined with ascetic cells was clean and empty of threats.

Wellstone said, "Upstairs and downstairs is all that's left."

"Basement," Gladlow said grimly, "Let's get it over with." He stood at the top of the stairs and held his hand out to Meese.

"Every time we go to the tavern," Meese said, digging in his pockets, "You've forgotten your purse." He dropped some coins in his hand.

A copper flared with white light and Gladlow tossed it down the stairwell. It flew over twelve steps, bouncing off the second to last, and rolled across a hard packed dirt floor. The circle of light on the floor blinked out as another glowing coin was flung into the far corner. The basement seemed to be filled with wooden tubs, a large tank, and open stone sarcophagi. The group spread out, this time Gladlow's lit ring on one side of the room, Meese's torch on the other, and moved slowly towards the coffins. They carefully peered inside each sarcophagus. There was nothing in them or the rest of the room.

Pel said, "These crypts bar from the outside. Four crypts, four wights. The two from the cave and the two outside."

Meese said, "I can't find that last coin."

Wellstone added, "The cells upstairs would hold the people we found outside."

"It was a silver."

Carlin asked, "Are you saying the whole sect is dead?"

"This congregation anyway." Wellstone sheathed her sword. "Probably everyone on the island."

Pel was a bit stunned by the idea. Their whole existence had, one way or another, been dominated by the Umbra Sedulous since the fight at the tower. The sect had nearly killed them twice, and in desperation they had brought the fight to them, only to find a powerful force had beaten them to it. Did their lives just get easier for the foreseeable future, or much, much harder?

· · · ·

"Nowen, when was the last time you checked for the amulet?" Gladlow led them back up to the ground floor.

"Sorry, the enchantment ended while we were in the courtyard. I'm sure it's in the building though. Should I recast?"

"No, we'll check upstairs first."

As Gladlow turned that way, Pel stepped in front with a playful smile and started up the stairs. It had him thinking as he often did lately. She really was a beauty. He thought it as if reassuring himself that he wasn't a complete fool. That smile and that view, as she rose in front of him, made for a heart-pounding couple of seconds before he registered the scream behind him. He turned to see the bone armor complete its charge and throw a gauntleted fist at his chest. He threw a shield enchantment just as the first blow struck, warping the air in front of him. He wasn't injured, but the force slid him backward, and the second blow knocked him onto the stairs just as the spell crumbled. It wasn't something he usually kept prepared, but beginning with the cave battle, this was the second time it had prevented something from plunging into his chest. He needed to get out of the stairwell, so he pushed himself off the steps and dove forward and to one side. He hit the ground awkwardly, rolled away to stand, and finally got a good look at the monstrosity. The armor was carved slightly out of proportion for a Human, making the thing stand seven feet tall. The blue vestments were draped over each shoulder exposing an elaborately decorated breastplate. The thing turned towards Gladlow, raised its hands, and recited a booming litany of indecipherable words.

Gladlow howled, "Get down!" and threw himself behind a pew. He heard its footsteps plodding towards him and the words continued without pause. It wasn't a spell. He called out, "It's not a—" and was cut off by the wooden bench slamming into him. He rolled away and the second blow splintered the bench. It seemed to be focused on him so he decided to spend his energy on dodging its attacks and allow his companions a chance to destroy it. He wasn't above yelling suggestions as he ran around more pews. The thing just walked in a straight line, parting furniture before it.

Carlin swung her mace in a wide arc and connected with the back of the ancient helmet. It bobbled in midair to the hollow bong of metal on metal. A shard of steel rattled down through the chest and fell from its tasset. "There's nothing inside." She ducked as it swung a backhand towards her.

Pel swung her blade like an axe, taking a wedge of bone from its leg. Wellstone, with perfect form, thrust her blade through the spot its throat should be. To no effect.

Wellstone said, "Maybe I should take the legs?"

Pel jumped in front of the effigy and countered its attacks with deflecting blows from the back of her sword. It marched forward, swinging punches like a brawler kicked out of the tavern, destroying its gauntlets on the unsharpened spine of the Orc blade. This went on for a few seconds as Wellstone and Carlin rained attacks on the bone sections of its shoulders and legs. Meese battered at a shin and Nowen stood helplessly as Gladlow had warned them from casting. Nowen had little left and Meese might do more damage to them or the building than whatever it was. The armor ended its speech about the same time Pel finally made a mistake. She twisted to the side to prevent her backwards blade from splitting her skull and leaned into the haunted armor's second swing. It connected solidly with the back of her shoulder and knocked her sideways. With its path clear again, it lengthened its stride towards Gladlow. He met it with a honey-colored globe tossed into its midsection. The bone tasset began to smoke and fizz where the spirits of salt splashed. Pel recovered quickly and timed her next attack to mirror Carlin's. At the same instant, mace and sword struck opposite legs behind the knee sending it stumbling forward onto its face. Carlin was standing on its back in an instant, landing a crushing overhead swing onto the ancient headwear. Pel separated one of its legs at the knee and Gladlow dropped another acid globule onto one of its arms. Everyone hacked at it a few more times before realizing the pieces of armor were lying loose on the floor.

Gladlow started to chastise Carlin but tried to temper it. "You were quick to attack. What if—"

"I know," she said, "I'm sorry I didn't duck. I knew it wasn't a spell. It was the *Litany of Labors*. It's just a morning prayer." She reached into her pouch and approached the altar. She dropped a coin onto the offering plate with a wink at Meese.

"Was that my silver piece?"

Pel was already standing by the stairs, so Gladlow grinned and graciously allowed her to usher him upward again. There was no door, the stairs ending at the entry of a spartan room. Though modest, it had a real bed and comfortable furniture. A desk was stationed by the window and an armoire stood opposite. Pel picked up something from the floor and handed it to Gladlow. It was a silver medallion depicting a skull with a scroll for a tongue. He passed it to Wellstone and began a search, tossing items of interest onto a shirt from the armoire and bundling it up.

"Pel have a look." He gestured and she pulled a mail shirt and coif from a hook.

Wellstone began reading aloud:

Prelate Meffin, your request to make contact with the reptiles is denied. They have been deemed too difficult to intimidate. Plans to make use of the hobgoblin freebooters have already been implemented. There will be no more wasting of time and resources on trivialities. I trust your mission is clear.

In future, the Fashkin woman isn't to contact me directly. You will verify her reports before subjecting me further. I think it ill conceived to trust such a one.

Middas reckons, Senechal Orn

She refolded the letter and swept a few more papers and things into her shirt to follow Gladlow downstairs. A small pile was made on the floor, Meese adding the now unanimated breastplate to the random jewelry and bottles.

At Gladlow's look, Meese said, "I saw your acid splash it and Carlin rang it like a bell, but it isn't even scratched." He nodded to Nowen who opened his spellbook and performed the probing incantation before squatting and stirring through the pieces.

Wellstone said, "I'm checking something outside."

Carlin was torn between witnessing magic and following her Chief. She whispered to Meese, "I don't see anything."

"No one but the caster does. Pretty boring." He received a pat on the shoulder as she left.

Pel looked at Gladlow questioningly and he shrugged. He said, "Nowen."

The man stood and brushed himself off, even though he hadn't gotten dirty. He said, "Meese is right, as usual. I don't know why I bother with that spell. Just the chest piece is enchanted. It's protective in nature, but there are divine aspects, which is not my area of expertise."

Gladlow said, "There's something even more interesting about it." He tapped the inlaid decorations. "That's lapis, isn't it?"

Nowen looked skeptical. "Can I cast the query spell using stones inlaid on magic armor?"

"Tomorrow you're going to find out. You can also find out if it can be used to cast the spell on itself." He went outside to check on Wellstone. She was examining the bodies again. "What is it you're looking for?"

She said, "Fashkin. There are a few women, but all of the clerics are men."

"So we have someone that's unaccounted for."

"Not only that," she said almost to herself, "the woman who took credit for the tower ambush isn't here."

Pel asked, "Do you think they're the same person?"

"It seems likely. The mystery woman was a cleric, and this Fashkin is high enough ranked to be giving reports to Senechal Orn. I don't know much about clerics of the Umbra, but it looks like women in their ranks could be rare."

After a short discussion, it was agreed to stay the night, but with some preparation and fortification. The gate was closed and barred.

It was agreed to finish burning the complete bodies, especially the two wights. Vultures were left to feed on the Hobgoblins in the open courtyard. Wellstone and Voorsh scouted around and decided on an escape route into higher ground. They would use a ventilation window on the side of the building to escape quickly. They stacked crates as steps and barred the window until needed. The front doors of the mission were stout jungle hardwood and barred securely. Gladlow thought it would be a bit on the creepy side after dark, but it was a secure structure.

It was rare for them to have any space to move around and everyone split up for a while. Gladlow left the women to loot the footlockers for clothing. Both Pel and Wellstone were desperate for footwear. He went back upstairs to poke around and check the desk and armoire more thoroughly but found only a spare tunic between the bed and wall. He would clean up before putting it on, and he wanted to make sure everyone had what they needed first. When he still had his robes, he had felt foolishly overdressed and a bit guilty while the ladies had so little. They were damnably hot as well.

"What are you staring at?" Wellstone said from behind him.

"Hmm? I was just thinking."

"About the bed? I can't blame you. It looks nicer than the cells the damned mendicants were forced to sleep in."

"I was just thinking that window is the best place to keep watch."

She said, "You're right of course. You usually take first watch... and who do you wake to take second? I'm not sure how much watching will get done."

Gladlow turned but refused to take the bait.

Wellstone said, "It's natural of course. You've just put Nowen in his place, and feel that maybe it's time to tell some more truths..." She lit a small hanging lantern in the corner.

Before he could retort, the other ladies filed into the room. Each had a few articles of clothing, mostly white linens and blue vestments. He had to admit he was curious what Voorsh had planned but knew it was time to make an exit. Pel looked worried, and he realized he must have an angry look on his face. Damned mind-reading Wellstone. He let it go and forced a smile on the way out.

The lads were lounging around in the cells, so Gladlow went to the basement to see if his plan would work. The enormous tank was filled with fresh water, and it was just about the only thing outside of the Prelate's room left unmolested by the Hobgoblin looters. Gladlow examined the tubs and containers, selecting a large vat sitting alone. It smelled of musty soap and was so heavy he could barely move it by throwing all of his weight against it. Perfect. He cast his size-changing spell, and the vat shrank to half its volume. It was still heavy, but nothing compared to before. He quickly dragged it to the water tank, positioned it under the wooden tap, and let the spell unravel. The tub returned to normal size and he cracked the tap to let it fill. He felt a twinge of guilt using his magic so frivolously, but back home he made a point of using every bit of power every day, utterly exhausting himself before performing his meditations. It was one of his secrets for maximizing his efforts. It meant he had more casting experience than most of his peers. The water was cool but tempting in this warm climate, so he quickly stripped and climbed in. He drank his fill from the tap, closed it, and dunked himself before leaning his head back against the edge.

Chapter Thirteen

Wellstone shouted when she saw the young man sleeping in the tub. The poor thing jerked awake at her exclamation. "Oh, the clever lad beat us to it! This is so much better than what I had planned."

Gladlow rubbed his face and said, "I fell asleep. Give me a few minutes and it's all yours."

Carlin, Pel, and Voorsh turned to go, but Wellstone was already half out of her clothes. "Who knew chaffing would be the thing that almost took me down?" She reveled in the look of panic he suddenly had.

"I said just a moment—"

"It's lucky my pants haven't caught fire from my thighs rubbing together!"

"Damnit, Wellstone, I know what you're trying to do, and I'm not getting out of the tub with you lot here. Vacate! Now!"

The others laughed hysterically, except Voorsh who crept closer.

Wellstone said, "I don't think you're prepared for how awkward that bath is about to get..." She pulled her shirt over her head and splashed into the water, Voorsh slipped in like a crocodile without causing a ripple, and Carlin already had her leggings off. Pel turned her back but pulled her shirt over her head. That made Wellstone laugh too. There was no way he was staying with Pel present.

Gladlow said, "You horrible women," and stood up, covering himself as best he could while climbing out.

"Two hands, there's a lad." Wellstone dunked herself and came up with a sigh.

He turned his back and stepped into his trousers as quickly as he could.

Carlin stood behind him and asked, "Can you help me in, Gladlow?" He almost turned around and that started the laughter again. He did an admirable job of keeping his back to them, without a peek until Pel was safely in the water.

At the stairs, he turned and said, "Don't drink all of that."

Wellstone looked in shock at the bottle of rum on the edge of the tub. She said, "Ha, you shouldn't have abandoned the poor thing, you foolish—" Her hand passed through the bottle and it vanished. She looked at the stairs in time to see Gladlow firing a rude gesture over his shoulder as he stomped up the stairs.

Wellstone said, "I hate to say it, but I think he won that round. I may weep."

Pel asked, "Why are you being mean to him?"

"I went a bit too far earlier, so this was by way of apologizing."

"That makes no sense."

Carlin said, "It doesn't, Chief."

Voorsh felt obligated to comment. "I don't understand."

Wellstone was busy dislodging every grain of sand from her body, but said, "Our Gladlow has recently decided to take the leadership role very seriously indeed. I approve, by the way. The problem is, subordinates make his skin crawl. So, I'll defer to him when it's life and death, and take the piss the rest of the time."

Pel said, "That is generally what Meese does."

"Exactly. His only real friend for a long time. It shows the boy how much I care about him."

Carlin asked, "That's the sweetest, meanest thing I've ever heard."

Wellstone was watching Pel as she examined her shoulder where the armored thing had punched her. There was no broken skin, but it was already turning dark purple. It must have hurt, but she was smiling sweetly. Wellstone asked, "What exactly has you in such a fine mood, Miss Pel? Can you spare any?"

"What? I was just thinking about the mail we found. It should fit, but I think I'd miss the armor spell."

Carlin said while pantomiming a rubdown, "You mean you'll miss having his magic *all over your body*." She broke into a fit of giggles.

Even Pel smiled at that, but said seriously, "I never planned to wear armor again."

Wellstone asked, "Bad memories, or chaffing?" She pointed below the water.

Pel laughed and said, "I do have bad memories of chaffing. No, I've spent the last five years looking for work that required less fighting. I thought for a minute diving might be good enough."

Carlin said, "Most people probably think that's looking awfully low, but I understand. It's insanely dangerous, but how else do you get to see that kind of beauty every day?"

"It's lonely too," Pel said, "but you're surrounded by people so it doesn't seem so bad."

Wellstone asked, "We haven't talked about it, it's raw for me too, but did you have many friends on the *Indomitable*?"

Pel seemed to close up again. "No. Just my raft-mates. We looked out for each other. I worked most with Hara and Becker, but I didn't even know they were lovers..."

"That's me as well. There were people I liked, certainly, and I'd do anything to bring any one of them back, even that bilge mucking rat, Rillan. But I don't think about any of them more than if I had just moved to another post. Carlin here was the only one I would have wept over, and somehow I was spared that."

Carlin threw her arms around her friend, then splashed water on her own face to obscure tears. She asked Pel, "You say diving was good, and you were happy?"

Pel shrugged.

"Were you happier then or now?"

Pel seemed utterly surprised by the question. "I... it's hard to say I'm happy with all of the death and destruction—"

Wellstone said, "And undeath and destruction..."

Carlin asked, "But you're happier *now*, aren't you? I can tell. So am I."

Pel nodded. "I suppose I am. But it's been horrible. You know it has."

Wellstone asked, "What feels different?"

"I don't know. I don't want to leave. I always do before getting to know people."

"I'd like to take credit and say we are very special people, but it's probably just you growing. You would have been good friends with Hara and Becker, if it hadn't been taken from you."

Pel looked miserable. "I would have ruined it and had to leave."

Wellstone said, "Nonsense. But there's no need to bring all of your friends down with moping. So, my fine ladies, what should we talk about?" She made sure not to look at Carlin, making her ploy too obvious.

Carlin said, "Oh! I know. Who—"

"No. No boys."

"You *promised*. Please, Helena? I just saw my first bum in *weeks* and you expect me not to talk about boys?"

"Fine. Do as you like, I'll just close my eyes—"

"No," Carlin said, sounding deadly serious. "You'll go first, and we'll follow round that way. Who was the first person you went to bed with?"

Wellstone said, "No, no. Veto. No one wants to hear about mistakes I made before the discovery of fire. Pick something else. What are you laughing at Miss Pel?"

"You always joke like you're an old woman, but you look twenty. Sorry, go ahead sweetie."

Carlin said, "What then? Most serious one?"

Wellstone said, "Hmm, I suppose. Well, I was engaged to be married. I still am, I'd bet. Since they didn't ask my permission, why would they take my leaving as a refusal?"

Carlin was stunned. Wellstone probably should have told her about it before, the girl had been her best friend for years, but it was always a subordinate relationship before the ship went down.

Pel asked, "Do your people arrange marriages?"

"Not officially, my clan anyway, but family can pressure you and destroy your life if you don't go along."

Carlin asked, "Who was he?"

"First son of a powerful family, the Whitmakers. They felt he *deserved* a wife and would pay to get him one. My family wanted the benefits joining the families would offer. I just wanted one of the Travertine brothers. I never got around to deciding which one."

Pel was smiling. "You were seeing both brothers at once?"

"Three. Bertie, Notts, and Lauter. I was young, and we didn't do anything too serious, but I made sure each of them felt they were my favorite. And each of them was. I don't think I cared which one I ended up with, or that they cared either, as long as it was one of them. I was completely in love with their family. I wanted it so much more than my own."

Carlin asked, "What happened?"

Wellstone felt her heart harden like it only did when she thought of this. "I said no to the Whitmakers and my family. It was my right. So together they set about convincing me... by taking away everything else in my life. They pressured my captain to restrict my duties and my friends to make themselves scarce. I left when they began to destroy the Travertines' business. It was also my right to leave. I traveled to the nearest of the big towns and joined the city watch."

Pel asked, "Have you been back?"

"No. I told them I would return on my hundredth birthday. I always planned to go back and raise a family, on my terms. That's all. Next." She dunked herself again and slicked her hair back.

Carlin turned to Voorsh and asked, "Anyone serious?"

Voorsh said, "My people are not the same..."

"Don't worry, you can also just say if there's a man you like."

"We form pairings. Men, women. Friendships, sometimes long. Entire life. Children are not our own, they belong to the tribe."

Carlin asked, "Do you have any other close friends?"

"No. Only my brothers and sisters, my clutch. They are the ones you ask for help. And Keeshka. She knows I'm from her final clutch."

Pel asked, "Keeshka is your mother?"

"Yes," Voorsh said with a shrug. "It is not usually known. It is bad form to give more attention to one child unless they apprentice. Keeshka requested me. My size and markings show I am hers, as my children's do."

Carlin gushed, "Oh, Voorsh! You have babies?"

"I did not want to at first, but I am glad. I could not leave the village for my duties if I had not given children to my people."

Wellstone asked out of morbid curiosity, "So... how does your courtship work?"

Voorsh said, "We can birth anytime. Most in spring and summer. Men are ready most times, unless injured or upset."

"Sounds about right."

"Women only sometimes. When a man wants a woman, he will stay near and do things for her. Show off. He hopes when she is ready, she will choose him."

Wellstone smirked, "Also familiar."

Carlin asked, "Did someone show off for you?"

"No," Voorsh said, though there was no sadness, "I am very small, like Keeshka. She told me no man wanted her until she was much older. She suggested I choose a man for what I like about him. I chose

Sessek. He shows the most intelligence. I also asked many women and they told me he was quick and polite. No biting."

Wellstone said, "I'm not sure *no* biting is my preference..."

Carlin said, "Hush up. Sessek is the hunt leader? We called him Blue Scar before we knew him. Voorsh, how was it?"

"Quick and polite."

Wellstone said, "In all seriousness, that sounds better than a full half of my encounters. Voorsh do something about that tail or *we're* going to have to be married. Pel? You're up."

Pel asked, "Carlin, would you go next?"

"Only if you promise, *promise*, to tell yours."

"I promise."

"Alright. Just like you Voorsh, I've decided I like smart boys. I didn't have anything back home, but on the ship, I saw a few men. I had a little trouble finding the right balance. Either I didn't do enough and they lost interest or I would start to get serious and they would get controlling. Until James. James was so intelligent. We actually talked." Carlin was lost in thought for a moment.

Wellstone said, "I remember James. He was sweet. Not much to look at."

"Don't be mean. He asked me to marry him and I said no."

"Hmm, too ugly?"

"Stop. No, he wouldn't wait. Either come back home with him or he was leaving without me."

"Just as well, not even you could make those children beautiful."

Carlin didn't respond. She was watching Pel who looked like she wanted to be elsewhere. Wellstone was proud of her when she said, "Pel, you don't have to. It's just supposed to be fun. We can talk about anything."

Pel said, "I've only been with one man longer than two nights. No more than one night for years. My first and longest was my instructor, my father's best friend. My parents trained me... well, since birth. My skills were well developed, but I was given into this man's care to build strength after I gained my full height and to have more peers to spar with. While my parents campaigned, I stayed with his other trainees in the barracks. I became his star pupil. I pretended to advance slowly. I enjoyed the praise he heaped on me, and the admiration of the other students. He became infatuated with me, and I believed him when he said he loved me. I gave in and he made me keep it secret. When my parents returned, he ended it. Told me they would be ashamed of me if I told them. I was... distraught. I told another trainee, we weren't close, but she always seemed... wiser. She kept her friends from getting in trouble, without anyone disliking her for it. I always admired that. She immediately told my parents." She took a deep breath. "I couldn't bear to tell you the things he said about me, how he tried to put the blame on me. My mother wanted to bring a grievance to tribunal, but I refused to speak out against him. I didn't want to be shamed in public. So, my father challenged him with an insult. He didn't have to accept... but I'm sure he thought he could win. My father had past injuries, weaknesses that his friends and training partners could exploit. All I could do was challenge him as well and publicly speak my grievance. It forced him to take the challenges in the order of most insulting to his honor."

Wellstone said, "And he never knew you were holding back with him. Did you kill him?"

"No, but I did win. He was bigger, stronger, and I underestimated how desperate he would become when I didn't fall immediately. But I had been sparring with him for a year. He had weaknesses too." Pel looked around at them. "My grievance was entered into the record as truth, and he was exiled from our town. He was murdered later that year."

Voorsh asked, "How did you feel when you learned this?" Wellstone looked at her in surprise, it seemed an unexpected question from one of her kind.

"Relieved. I was glad he was dead, but glad I wasn't the one who killed him. He doesn't deserve to take up any more space in my heart." It was then that Pel shed the first tears they had ever seen from her.

Wellstone said, "Pel, I owe you an apology. I've teased you about Gladlow too many times. I want you to know it wasn't meant to be unkind. It's not that I think you two should be together or that you should do anything you don't want to. It was just a pleasant thought that two people I like very much might find something together." She had to wipe her own face. "I think my people can get that way living out amongst you. We can imagine knowing you through your whole short life and it's painful to think of it not being a full one. Meese admitted to me he was trying to give the two of you every opportunity to get together, even if it meant his friend might be heartbroken. He didn't want him to be afraid to try."

Pel said, "I would have hurt him. I *tried* to ruin it..."

"Nonsense. Carlin, give her a hug. Pel, nothing has been ruined. Do you even have feelings for him? I mean, do you actually want to pursue him?"

"Yes, but I don't want him to hate me."

Wellstone said, "Let me reassure you, if he had been here when you talked to us, he would feel the same way we do. Angry on your behalf, sad that you had to go through it, and proud to know you. You're worried about what he's feeling, but what do you feel?"

Pel struggled to answer. "Sometimes I want to kiss him, other times I'm just standing there wishing he would hurry and kiss me." Carlin was squeezing her and trying not to make a sound, but Wellstone knew she was about to explode.

"A lot of kissing. Got it. And you think the second you make contact, you'll jump him?"

She smiled, "Sometimes, but he'll expect me—"

"Stop. Want to? Yes. Dump his money in the offering plate and pray to the death god that you will? Also yes. But I assure you that jumping him would come as a big surprise." Wellstone sighed. "Do you want me to tell you what to do?"

She nodded.

"Listen, you didn't mean to, but you took control early on, and he's been good to respect your wishes. Someone should congratulate him on the bare minimum required to be a good person. My advice is to start small. Don't sleep with him. Too big. Tell him something personal, kiss him on the cheek. Don't punch him on the arm. Too small."

Pel and Carlin were laughing. Pel said, "I forget, was it sleep with him, or *don't* sleep with him?"

Wellstone said, "I know you want to keep him interested, but I promise, a hug from you will sustain that boy for a week. When you start having that worry, go smaller again. Don't be afraid to talk to him about it. He tries so hard to be a good chap. Let him."

Wellstone joined Carlin and Pel in a hug. Carlin grabbed Voorsh and dragged her over to them.

Meese stomped down the stairs with a linen over his shoulder and a tooth-stick in his mouth, turned around, and stomped back up.

• • • •

Pel crept up the stairs to find Gladlow sitting watch by the window. The room was lit only by moonlight, giving objects a bluish cast.

She said, "You can have your light back. It was nice of you to leave it for us."

"Probably best to keep it off. No need to let the island know we're here."

Pel went to sit on the edge of the bed but found only hard wood. "What happened to the bed?"

"I moved the mattress and covers to the dormitory," Gladlow said. She couldn't see his face, but she could hear he was smiling. "We'll all sleep there near our escape hatch."

"Do you think we'll be attacked?"

"No, but I'm learning not to take any chances. There're too many unknowns. We'll start finding answers tomorrow."

"I'm afraid to even feel hopeful that the danger is over."

Gladlow turned in his chair to face her. "Yes, exactly. I was only hopeful that we'd done enough damage to give us time. We destroyed two of their... murder squads, right? But now, it looks like they're wiped out, and I'm even less confident."

"Right, too many unknowns." Pel took a deep breath and said, "This morning was the worst. Not being able to talk to you."

"Worse than wights. I agree."

She felt her face turning red. "I look forward to it. This morning I felt cheated."

"I was just teasing. I look forward to it too."

Pel was glad he couldn't see her face well. She felt like she was doing it wrong. She almost laughed out loud. Telling him she liked his conversation? Too small. Wishing the mattress was still on the bed? Too big. "I wanted to tell you something. I haven't held a sword in... probably three years. I stopped wearing armor years before that. I didn't always like myself very much. I feel different about that lately. I want to thank you—"

"Please don't thank me as if you haven't done just as much for me. For all of us."

"Thank you for being my friend. The way you look at me, sometimes—"

"Pel, you have nothing to worry about. I'll be more—"

"I don't want you to stop."

"I won't stop being your friend, Pel..."

"No, I... don't want you to stop looking at me like that. I'm staying with you to see this through until everyone is safe." She put a hand on his shoulder and kissed him quickly, closed-lipped, on the corner of his mouth. She dropped back to the bed and they sat quietly for a few moments. "I feel like maybe I should have left just then..."

Gladlow laughed. "On the bright side, I don't think it would be any more awkward if you left now. How could it?"

"Stop." She found herself grinning like an idiot. "I really just came to talk for a while before bed. Wellstone says I'm off watch for one more night."

"Good."

She said, "So, what's that you're holding? I can't see much of anything."

"Something I was reading before the daylight ran out. It's a spell that's still getting the better of me."

"You can't cast it?"

"I should be able to cast it from the scroll, but I'd only get the one. I have to understand it intimately to duplicate it."

She asked, "What does it do?"

"It summons an enormous wave... but I'm a bit out of my *depth*." She could hear that grin in his voice.

"Idiot."

"Seriously, the energy required is more than I've ever managed. But I've been pushing myself hard recently. I thought I'd give it another look."

"You can tell by reading it whether you're ready? What does that feel like?"

He leaned back and said, "Have you ever dug a well? It was one of my responsibilities when I was little. I would stand in the water and fill a bucket of mud to be hauled up and thrown in the fields. Soil from deep down was good for crops when an area had been farmed for a long time. So every bucket of mud and water just filled in with more water. The water level always stays the same, but it gets deeper and clearer. That's how I think of magic. People are wells that deepen as we learn, and especially as we draw and use magic."

"You say people, not mages..."

"And I mean just that. Mages, and priests for that matter, are always looking for young people who will be adept, like looking for a spring to develop, but I think anyone can learn it eventually."

She said, "You can dig deep enough anywhere and find water. It's a nice thought."

"How long would it take me to learn decent sword technique? I mean, just enough where my instructor wouldn't be embarrassed."

"If you knew nothing, four years. But I've seen you fight, and you know your spear well. With regular instruction, I'm sure you'd be rather good in half that. You could halve it again with serious focus."

Gladlow asked, "Do you read? Write?"

"I read well, my writing is terrible."

"You could certainly learn to use magic in less than two years. That's what it takes most students, but a good portion of early training is literacy. I would make a generous bet I could teach you a minor arcana in a matter of months."

Pel said, "Are you teasing me?"

"Were you teasing when you said I could possibly learn the sword in a year?"

"It's not the same thing."

"Isn't it? Fighting can't be just physical, not the way you do it. What's the hardest thing to learn?"

She snorted and said, "Staying calm when something is trying to kill you."

"Right... that might be even harder for mages. Try not to stutter when someone is swinging a sword at your head."

"Gladlow, can I ask you something? You called that spear your childhood weapon. I've never heard that phrase before."

He was quiet long enough for her to start regretting the question. He finally said, "We played with spears as children, and it turned into training as we grew. When you become a man, you're given a weapon by your father, or sometimes your mother's brother. The spear was a tool for hunting, fighting an enemy with one wasn't looked upon favorably. It was a weapon for women and children to defend themselves and the village."

"You said you never learned another..."

"I'm not considered a man by those people. I was given over to the occultists for training. Priests weren't considered men either."

"Would you like me to teach you the sword?"

Gladlow was only quiet for a moment this time. "No. Part of me wants it badly, but I don't listen to him anymore. I think some help with the spear would be a better course."

"It would. Your basal technique is solid, your attacks are strong, but you don't put much effort into defense. Shorter spears like that are effective for defense. My mother... was a master with the spear. Children traditionally learned their father's weapon, but I loved to spar with her. I would be happy to show you what I learned."

Gladlow said seriously, "Thank you Pel, I'd be honored," before he grinned and said, "Now what spell will you learn?"

"No, that's silly."

"It's not. Do you want something useful? Something fun? A dirty trick to pull in a fight?"

She didn't want to hurt his feelings or miss a chance to spend time with him. "You choose something easy to learn. I'll try."

Gladlow stood up and held out his hand. She took it and he pulled her up and led her to the stairs. He followed her down a couple of steps before lighting a coin from his pocket and handing it to her.

She said over her shoulder, "I suppose that's useful and all, but I think I'll just have Meese teach me how to start fires."

He called after her, "You could just buy matches. Tell him I said that."

Chapter Fourteen

Wellstone gently shook Gladlow to wake him, but the big idiot brushed her away and tried to roll over. There was no room to move on the little cot and he slowly eased back to his original position, which was flat on his back with his mouth hanging open. She patted his face a few times, ending with a gentle slap. He must have been exhausted, he normally was a light sleeper. She was going to have to wake everyone anyway, but she had wanted to start with him. She peeled his eyelids back and waited.

He didn't move but said, "What the fu—"

"Gladlow. Get up. It's Carlin."

Wellstone led him by the hand into the main room, where what little moonlight filtered through the deck prisms wouldn't be enough for him to see. She forgot in her distress that her night-vision was superior to Humans. She was casting about for something when he spoke.

"What is she doing? Carlin!" Gladlow's voice called out as he bent to pick something from the floor. One of the pieces of false armor flared in his hand and he waved it in front of the girl's face. She was kneeling in front of the altar and mumbling quietly. She was wearing the enchanted breastplate.

Gladlow looked to Wellstone in alarm. "Helena, what happened to your face?"

"What?" She touched her face and found it sticky with blood. It seemed to be a small cut on her eyebrow. "She threw an elbow back when I tried to stand her up. I'm alright. What—"

"She's writing. Carlin, can you hear me?"

Wellstone walked around the girl and looked. She was writing steadily in the journal Nowen had given her. Wellstone knew it was already a quarter full with notes and sketches of animals, plants, and Voorsh. She looked to be on the last remaining pages. "I thought she was praying. Why is she wearing that thing, Gladlow? She wouldn't have put that on without talking to us. Why isn't she answering—" Wellstone stopped herself when she heard the panic in her own voice.

"Wake everyone. Ask Pel to keep watch. One of us will relieve her soon."

When Pel was on her way upstairs, and the others were in tow, Wellstone hurried back to the altar.

Gladlow was on one knee speaking to Carlin. He stood up as they entered. "I haven't gotten a response from her. While you were gone, she finished a page that was readable, but very old-fashioned. Prayers maybe. She's now started a journal entry about a beetle in her regular writing. She even left a space for a sketch."

Voorsh asked, "May I try?"

Gladlow and Wellstone looked at each other and gave the little Lizard the go-ahead motion. Wellstone added, "Be careful, she's not herself."

Voorsh squatted in front of the young woman and said clearly, "I will stop you," and reached for the lead stylus in Carlin's left hand. Without looking up from her work, Carlin swung her right fist in a vicious arc, only to be blocked expertly by Voorsh who seemed to be ready for that exact outcome. "I have seen this." She stood up and turned to the others.

Wellstone said, "Can you explain it to us? Is she in danger? What—" She stopped herself once again with a deep breath.

Voorsh said, "It is difficult to explain. There is a... thing in our village, a large rock. It has always been there. It is the Geth-Terna."

Gladlow looked to Nowen who thought for a moment before saying, "Quest-Stone?" He added a shrug.

Voorsh was nodding. "Yes. A villager chooses a charm from the stone. Soon they will begin a task until it is completed."

Gladlow asked, "What do you mean by charm?"

"Small, silver. Also, bright metal. They are made by the metal worker and added to the proper places on the stone." She showed a small tarnished disk with a hole in the center, smaller than a coin. It was attached to her satchel strap by a single leather thong threaded through the hole and knotted. "I only have one. I found the experience—" she said a word in her language and waited for Nowen, who was by then thumbing through his phrase book.

Nowen said, "Threatening?"

Voorsh shook her head. "Feeling of wrongness."

"Disturbing."

Voorsh repeated the word to memorize it. "I found the experience disturbing."

Gladlow said, "Describe what happened, from the beginning, but quickly."

"We are not forced to take a charm, but most do when young. Some people have many. They find comfort."

"Voorsh, what happened when you took yours?"

"I made fishing nets, from dawn to day's end."

Wellstone was becoming impatient. "Voorsh, dearest, what was the disturbing part?"

"I did not know how to weave nets. I do now."

Meese looked at Gladlow who was already nodding. Meese said to Wellstone, "*Geasan* are spells of compulsion. A person inflicted with one will do nearly anything to complete it."

Gladlow added, "The sort mages cast aren't like Voorsh describes, it would have to be a task that you know how to do..."

Wellstone asked, "What in the hells is she being compelled to do?"

Gladlow said, "I think she must be doing it." He knelt back down in front of her. "Carlin, I think you can hear me. I think you know I can stop you. You won't get much writing done if you're asleep or paralyzed, will you?" She gave no response, so he tried once more.

"If you don't answer me, this stops now." He stood back and began a complex hand gesture and his usual gibberish words.

Carlin said, "Please don't," but continued to write.

"Convince me you aren't in danger."

Carlin said, "I made a mistake. I gave in. A little. I have to finish. I'll explain. When I finish."

Meese said, "I don't have a better idea. It's creepy, but let's face it, she's acting like Gladlow when he gets a new spell, or Nowen at a party."

Gladlow said, "Nowen, get her some more paper, she's nearly out. Voorsh, what else can you tell us about your Geth-Terna?"

Voorsh gave a half-shrug, "It has always been there."

Wellstone said, "Can you describe it?"

"Yes, yes. It is big. Gladlow can touch the top. It is the same rock as the island. There are many holes where charms rest. It is in the... old middle of Uljar-Molik. We feasted surrounding it. It was open to the sun and air. It was damaged by Odd-Gollins when they first began to attack. They took many charms. We built a hut around it to remove temptation."

Gladlow asked, "Hobgoblins? Were they affected by the compulsions?"

"Most were killed before they escaped. They always... think we are less?"

"Underestimate."

"Yes. They estimate us under the truth. The morning after the attack, Trolsht found a... Hob-Goblin working in his fields."

Wellstone said, "No joke?"

"None. Trolsht let him plant nine rows of sweet-root before killing him."

Meese said, "I don't blame Trolsht, but it may have been a bigger deterrent to let him go."

"That is what Keeshka said. Let him go to tell the tale."

Gladlow said, "That's a good thought, but it wouldn't have worked. No Hobgoblin would return and tell the truth about something like that. They're superstitious, especially about foreign magic. He would likely have been killed or cast out."

Meese said, "Or retired as a farmer. Do they have farmers? That doesn't sound right."

Gladlow answered as if lost in thought, "Of course they do. A bit more meat than Humans, and they like stronger spices..." He realized he had lost the subject at hand. Nowen was holding a new journal open to the first page, and they all watched as she finished the old one and began scribbling in the new. "Nowen, take over for Pel. We'll relieve you—"

"This is hardly her area of expertise—"

"That's why I sent her to watch, but she can't see in the dark."

Meese said, "I'll go. None of us are experts at whatever this is." He leaned his torch-staff against a pew and moved to the stairs. As he passed Wellstone, she was surprised by his hand on her arm. He said to her, "We've only got old stories to go by, but none of them tell us she's in for anything more than a cramped hand and crossed eyes."

She managed to be distracted for a brief moment. The touch was a very Human thing to do, and of all the habits he could be infected by, it was the one she approved of most. Humans were certainly the chattiest race she had encountered, but they were probably the touchiest too. Among the Dwarrow, the closest of friends or brothers slapped backs or clasped hands, but you would be deemed mentally unfit if you went around hugging people as Carlin did. Wellstone remembered there was a young man on the *Indomitable*, still a boy really, who ran errands and messages. One day he was patiently waiting for Carlin and Wellstone to finish their business and deliver his message when Carlin suddenly hugged him. It was one of her full body, squeeze-the-breath-from-you hugs, and the lad openly wept. Carlin hadn't heard he lost a friend days before, but she knew something was wrong and responded in her typical way. Wellstone had never bothered to learn his name, let alone notice his suffering. There might be drawbacks, of course, Carlin was probably responsible for the poor lad's voice changing overnight.

Pel was met at the bottom of the stairs by Gladlow and informed of the situation.

She asked, "Are you certain we shouldn't just force her to stop? How long will it go on?"

Wellstone said, "She claimed she would explain when she finished. I don't want to risk hurting her. Or her hurting herself."

Gladlow said, "I'm more concerned with the other thing she said. She made a mistake and she gave in. This has to be related to her nightmares, doesn't it? Proximity to that artifact or the altar has given something greater influence over her. Whether she meant to or not, I think she somehow agreed to this."

Pel asked, "What about the armor? Is it doing this?"

Wellstone said, "I couldn't unlatch it. It might as well be welded. I was trying to stand her up when she lashed out."

"Gladlow, would your unlocking spell work?"

He shrugged after thinking about it. "Possibly. I think it would take a casting for each latch though. If we see any more hint of danger, we'll put a stop to this."

They whiled away the time until dawn with studying what little they had found in the desk upstairs. Originally the plan was to stay at the chapel long enough to hunt and resupply, but they all seemed to be in unspoken agreement to vacate immediately.

Wellstone stopped pacing long enough to sit on Gladlow's pew and brandish a smudged paper at him "Look at this."

Gladlow put down his spell book and took the paper. "It's the ink blotter from the Prelate's desk." He didn't sound impressed.

"Look at those circles there, this square, and this line here."

He looked at her for a moment but decided to indulge her. She took it from him, turned it over, and pressed it back in his hand. She tapped it again. He squinted at it but finally shook his head. "Helena, it's covered in ink smudges. I can't read a thing."

"Not the words, the circles. What does that look like?"

"It looks like someone penned something and used the blotter as it was intended."

She pulled out the journal with their map and held it next to the blotter. She knew she wasn't crazy, but she needed him to see it on his own to confirm.

Gladlow said, "I'm sorry—" He stopped and held the two pages next to each other. "These blots are in the same configuration as the towers, but any two blobs would—"

Wellstone said, "And this line here would be the beach, this other one is faint, but it matches the river and the path towards the village..."

"I see it, but it doesn't match, it's at the wrong angle."

"The blotter was used again, moving the position. Turn it, and it matches the other parts."

Gladlow could see it. He said, "This square—"

"Is the chapel we're sitting in. Now look, there is one big smudge that isn't on our map. It would be right here."

Pel noticed their excitement and came up from behind Gladlow to put her arm over one shoulder and her chin on the other. Meese stayed near Carlin with Voorsh.

"That's off the main trail on our map. Helena, you think it's on this higher one?" Gladlow asked almost to himself, "What is it?"

"I don't know Gladlow, it's a smudge."

He said, "Still. The only things they drew were this chapel and the towers. It could be another tower."

"If you say so..." Wellstone grinned at his annoyed look. "So, we have a destination if we can ever leave here. There's something I've been meaning to talk to you about."

Gladlow looked suspicious, but said, "What can I help you with?"

"I understand the pains you take to maintain an image of vast knowledge, and that it isn't just your incessant need to show off—"

"Your point..."

"We're going to need a list of your spells."

Gladlow stared at her blank-faced. Pel's face was right next to his and she raised an eyebrow as well.

"For the sake of strategy, wouldn't it be more sensible for all of us to know the capabilities of every—"

"No. It wouldn't. Second-guessing my capabilities, or letting anyone else do so, would have killed me before my thirteenth birthday. If you have suggestions, you'll need to work with what you've observed."

Wellstone held her hands up in defense. "No need to be tetchy." She flicked her eyes at Pel. "Who do you still need to impress?"

Pel said right next to his ear, "Certainly not me."

Wellstone suppressed her victory smirk when she saw him give in. He said, "I haven't exactly been holding back. The two I didn't plan to prepare daily are a minor shape change and invisibility. I made scrolls with a couple of each in case my plans go cockeyed. I also brought three new spells, one for each of us. I haven't quite puzzled out my own."

Pel gently bumped her head against his and said, "You'll get it soon."

Wellstone said, "We've seen Nowen's... does that mean you brought something for Meese as well?" She looked over at the man and he was red-faced with embarrassment. She went on, "Why the generosity Gladlow?"

He cleared his throat, unprepared for an obviously emotional subject. Mages were strange creatures. He said, "I knew we might be away for some time, and I couldn't count on the researchers to provide anything new, they aren't our mentors after all..." He almost didn't say anything more, but added gruffly, "Those two would never learn anything new if I didn't force it on them." Gladlow dug through a leather case and pulled out a scroll. "You might as well take it now. I have enough to carry."

Meese stood up and took the scroll shyly, "Lad, you didn't have to do that. You've spent everything you had on this damned outing..."

"I know I haven't been able to find the ones you wanted, but this should keep you busy for a while. Who doesn't want to fly, right?"

"Fly? You *didn't*. Thank you so much." Wellstone could see right through his smile to his crushing disappointment.

Gladlow seemed oblivious. "Go ahead and look. Do you think you could use it in an emergency?"

Meese unfurled the roll of parchment. His fake smile turned into a puzzled frown and then to childlike wonderment. He said, "You absolute prick."

Gladlow was laughing so hard he could hardly speak. He managed to gasp, "Your face."

"You unrelenting shit. All I could picture was Instructor Danksmuth getting tangled in his robes." Meese turned to Wellstone to explain. "In this climate, some mages don't wear much under their robes... flying in robes can be tricky..."

Wellstone said, "So everyone saw this Instructor Dank-whatever's balls. We understand. So what is it, really?"

Both wizards looked at her like it was the stupidest question they ever heard. "What do you think?"

"Oh, for... *another* fire spell?"

"A big one," Meese said, "a very big one." He chucked his friend on the arm.

Pel asked, "Gladlow, is that why you chose one that summons water?"

"Can't have him burning the whole island down."

Meese said, "I'm certainly going to try."

The carefree moment didn't last, and Wellstone went back to pacing. "Gladlow, when do we decide enough is enough and do something to help her?"

"If we can't get her to drink soon, we'll try something drastic."

Carlin called back over her shoulder, "Not much longer, I think. Soon."

Soon was two more hours, but Carlin dropped the stylus and stumbled to her feet, knees cracking. The others gathered around and she grabbed the collar of the breastplate and pulled. The latches clicked open of their own accord and she let the armor clatter to the floor. She turned and threw her arms around Wellstone and let herself be led to a pew.

Wellstone started shoving people back. "Give her some room to breathe. She'll talk when she's ready."

Gladlow was there with water and she downed the entire flask in one long drink. She belched and started crying, though she collected herself quickly. Gladlow said, "Let's go upstairs so we can all be in one place." While they settled in, he stood by the window to keep watch.

Carlin began without further prompting. "I was having a dream, strange but not frightening. I was home at my family's mortuary. I had forgotten that it always smelled of rosemary. There were two corpses, a man and a woman. He looked like he was just sleeping, but she was crumbling to dry bones and dust. They didn't move, but they were speaking to me, talking over each other. They were both asking for my allegiance, but he became more insistent, demanding I serve him, while she began to... bargain. She wasn't begging, it wasn't so desperate, but I had the feeling it was her last chance." Carlin stopped for a moment before she said, "Gladlow, I haven't been hearing a calling. I've been hearing two." She rubbed her face. "I knew I was dreaming, I felt in control. I remembered what you said, that we have free will. I silenced him. I willed him to be just another corpse, and he was quiet. She flattered me, said I could hear her because I was kind, that I had a *gift* for kindness. She gave me the armor, said it was mine, that it would help me protect all of us. That she owed a debt to us." She looked to each of the three mages. "I saw the three of you in Shek's lair. Gladlow, your illusion spell, can you show him to me?"

"Carlin, why would you want to see that horrible thing?"

"Even after everything, I still want to know it was more than a dream. Or maybe I'm hoping it wasn't. Please?"

He gestured and a half-size taxidermy replica of the ghoul appeared in the center of the room. Carlin looked in its face and nodded. He let the illusion fade.

She said, "Next, I saw all of us in the cave. I saw..." She stood and hugged Pel tightly. "The two wights were rogue and we killed them."

Wellstone said, "That raises a few questions..." She gestured for the girl to go on.

"She thanked me and asked if I would accept the gift and listen to her plea. I said I would listen, and I could see her the way she used to look." She accepted more water and took a deep breath. "The rest is a blurry memory, but when I saw her I knew things about her. Them. Jeme and Middas have always been together. Sometimes worshipped as one being, other times and places they are lovers, or twins. Chief, did you know I was a twin?"

"I know sweetheart."

"They represent death, birth, undeath, and resurrection. They're supposed to represent balance, but Umbra Sedulous slowly began to worship only Middas, and Jeme has faded to nothing. The armor, and others like it, were worn by her clerics, yet Umbra only used it to create an enchanted guard for the worshippers of Middas." She seemed exhausted.

Wellstone asked, "What was all that writing?"

"She offered me... I don't really remember. Many things. I refused over and over. Until she offered a final deal. I didn't have to serve her, worship her, but if I would do one kindness, she would reward me, and I would be left alone. All she wanted was to give her teachings, her stories and prayers, to someone worthy. If I wouldn't be her champion, she would trust me not to let them vanish. I didn't refuse that right away, and so she flooded my mind with things from her... not life. Existence? There are other worlds..." The young woman seemed to go into a daze.

"Carlin?" Wellstone put a hand on her back. "She found something you couldn't say no to."

The girl looked at her and nodded. "She learned about me too. She saw the work I do, what I'm searching for... She gave it to me, then said to do what she asked or she would take it away. I didn't have a choice."

Gladlow asked, "What are you searching for?"

"Medicines. My people, my family in particular, have passed down medical knowledge since before we had writing, but now we compile it in our town libraries. Some study the old writings, but it has always been my intention to add new ones of my own. I've begun a field of study that's almost entirely new to my people, marine life. We believe every compound, even poisons, can have valuable medical applications. I said yes. I woke in front of the altar, wearing the armor, and couldn't stop writing."

"What did she give you?"

"Knowledge of a few animals and plants that she kept for her worshipers alone. Now they're mine. The one that I couldn't refuse... the blue aster. It thrives on these islands but can grow almost anywhere. A mild healing potion can be made from it for little more than the effort to brew it."

Wellstone knew the answer before she asked, "What do you plan to do with it?"

Carlin gave a radiant smile, and said, "Tell *everyone*. I'll bring the seeds and the recipe everywhere I go. I'll share it with every village, every library. My people will study it for generations and find even better ways to use it. Uljar-Molik will be the first when Voorsh brings the knowledge back with her." The little Lizard imitated Wellstone by rubbing the girl's back.

Meese said, "That's something the Institute would pay you well to research."

"Well, equal shares. What requirements would they have?"

He said, "Likely none at all. They've thrown money at worse people than you, with worse missions."

Gladlow said, "It's true. Previously hoarded knowledge, ready to be given to the world? You could probably trade a pamphlet on this blue aster for a grant to study anything you want. As for shares, I think we all trust you not to forget about us if your plan to give everything away accidentally makes you rich."

Pel had been quiet until then. She asked, "What, exactly is the bargain you made? What's required of you?"

Carlin said, "Only that I record her scripture. I considered leaving it here, but I don't think I'd feel right about that. I think I should read it. I'll decide if anyone is worthy of it. Or if it's worthy of spreading."

Nowen said, "I'd like to find out what I can about the armor before you put it back on."

"Go ahead. I won't be wearing it again."

Chapter Fifteen

East of Arux-Troth Basin, plateau trail

Meese was relieved to be away from the chapel compound, and he thought everyone else felt the same. They had left early in the day with nothing but copious amounts of water to fill their stomachs. They would need to find food soon, but for the time being, they marched, keeping a lookout for a decent camp. He had hoped they would find one early and spend the rest of the day on food, but they continued on through midday before finding a rock overhang that promised some protection from the coming rains. An evening meal still happened in spite of Meese's worries, stewed in a looted pot, with half a dozen ingredients, six of which were breadfruit. They were sheltered from the night's downpour, and it seemed whatever might be out to get them decided to stay dry as well.

The following day they continued their trek along the elevated trail. Nowen was being more solicitous than usual. It seemed Carlin managed to give him the same scare as everyone else, and even his shriveled sense of camaraderie had flared up. As had become their custom, the person with the least sleep or the most injuries marched in the middle of the group where there was less need to pay attention to one's surroundings. It also happened to be where Nowen always was unless kicked to the front or back. He now carried the breastplate and walked beside Carlin, with Voorsh flanking her on the other side. The only further addition Carlin made to her journals was a new sketch of the blue aster flower. Meese just thought it looked like a daisy, but that comment got him a slightly dirty look from Carlin, Nowen, and he thought, Voorsh. They were convinced they could find some soon. Meese suggested the locator spell, but Gladlow asked that they conserve their strength until they found another secure location. He had become convinced Wellstone was right and that they were on their way to the newest research tower.

Meese suspected Gladlow would now be willing to leave this place without a backward glance. His one-time obsession with the island had palled in the face of the danger and horror they had found in place of academic achievements, and anyone could see the obvious change in him and Pel. They were unconsciously inseparable. The touchy, flirty friendship they were settling into wasn't what Meese had expected from a couple of adult Humans, but it was obviously mutual, and who could really demand better than that? He looked over at Helena and found her already looking at him. Damn it. The cursed woman was either a mind reader or determined to convince him she was capable of such a thing.

She said, "No need to arbitrate that anymore, they seem content for the time being."

"He already gave me a rap on the knuckles, no need to heap it on."

"I was directing that to myself, thank you."

Meese said, "So, you've been meddling." He couldn't help but ask, "Then you know what's going on with them?"

She pretended to think about it. "I don't know if I should say..." He could tell she was just winding him up but knew she wouldn't be able to resist if he kept quiet. She relented immediately. "The two of them seem to have been left out of all the childhood infatuations and lovesick crazes. Which sounds preferable to old cynics like us—"

"Until you think about what they missed." He couldn't help but look at her in open admiration, which she took as her due. He said, "A little late for first love, but I'm ashamed of myself for thinking of it so cheaply."

"It *is* sweet. I give them a week before they cheapen it themselves. Vigorously."

Meese said, "If it wasn't for the frustrations of leadership and the constant threat of death, I'd say I've never seen him this content. I think you'd be surprised what he'll endure to keep things as they are."

Wellstone said, "I wish enduring wasn't such a large part of being young." She threaded her arm through his and matched his steps. He was left thinking that it was never too late to start making up those losses.

"Helena, since we've dispensed with courtesy—"

"Complete banishment of courtesy, yes."

"Since our affront to courtesy has utterly destroyed our dignity and humiliated our families, can I ask you about yours?"

"You may inquire as to my lineage." She said it lightly, but there was no mistaking it as a promise to answer.

"Wellstone is an old name, even I've heard of it—"

"Even you? I would imagine you know a great deal about the founding families."

Meese sighed, "Right. I was referring to my lack of introductions. But it slipped my mind that we've murdered courtesy and buried it in a shallow grave."

She said, "You didn't mean Wellstone is an old name—"

"I meant a terribly rich one."

"What's your question, kinsman?"

"What in several hells were you doing on a ship past the edge of civilization?"

She said seriously, "Upholding the law." But she smiled and asked, "Do you mean, what is a person of means doing on a ship past the edge of civilization? Or a woman?"

"I meant what the fuck were you doing on a *ship*?"

She burst out laughing and nodded. "That sir, is a fair question. I've met a few dockworkers and such, but only one of our kin crewing a ship. He was a complete madman who was convinced he was meant to die under a tree."

Meese said, "Uhh, he could just as soon stay underground. I only learned to swim *months* ago." He shouted the next part, "Because *that* towering bastard threatened to leave me behind. How did you end up on the *Indomitable*?—Sorry, I don't mean to be discourteous to those we've lost, but that's a stupid name for a ship. What were they thinking?"

"It was rather asking for it." She pondered a moment before she asked, "Have you known any rich folk?"

"Some. A few students, some faculty."

"What did you think of them?"

Meese said, "All things considered, they're best avoided."

"I felt the same way. My interests as a youth were martial in nature. It was unusual, but girls are indulged. What does it matter what she studies? It will lie fallow while she's pregnant for most of a few decades." She was quiet for a moment. "I know you were curious if maybe I was exiled. I wondered the same about you. It's funny that's the first thought when one of us is seen out in the world. Well, I cast myself out. I won't go back for another fifteen years, if then. When I needed work, I had one set of skills to draw on. I joined the city watch. I accepted every assignment offered, I said yes to every favor asked. Eventually, I was made constable of the district with the shipyard and docks. When that great bloody ship was built, the office of constable was moved onboard."

He asked, "Do you like swimming?"

She said seriously, "Not anymore."

They walked arm in arm a while longer before she said, "Your name..."

"Yes."

"Who gave it to you?"

Meese smiled. It was rare that he had been asked that. Humans didn't often notice anything strange, and his kin were too polite to ask. "The story is that I sort of gave it to myself. Have you ever spoken with anyone from Gossanmere-in-Felsic?"

Wellstone swung her fists drunkenly and launched into a nasally, sing-song accent with rolling r's. "Yer maw kenna call ye for dinner effen yer bloodered oot yer ears."

Meese laughed so hard his eyes teared up. "That's it exactly. Graben Gneissfall of Gossanmere-in-Felsic was the man who broke through into the central vault. I was too young to remember it, but he said, 'Look at the wee mice,' and handed each child to his friends in the tunnel. He and his miners cut their way into three strongholds and rescued ninety-two children, the most of any one team." He unabashedly wiped a hand across his eyes and Helena returned her arm to his. "For years he visited us. Some of my earliest memories were of him saying, 'How urr ye, mah wee meese?' and maybe I thought he was only speaking to me."

Wellstone asked, "You never joined a clan?"

He said, "By the time it was offered, I was too angry to accept. As others were adopted, they were replaced with Human children, and I was the last of us long before I was apprenticed at sixteen. There was some question as to which stronghold I came from, and what my bestowal was to be. Graben died in a mine when I was ten. I thought about asking his friends if they remembered me, but I just didn't. I took the apprenticeship and didn't go back until years had passed." He felt like being quiet for a while, and mindreader that she was, she let him.

They eventually talked of less serious things, and though they didn't walk arm in arm for long, the feel of it lingered.

* * * *

Pel was trying to listen, she had asked the question after all, but she found herself focused on his lips and his voice without paying much attention to the words.

Gladlow said, "It's a simple probative spell that can tell you the basic functions of something, like its purpose and its usage."

"Mmhmm." They really shouldn't be leading if she wasn't going to pay attention. She put her eyes to the front and swept the path for danger. The jungle had thinned to almost nothing, trees being replaced with sandstone outcroppings on the high trail and plains of grass on the lower. "And Nowen says it has no purpose?"

"Well, the spell is telling Nowen it's a scroll... with no discernible function other than *being* a scroll."

"Is the spell intelligent?" Pel turned back to him in embarrassment. "I'm sorry, I probably sound like an idiot—"

Gladlow said, "Not at all, because we don't know if a spell is intelligent. The current consensus—no, sorry." He visibly forced himself to stay on subject. "The query spell works by reading the enchantments on an object, that's really what it identifies. If the object was just created *with* magic, which I suspect it must have been, but had no further enchantments bound to it, the spell would tell him *that*."

"So, the fact it tells him it's a scroll—"

"Is very damned strange." He was lost in thought for a moment, then said, "I have a theory, and I've shared it with Meese, but Nowen might take offense..."

"Is that an unusual problem?" She winced at the cattiness in her voice.

Gladlow sighed, "It is *not*... but we butted heads recently, and he's having a difficult time too. He only acts like he's above it all. He was right though, Meese and I were prepared for the worst—not actually, this was much worse than we prepared for. Nowen just learned a detection spell and packed a phrasebook."

"Why do you think he'll take offense?"

"My theory is that the shell object you were supposed to smuggle back, has a purpose or function beyond his current comprehension. A scroll is the nearest thing that he understands."

Pel blew air from her lips and said, "He may go into fits."

"That's not the worst part. The next logical step is for someone else to cast the spell." They walked in silence for a few minutes before Gladlow made a decision. "I'm going to leave it alone. Greater researchers than us have examined it, maybe we'll talk to them soon. Maybe they all learned the same thing, or maybe they used more advanced methods before hiding it in a gold lined crocodile to be hand delivered by the most magnificent woman south of the equator."

"You have someone stashed away in the north? I'll *kill* her." She grabbed his hand and held it for a few moments. She was becoming less self-conscious in front of her friends, but they were *actually* in front of everyone right then, so she squeezed it hard and let it go. "Nowen's spell worked on the breastplate? Are you sure it's not safe for her to wear?"

Gladlow shrugged and said, "That's not it. I'm not sure of anything. Nowen learned it will resurrect the wearer if they're killed, and offers enhanced defense until that time. The resurrection will unravel some or all of the enchantments, but even so, I never imagined it could be something that powerful."

"Why don't you want her to wear it?"

"Listen, she was told it was a gift for the group and she's also afraid of it. She's going to ask you to take it. I'm... afraid for *you* to wear it. "

Pel was surprised but knew he was probably right. "I'd prefer she has it, if it's safe, but this mail you found will fit her fine, she's welcome to it instead. What worries you about me wearing the breastplate?"

"I don't trust it. I don't trust this Jeme entity. Why was Carlin wearing it? It was able to speak with her before she put it on, but the moment she did, she was afflicted with a compulsion and the armor couldn't be removed until she completed the *geas*." Gladlow sounded angry.

Pel said, "I think I see your point. You think the *geas* might be part of the armor and not the direct influence of this god..."

He said, "Exactly."

"Wouldn't Nowen discover that with the discovery spell?"

"Not if it was purposefully hidden by the enchanter. I think."

Pel thought about it for a few moments. "She accepted the gift of the armor and was immediately under Jeme's influence. What happens when you accept the gift of Jeme's resurrection?" Gladlow just nodded and lapsed into thought.

She managed to watch her surroundings for a couple of hours while she pondered the implications of what they had talked about. She had to admit, she thought the risks of the armor were worth it. If her choice was death or serving a god, she thought she might relish some purpose to her life. On the other hand, she had a way of letting things happen rather than making plans for the future. She was considering how one might make such plans when she noticed the tower. It was far in the distance, but too unnatural a shape to be anything but purpose made. It was past midday before they made their final approach, but they had such high hopes of comfort and assistance that they all agreed to push on without rest. This structure was twice as large as the signal tower had been, two stories tall, also with a flat roof. The upper floor was encircled with arrow slits, while the rest of the structure was featureless sandstone. It sat on a low rise with a good view of the immediate area and the lower plains to the east. They were forced to approach out in the open, with no cover.

Nowen said, "There's someone on the roof." Pel could see he was right. She had been watching a red and blue bird circling the middle of the tower and hadn't noticed the hunched figure sitting with feet dangling over the edge. They appeared to be wearing rust red clothes and a purple cone hat. They were nearly a hundred yards from the building when Nowen said, "It's a Hobgoblin."

Gladlow said, "It's a young one. Adolescent."

They all stopped there and Pel was able to see it wasn't red clothes, but its own fur. It looked to be wearing only a leather skirt, sandals, and a purple cone hat with tassels. It was sitting sideways to their approach, it may not have noticed them. She said, "We should pull back to cover. If the tower has been taken over, we could be showered by arrows any second."

Wellstone said, "I think it's too late to sneak away." She was pointing at the bird who had changed course to swoop past the figure, who immediately looked their way. It climbed to its feet and moved to face them, sitting back down on the nearer edge.

Pel asked, "What's in its hand?"

"It's a book," Nowen said, shading his eyes.

They all looked at each other in various states of surprise and confusion.

Gladlow said, "I'll approach alone—" and was immediately shouted down with protests. He made a patting motion with his hands and continued, "My shield will let me get away if it's an ambush."

Meese said, "I'm going. I have the shield ready too."

Gladlow became visibly frustrated by the arguing that ensued, saying, "Can we please not fight in front of the Hobgoblin? I'm going alone. Be ready for my signal—"

"What's the signal?"

"Running is the signal, Meese. Don't set fire to anything unless you see me running." Gladlow stalked away, shifting his spear to his left hand. Pel thought he looked nothing like a wizard at this point, so observers wouldn't guess he was capable of attacking at range. He stopped far enough away from the tower that he didn't have to crane his neck too badly to address the creature on the roof. They all stood around impatiently, as there was nothing to see but the normal movements of people talking, nodding, shrugging, and hand waving. Gladlow turned and made a hand sign to his left, then a beckoning motion. When they all arrived, Gladlow was standing with a hand pinching the bridge of his nose. The Hobgoblin had retreated so that only its face was peaking over the edge of the tower. The blue and red bird landed next to it, breathing heavily. Pel thought it was unlike any bird she had ever seen.

Gladlow asked in an overly calm voice, "So, absolutely no one remembers the hand signs we agreed on?"

Voorsh said, "You asked for Nowen, but I thought I was wrong..."

"Holy Silent One, it speaks." The Hobgoblin's voice was a bit growly and lisped, but it had the exact accent of the northern sailors from the *Indomitable*.

Wellstone said, "We're a bit gobbed ourselves." Just as she spoke, the bird dropped off the edge of the roof and flapped wildly to slow its fall. It wedged itself into the nearest arrow slit and stared at them with enormous unblinking eyes. Pel could see it more clearly at the reduced distance and realized it wasn't really a bird at all. It looked like a chubby gecko crossed with a blue and red turkey. Its fat tongue licked one eye, then the other.

Gladlow said, "Dugg and Bustard, meet Voorsh. This is Wellstone, Pel, and Carlin. Nowen and Meese," pointing to each in turn. "We're baking in the sun, can we trade for some water?"

Dugg said in a sarcastic tone, "I'll just be right down to open the door."

"Well, I'm not going to stand here with my mouth open waiting for you to pour it over the edge. What do you need?"

Dugg scooted forward and said, "I have everything I need for a week—"

"Five days," said Bustard. Its voice sounded exactly like a little girl.

"Shut your mouth, Bustard."

At the sound of its voice, Wellstone pushed past everyone to the foot of the tower. "Bustard, do you remember me?"

"I... remember."

Dugg said, "He's lying. His voice gets even higher when he's lying."

Carlin rushed forward. "The spiders! You warned us."

Bustard was silent.

Dugg asked, "What's this about spiders, now?" He was leaning over the edge so far, he was in danger of falling. "What was your name again, lovely?"

Carlin casually shifted her bag so the strap crossed her chest, holding her tunic closed. "We were attacked in the western jungle by giant tree spiders and... a spider-boy."

Bustard looked around in panic, craning his neck to see around the sides of the tower.

Dugg said, "Huh. Anansi. They're nasty work. They don't attack unless they know they can get ya. We wiped them from our territory, but there's plenty in the northwest trees."

Gladlow asked, "What are you doing so far from your territory?"

"I know you think you're clever getting me to talk, but I'm happy to tell you. We're the Bloody Chummers and everything north of here is our territory." His focus went back to Carlin. "So, you owe us for one rescue..."

Wellstone said, "She'll be happy to give Bustard a big kiss, but you said he was lying. What did you mean?"

Dugg sighed and rested his chin on his hands. "They remember everything, but never when you want them to. They're smart, but like a smart person on a permanent bender. Yer warning may have come from Bustard or one of his friends he's taught some words to. Corey says he cursed in front of Bustard one time, and now every bird on the island knows who does what to whose mam."

Bustard released a scorching phrase made funnier by his little girl voice. He seemed pleased by the attention.

"See? That gives him no trouble, but ask him if he delivered a message and he'll say, 'I... did it.'"

Gladlow said, "How is Corigain? I didn't think we'd see him out this way."

Dugg had scooted back so his eyes just peeked over the edge.

"Listen, Dugg, I'll be honest with you. I came to the island to join Wulfric's research party. These ladies survived their ship being sunk by a godsdamned sea monster, the island is crawling with undead, and no one I came to meet will stay where they're supposed to. *Where is Corigain?*"

Bustard sounded sad when he said, "Corigain went away."

Dugg said, "Shut it, Bustard. He's right, though. They all left."

Gladlow asked, "How long ago did he leave? Who is *all*?"

Bustard said, "Nine days."

Dugg said, "Pfft. He thinks nine is the highest number. More like eighty days. All the wizards and witches."

Gladlow asked, "Witches?"

"Woman wizards?" He said it like he must be talking to idiots.

"Right. They're just called mages."

"Whatever. Wizards and mages. I think it's time to talk price."

Wellstone said, "Allow us to confer." She took a few steps away from the tower and waited for everyone to join. "Are we knocking him off of there and making him talk, or are we trying to buy information?"

Meese said, "I'm more interested in getting into the tower."

Nowen said, "He must have the password, right? Do you think he overheard it? Or did they actually give it to him?"

Pel asked, "Give it to him? Why would they do that?"

Gladlow said, "I don't think they would. We have a strict protocol. But he has it now, and he knows we want it, so let's try to deal fairly and get this done."

Wellstone said, "We don't have much to offer. What if we can get him down without killing him? We'll just scare him a little and he'll give up the password."

Gladlow said, "We're not attacking him. If we do this honestly, he'll see reason. If he tries to cheat us, you can do what you want with him."

Carlin said, "I don't want to hurt him either, but what makes you want to trust him?"

Dugg called down, "He doesn't trust me. This *migasht* is the only one of you who knows I can hear every word you're saying." He was on his hands and knees, leaning over the edge with his bum in the air.

Gladlow turned his head upward and let out a stream of Hobgoblin that sounded threatening to Pel. Of course, she didn't know what non-threatening Hobgoblin would sound like. Dugg sat up and raised his hands innocently. It was a very Human gesture.

Pel whispered, "What did you say?"

Dugg called down once more, "He said, if I called him that again, I'd soon get to see the inside of me own bum. Not all of our sayings translate very well. That one holds up."

Gladlow asked, "What do you want, Dugg?"

"I'll keep it simple for you lot. I have a Goblin problem I need taken care of. Do that for me... and I'll share the password."

Wellstone said, "We could try this another way. Bustard, sweetheart, what's the password?"

"Mirabar Clanger."

Dugg collapsed dramatically with his head and arms draped over the edge. "Damnit all, Bustard."

The accommodations of what they were calling the watch tower, were much the same as the signal tower. Four bunks and a large table. This tower had the addition of a sitting area complete with leather couch and chair. The group spread out into the room while Dugg pouted in the chair. Pel kept him in sight at all times. He had a lumpy pouch on his hip, but it wasn't big enough to hide a serious weapon. The place was a mess. He looked to have been sleeping on the couch and eating what was left in the cupboard.

Gladlow said, "Look here." He was standing in front of a painting of four obvious explorers. They were geared up for mountain climbing and hiking, yet they were posed in a library. "That's Corvin, there."

Pel answered, "The one who found the island?"

"Right. You see his hat?"

"I do. It's... unusual."

Wellstone said, "It looks like he has a melon stuffed under it."

Gladlow laughed. "He could have a dozen melons under it. It's bigger on the inside than the outside. It was his sixth-year project, like my ring. It's not a requirement anymore, but the resources are still traditionally offered if you can get your design approved. When his instructors graded it, they said that bulge in the middle was evidence of an unstable holding enchantment. He told them it was evidence he was a better enchanter than haberdasher. He got a B and never took it off." He stood there smiling proudly.

Pel put her hand on the small of his back and asked, "What grade did you get?"

"Oh, his was more difficult—"

Meese said, "He just repurposed enchantments. Gladlow's was entirely new."

"He was the youngest on record to complete that course. I was a year older."

Meese made a letter A with his fingers and winked at Pel.

Gladlow reached out and rattled the painting. He felt along the back edge of the frame until they heard a click. The painting slid to the left revealing a familiar fist-sized hole.

Meese asked, "Same trick as before?"

"Looks like it."

Meese generated his ghostly green hand and soon the stone cabinet swung open. "Don't anyone touch anything. There's another glyph on the door."

Pel stood back while the mages pulled journals and papers out to lay on the table. Dugg was crowding behind and craning his neck to see inside. Pel could see what Gladlow meant by adolescent. Dugg was seemingly full grown, a bit under her height, but there was a round fuzziness to him that took away a good deal of the threat. Pel was fascinated, not having ever seen a Hobgoblin who wasn't swinging a weapon. Anything that wasn't papers or books, they left in the cabinet when they locked it back. Nowen and Carlin stayed by the table to look through the small pile. Voorsh systematically searched the rest of the room. Pel had expected her to be upset by the presence of a Hobgoblin, but Voorsh showed no interest at all. Gladlow was already climbing the ladder, so Pel followed and stepped off onto the second floor. A hallway curved around the entire tower, granting access to the arrow slits. The oak door across from the ladder was the only access to the circular room in the middle. Pel stepped aside as Wellstone climbed up after, followed closely by Dugg. Bustard flapped up through the hatch and landed on the floor. He walked down the curved hall and watched them from around the corner.

Dugg said, "There's no way in. The password doesn't work."

Everyone jumped in surprise when Gladlow barked a guttural command. The door opened at his touch, the chamber dark until he lit his ring. The entire room was stacked full of crates and bags, many of which had been opened and rummaged, causing the contents to expand and crowd the room. There seemed to be a great deal of clothing, as well as odd pieces of equipment like ropes and candles. Wellstone picked something up from the ground and handed it to Gladlow.

He said, "It looks like they locked it and slid the key under the door. We'll look through that mess later." He relocked it and pocketed the key. He ushered everyone back down and said, "Dugg.

I'm going to need you to tell us everything. I'm sure we can work out some sort of compensation."

"I told you, I don't need anything but help with a little Goblin problem—"

Pel asked, "Why would a Hobgoblin—"

"Hob."

"What?"

"It's just Hob. Why do you milk-faced chuffs—" He stopped when her blade slid free of the sash on her waist. He stared for a moment, but it wasn't fear, it was recognition. "You lot. I heard about you. The woman with the Orc sword and the *migasht* wizard—"

Gladlow cut him off in his own language when the Hobgoblin gestured to him.

Dugg held his hands up innocently again but turned to Meese. "You fit the description..." He made a gesture indicating a short person. "But he looks like a sheepherder, and I thought she'd be bigger."

Pel asked Gladlow, "That word he keeps calling you. Will it make me kill him?"

Gladlow hesitated the briefest moment before saying, "It means mongrel."

The tip of her blade was gently lifting the Hobgoblin's chin before anyone could react. Dugg flinched hard at the sound of two clay balls dropping out of his split pouch and rolling across the floor. He said, "Damnit all, you could have killed us..."

Gladlow squatted down and carefully picked one of the orbs up. It was made of rough clay carved with runes and baked hard. He made a gesture as if to toss it back, but Dugg shouted, "Don't mess about you... Don't even toss it from one hand to the other or it will go off. I saw a Goblin trying to act hard. When he tossed it up and caught it..."

"It killed him?"

"Well, no. It knocked him on his dirty little arse, though. I like my hearing sharp, thank you. I can get you those for—"

Gladlow said, "I have two, thanks."

Even with a sword at his throat, Dugg didn't stop negotiating. Pel realized he was much smarter than she would have thought possible. He knew they weren't going to kill him. She said, "Sit down. Piss me off again and Meese will burn your hair off."

Dugg sat but said, "No need to be perverse." He smacked his lips like he had a bad taste in his mouth.

Gladlow flopped on the couch across from him and looked around at his friends studying and searching. "I think we'll find more by searching the place than listening to you. You can go."

Dugg said, "What? You can't just kick me out... yes you can, but should you?"

"You didn't have access to anything but the front door. I don't see any reason to believe you're anything more than a research subject. Was it Whitecloud who let you hang about? All you had to do was answer questions about your people?"

Dugg sat glaring but was silent for once.

"You've eaten our food, enjoyed our hospitality, and kept the password for us. You have my genuine thanks. You can go."

Bustard landed on the back of Dugg's chair and said, "He's hiding."

"Shut up, Bustard." Dugg was back to pouting.

Gladlow asked, "What's he hiding from?"

Bustard looked confused. Dugg fussed at him. "Do you even remember why we're here?"

"I... remember."

There was a grating sound of stone on stone and everyone jumped up. Pel pointed at Dugg who sat back down in a huff before she followed Gladlow.

Voorsh was standing by the ladder. She said, "I have found a cave."

It turned out to be a wine cellar, though a small one. There was enough room for one person to climb down the ladder and pass up a cask, of which there were seven.

Soon everyone was feeling much more civilized, and Gladlow was ready to try one last time to interrogate the Hobgoblin youth. Voorsh was stretched belly down across the rug with Wellstone resting her head against the little Lizard's side. Carlin and Nowen remained seated at the table, while Meese had claimed the nearest bunk. Pel was in awe of how enjoyable it was to lounge on a couch with Gladlow's arm thrown casually over her shoulder. Mages had a knack for comfort that she was beginning to admire, but she wouldn't have minded too much if they were sitting on a stone slab instead of that work of art in leather and oak.

Dugg said, "I should be grateful to whatever gods watch over me that I didn't find this wine a week ago."

Gladlow asked, "It was Whitecloud wasn't it, that you made a deal with?"

Dugg squinted his eyes at the man for a moment. Pel imagined he was aware of the new ploy, but he decided to answer. "It was Vossy."

Gladlow barked an unamused laugh. "Vossy, that paper poaching prick. I was annoyed at Whitecloud for expanding away from Uljar-Molik, but it isn't even Vossy's field." Gladlow sounded genuinely annoyed.

Pel asked, "Is that what you were going to study? Hobgoblins?"

This elicited an actual growl from Dugg, but at her look, he took a deep breath and said, "It's just Hob. It's even easier to say, why not just say Hob? Do you want to be called Human-dog all the time?"

"That's *exactly* what I've been called by Hobgoblins—"

"Not by me..." Dugg suddenly looked uncomfortable by all the attention. "What's so wonderful about dogs, anyway? They don't even have thumbs." He said into his wine, "Useless."

Wellstone said, "Dogs rarely rob and murder their Humans..."

"Well, that's a kick in the fork, but a fair point given my own problems. Lady Pel... I beg your pardon. You asked your man there a question...?" He seemed embarrassed and sincere, but it was the *your man* comment that mollified her.

Gladlow said, "I have to be fair and admit there have been no reports of a significant Hob population on Arux-Troth. My papers on Orc culture—"

An involuntary snort was pulled from Dugg, but he put his face back in his wine.

"—earned me a request. I chose to assist Wulfric's Corvin hunt. It would have allowed me to interact with the other researchers and maybe find another paper to write. Vossy knew damn well that, even being my senior, contact with the Hobs would have fallen to me. Only a few very senior mages, like Whitecloud, could get away with throwing their weight around."

Dugg chuckled and said, "I liked Vossy, none of the others wanted me around, but he didn't even speak Hob before I got to him." He gave a nasty smirk and said, "He's in for a surprise when he makes contact."

Wellstone asked, "What did you teach him you cheeky little shite?" Pel recognized Wellstone's overly relaxed attitude. She would get the Hobgoblin talking if Pel could keep her temper in check.

Dugg said, "He'll sound like a nurse talking to her babes. It's going to be hilarious when he calls some Hob trader his little sweetie."

Pel thought the group overdid the laughter a bit, but Dugg seemed to appreciate it.

Wellstone said, "A veritable fortress to stay the night, and the wine from a wizard's secret room... It puts me in mind of how we've neglected our Traveler game of late. We wouldn't want to flout our good fortune. Who got the pass last time? Carlin, wasn't it?"

Carlin jumped up from her chair and joined her friends on the couch by sitting in Gladlow's lap with her legs across Pel. This was obviously something she and Wellstone had planned, or perhaps Gladlow? Pel looked at him, but he was adopting Wellstone's relaxed attitude and attempting to look bored by the proceedings. Pel just gave a mental shrug and leaned into *her man*.

Dugg was enrapt in Carlin's nearly contentless story about a summer spent diving with James. During the tale, Pel became certain this was Gladlow's idea. It was true that Dugg was focused on Carlin's story, but his eyes often lit on the man with the two women in his lap. Pel imagined the youth was looking at his idea of a dominant male. She shifted to slide one hand up to Gladlow's chest and rest it there. Carlin spent ample time describing sea life, and how she learned to be more comfortable with increasing states of undress, before she ended with her refusal to marry and a tearful goodbye.

Gladlow pushed Carlin up, patted her bum, and said, "James was a fool not to stay and win you over. Would you pour another round, sweetheart?" Carlin went about her task cheerfully, and while Dugg was looking away, Pel put her hand on the one Gladlow had on her shoulder, and slowly squeezed until he silently begged for mercy by frantically patting her leg. He asked, "Dugg, you think you might be up for a round? It's traditional for newcomers to go next." Before the Hobgoblin could protest, he intoned, "The ancient rules are simple. Tell only what you choose, be it story or query, but lies bring misfortune on the road—"

Meese said, "Unless it's to make a story more interesting—"

"Of course, but no *real* lying. It can be a personal story, a legend you may know better than the rest of us, or you can just answer questions from the group."

Meese said, "Don't choose Query if you've plans to be false, better to let the gods hear an amusing tale."

Dugg said, "The gods."

"It's an old belief that the gods watch folks on the road, and therefore are listening when we tell our stories. I don't know if that's true, but the rule about lying isn't to be trifled with. I once heard a man lie during a game of Traveler, his wife was there so who could blame him? Next day? Impaled on a snake." Meese drained his cup and lay down on the floor next to Voorsh.

Gladlow asked, "How much have you had to drink?"

Meese said, "Exactly."

Gladlow said to Dugg, "The easy way out is to tell us something personal, like your Goblin problem, there has to be a story there..." Dugg's face started to clench up, and Gladlow continued quickly, "But I'd like to officially request the story of the Bloody Chummers. Remember, tell it as you like. If there's anything we shouldn't know, keep it to yourself."

Dugg seemed nervous. He said, "I'm not sure where to—

Meese said, "Long ago—that's best if you don't know how long ago. You can also say, fifty years ago—but just put how many actual years—"

Wellstone cut him off. "Another beginning is 'I don't know if it's true, but this is how it was told to me.' That one's best if you have a Hob tale passed down through the years."

Pel said, "Gladlow likes to start with, 'This is the part you know...' because then he gets to lecture you on the part you don't." She laughed when he grabbed her ribs and she pressed his hand to keep it there.

Gladlow said, "Start at the beginning."

Dugg said, "The Bloody Chummers... no, I should start back more. Twenty years ago, the Bone Splitters were at war with the Skull Drinkers. Not war like Humans do, they fought each other constantly, but there was mercy and recompense. One week they'd be drinking together and making plans for a joint venture, the next they'd be fighting over whose child belonged to whose clan." He said as an aside, "Men and women snuck back and forth constantly between the two camps." He took a drink and continued, "The Orcs nearly wiped out both clans. They arrived on ships and wanted our territory for themselves. We were close enough to the Human settlements, they'd have years of raiding to look forward to and they didn't intend to share it. My... the Bone Splitters had a young warrior named Lenogg who rose through the ranks quickly with the loss of so many. He formed an army from the remnants of the Splitters and the Drinkers, and attacked the Orc docks when most of their warriors were away on raids. He captured three ships and set the rest ablaze. There was a bloody struggle between the two clans over the ships, but Lenogg came out the winner. He had kept better track of who was related to who and used those loyalties to isolate the troublemakers. At first, they sailed about, looking for a place to make a new camp, but years of failures—and learning to sail—made them realize how dependent they had become on the ships. Piracy had been a thing of chance, but they began making plans and targeting the smaller trade routes. He renamed the galleon *Frenzy* and became Captain Lenogg. We became the Bloody Chummers. We found a Goblin nest in the northern cove and took some of them on as crew. Eventually, we built the docks and set up a permanent camp. We named it Ningolohk. That... that's the story of the Bloody Chummers."

Gladlow stomped his foot in applause and said, "That's a story to be told and told again. Thank you, Dugg."

Wellstone had relocated to rest her head on Meese, who seemed to be asleep. She asked, "You were born on the *Frenzy*, weren't you lad?"

"How did you know that?" Dug asked.

Meese said with his face still on the rug, "Don't fart lad, or she'll tell you what you had for breakfast."

Wellstone said, "Shut up, Meese. You said 'They sailed about,' but then said, 'We became the Bloody Chummers.'"

Dugg said, "Right, I was. We don't have many children when times are lean. It isn't allowed. A whole mess of babes happened when we settled the cove. I was born just before."

Voorsh was then resting on her back and spoke with her head upside down. "There has been little fighting for two years. Why did you attack my village?"

Dugg's face went blank and Pel could see the tension in his body. He was ready to bolt.

Gladlow said, "Now's not the time, Voorsh—"

Wellstone said, "I imagine it's all about the tribute, right mate?"

Meese said, "I warned you..." and lapsed into silent chuckles.

Dugg was staring at her in shock, but she continued casually, "The Chummer's tribute disappeared, just like the Crown's. Boazoch destroyed the *Indomitable*, but your Captain Lenogg managed to scrape together another, am I right?"

Dugg was nodding almost involuntarily. He said, "It took everything we had, and that filthy beast only left us the *Frenzy*." He looked at Voorsh. "We needed supplies for a trade mission. If it fails, half of us will starve. The council barely passed the vote to attack. I don't get a vote yet, but I advised against it."

Gladlow was sitting forward and gave up all pretense of disinterest. "*Council*? What do you mean by trade mission?" His voice was dripping with disbelief.

Dugg sighed and said, "I managed to keep all of this from Vossy, but he didn't offer the good wine." He raised his cup in a mock toast and emptied it.

Gladlow dumped his wine into the youngster's cup and said, "I want you to tell us everything. As a show of good faith..." He made a gesture and a detailed replica ship appeared floating in the air. Pel recognized it as the sunken ship from the little beach.

Dugg leaned forward to touch it but stopped short. "That's the *Rampage*. Boazoch destroyed it."

"It's sunken in fifty feet of water off of the south shore. It can be salvaged. It's intact."

Pel said, "I think they ran for the lagoon but were swamped. Any crew that escaped were killed by the eel-men as soon as they tried to make camp."

Dugg snarled, "Those... *things*. Disgusting scavengers. We encountered them for the first time a couple of years ago, but there are hundreds now."

Gladlow said, "The trade mission, Dugg. Not piracy?"

Dugg looked embarrassed. "We've been trading... but pretending it's piracy." He scratched his ear vigorously and took a deep breath. "I might as well tell, it's what I really need help with. I was waiting here, hoping the witches would come back. The *Frenzy* has been trading seastone for supplies at the pirate coves, and to the Human pirate crews. The Humans love seastone. Everyone thinks we raid it from the Lizards, but... it comes from our own mine."

Pel asked, "You have legitimate resources, but are pretending to be pirates?"

"Everyone knows how tough the Lizards are, it helps our reputation."

"And reputation is everything to a pirate."

Dugg nodded. "The Human ships are barely pirates anymore. They're so brutal, even the Orcs don't cross them, but they've struck a balance with their own leaders."

Wellstone said, "You mean the Crown. It's true, the Human pirates are ignored by the Crown if they don't target Crown vessels."

"Not only that, they retaliate if anyone else is found to attack them. It happens, mostly the Orcs, but it's the only time even they tread carefully."

Gladlow said, "They're doing it to prove they don't obey anyone's orders. Those attacks are probably oneupmanship between squabbling Orc vessels."

Dugg looked impressed. "We can only manage the Orcs because they don't have our discipline. Using ships they built, but crewed by Hobs, we can take them. They spread themselves thin, each ship becoming a separate tribe. When factions merge from time to time, we can't match their numbers."

Everyone seemed to be lost in thought for a moment, so Pel prompted him again. "So, Boazoch sank two ships but left the *Frenzy*. I understand the desperation, but why risk attacking the Lizards? I haven't heard of a force like theirs since the wars, and even that was mostly rumor."

"I had a theory," Dugg said shyly, "that I shared with Whitecloud. She ignored me until I told her this. I think the Lizards are why my clan is changing. Captain Lenogg changed because of them. Hobs have always liked to fight. Everything is a challenge, a contest. The Lizards were seen as a worthy opponent for a long time. We thought they were incredible fighters, but undisciplined, like the Orcs we hate so much. We always thought it strange that they didn't retaliate. It was Lenogg who realized the Lizards changed their ways instantly when they suffered a loss. That's the *opposite* of undisciplined—"

Meese said, "The word is *disciplined*."

Wellstone smacked the back of his head. "Go on."

"They didn't see us as any more of a threat than... bad weather. If one of their foraging parties was robbed, the next party sent out was double in size and better armed. Their walls, their guards, and most of their buildings were in response to us."

Gladlow asked, "How does that change the Hobs?"

"It changed Captain Lenogg. The way he talked about them changed. We didn't bother them anymore. We started to deal with the Humans differently too. Fairly, when we could. I don't know everything he's done, but he began supporting elements that wanted to bring back the old ways, but at the same time he started making changes and *presenting* them as a return to the old ways. I hated that. At first. But it looks like it's the only reason we've made it this far."

Gladlow said, "You mean old ways, as in before the wars..."

Dugg said, "That's right. Only, no one has ever been able to agree on what that even means. Lenogg has recruited or outright taken over other clans, or the leftover pieces of them. Each faction is given a vote, or a piece of one, in council. The older Hobs brought in are almost all used as ship crew. The younger are assigned to learn a trade."

Gladlow sat back, stunned. "That means... what does it mean? It means he's... engineering a different culture for Ningolohk. One that changes with just one generation."

Wellstone toasted him and said, "I thought my father was controlling. You have my sympathies Dugg." Which set Meese to laughing again.

Dugg said, "Is she a witch?" He looked around comically. Pel assumed he was feeling his drink at least as much as she.

Wellstone went on, "What is it you need to resolve before your papa comes back?"

Dugg rallied and said, "I want to make a bargain. What do you need from me?"

Gladlow said, "See the symbols etched into the floor? That's a teleport circle... a magic pathway. It may be the only way off this island. Bessemer and Wulfric can use it. Maybe Whitecloud. Where are they?"

Dug said, "I was here with Wulfric's group. They paid me to get them through East Gate. They paid a lot. They could have gotten around easily, but they wanted to follow a specific path. They didn't want to chance missing anything. This tower was empty for a long time, but I always checked back." He lifted a hand. "They were interesting. One night, I saw lights and came to find Vossy here. Bustard was with him."

Bustard woke up and said, "Vossy's no good."

"Umm, alright Bustard. Vossy said something bad happened. He was just there to get supplies before flying away. He *flew away*." Dugg shook his head. "I had been forbidden to have contact with the witches. I didn't tell my father before letting them through the gate and caught Goblin duty for it. So I told him this time. In a couple of days, Vossy showed up with Corigain—"

"Corigain!" Bustard flapped his wings and bobbed his head.

"—Betta, Bijou, and Whitecloud. Vossy was furious because they wouldn't go with him straight away. He said he didn't know if his people could hold out. Whitecloud refused to break our laws, and the others agreed."

Gladlow said, "Their research was everything to them, they didn't want to cause conflict. I'm a little surprised they didn't sneak through."

Dugg said, "They talked about it. It was because I knew. They decided to make a bargain. I set up a meeting with Lenogg."

"Maybe they couldn't resist a chance to meet him face to face. Could we make the same bargain?"

Dugg said, "You don't want to try it. He won't deal like that again."

Gladlow asked, "If we help you with your problem, can you get us through your east gate?"

Wellstone said, "Hold up there, Gladlow—"

"I asked if. Is it something that can be done?"

"I want to hear how their negotiations went."

Dugg sighed. "My father figured them out instantly. I had told him everything. He managed to threaten and bargain until they *wished* they had snuck through." He turned to Gladlow and said,

"Getting you through East Gate isn't that hard. It's Witch Gate that will be a problem."

"What's Witch Gate?"

"That's the gate Bijou Bessemer built for us."

Chapter Sixteen

Arux-Troth Basin, northern jungle

Meese said, "This is insulting. You know why *we're* going after the Goblins don't you?"

Dugg said, "We're only scouting, and I'll not be joining any scrap. It's just, you'd never find it without me." He had said several times that he wouldn't be doing any fighting, yet he was armed with the wight's longsword and his own returned property.

"We could have formed groups so that the experienced folk could help the less prepared..."

Voorsh said, "I have gratitude for your experience, Meese and Wellstone."

"Or all the ladies and all the fellows..."

Voorsh said, "That does not make sense."

"Instead, they sorted us by *height*."

Dugg said, "If I know the little rats, they've already turned the place into a warren of tunnels and tight spaces. Your great Humans, with their broad shoulders, would take forever to get through. I'll not be much good either—"

"We know, you won't be helping."

Wellstone said, "Don't mind him Dugg. He's just feeling the separation from his husband."

Meese made a rude sound.

Voorsh explained to Dugg, "They are making a joke. Meese and Gladlow are not mated."

Dugg said, "Right..."

"Gladlow has not mated with anyone."

Wellstone and Meese laughed uproariously, but he said, "Oh, poor lad, I shouldn't be laughing."

Dugg said, "I thought those two were his wives."

Wellstone could barely stop laughing long enough to say, "Not enough magic in the world..."

Meese said, "Stop now, you're just confusing these two. Gladlow and Pel are... courting. Carlin is just friendly."

Voorsh asked, "Do Odd-Gollin men have many wives?"

Dugg said, "What—"

Wellstone said, "It's just Odd, no one likes being called Gollin," and continued her hysterical laughter for a moment more. "Sorry sweetie, I shouldn't tease you. I've never heard anyone pick up a language like you." She patted her with one hand and wiped tears with the other.

Voorsh said, "Forgive my mistake, Dugg. Do Hob men have many wives?"

"In some clans, it's common, especially the leaders. With the Chummers, you can only have one legal wife, but important men can be granted permission for an honorary second."

Meese asked, "Why is that?"

Dugg shook his head. "I don't know, truly. I think it's to make better babes for the clan. You'd have to ask a prater."

Wellstone asked, "Do we want to know what a prater is?"

"A prater, you know? A prater." He could see their blank looks. "Maybe I'm using the wrong word, but that's what the Humans called it. Praters are smart. Some of them keep the numbers, track lineage, or predict yields. A lot of them are occultists. They all talk. A lot. It's usually a prater that recommends an honorary wife."

Meese asked, "People don't choose their own... life companions?"

Dugg said, "Mostly they do. The clan doesn't need to meddle to get promising children. Some choose for looks, or wealth, but most make at least one try for someone who could beat them in a fight. My father's sister was known as Adwa the Dawn. She captured the *Frenzy*. Not by herself, but she got the credit by everyone who fought with her. She had suitors before that, she's a real beauty, but after, it was endless requests by the praters to marry her off. They didn't care whether it was as wife one or two."

Voorsh asked, "Why was she called Adwa the Dawn?"

"It was a joke by the Human pirates, but a respectful one. They said she was a dreadful sight for sailors. She has this lovely red coloring, you see?"

Meese said, "I don't get it." Voorsh was also shaking her head.

Wellstone said, "A red sunrise can mean storms on the way. Not the most reliable indicator, but people have been repeating it since wood began to float."

Meese asked, "So, anyone managed to land that fish?"

"Meese, don't try to join the nautical talk."

Dugg said, "None. Everyone hoped she would have children after that. Her injuries keep her from battle, anyway. Now she just fights off advances while she runs the public house."

Voorsh asked, "What is a public house?" Just as Wellstone asked, "Why do you need a public house?"

Meese answered Voorsh, "It's like Whitecloud's hut but for more people. It's a place for visitors to stay."

Voorsh said, "Like your taverns."

"I don't know. Dugg, what's your public house like?"

"We built it to be a tavern, but the Humans say it's no tavern. It's a public house. After her injuries, Adwa felt she was useless. She leapt at the chance to earn for the cove and became Adwa the Sutler. Lately just Sutler."

Wellstone asked, "Humans visit your port?"

"Yes. We've an eye for profit. Trading from our own port costs us nothing. Right now, the *Wyvern Wind* is docked to replace some rigging. I don't know why they chose us, but it's good money."

"I guarantee it's so the authorities don't see the damage they suffered. It might identify them."

Dugg said, "That sounds right. They make their money from trade, but they only trade stolen goods. They told a story about getting caught smuggling and escaping capture."

Meese asked, "How do they get around Boazoch?"

"No one gets around it. Everyone pays."

Voorsh asked, "What did Boazoch request from your people?"

"What do you mean?" Dugg looked at her like he didn't understand the question.

"What tribute did he demand? He requested more sweet-root from Uljar-Molik, but we sent other gifts as always."

"It can talk?" Dugg looked shocked. "Wait. You pay in sweet-root?"

Wellstone asked, "What do you pay in?"

"Gold. A lot of it." He was still shaking his head in disbelief.

"How did you know what to pay the first time?"

"We did what the other ships did. A few might try to soften him up by putting a fresh kill on the raft, but we've heard tell of ships brought to the bottom for trying to substitute gold."

Meese asked, "You thought the Lizards were giving him gold?"

"Well no. We know they worship it—him, but they don't have boats..."

Voorsh said, "Maybe we will make boats when the Crown can't kill us for leaving the reefs."

They were all stunned silent for a moment. Wellstone recovered first. "Voorsh, what do you mean? The Crown...?"

The little Lizard said, matter-of-factly, "Seven years after my birth, the Human ships would kill all found outside the reefs."

"How old are you now?"

"Two tens."

"Twenty."

"Twenty. Thank you."

Meese asked, "Voorsh, do you remember it?"

She said, "I do remember. The first time, many, many were murdered. Once more, and we understood. We were careful not to be seen. We can hold our air for many minutes. But Human divers killed us under the water. Soon we were forbidden to leave the reefs."

Dugg said, "You've paid tribute faithfully. Did you ever ask Boazoch for help?"

"We do not ask for help from a god. We pay him to be left alone."

• • • •

Eastern Plateau, sandstone bluffs

Gladlow took his eye away from the spyglass and handed it to Pel. They had found it while digging through the watch tower's upstairs storage room. He turned and sat his back against the rocks they were hiding behind, lost in thought looking at her new boots, acquired at the same time as the spyglass and his trousers. He didn't know whose bag the pants came from, but they were black and white striped and a foot too short, with his boots making up the difference. They planned to inventory the room, but it was a huge undertaking and they didn't want to waste daylight. Their vantage point was only a two-hour walk from the tower, but a steep climb to the bluffs with a clear view of the mine entrance. It would be a six-hour round trip from tower to mine, but they were only scouting and foraging today. Dugg had until the *Frenzy* returned in sixteen days to get his problems sorted, but Gladlow wouldn't rush deciding this one.

Pel said, "I see it up on the ledge, but I can't make out anything but brown and gold fur. What do you think it is?"

Gladlow said, "It's a manticore. A big one."

"Damn. Have you ever seen one?"

"No, just drawings, but I watched it stretch and roll over."

Pel was still peering through the device. "It doesn't look that big to me..."

He said, "Look below him at the mine entrance, those are Hobs and Goblins."

"I see what you mean. The Hobgoblins in the village—"

Gladlow cleared his throat.

"The *Hobs*," He could hear she was smiling, "that attacked the village were a little under six feet tall. That beast has to be twelve or fourteen feet long." She lowered herself next to him. "I've never dealt with something like that. What do you know about them?"

"Mostly the things you know by looking at it. Wings, teeth, spiky tail. Fast, strong, and just smart enough to extort the Hob miners."

Pel, unconsciously it seemed, put her hand on his thigh and asked, "Do you think it's possible to drive it away?"

"I don't know about that. Dugg says it calls itself Murra the Outcast, and it's pretty old. It might be more clever than average, but I doubt it will leave such a comfortable lifestyle. It has Gnoll servants to tenderize its meat, and an army of captives to amass wealth while it naps."

She said, "Gnolls I've dealt with. Berserk fighters, no tactics. I think we should take them on away from the mine and eliminate a couple of Murra's allies."

"We haven't even decided to do this..."

"Really? What else are we going to do? We could try to make our way through the east territory, but Voorsh thinks it's too dangerous. It would be a slow trek, climbing in and out of caves and sinkholes, and we'd likely end up fighting something anyway. Or we could swim for it and deal with hundreds of eel-men."

Gladlow said, "I know, but it seems like looking for trouble. I don't want anyone else to get hurt."

"We could hole up in the tower and wait for rescue. Or live with the Lizards."

"Would you want to do that, rather than keep looking for a way off the island?"

She looked sad when she said, "It doesn't sound so bad to me anymore, but I don't think you would stay long." She put her head on her knees for a moment. "It's the same reason I'm a little afraid to find a way back."

"What do you mean?" He put a hand on her back.

"Gladlow, you have a big life. It's already filled with friends, and work, and studies..."

"Pel, in my mind I already have this huge space in my life cleared for you. My work fell apart, and I'll likely be disciplined for coming here anyway. As for my friends and my studies, you already put up with them. There aren't any more waiting for me. I'm desperate to get back so we can spend time together because you *want* to, not because you're trapped here with me."

She asked, "Remember, on the beach with the longboat? When you asked me to come with you?"

"I remember."

"That's the moment I stopped being trapped. Let's keep going. There's too much we don't know to just sit and wait for the next thing to happen."

Gladlow nodded and said, "Agreed. We'll start by eliminating Murra's support. Dugg said they walk their trap line every night, so we'll pick a place to attack that's furthest from the mine. Are we... just going to kill them?"

Pel hesitated a moment before saying, "I'm not sure what else to do. Gnolls aren't just different than us, like the Hobgoblins—Hobs. The only vocations they have besides hunter, are slaver and animal trainer, and it's all the same to them. I know not everyone has to be an enemy... but if I had to draw a line, I think it would be with Gnolls."

Gladlow was nodding. "I was thinking the same, but I don't have your experience with them. It's just not a decision I want to assume when we have time to plan."

She said, "We could give them a chance to run, but they won't take it unless we beat them to within an inch of death. Total domination is the only thing that holds their attention."

"When Dugg drew the layout of the mine, he described the meat left to age in front of Murra's chamber. It included Goblin and Lizard. The Hob warriors he sent will surely be hanging there now. I think killing and eating things that can speak is a good enough definition of evil for me."

"I like that you think about it. It's one of the reasons I put away the sword, I had stopped thinking about it."

Gladlow asked, "How do you feel about fighting now that it's been forced on you again?"

She said, "I don't feel forced. I picked it up again gladly. I suppose it feels more natural than it used to. It does feel good to be useful, to be good at something, but I hate... I don't know."

"You hate being praised for it."

Pel gave him a radiant smile and nodded. "I don't want to be... only that *one* thing. How did you know?"

"I was an angry child, but I could control myself most of the time. When I was being trained to fight, they only praised me when I let it out. When I hurt someone." He sighed. "Now I'm grateful I was so weak. I didn't want to be that thing at all."

She put her head on his shoulder and they sat quietly for a while. She eventually asked, "Should we go look for the others?"

"They're supposed to meet us up here, it's a good landmark. We'll give them a while longer."

Pel said, "So, Wellstone will come back with a plan for the Goblins. If we take the armory back from them—"

"We'll be even with Dugg for the information—"

"And have some armor and weapons for ourselves. Then we start by taking out the Gnolls, isolating the manticore. Then what?"

Gladlow said, "Dugg says Murra is due to go off on one of his away trips. It was Dugg's plan to arm another group of Hobs from the armory stash and lie in wait for Murra to return. It's not a bad plan."

"Where does a manticore fly away to? The beach?"

"Sounds nice. He's always gone exactly two days, he brings trinkets like polished seastones, and fresh meat, not the rotten filth he eats. I would guess he's going to see a woman-ticore."

Pel groaned and said, "You're such an idiot, I can't believe I spend so much time thinking about kissing your stupid mouth."

"What? You're thinking about..." He leaned away to look at her face.

"What's wrong? It was just a joke—"

"Right." He shook it off with a perfectly natural chuckle.

"I obviously don't think you're stupid."

"What?"

"Gladlow, tell me what's wrong."

"Nothing's wrong. You said you were thinking about kissing me..."

She moved around to face him and looked at him like he was speaking the wrong language. "You've been thinking that I wasn't going to? Ever?"

"I had... I hoped that when we were away from here, you might feel differently about me, I wanted to try, but it was alright if you just needed a friend—"

"Do you just want to be friends?"

"No!" He took a deep breath and pushed the sudden panic down. "I feel like we're having a fight, but what you said is the best thing anyone has ever said. I was just surprised... that you said it." He gave a feeble shrug.

Pel said, "I'm the idiot. I haven't told you anything, have I? I let you talk and talk—"

"I don't talk that much..."

"And talk." She was smiling again. "But I haven't shared much with you."

He put his hands on her arms and said, "That's alright—"

"It's not. I should have told you I'm thinking of a lot more than kissing you. I should have said I just needed to wait a little while. I'm sorry I'm bad at this, but I've never been—" She covered her mouth and snorted, "Never mind."

"You sure are saying things *now*." He couldn't stop smiling, but there was something he knew he should say. "Pel, there's a couple of things I should tell you before we get to... more than—"

"Stop. I don't want you to share anything else until I catch up a bit. I want to keep things the same a little longer if that's alright?"

"Of course it is—"

"Just because I'm so happy right now. Are you sure?"

"About keeping us the same? Yes, I'm sure. We'll just keep thinking about what we'll do when we get out of this place. The things I need to tell you are important, though. It's not right for me—"

Pel said, "Traveler rules. Tell me one thing. The least important one. Then you have to wait for my turn."

Gladlow considered cheating but decided his incredible good fortune shouldn't be risked. "I'm a little younger than people assume..."

"How old are you?"

"I'll be twenty soon."

"How soon?"

"A year." He tried his most charming grin, it usually got a better response. "I'm sorry, did that... change everything?"

Pel had her hand back to her mouth and her eyebrow raised. He couldn't read that look at all... but it turned into a sweet smile. She said, "I'm twenty-four, but I feel like I've skipped over living the last five. I don't care, Gladlow. Not at all."

He pulled her half into his lap and asked, "When you said keep things the same, did you mean exactly the same, or is kissing my stupid mouth still negotiable?" He leaned in and—

"That's a really steep climb," Carlin said as she topped the rise. Gladlow's lips landed on Pel's cheek as she turned to look, making her laugh. Bustard could be seen flapping circles around Nowen, twenty yards behind. Carlin continued, "We found them. Look." She dropped a small basket of blue-black daisies, roots and all, in Pel's lap.

Gladlow said, "Unbelievable, Carlin." Pel punched his arm and stood up. He followed, taking the spyglass and looking once more. Murra the Outcast hadn't moved, but the figures going in and out of the mine never slowed.

• • • •

Northern Basin, hidden armory

Wellstone lay perfectly still, as she had for nearly two hours. She knew she had seen something, but she was beginning to doubt. She had just mentally allowed herself a few more minutes when a colorful bird fluttered to the vines hanging from the limestone wall she was watching. The bright green and yellow creature landed on a previously unnoticed ledge to peck something off the surface. She could see the entrance to the abandoned mine Dugg had led them to but was assured it was heavily barred from the inside. Originally the Hobgoblins had harvested limestone blocks from several locations in their cove, before reaching a point when they didn't wish to cut into it anymore. An effort was made all over the northern half of the island to start new quarries and mines to further their wall aspirations. A stroke of luck found the seam of seastone close to the surface and mining operations began as soon as they realized the blue stone with sea foam patterns could be a modestly valuable resource. A few Hobgoblins and many Goblins were set to the jobs of mining, cutting, and polishing the stone. It was a disaster for a long time, but artisans began to emerge from the builders, war engineers, and scullery staff that were tasked. All other attempted mines, like the one Wellstone had been staring at, never yielded more than limestone. When this one was abandoned, captain Lenogg had a massive door installed and stashed enough supplies and weapons to equip a small force to retake the cove, should a coup arise. Dugg said he may have failed to tell his captain that he hadn't cleared out the stash when he was ordered to. It became the hideout for his personal entourage of most trusted companions.

Wellstone realized the little bird had vanished from sight, but she hadn't seen it fly away. The vines to the left and fifteen feet above the entrance suddenly shook and the bird's dead body flew out and tumbled to the ground, where a small hand moved a bush to get a look. She thought she heard a nasty chuckle, but everything was still again. She carefully retreated backward and returned to base.

Base was a log in a clearing, upon which sat Meese, Dugg, and Voorsh, eating all of the food they had brought.

Meese had the grace to look guilty. "You were gone so long, we assumed you were dead."

Wellstone asked Voorsh, "Sweetie, would you take over lookout?"

Voorsh nodded and held out a loose handful of dried snacks, noticed Wellstone's hesitation, and quickly ate the beetles out of it. Wellstone accepted the remaining seeds and berries with a shrug as the little Lizard ran silently into the tree line. She fought her natural hesitation to take Dugg's offered water flask, but she thought she covered it well. The youngster was obnoxious but better groomed than her own crew of late. She was having trouble shaking the lifelong impression of Hobgoblins in greasy, blood-soaked leather.

She said, "Those are the most disciplined Goblins I've ever seen. They're excellent guards."

Dugg said, "They should be. I chose the best."

"Good job, shithead."

"I thought they were loyal..." He trailed off when he heard how that sounded. "Maybe I should have paid them."

Meese asked, "How did they manage to take over an armory?"

"It's not a fortress, we just stashed some equipment here. I had plans for it, so I left a couple of trusted Hobs to watch over it."

"How did the Goblins know about it?"

Dugg looked exasperated, "A couple of them, my assistants, were with me when I gave the orders."

Wellstone was grinning. "So your butler conspired against you with your valet. That's some hard luck, Your Lordship."

Meese said. "That doesn't explain how they managed it. How did two Goblins defeat two Hobgob—Hob guards?"

Dugg glared at his verbal slip. "Well they recruited reinforcements, didn't they?"

Wellstone said, "There is no way Goblins would attack prepared Hobs unless they outnumbered them, what, four to one? Five to one?"

Dugg reached into his pouch and pulled out one of the clay orbs. He held it up for a moment before he said, "This is a Pummel Shell. Hob magic from the Gut Slashers clan. Most of the occultists in Ningolohk are Gut Slashers. They're hard to make, but we worked the Slashers hard to supply our boarding crews. Now ships carry a few just in case. When you toss it, it explodes on the next thing it touches. A person, a deck... water. It's loud and bright but doesn't do much damage, so it's good for capturing ships. They made larger ones to fire from a ballista, but they couldn't get them to set off properly—"

"Dugg..."

"When the *Frenzy* went on the trading mission, I was left in charge. Mostly. The garrisons each have a captain. In all non-martial matters, I was in charge. Except the artisans. And the occultists. They have their own orders. My biggest job was keeping the mine running, and that meant keeping the miners fed, and that meant making sure that the hunting, and fishing, and gathering was done. Hobs think everything but the hunting is beneath them, so it all falls to the Goblins. Well, my grandmother always said, 'When all you have is rotten melons, you make grog.' So I taught some of the Goblins, the ones who could pay attention long enough to teach... how to use the Pummel Shells. I just gave them enough to go fishing. And it worked!" He said, "Until they went fishing for the guards at the supply cache."

She said, "Oh, Dugg..."

He said, "Even without the extra equipment, I got a group of volunteers to attack the seastone mine, but they were killed. Murra took an even bigger cut as punishment."

Meese asked, "Cut? Does the whole cove know what's happening?"

Dugg said, "There's no hiding it."

"Why hasn't anyone put a larger force together and taken care of this?"

"The council was apparently told not to interfere with my responsibilities. Half of them would love me to fail—or die, that would be fine with them. The other half won't go against orders unless it risks security."

Wellstone said, "This seems like a pretty big breach if this mine is so important."

"They don't see it that way. The seastone being paid to Murra is still there. The *Frenzy* crew will just kill him and take it back, and I'll be on sewer duty because the mine operated so slowly while they were gone." He looked at them and made another bid to recruit them to the larger job. "When the *Frenzy* returns, there's no way to get through the cove. You'll have to find a way around. If you help me take back the mine, the council won't interfere with me letting you through Witch Gate." They weren't protesting so he took that as encouragement to go on. "I'll mostly tell them the truth. I'll say I hired you to kill the manticore—or drive him away, I won't tell you your business. I'll say you're a ship's crew that was cast away by Boazoch on the south side of the island. We'll put you in the public house, they'll be watching you closely, but you'll have until the ship returns to decide what to do. I can sneak you through East Gate, like the witches, you sign on with another ship, or you can leave the way you came."

Meese said, "As long as we decide before the *Frenzy* returns. What happens if we're there when it does?"

Dugg made a hissing sound through his teeth. "If you've signed on with a crew, nothing. Lenogg won't risk the cove's reputation... Otherwise, I don't know if you could talk your way out. I wouldn't try."

Voorsh came running back. "Eight Gollins have left. It looked as a hunting party would. They went west, into deep jungle."

Meese said, "That would have been a stroke of luck if we were all here and ready. How often do they hunt?"

Dugg said, "It depends on what they get. This crew is pretty good, and Goblins will eat anything. They probably won't have to go out again for a week."

Wellstone said, "We can't waste the opportunity—"

Meese cut her off, "No. Absolutely not."

She put a hand on his shoulder and felt guilty knowing the touch would shut him up. "There are a couple of guards locked outside the gate and more on a ledge above. It must lead inside, there's no way they're making that climb several times a day. If we did this, hear me out, I would climb up and open the gate for the rest of you."

He knocked her hand off his shoulder and said, "How in four hells will you do that without being seen by the guards?"

She said, "With this," and held out a scroll. He was frowning deeply, but he snatched it away and unrolled it. She said, "I read a bit of Elvish, did I pick the right one?"

"I can't believe you took this from Gladlow—"

"Can you cast it?"

Meese said, "Of course, I can cast it. I have a copy in my own book. I just don't keep it prepared."

Wellstone said, "It seems strange is all. It sounds pretty useful, all around."

Even annoyed, his smile was unbearably cocky. "Why would I want to be invisible?"

Chapter Seventeen

Eastern Plateau, watchtower trail

Carlin was feeling 'not oneself', as her mother had called it. She was convinced she was still feeling the influential pulls of otherworldly entities, but had to admit, she might have just been feeling a little left out. She and her brother, being the youngest as well as twins, had absorbed most of the praise and affection the family was able to generate. When her brother died, the volume of attention remained but took the form of overbearing care and solicitation. She realized she was never viewed as her own person, and in his absence, was seen as half. Sometimes less. She knew this was the source of her resolve to reject these supposedly divine callings, it was the source of her rejection of two marriage proposals, and the impetus for leaving home. The entire universe seemed to believe she would never be whole until she gave herself over to something or someone. She fundamentally rejected this, but constantly felt the pull. Disappear into something greater than herself. Be half of a whole again. She was... a little jealous of Gladlow and Pel. Not of one or the other, but both, just a little. She knew it was only that she felt a reduction in attention after her ordeal, and she was by this age adept at suppressing her childish impulses to be the center of attention. She often compromised by lavishing affection on someone who needed it. It struck her as funny, as it had many times, that being aware of one's faults did not necessarily mean they were easy to eliminate.

Carlin said, "I've decided to wear the armor."

Pel nodded immediately. Carlin was unsurprised she would support her in this. It was their group's greatest piece of defensive equipment, and she would want it to be used. Pel knew she was the more logical choice, but would be happy to have one of her loved ones better protected. Gladlow was a different matter. His frown was even less of a surprise. His extreme distrust of the divine seemed to be well founded, and he saw the enchanted breastplate as a trap to be avoided. It was one of the factors that decided things for Carlin. He was torn between wanting Pel to be more protected from injury, possibly even from death, but would resent the danger put on his sweetheart's free will. Carlin decided to take the burden from them all.

Gladlow said, "I don't think that's necessarily—"

"I've made up my mind. There are only a few possible outcomes. It protects me, and all of you don't have to risk yourselves quite so often. Or, I'm killed but it prevents my death. If our worst fears become a reality, I have three wizard friends to help me figure out what to do."

Nowen said, "You'll have more than that. The Institute can bring incredible expertise to bear on something like this. Of course, all three of us will end up paying back those favors for years. It will be worth it." That was probably the nicest thing Nowen had said to anyone in fifty years, judging by his pained look.

Gladlow said, "If we handle things the right way, we could have the Institute paying you for the privilege of helping." He seemed to be trying to cover his relief, but Carlin genuinely hoped he *was* relieved. He asked, "Can I offer a piece of advice? About magical protection?"

Carlin smiled and said, "I suppose, if you're the expert..."

"Pretend you don't have it. Convince yourself it isn't there, that it doesn't work. Someone trained to use armor knows what it can do, can use it like their weapon or shield. A novice to it, like mages, might not duck when they should. Or worse, step into something expecting more protection than it provides." He sounded earnest when he said, "The best thing about the armor spell is that there's no evidence it's there." This turned into an embarrassed look. "End of lecture. All other armor questions should be referred to Wellstone and Pel."

Carlin wrapped her arms around him and laid her head on his chest, but she kept it brief. She moved to Pel and squeezed her hard. "I hope we can do more training. I know I've been lazy about it."

Pel said, "You've done great. Soon you'll be better with a bow than I am." She gave her the big-sister look that Carlin loved. "We do need to talk about throwing down your shield when a fight starts..."

Carlin turned to Nowen who looked a little panicked. It had taken some time to show him she could be affectionate without wanting to sleep with him. The secret with Nowen was consistency. He believed what was proven more easily than what was promised, and he never argued with what was proven. She said, "This is in anticipation of the help you'll be giving me on my new project," and gave him one of her maximum affection, but not too sisterly, hugs.

Nowen said, "Anything I can do to help," with what little breath he could bring to bear.

Carlin said, "Now come on, I didn't mean to hold us up."

They soon arrived back at the watch tower, where she set Nowen the task of searching the upstairs storage for a list of items, while Pel and Gladlow curled up with a map to make plans and canoodle. Carlin laid out her compounds and reagents, considering each before packing them safely back in their padded compartments, or setting them to one side. She wrote down a quick list of steps and began making each component. Seaweed alginate she normally used for sealing ulcers, was added to a small amount of the Anansi venom. The thickened substance was evenly painted onto the heads of her six finest arrows. A layer of the muslin she used for filtering was laid on each side, trimmed to size, and sealed with beeswax. She would need to be careful where the arrows were shot. It would take weeks and a laboratory to make an antivenom specific to the spider-boy's venom. She had marine derived antidotes and antivenom, and hopefully, the blue aster draughts by morning. They would have to do for the time being. She felt somber at the thought of using these methods for harmful purposes, but it would be good to finally contribute to the safety of this chance family she had grown to love. Skeletons, cadavers, and wights had made it difficult to turn down the mantle of Jeme's cleric. If she could devise a nonmagical defense against the undead, she would never again leave home without it.

The couple sitting in the bunk had lowered their voices, which meant they were talking about things not having to do with the group. Gladlow's voice carried so that Carlin was able to hear his half of the conversation. Lately, it had begun to feel wrong to eavesdrop, so she climbed the ladder to the second floor, where Bustard could be seen flying around the tower as he passed each arrow slit. Order was beginning to rise from the chaos of the round storage room. Crates of native artifacts and specimen samples were neatly separated and stacked on the left half of the room. Books and papers were beginning to fill in the gaps. The rest of the room still looked like a peddler's wagon had been thrown at a swaphouse. She smiled at the thought. It was easily something the Chief might say, but she imagined it in Meese's voice.

Nowen asked, "You like it then?" and stepped aside to give her a better view. He was gesturing at a small table littered with objects. She could see the containers she had requested, bowls and glasses, but they were surrounded by a mess of randomness and wax trimmings.

Carlin pasted on a smile and said, "Oh, you cut all the candles." She nodded happily. "They're *shorter* now."

"For this." He slid a candle lantern forward. The small device had been stripped of the bone windscreens and the metal supports had been bowed outward to make it round and squat. He fit a small clay pot on top and a shortened candle underneath.

She said, "That's... enormously clever, Nowen."

"Oh, it's nothing. I saw something like it in Gladlow's—" He stopped, pointing strangely at his mouth. He shrugged. "One of his scroll customers. She has a curio shop that looks very much like this room, but worse smelling. This little cooker is part of what she called a candle kitchen. The clay pot makes it heat slowly, and I trimmed the candles to burn for the correct time in your recipe..." He seemed to be taking her silence as displeasure and speeding up his explanation. "There're plenty of uncut ones, so you can make it more precise, and I trimmed the screens to fit in the base so you can stack them to raise the candle as it burns down, which I know is primitive compared to the counterweight device she had—"

"Nowen, hush." She grabbed his ears and gave him a loud kiss on the mouth. "Show me the rest." They spent some time choosing a watertight container to carry her new candle kitchen.

Carlin considered clearing her throat or stomping loudly down the ladder to warn of her return but chose to hang upside-down from the hatch instead. Gladlow and Pel were at the table, so she swung down and grabbed the ladder. Nowen and Bustard followed.

Gladlow said, "We're going to use the time we have to find the Gnolls' trapline."

Nowen began to protest, but Carlin cut him off with, "That's a good idea."

"I know you're eager to work on your blue aster—"

She waved that away. "I'm too excited to sleep much tonight, so I'll work on it when it's quiet. I don't feel like sitting around waiting for the others to return."

Pel said, "That's how we felt. Come take a look."

Gladlow showed them the map where they added the seastone mine. "Dugg said the Gnolls check their traps every night, but they move slowly to hunt if there's an opportunity. We think that limits them to this area to the west of the mine. If we avoid walking into one of their traps, we can pick an ambush spot to use in a day or two when our scent clears."

Carlin said, "That's still a big area..."

Nowen said, "If we use the locater here, and walk straight across here, that will cover most of the area. I think we'd have a good chance with one casting."

Gladlow said, "I'm not so sure. It's very specific. What are you searching for?"

"Point taken. If I haven't seen it, I have to visualize it clearly. Even if you described the exact trap, I'm not sure I'd be able."

Carlin asked, "Do we know what kinds of traps they use?"

Gladlow shook his head. "I didn't think to ask, but they bring back all size game. Some of the traps have to be pretty big. Is a pit something you can locate?"

Pel said, "For big animals, the traps aren't deadly. The larger ones will have a chain staked to the ground. Can you locate the nearest chain?"

· · · ·

Northern Basin, hidden armory

Wellstone loved being invisible. It was a new and bizarre experience to be disembodied, and she wasted long moments waving hands in front of faces, both her friends and her own. In all her years, she had never realized how much of one's body is in view at all times. Shoulders and breasts, suddenly and conspicuously absent from her peripheral vision, gave her a distinct feeling of insubstantiality, but the unnerving part was the missing frame of her face. The sides of her nose, her upper lip, her cheekbones, now utterly transparent, cleared her field of view and gave her the illusion of being thrust forward out of her own skull.

Meese asked, "Are you listening, or are you waving your hands in front of everyone's faces?"

Wellstone whispered in his ear, "I can do both."

He let out a put-upon sigh. "Then what did I say?"

"You said, 'Are you listening, or are you waving your hands in front of everyone's faces?'"

"I said don't do anything that can only be explained by there being an invisible person around. Don't touch anyone. Tweaking someone's nose, maybe even brushing past them, will make you visible. Good luck."

There was nothing but silence.

"Wellstone, did you already leave, or are you messing about?" He waited for a moment. "If I can hear you trying not to laugh, those Goblins surely will. You have less than an hour, get moving."

She made her way quickly to the clearing and only hesitated a second before jogging into the open. She peeked around the bush to see two Goblins leaning against their spears, practically asleep on their feet. She chose a stout vine out of reach of the ledge above and began her climb. It was impossible to climb without moving the vine, but she did her best and rose above the level of the ledge before two Goblin archers peered out from their alcove to investigate the rustling of leaves. She climbed a good six feet above them while they looked over the edge, assuming the movement was something on the ground. Finding few handholds in the limestone, she was nevertheless able to creep along the wall without disturbing the vines further. Behind and above the two archers, she was forced to transfer her weight back to a final vine to make her descent. She froze and flattened herself against the wall whenever her vine rustled, causing the two Goblins to look up and about. She dropped silently to the ledge, but one of the creatures still whipped his head around to look. She stood still, holding the vine steady until he returned to looking over the edge. She had an indecisive moment, looking around for ideas, when she noticed the rope and bell further in. If that was their alarm, then getting them off the ledge was the next logical step. She drew her sword slowly and crept up behind the two Goblins. Grabbing a vine to ensure she wouldn't follow them over the edge, she thrust her sword into one and kicked out as hard as she could at the other. The first fell dead, sliding over the edge, but the second was not as heavy as she anticipated and her kick sent him flying forward to land on his face, feet folded over his back. Her short-lived experience as a vengeful spirit was over, so she ducked back before the two guards on the ground rushed out to look up. She heard Dugg's voice but didn't speak Hobgoblin. Looking out into the open grass, she saw her friends approaching. The two guards brandished their spears, but Dugg walked right up to them, within easy stabbing distance, and dropped his hand to the sword on his hip. He continued to speak while Meese tried to look mean and Voorsh tried to look crazy, bobbing her head and swaying back and forth. One Goblin bolted into the trees, the other ran to the heavy door to rattle it ineffectually before following his companion.

Meese asked, "What did you say to them?"

Dugg said, "I told them they all look the same to me, so be sure to report for their punishment tomorrow. They'll probably join a foraging team and sneak back into Ningolohk, but they might go warn that hunting party. We should get inside and get this done.

Wellstone didn't need further prompting. She took a few moments to slash all of the easily accessible vines, leaving one to be hauled up and coiled on the ledge. She cut the rope to the alarm as well when she crept past the bell and stuck her head through the hatch in the floor. There was little light, but her eyes adjusted quickly. She made her way into a limestone hallway ending in a partial cave-in. Where the limestone ran out, wooden timbers held up a Goblin-sized opening into a dirt tunnel. She stayed in the original mine tunnel and stepped through the doorway near the middle of the hall. The short connecting hallway had been built up with cob to shrink the passage. Dugg was right, the Goblins were modifying everything to fit their scale. It reminded her of mud wasps filling in keyholes. She came out in the main room, a large rectangular chamber filled with the remnants of wooden mine tracks and carts. Seeing no movement, she trotted to the huge door and lifted the timber barring it. Her three companions piled in and re-barred the entry.

Meese asked, "What's the strategy here?"

She said, "It looks like the adit has been barricaded at the end there. We'll go back the way I came. It will be clear behind us, so we'll just sweep—"

A *thok* sound drew their attention to an arrow sticking out of Voorsh's shoulder as another whizzed between Meese and Dugg. Voorsh charged in the direction of the shots while Wellstone directed everyone to the hallway. It took everyone a moment to squeeze through the narrowed passage, and their assailants loosed two more missiles at the group crowding the exit. One clattered on the rock wall, but the other hit Wellstone squarely in the back. Voorsh arrived to shove her through the opening, and they all piled into the hallway.

Wellstone asked, "How bad is it?" while desperately feeling around over her shoulder.

Meese looked and asked, "How bad is what?"

"I was hit—"

"It must have glanced off the armor spell. You got away with a bruise, but Voorsh isn't going to be that lucky."

The little Lizard had already pulled the arrow loose. There was a bit of blood, but it wasn't flowing freely. She said, "It hurts a very lot, but it did not go deep. There is a wooden wall with openings for arrows. No door."

Wellstone said, "That means the plan still holds, we just won't get another sneak attack. We can still climb out the way I came and get away clean..."

Dugg seemed to be the only one considering it, but he said, "We made it this far. That's twelve Goblins outside, and the two shooting at us. It's only been a couple of weeks, how many could there be?"

This time Meese led the way, left forearm up, magic shield ready to trigger. He kept the cap on his torch staff, three of the group able to see reasonably well. Voorsh kept a hand on Wellstone's shoulder and stayed to the middle as the most injured traditionally did. The dirt tunnel curved to the right and rejoined the original mine with another narrowed entryway. Dugg was the only one who had trouble getting through, but he managed without too much delay. They arrived back in the main adit, this time behind the barrier. It looked to be a storage room, but the barrier was a jumble of scaffolds allowing places for four, now absent, archers.

Meese released the perpetual flame at the end of his staff. "The shelves have been converted to bunks. Look around but let's keep it quick."

The group proceeded to rummage while Meese watched the door at the end of the room. They joined him with little to report. Dugg said, "A few bits of trash. Goblins leave nothin' for their fellows to steal."

Wellstone said, "Nothing. Voorsh?"

"No things. But I counted twenty and two bunks recently used."

"Well done, I should have thought of that."

Meese said, "That means we could still have ten to deal with, and only if none of them are spooning at night. This is a stupid way to die. We should call it off."

Dugg said, "I don't know what else they've done, but through that door is where we stashed the armor and weapons." He pulled the Pummel Shells from his pouch and held them in one hand. He drew the longsword with the other. "If we do enough damage right away, I think they'll surrender. They can count high enough to know they're only at half strength."

Wellstone said, "Voorsh and I can each occupy two. That leaves the rest for whatever tricks you and the boy can pull to keep us from being swarmed. You'll have to decide."

Meese said, "Single file behind me. I can block most of the arrows, but only if they're aimed at me. The two of you rush the archers if it's an option. Dugg, don't hit any of us. I'll be trying for the biggest group. Stay out of my way."

There was no point in waiting any longer. Wellstone opened the door and followed closely behind Meese. The same size and shape as the previous sections of the adit, the room was a wide, rectangular limestone hallway. Stacks of crates and baskets teetered in four and five foot tall towers. Hobgoblin leather and chain armor was arranged on makeshift wicker armor stands, giving the appearance of a dozen soldiers standing at attention, if a bit drunkenly. The room was dark but for Meese's staff, the ersatz flame making the armor shadows move. The light failed at the far end of the room where the limestone seemed to have run out again. The floor transitioned to dirt, and there was only darkness further on.

Meese whispered, "This is absolutely an ambush, right?"

Wellstone nodded and moved to cover their right flank, signaling to Voorsh to go left. The Lizard was still the only one to remember the signals Gladlow worked out. Even Wellstone had just shrugged and shook her head the last time he tried to go over them. Dugg seemed to understand that he was to watch the rear. They crept forward and Wellstone got a look at the hazy shapes behind the armored figures. Bundles of sticks and piles of rough-cut boards filled every space. A few half-constructed wicker seats were abandoned in the path already being crowded by hay and dried grass filling loosely woven baskets. The Goblins looked to have a major construction project planned in their rustic cob and thatch style. Wellstone felt something about to happen. They were far enough from the door that they could be surrounded, the attack would come any second. Unless they had grossly miscalculated their numbers, the Goblins should still be manageable. A portion would attack from either side, attempting to cut them off. The main force would attack from the front, giving Meese a clear opportunity to... Wellstone looked at the straw scattered under their feet, the wicker, the grass.

She started to speak when Meese cut her off with, "Close your eyes!" She looked instead. Several objects were already on an arching trajectory. Four orbs with glowing runes, left tracers in the air as they spun toward them. Dugg threw his own shells with a curse. She closed her eyes and covered one ear just before the pummel shells struck. She experienced a teeth-rattling boom and a flash of light barely restricted by her eyelids. She opened her eyes and realized their error. Apparently, a magical barrier wouldn't set off a pummel shell. Two of them had bounced off Meese's shield, one striking a wicker man, the other exploding at her feet. Wellstone looked right at it. For a few precious moments, the world was only an impression of events. She knew Dugg's shells went off up ahead. She knew several Goblins were appearing from both sides, but they seemed to be equally affected by the delayed explosions. Meese was already casting at a mob charging from the front. There was something about flames... she shook her head violently to clear it.

"No Meese, you'll kill us all!" she managed to shout just as she was forced to parry a flurry of attacks from a Goblin wielding a shortsword in each hand. His companion was similarly armed and would be on her momentarily. She took a risk and lunged at her assailant, her blade's reach a serious advantage if she could keep a distance between them. She felt it bite flesh and chanced a look to see the results of Meese's spell. She thought he must have heard her, as the room wasn't ablaze, but the Goblin in front stumbled to a stop and fell on his face. The one behind tripped over him and landed on his side, sliding forward a few inches. Then the next and the next. Four assailants lay still on the ground and a further two were stumbling forward, likely recovering from Dugg's pummel shells. Wellstone was not in full control of her senses, as she forgot about her own attackers. A Goblin's blade slashed her shoulder, this time unimpeded by the armor spell. She spun in time to block the second blade and stumble back. Dugg was shouting in Hobgoblin, but it only seemed to affect the two latecomers, who at least hesitated in their charge. Wellstone held up her blade but was unsure of her ability to defend. Meese pulled her with him when he stepped out of the path of his next spell. He gestured and flicked his hand. A small basket on top of the heap flew in an unnaturally straight line, directly into the Goblin's chest, exploding in a cloud of dried grass and separating him from his weapons as he flew backwards, the two shortswords dropping to the ground.

Dugg said, "Drop your weapons, you little traitors, and we'll let you live. Voorsh, let him surrender." Her first was beyond making choices, but her remaining opponent made the wisest one, dropping his weapons and placing his hands on top of his head. Wellstone thought he looked as if he had done this before.

Meese said, "We should tie these four up, they'll wake in a few seconds." He looked at Wellstone and said in a high pitched voice, "No Meese, you'll kill us all!"

Chapter Eighteen

Seastone Mine, the den

She didn't know why Murra called himself the Outcast, it could have been for any number of reasons. He was probably shunned for being a backbiting schemer. He was always one step ahead, watching and waiting. When the two sister-clans destroyed each other, Snurrl was there to scavenge the carcasses. Best meal she'd ever had. She was also there to take over and beat the survivors back into a clan-shaped mass under her skull-cracking, neck-biting leadership. She was Alpha for the days of one hand before Murra and his fat subordinate, Yug descended on them, in broad daylight no less, and slaughtered the little patched-together clan. It was an impressive display of strategy, attacking while they slept. Murra was a genius. He also felt no mercy or loyalty. Murra not only killed her clan, their thralls, and their precious animals, but also his own pet Ogre. Yug was getting a little long in the tooth—literally, he was in danger of gouging his own eyes out when something made him laugh, like an animal with broken legs or eating someone ass first. Murra let him finish his work before crippling him from behind and giving Snurrl and Growfra his old job. Tenderizing their master's meat. They began with Yug and had served loyally ever since. Growfra rarely complained, but Snurrl had gotten a taste of power and wasn't ready to give up the dream of a new clan. Lucky for them, Murra seemed to like the beasts and allowed the couple to keep a few cubs. He remained unaware of the danger living under his hideous nose. All she had to do was protect the animals, feed the right people to them, and her clan would rise again.

"My chieftain—" Maggot's voice cut off as her fist lifted him from his feet and sent him into a pile of furs where he was vigorously licked by a pair of beasts.

Snurrl growled, "No say that. He hear."

"Right, right. It won't happen again." The Goblin rolled to his feet and knelt before her. She hated the filthy little runt, not because of his uppity speech, but because she was brought so low as to have a thrall such as him. You had to start somewhere. She jokingly thought of him as Maggot the Outcast, though she knew why he was exiled. He was a killer of his own kind, not in fair scraps either. He killed his sisters and brothers while they slept to take what they had. He was kicked out except for an eye and several fingers, those being left behind in the biting, gouging, fracas that was a Goblin shunning. His missing ear was her doing.

"Report."

"Yes ma'am. There're four—that's this many." He held up the remaining three fingers from one hand and added one more.

She studied the display carefully. "Strange. Small group. Are you sure?"

"Four. Weapons but no armor except—"

"Easy hunt. Good." It was a bit before she planned, but the Hobgoblins and the Lizards didn't travel in small groups. Only a few of her beasts were ready to rise. She would have to hide her new sisters and brothers until more grew to full strength.

Maggot said, "You should know, they aren't Hob—" She hit him again, but open-handed. Practically a reward. It was almost a shame to infect her beloved animals with intelligence and ambition, those things not having served her well. It would be different this time. Some of the affection and loyalty of her hand-reared cubs would linger in her risen clan members. They would at least have the courtesy of biting her in the front.

. . . .

Eastern Jungle, Gnoll trap line

Pel was a bit worried about everyone's attitude. Gladlow could usually be trusted to take walking point seriously, but even he was distracted. She realized it was her fault, she had after all just blurted that she was scheming to sleep with him. It seemed to be worrying her more than him, though, she was glad to see. She knew her habits, she was just trying to break them for the first time in a long time. The familiar worry that he would lose interest made her want to do something to prevent it, but that fear was easily put to rest by meeting his eyes. She often saw as much desire in his look as from any man, maybe more than most, but he had many other looks for her. Often he was smiling like he had thought of something that would make her laugh, other times he just needed her to look his way to prove he himself hadn't been forgotten. The strange thing was that he most often looked content, like her being near was all he needed. She had brought up the beach to him, where he proposed this mission of collecting research and escaping the island. She thought he had included her as a kindness, and out of respect for her abilities. That he saw it as the right thing, even if it was awkward. After getting to know him better, she knew those things were true, but she was beginning to admit that he couldn't bear to be separated from her. Waiting was going to be harder than she thought.

"There's a mouth in the ground."

Carlin said, "Stop! Don't anyone move. Bustard, what did you say?"

Bustard landed on a low branch and looked at her in bewilderment.

"Bustard. Do you see a mouth on the ground?"

He looked at the ground a few feet in front of Pel and said in his baby voice, "Careful, he bites."

It took them a few moments to find what Bustard saw, the trap was so well hidden.

Gladlow used a twig to uncover enough to see how it was made. An iron-toothed jaw lay open on the ground, nearly three feet across. He said, "Godsdamnit Nowen, she almost walked right into it."

"I can only tell you the direction, not how far away it is." He did have the grace to look apologetically at Pel.

She said, "It's my fault. I was distracted." And she had been, she was embarrassed to admit. She was annoyed that Carlin was spending more time looking for flowers than dangers, Nowen was walking in a trance while he concentrated on his spell, and Gladlow... He was acting a bit overconfident, but otherwise alert. She was the one not paying attention. She said, "This is probably the far end of their loop. We should take the warning and go back."

Gladlow looked worried but put on a smile. "It was a close one, but everything's fine. We'll head back. If I see any more of those giant rodent things, I'm shooting a couple." He made the gesture for his hornet spell and waggled his eyebrows. They turned and headed towards the tower.

Carlin said, "That seems wrong somehow..." but she was smiling.

"It seems wrong to eat hardtack when delicious rats are scurrying around."

"Those aren't rats, they're called hutia, and they're too cute to eat."

Pel joined in with a smirk. "Nothing's too cute to eat."

Carlin said, "I thought I was tired of seafood, but now I wish we weren't so far from the beach."

Gladlow said, "I can eat seafood at home. Nowen, can you locate the nearest roasted duck?"

Nowen grunted.

"What's wrong? That was good work with the locator. I didn't mean to snap at you."

"That gave me a scare too, it's not that."

They walked in silence until he said, "I haven't made any progress on my research. We're out in the middle of nowhere, and I'd rather be at a cultural site. I'm not complaining, we're lucky to be alive. Blah, blah. Anyway, that's what's bothering me."

Pel said, "You're researching the Lizards, right? Voorsh has to be a goldmine."

Nowen rolled his eyes and shrugged.

Carlin said, "He's not studying the Uljar-Molik directly, though they are the largest clue he has to work with." She waited, knowing it would prompt him to speak.

Nowen said, "There have been several researchers to observe the tribe, but there are some things I've noticed from reading everyone else's papers. You heard it yourself when Voorsh said of her people, 'We have been here always.' She said the same of the Geth-Terna. When I spoke to her about it, she was being literal. Her people believe they have been here always."

Pel said, "Is that unusual for a people without written history? How far back can memories go?"

Nowen said, "Oral traditions can go back thousands of years. Always hundreds." Nowen was getting warmed up to his subject now. "Their unusual advancement, as compared to other known Lizard tribes, speaks to a long oral record, and they do have relatively sophisticated pictograms, also unusual for their kind. But their recorded, or remembered, history only reaches back a short while."

Gladlow asked, "Is it less than fifty years?"

Nowen actually looked pleased and smacked him on the back. "As far as I can tell, exactly fifty."

Carlin said, "I don't understand."

Gladlow said, "The Quakes. Corvin traced all of the falling rock back to this island. He estimated that this basin was created by the event. How could the Uljar-Molik have been here always and survived intact?"

Nowen added, "They have no concept of the event. No legends. Nothing. Voorsh remembers the names of everyone who's made a significant contribution to the tribe. Each invention and discovery, great warriors, explorers like herself, they all have at least a small story. It's part of her purpose but they only go back a few generations."

Carlin said, "That's what had you so agitated in the cave. You said there was nothing new."

Nowen said, "I grew frustrated. Every pictogram I translated, turned out to be a reference to something other researchers had already written about. I did eventually record a few that I believe were previously unknown. Nothing before the last ten years. The only purpose it served for me, was a rapid course in Uljar-Molik pictograms."

Gladlow asked, "Did Voorsh say there are other caves like that one? Other historical sites?"

"She did. Someday I'd like to examine them. She claims no one other than her tribe has ever been. But I fear I would only find the same stories going back five decades."

Carlin asked, "Have you discovered anything in the tower?"

Nowen looked embarrassed. "I haven't gotten past sorting—"

"You mean you've spent so much time helping me, that you haven't had time."

"Your work is more important right now, maybe even to our survival."

Pel looked wide-eyed at Gladlow behind their backs and he responded with a bewildered shrug.

Carlin said, "I'll be upstairs late tonight if you'd like some company. I should have plenty of time to help between batches."

"I'd like that very—"

"The dogs are coming." Everyone froze at the sound of Bustard's announcement. He had been circling above, but landed on a high branch.

Carlin asked, "Can you see the dogs?"

Bustard looked northeast and said, "I... can see."

Gladlow asked, "How many are there?"

"Nine."

"We're not actually talking about dogs, are we?"

Carlin said, "Well no. There's nothing like that recorded on the island—"

Gladlow asked, "How does Bustard know what a dog is?"

Pel asked, "Did Dugg say anything about these Gnolls raising pets?"

Gladlow realized first. "You mean—"

"We just crossed into their territory, and hyenas are incredible trackers. The Gnolls must have set them on us."

Nowen asked, "How did they know—"

"It doesn't matter now. If they were wild, we could scare them off, they're smart. But these will be trained not to back down."

Gladlow said, "We should climb a tree or something and pick them off—" He stopped to listen to strange sounds coming nearer.

Pel said, "Too late." She took his boar spear and handed him the Orc blade. "It will make you look more threatening, but I wouldn't hold back any spells for later."

Gladlow stepped in front of her and raised his fist. She didn't protest, she just prepared to step around him after his spell went off. They only had to wait seconds before the front of the pack burst through the trees. More rushed in behind, and there was no circling or other strategy to the first wave. They charged straight into a blast of sound and air. A handful were sent back tumbling, and most didn't get up. Two made it through, one charging directly into Pel's spear, the other snapping at Carlin and receiving a mace blow across the muzzle. Nowen sunk his foot-long blade into its neck. At least a dozen others cowered at the sudden clap of thunder, giggling in distress, but rallied quickly. They reverted to their natural tactics and began circling in smaller groups, ready to wear their prey down.

Nowen said, "Let me take the next group that charges."

"On my mark," Pel called out, "turn your backs to that group of five. They'll rush us. Now."

They all turned to face the other groups circling and just as she predicted, the group charged their backs only to fall to the ground, asleep. Pel screamed and dispatched one, shaking her spear in the air. She said, "That trick won't work twice. Put on a show and it might make them hesitate next time. Look them in the eyes."

Gladlow's deep voice roared out across the jungle as he brought the sword down. Carlin squealed in disgust as she swung her mace. Nowen pointed menacingly at the remaining animals and left the killing to his companions. Whooping sounds echoed back and forth as the remaining eight gathered to one side and kept their distance. Carlin dropped the mace through her belt loop and readied her bow.

Pel said, "Ready yourselves to attack on my—" Her speech turned into a scream as she saw Gladlow hit high between the shoulder blades with a giant wooden mallet made from a cross-section of a foot-thick tree. He fell to the ground like a discarded rag-doll. The Gnoll masters had arrived and their pets had kept the prey distracted while they attacked from behind. The second wooden hammer struck Carlin as she turned. Jeme's breastplate took the blow dead center and she was thrown from her feet. Pel charged and ducked a wild swing to thrust the boar-spear deep into the Gnoll's midsection. Its hyena face topped a lanky body over seven feet tall, and it was raging and giggling through drool-soaked lips. It tried to dislodge her with a backhand, but she didn't feel the blow. It reared back to bite, but it turned into a howl as she ducked and twisted the spear, coming up under the shaft and lifting with every ounce of her strength. She felt the oversized shaft flex as the monster was lifted to its toes, but its flesh gave out first and parted before the spear's iron blade. It flopped backward and curled around the killing wound. The hyenas charged, but eight became four as they passed those suddenly slumbering under Nowen's second spell. Gladlow was, impossibly, getting to his feet, but the hammer was being raised for a second blow when an arrow stuck in the Gnoll's hide. It brushed it away in annoyance and resumed its attack. Pel was running, but wouldn't make it in time. The Gnoll raised the hammer high, but it didn't come down. Its back arched further and it fell to the ground, completely immobile but for its spasming muscles. Nowen went down under a charging beast, with another hyena leaping at each of his companions. Gladlow lobbed a bubble of acid into the face of his adversary. Pel's hyena died on her spear, while Carlin was bowled over just as she fired an arrow. Gladlow's opponent locked onto his arm with a sickening crunch before a red hornet impacted the beast from behind and it dropped, dragging Gladlow with it. Nowen sat up trying to push a dead hyena off his legs and withdraw his dagger from its throat, while Carlin joined Pel in prying dead jaws from Gladlow's arm. When they were all on their feet, Gladlow asked, "What about them?" indicating the four sleeping beasts. "Will they attack?"

Pel said, "With their masters dead, I think they'll avoid us."

"Understood." He took the spear, his left arm clamped to his side and dispatched the Gnoll paralyzed on the ground. He checked the other, but it had died at the end of a trail of gore.

Pel went over their injuries, and it looked like she was the only one unscathed. Carlin's face was bloody, but it was only from being struck by a beast's skull. Nowen's yellow robe was turning red where teeth had sunken into his hip, and Gladlow's arm was a mess. She looked at his back and neck and could see where the hammer impacted. How he was still conscious was a mystery to her. She put a shoulder under his good arm and led the group away from the beasts before they woke.

Gladlow mumbled, "We should hide the bodies..." and started to turn around.

Pel said, "Trust me, their pack mates will clean up."

"If Murra flies over, he'll see—"

Pel said, "You're not thinking clearly, which is a relief. I was beginning to think you were indestructible."

"What?" Gladlow's feet were starting to drag.

"I've seen a blow like that kill. How do you feel?"

"Tenderized." He chuckled stupidly.

"Alright, one foot in front of the other, big man."

Carlin propped him up from the other side, and they stumbled along together.

"My arm hurts."

"I know it does." Pel patted his back.

Carlin said, "It will take two hours to make the first batch of blue aster."

Pel asked, "How sure are you that it even works? Should we test it?"

"I've already tested the components for toxicity. I ate some. Most plants in the aster family are edible anyway, and the few medicines wouldn't be dangerous in these amounts. But I'll take the first draught to study its effects. I've got some herbs that will lessen his danger while we wait—"

Pel asked, "Is it true he shouldn't sleep?"

"It's best not to risk it. At the very least it will be easier to observe his condition if we keep him awake."

Gladlow said, "I know how you ladies can keep me up tonight..."

"Gladlow!"

"Traveler!" he shouted. "Or you can lay bets on a wizard duel. What do you say Nowen? Can you beat me now that I have a brain commotion?"

"How would I know the difference? I usually win."

Pel asked, "An actual duel?"

Gladlow said, "A test of luck and daring..."

Nowen said, "It's an illusion game. Dice and chits are used to simulate attacks on an illusionary champion." He seemed to be regretting the explanation. "It's a childish pastime for students."

"Nowen won a trophy. That's how we met."

"I was stripped of my title for unsportsmanlike behavior," Nowen said hopefully, in an apparent effort to make it sound more lowbrow.

Gladlow snickered. "We cheated. A lot."

Pel was smiling when she asked, "You cheated at a children's game?"

"It's no longer a game when you're making money. It's work."

Carlin asked, "You cheated at work?"

"You wish you'd thought of it."

• • • •

Eastern Plateau, watchtower

Carlin sat on the arm of Gladlow's chair and waved his own lighted ring in his face. She said, "I don't like this. One pupil is larger than the other."

Pel said, "It's been like that since the signal tower ambush. That magic of his bunged it up. If you look closely, you can see yellow streaks in the brown."

"Huh. I hadn't gazed deeply enough to notice." She grinned at Pel who looked embarrassed. "Gladlow. Is your vision blurred? Are you having trouble staying awake?"

"My left eye is a little sensitive to light now, but it's no different than yesterday. I am having trouble staying awake, but I think it's regular exhaustion."

Pel said, "He starts to drop off unless he's talking." She smirked. "He'll be fine till morning."

Gladlow was mock offended. "You *asked* about Bugbear courtship rituals... didn't you?"

Carlin asked, "Nausea? Headache?"

"Ask me about my arm."

"How's—"

"It shitting hurts, Carlin. It's sweet of you to ask."

She said, "Alright. I suppose it's time. I didn't feel any negative effects. In fact, it's very pleasant." She poured a blue liquid from a repurposed potion vial into a cup of wine. "It's bitter."

Gladlow took a skeptical sip. "That's... good. The wine was too sweet anyway." He downed the rest of the cup and stared at his bandaged arm. "I don't feel anything."

"It's not a magic potion—I mean, it is, but it's more..." She shrugged.

"Intrinsic magic."

She sat next to Pel on the couch and put her chin in her hand. Pel took a similar pose, but couldn't keep a straight face.

He said, "I know what you're doing. You act all interested now, just so you can make fun of me later for being a know-it-all."

Carlin said, "If you were explaining natural processes to me, I'd be insulted. This is new. You can be the magic expert."

Gladlow narrowed his eyes at Pel and she said, "There's no way I'll stay awake through this, but I'm not the one with a concussion."

"Fine. What do you want me to talk about?"

Carlin said, "Give me the theories on intrinsic magic."

"Alright. It's tied to a theory of all magic, so bear with me." He paused to think, but Carlin could tell they had managed to embarrass him. She rarely saw him unsure of himself, and it made him seem young. He overcame it quickly with the prospect of a good lecture. He gently rubbed his hands together, an affectation he himself mocked from time to time. "Imagine magic as a tapestry woven of musical strings, infinitely big and complex. Every movement of every living thing causes strings to vibrate, every object at rest serves to dampen them. Everything in existence connected to this tapestry of strings. By definition, there is an order to it, though we experience it as cacophony, as utter chaos. However, if you touch a particular substance, move your hand in a precise way, and speak the right words, certain strings are lifted from the tapestry to strum a chord. This is a spell. An infinity of combinations means infinite possible spells. This is the prevailing Elven theory of magic." He tapped a finger to his lips for a moment in thought. "When I cast the alchemical spell, by concentrating I can hold a sphere in stasis, as if waiting to strum the cord. Through ritual, I can cast the same spell as I write it onto a scroll. The words hold it in place until it is read by another mage, using no power of his own. A spell is woven into the brewing process of a healing potion. Intrinsic magic is different. Everything has a little, that part that connects it to the strings, but a powerful being, such as a deity, possibly even a powerful enough mage, can make further connections so that a single substance or plant strums a chord on its own. Jeme made a flower so intrinsically linked that no further effort is needed. Whatever the substance it makes, the brewing process is likely just to extract it efficiently. You might improve the process, or even breed the plants to make more or less."

Carlin nodded. "I've already thought of an angle for my research. The draughts don't keep for long. Jeme's clergy was meant to brew it as needed with lots of ritual and pomp. I'm going to find a way to preserve it. The wine is my first attempt." She leaned forward to look at Gladlow. "How are you feeling now?"

He seemed surprised. "I feel good. Normal, but relaxed. Like that perfect amount of drunk that you try to maintain, but that only lasts for a short while." He flexed his hand. "It hurts like four hells, but I don't mind so much."

"I'm thinking of calling it Jeme's Recovery, or just a recovery potion. That's what it does, greatly reinforce your body's natural recovery as you rest. I plan to write a paper for your Institute... would you look over it for me?" When he nodded dazedly, she patted him and said, "You should be fine to sleep, you're out of danger."

Pel helped him to his feet, with only a little wobble, and took him to bed. Those little moments were what Carlin was envious of. She adored Gladlow, but didn't want him, or not more than a little. She felt similarly about Pel. If they had been acting like a typical new couple, she would probably feel less jealous. All of the hand-holding and whispering made her feel more lonely than any fooling around would. She could only brew two draughts at a time currently, and the next one would go to Nowen. Maybe under the guise of caretaking, she could entice him to cuddle while keeping his hands to himself.

Two hours later Nowen sat reading while the blue aster did its work. She began another batch and looked from the arrow slit her work table had been moved to. It was dusk and the others had yet to return. She didn't think she could sleep but awoke to Nowen gently shaking her shoulder. She had drifted off with her head on his lap, but he didn't wake her until the candle had burned down. He massaged the feeling back into his leg while she poured the batch to cool. The Chief and the others still hadn't arrived. She conferred with Pel and was forced to agree that a search party would have to wait until dawn. All she could do was brew a final batch. That would leave five draughts. She had gathered enough root cuttings to start a garden plot of the blue flowers but had been careful to leave enough plants to live wild where she found them. She decided right then to map every location they were found. She would disseminate their use widely, but keep the map to herself, and encourage growing them rather than foraging. Nowen fell asleep with notebooks in his lap, so she sat and watched the candle burn.

"Pretty-pretty is coming." Bustard's announcements had begun to send a chill down her spine, but this one hardly seemed threatening. She could see nothing from any of the arrow slits, so she went downstairs to wake the others. With a grinding sound, the front door swung open.

Meese said, "We thought we'd just pop round to—"

"Wine now, jokes later." Wellstone pushed past him and began stripping her top. She lay face down on a bunk and pointed a thumb at her bloody shoulder. Carlin grabbed up the bag on her bunk.

Meese walked across the room until the floating bundle of wicker baskets and crates passed through the door. He signaled to Dugg to close it, and the bundle crashed to the ground as he released the spell. Bustard flapped over to Voorsh but thought better of landing on her. He settled on a chair back closest to her. So that's who pretty-pretty was. Carlin had long since stopped marveling at the Lizard's strangeness and begun admiring her fellow researcher's ability and character, but she had to admit Bustard was certainly observant. Pretty-pretty indeed.

Dugg had already retrieved a cask of wine, struggling the short way up the ladder with it on his shoulder. He dropped it heavily on the table and said, "I would like to propose a toast—"

Meese said, "You should pour the wine first."

"—to the completion of an honorable bargain and to the health of the—"

"It doesn't feel right to not be holding a glass."

"—and... Curse it. Where are the cups? I was going to say, honorable bargainers."

Gladlow had roused himself when he felt Pel spring out of bed. "Which bargain was that? What's happened to Helena?"

Dugg asked, "Who the shit is Helena?"

Wellstone said, "Don't get your back up, big man—"

Meese said, "Before you get mad at us, let's have a glass of wine, and we'll explain—"

Voorsh said, "The Gollins have been removed from the armory."

"Who is Helena?" Dugg asked as he poured wine across the cups and table. Bustard landed to drink a puddle. "Does anyone know if lizard-birds can have wine?"

"You did what? Are you going to explain how that's not stupid?" Gladlow crossed his arms and glared at Meese. "You're the only one I'm mad at."

Meese narrowed his eyes. "What happened to your arm—"

"Don't change the subject—"

Bustard said, "The dog bit Gladlow."

Meese asked, "What dog? Are you alright?"

"It'll be fine in a couple of days. We were talking about—"

"The tall dog hit Gladlow's meat."

Dugg said, "Tall dog. You were attacked by the Gnolls?"

Meese yelled, "The Gnolls? Is everyone safe?"

Gladlow relented. "Yes. We were ambushed, but we made it out."

"You're sure you're not injured, lad?"

"I'm fine—"

"What's wrong with your leg?"

"There's nothing—"

Meese kicked him in the shin and when Gladlow bent over in pain, pulled him down by the hair and slapped his face.

Gladlow shook him off. "Stop it, you moron."

"You were going to lecture me about taking a risk—"

"We were ambushed! Were you?"

They stood and glared at each other. They didn't break eye contact as Dugg handed cups around. He asked quietly, "What was the... final result of your... interaction with the Gnolls? I only ask for toast purposes."

· · · ·

Eastern Plateau, sandstone bluffs

"I'm telling you, I haven't been inside the mine for a while—"

Gladlow said, "You told us about the Gnolls and their trapline, how could you not know they had a godsdamned pack of hyenas?"

Dugg waved his arms around in obvious frustration. Gladlow had been raking him over the coals for the entire trip to the overlook that spied on the mine. "I didn't know it was a pack—"

"Clan," Carlin interjected helpfully.

"I didn't know it was a clan. I heard they had some pups—"

"Cubs." Carlin raised her hands in defense against the looks they threw at her.

Gladlow took a breath and tried to make his point again. "The information you gave us was worse than useless, it almost got us killed—"

Dugg said, "Who told you to go after them?"

"We didn't go after them, Dugg. They came after us. We were checking the trapline you told us about. Their big weakness, you said. The plan was to—shut up Dugg. The plan was to wait until Murra left, take out the Gnolls, and lay a trap for him. I'm asking you, will Murra leave if the Gnolls aren't there to watch over the mine?"

Dugg made a hissing sound with his teeth as he thought. "Maybe. The Gnolls weren't allowed to be near the miners. They were just kitchen staff, you know? Catch the meat, age the meat, pound the meat on a big flat rock." He scratched behind his ear and said, "He won't notice anything for a couple of days. They had to have been taking those beasts out at night sometimes, right? Yes. I think even if they don't come back soon, he'll keep to his habits. He has plenty of meat for a week, but he'll be annoyed at having to do anything himself."

Gladlow asked, "Will he look for them?"

"It's hard to say. He's a lazy beast. Is it more work to look for his servants or to go without?"

Pel said, "We should do what we can to obscure the ambush. As you said last night, he may fly over. If there's nothing to see from the air, maybe he won't look closely."

Gladlow said, "That's a good plan... but I think we should cut our losses. Dugg, you said yourself, you haven't been in the mine in some time. Who's to say your other information is any better?"

"I say. I give you my word. I have nothing to gain by lying to you."

Funnily enough, Gladlow knew he was the person in the group most likely to trust a Hob's word. He didn't think Dugg tried to get them killed, he thought Dugg was an arrogant little prick and half an idiot, like most kids his age. Gladlow reopened negotiations by glaring.

Dugg said, "Listen, I helped with the Goblins, didn't I?" He looked at Meese, who shrugged.

"He fought very little," Voorsh said, "he did yell at Gollins. It helped."

"See there? Leadership is more my trade, but I put my neck in the noose right there with you."

Gladlow said, "Intimidating Goblins was useful. That time. As you said, it was an honorable bargain. Now we've eliminated another of your problems, and I have nothing to show for it but this." He held up his left forearm, which he had left unbandaged. The punctures were closed over with pink flesh, and the bone was straight, but it was an alarming sight to see the swollen red bite highlighted in black bruising.

Dugg said placatingly, "It's all part of the same deal, but you're right. You're ahead on your part. Listen, get rid of the manticore, and I'll start the mine operating at double shifts. The cove will practically be cleared out. If I keep my requests reasonable, my allies in council will back me. You'll have the run of the place until the *Frenzy* returns."

"We keep everything the manticore has taken." This was spoken by Wellstone as she returned from the overlook trail. At Gladlow's look, she said, "Buying passage on a ship is going to cost." He had trouble believing she was talking about making a deal with pirates, but he decided to leave that discussion for private.

Dugg said, "How does that serve me? It does me no good if I don't return the ore."

Gladlow said, "It defeats the purpose of entering Ningolohk if we can't buy a way home."

"I'll give you... a tankard of polished seastone. Barter quality. And you keep everything you find but the ore and mining tools."

"And you get us out of the cove, in the way of our choosing, with our possessions." Gladlow added something in Hob that made Dugg hesitate, but he used a fang to open a small cut on his thumb. Gladlow signaled at Pel and she passed her bronze blade. He jabbed himself lightly and pushed a large drop of blood to the surface. The two reached out their hands, each smearing a thumbprint on the other's hand. Dugg said something in response and they gave a single lick to their palms.

Meese mumbled, "That doesn't seem sanitary."

Gladlow said, "No, but it's binding. Whatever else happens, Dugg has my trust. Wellstone? Did you find it?"

She said, "Dispatched. I did the poor twisted thing a kindness."

Carlin asked, "What are we talking about?"

"The Goblin that's been following you. It was Gladlow's idea to have Bustard look for someone on your trail."

Bustard said, "Nasty-boy watching."

Pel said, "That's how the Gnolls knew to send their pets."

Gladlow asked Dugg, "Do you think it was the Gnolls, or Murra who had us watched?"

Dugg thought about it and said, "I don't know. Snurrl could only speak a few words of common, and Growfra made her look like a genius..."

Pel said, "Training slaves and animals is their specialty."

"True. I don't think it was Murra anyway. If he thought of something like that, he'd make a Hob do it and eat the Goblin."

Gladlow said, "So we keep to the plan unless Murra doesn't leave."

Wellstone said, "He's asleep, sunning his belly. It would be cute if it wasn't so nightmarishly grotesque."

They made their way to the trapline, and just as Pel said, the survivors had feasted on the fallen. The four must have gorged themselves, as a surprising portion of the carcasses were gone. Interestingly, the hyenas didn't appear to have disturbed their kin, though plenty of smaller scavengers had. What remained of the Gnoll's bodies were lighter, and the group settled for dragging them under particularly dense canopy to hide them from the sky. They carefully explored the trapline, deactivating the mechanisms and cutting the lines. Lastly, they found a smallish pig in a snare and dressed it for the return to the tower. Voorsh carried the pieces of several traps intending to learn their use.

Gladlow decided it was a good time to broach a subject with her. He waved Dugg over as well. "Voorsh, what are your plans if we get through the Witch Gate?"

She gazed at him blankly, not answering right away.

"You're welcome to join us, of course. I know everyone would miss you terribly, but we'll understand if you want to take what you've learned back to Uljar-Molik."

She said, "Yes. This is the thing that pulls me away. However, I wish to stay with you."

"Dugg, is it possible? Your two clans have a lot of blood behind them..."

He said, "It would draw a lot of attention, but that'll happen anyway. Come to think of it, she might not be the biggest problem. Voorsh, and don't take this wrong, but would you be willing to pretend to be... from elsewhere?"

She said, "Explain."

Gladlow said, "He means it would cause less trouble for us if everyone thought you were from a different tribe. We don't want to offend you..."

"If others believe I am not Uljar-Molik, they will not fear retaliation for slights against us."

"That's exactly it. Dugg, how likely is that to work?"

"It's a guarantee. We can't hide the fact she's a Lizard, which may or may not cause problems, but lose the feathers and give her a single thread of clothing and everyone will believe she's from elsewhere. Besides, she speaks better than any sailor. No one has seen that before."

Voorsh said, "I do speak very well. However, I do not wish to be from another tribe."

Wellstone spoke up. "Voorsh, I couldn't help but overhear. I'd be happy to teach you everything I know about the art of disguise."

"What is this?"

"Hiding who you are by being someone you're not."

Gladlow couldn't help but smile. Of course, Wellstone would know how to convince her. Not only was Voorsh unable to resist learning something new, she was honor bound.

Voorsh asked, "Lying is a skill I do not have. Are you good at this?"

Wellstone said, "Lying? Not at all."

"That was convincing. I accept."

It would take two more days for Murra the Outcast to leave. The group began their wait by drinking a good deal of the wine and working on their own projects. Meese had brought back a selection of arms and armor, as well as what few supplies were left unmolested by the Goblins. He seemed determined to accomplish nothing. Wellstone and Voorsh spent their time working on the bits of leather armor, combining Goblin and Hob to make a complete set sized for Wellstone, while Voorsh modified the leather strip skirt favored by the Hobs, adding bracers and greaves for arms and legs. After some discussion, Pel decided to forgo mundane armor in favor of the spell, only adding a compact shield. She tried to explain she felt comfortable with a blade, but a bit panicked when encumbered by even the lightest armor. Wellstone seemed to have some insight Gladlow lacked, asking if Pel's people dueled without armor, to which she replied in the positive. Gladlow could see she felt it was a selfish choice but reassured her that he could spare the casting. He stowed his questions away for the time being. He had identified a narrow range of subjects guaranteed to upset her and was content to let her come to them in her own time. Carlin dove into the research left behind in the tower, identifying subjects that might be of interest to herself or Voorsh. She also struggled to find assistance with her hair. She was able to maintain it herself with some difficulty, switching between her family's traditional knots spaced evenly across her scalp to the springy ringlets that resulted from releasing them. Pel was eager to help, but her experience with hair consisted of periodically hacking hers off, possibly leaving just enough to braid out of the way, first when wearing a helmet, later while diving. Gladlow had pity witnessing the massacre and gave Carlin advice on broaching the subject with their Elvish friend. He explained that Elves maintained traditional hairstyles as well, but could be sensitive about touching other's hair as it was seen by some as beneath them. Nowen in particular might balk at the suggestion as he specifically would a request to trim one's hedges. She ignored Gladlow's advice and ruthlessly bullied Nowen into it.

Dugg stayed in the tower that night but would be away in the morning to recruit some trusted companions to establish themselves at the armory and prepare to take over as guardians of the mine when Murra vacated.

Gladlow said, "Don't take any risks on who you tell about our plans. No Goblins."

Dugg nodded sheepishly. "I've learned my lesson. I'm turning the armory over to my most loyal friends, and even they won't know anything more. These are people that will crew if I take a ship, or back me if I move on my enemies."

Meese asked, "We haven't just armed you for a coup, have we?"

"The only way for me to take Ningolohk is to not disappoint my father. And to want it in the first place. I'd rather sail one of our trade ships one day. Maybe even the one in the shipyards now. It has no name and no captain."

Gladlow asked, "I've witnessed some Hob construction, and was impressed by it, but I've never heard of Hobs building ships."

Dugg said, "Lenogg paid a fortune to a Human shipwright to train a few of our people. It's slow going, and expensive, but it will be ours."

Meese said, "Before you go, lad... would you mind explaining this?" He held out one of the small gourd flasks they had recovered from the sunken ship. "Your people have many things you excel at, but distilling liquor isn't one of them."

Dugg unstoppered one and made a face when he smelled it. He dipped his small finger in the hole and pressed it to his tongue. "Where did you get this? My ah-shah is the only person who knows how to make it."

Gladlow said, "We recovered it from the *Rampage*. The papers and maps were destroyed."

Dugg said, "I've only tried it once in training, and I thought my heart would explode."

Meese asked, "You drank that on purpose? It smells like a urinal trough."

Dugg said, "It's not something you mix with fruit juice and share with your bedmate. This is Hob posca. All but the *Frenzy* boarding crew are forbidden to have it."

Gladlow asked, "Boarding crew? It's not liquor is it?"

"It's a potion that makes you a bit stronger, a bit faster, and a lot tougher. You'll feel ready to drop afterward, so don't drink it when you're already tired. How many of these did you find? The Human crews will pay out the ears for it... I could find a buyer—"

Meese took it back and resealed it. "I think we'll hang on to it. Never know when we might need to sweeten a barter."

They sent Dugg off with a round of Traveler, which the young Hob had taken a strong liking to. Meese with his fellow mages, Nowen providing visual illusions, Gladlow providing sounds, told a legend of a misfit band that saved the world in an earlier age. Wellstone told one of her stupid criminal tales, stories that always pleased and of which she had an inexhaustible supply.

Carlin began shyly, "I'm writing a paper for the Institute on the blue aster, but I've never done any formal writing, just my journals. So I was thinking, I should practice, right? So for my turn, I'll be sharing what I have so far. It's called *Where are the Gold Urchins?* So far it's not so much my writing as gathering notes from both Institute and Crown researchers and filling in—"

Gladlow said, "Carlin, I think we'd all love to hear it."

She read directly from her journal. "The Antylia urchin is, so far, unique to the Antylia Archipelago. The Magical Research and Preservation Institute is responsible for the civilized world's awareness of its existence and value. Before the Crown interdiction on harvesting by anyone other than official Crown vessels, thereby curbing its study, the Institute had determined that these creatures' ability to aggregate valuable metals wasn't due to any known alchemical process. More likely the substances are filtered from the sea water or from the urchin's constant grazing. The renowned explorer Corvin put forward the theory that the urchin's choice of metal is made sometime after its birth, likely determined by the spot the larvae chooses to attach and turn itself inside out. The Institute's research shows that regardless of their differences, they are all of the same species." She looked around to make sure she wasn't boring the room and Gladlow gave her an encouraging nod. "Where are the gold urchins? Rumors and conspiracy theories abound in the port taverns and ship mess halls. Platinum is more rare, yet these are known to exist. The Crown is a favorite culprit, with many stories alluding to success with breeding them in captivity or else hunting them to extinction. The Institute's most recent theory is that they do exist but die young. Gold is much too soft to support the lantern shaped mouth structure, causing the young urchin to starve. A small number of Institute scholars also believe the urchins were created by magical means, possibly by an ancient undersea race, and not entirely successfully. Both theories are supported by the black urchin's somewhat compromised health. Pure silver would also be too soft to support a larger lantern, but the corrosion and the urchin's physical overgrowth in response are able to strengthen it sufficiently to survive. That's all I have so far."

Gladlow lifted her in a bear hug and kissed her cheek. "Well done, Carlin. It sounded just like one of Instructor Darach's Encyclopedia entries. That's a compliment, by the way."

Dugg fell asleep on the couch, a testament to his trust in the group, as well as their trust in letting him be. Pel took Gladlow's hand and led him to the ladder, and then onto the roof. She sat him down across from her and began to speak. She explained she had told this to the other women in the tub, and had wished ever since that he had been there as well. It had the lilt of a retelling, nearly emotionless, and he suspected it was word for word the same so as not to provoke more reliving of it than necessary.

After a moment, she continued, "I'm just starting to understand how angry I was. I punished my parents and I punished myself. I especially punished the enemies they pointed me at. I realized fighting made it worse. It was like it kept a wound from healing. I hated myself, and I hated them too. So I stopped, but without the army, I was lost. I could never seem to make friends or trust anyone. I was so afraid to talk about where I came from, I barely spoke at all. A few years ago, cracks started to show. I cried a lot, but I began talking to people more. Eventually, I would become desperately lonely and try to make a friend... or sleep with a man. The friend never seemed to stay, and I couldn't bear to look at the man the next day. Sometimes I felt I had to leave because I slept with someone, other times I would sleep with someone so I would have to leave." At that moment she showed worry for the first time, she hurried to add, "It wasn't so many... never more than once at any job or town—"

"Pel, that doesn't matter. I've slept with a few women, never for a better reason than being lonely. I'm sorry you've been so unhappy for so long. If I can do anything to help—"

"I'm happy right now, Gladlow." She hugged him fiercely. "The rules of Traveler say you can ask a couple of questions..."

"I have a lifetime of questions for you. Do you really want any of them now?"

She put on a brave face and nodded. He knew he still should tread lightly, but wanted to encourage her desire to talk. "Would you tell me what happened to your parents? You mostly speak of them fondly, but you seem to feel you didn't leave things well..."

She nodded again and said, "They're both gone now. My mother died on her last campaign. Not long after that, my father was killed in an unsanctioned duel. That was how they officially recorded his drunken bar fight. He had lost his edge sometime before, as he put it, he could no longer lead from the front. My mother carried on without him and died doing her duty. He couldn't carry on without her. I hadn't spoken to either of them in two years. They were ashamed of me for leaving but would send someone round to retrieve me whenever their men heard where I was. As much as it angered me, I would have been crushed if they had stopped trying." She grabbed his hand. "Last question."

"Would you go diving with me?"

"What?"

"That's what I've been thinking about when we talk of getting off the island. There's a port town called Young with reefs nearby. Less dangerous, more inns. Imagine spending the whole day underwater, no Tesco's..."

"Then a bath, food, drinks, and a big soft bed... I've never heard anything so wonderful." Her smile faded though. "Just you and me?"

"Just for a little while. Then we'll catch up to whoever you want. Are you afraid of everyone splitting up?"

"Yes. I know it's horrible, but I'm less afraid someone will be killed than I am they'll leave."

"I feel a change coming too. Everyone will have important things to take care of when we get back, but for the first time, I doubt Meese is going to follow me."

"Is it Wellstone?"

"I think so, but not like you and me. I've heard them making plans, but he makes a joke, and she makes a joke, and the conversation ends because they were both just joking... Whatever it is, they agree. I heard them talking about capital the other day, I think they might be going into business together..." He shrugged.

"That's actually very sweet."

"In some ways, their folk take a business partnership more seriously than marriage. Really, a wedding could be seen as a minor sort of business deal to them."

"And the others?"

"I don't know, but whatever happens, we won't let everyone just drift away."

Pel nodded but looked pensive. After a moment she said, "This thing we're doing... why are you doing it?"

He knew what she was asking, Meese had done the same. "You're asking if I want off the island more than I want to find the expedition."

She shrugged. "Everyone else wants out, maybe at any cost. I know you need to find out what happened to your people..."

"Pel, I wouldn't pass up a chance to get home even if I never learned the truth. The difference is that I think they might be one and the same. I think Ningolohk is the next step."

"Well, I don't care what we have to do, as long as we're all together."

Chapter Nineteen

Ningolohk Outer Territory, seastone mine

Meese scratched his armpit vigorously. The mine's old tool room smelled strangely of rotting leaves with a hint of decomposing corpse, probably from one or more of the decomposing corpses hanging in the mine entrance. Worse than the smell was the multitude of fleas infesting the piles of partially processed furs the Gnolls had bedded down on. Meese had voted for waiting down the small tunnel leading deeper into the mine. It was too small for a manticore, but it was also in use by the miners and they were trying to disrupt the mine's operation as little as possible. Dugg had warned the miners of the group's presence, but not their purpose, hoping that Murra would see the miners, if not hard at work, at least present and acting unsuspiciously. The whole group had been struck by the strangeness of Hobs, and even Goblins, dressed in work clothes and carrying bags and baskets instead of swords and spears. Instead of the mine proper, the group hid in the tool room at the front of the mine. As they suspected, the Gnolls hadn't let anyone near their kennel, and the taboo seemed to hold even with their absence. The door opened, Pel and Gladlow entered, propping their giant wooden hammers next to the door.

Gladlow said, "That might be the worst thing I've ever done." Pel shrugged.

Carlin asked, "Was it necessary?" while looking at their gore-splattered clothes.

"We spent too much time in his lair to go unnoticed. We're hoping the—" Gladlow paused to swallow bile.

Pel suggested helpfully, "tenderized meat..."

"—would mask our scent for a few moments when he arrives."

Meese said, "Well, I think it's time for one last outing—"

"No, we can't risk it. He might come back any second or another six hours—"

"I'll just pop down the mine then—"

"No more wandering about. The shift is changing, none of the new Hobs and Gobs have seen us, and we can't risk an incident. We need everyone acting normally—"

"Fine, I understand. Settle down."

Gladlow said, "Trust me, this is a stay at the Neru Pelati compared to where Wellstone and Voorsh are hidden." He saw Carlin's curious look. "Under stinking furs near the dinner we just laid out." He smelled his shirt in disgust. "I think—Meese, what in the hells are you doing?"

"I'm pissing in the corner."

"Even the godsdamned hyenas were housebroken—"

"Hush now, Murra might come back any moment..."

Carlin said, "Now I need to. I can't go if anyone is looking."

Pel looked at Gladlow. "I could go."

He said, "Ugh...me too."

The group managed to stay quiet for almost an hour before Meese started a fight, a very quiet one, with Nowen by testing what level of sound or proximity of finger might disturb the meditating mage. Three hours later, Gladlow had long since been forbidden to speak and was trying to communicate with signs while Meese pretended not to understand. When the manticore arrived, Meese was comically shrugging and shaking his head while the ladies stifled laughter. Even through the hardwood door, the roar of surprise and rage was deafening. They only stared at each other for a split second before piling through the door exactly as planned.

Gladlow yelled, "Call out!" as he and Nowen ran across the wide hall to the entrance of Murra's bedroom. The ripening corpses of Hobs and Lizards stood out from the hanging deer and pig partially obscuring the tunnel.

Through the roars, Wellstone screamed, "Attack!"

Meese pushed in between Carlin and Pel, both with shields raised, who in turn pressed close behind the two mages in front. Both released their hornet spells at first sight of the beast, there being no chance of hitting an ally, then ducking to either side, joining Wellstone and Voorsh behind a bit of cover. The two shield maidens stood closer to the middle, with only their legs hidden. Meese stepped into the open as he cast his spell, chosen and argued over at length for its reduced likelihood of setting the giant nest ablaze. He managed to maintain focus and hold the spell while getting his first view of the monstrosity called manticore. Seeing paintings of lions let him recognize the twelve-foot-long body with one massive forepaw clamped in the oversized bear trap. The beast had climbed down the widened air shaft to step directly on it, apparently rolling away from the pain and catching a giant batwing in the second trap. Paintings and etchings didn't portray the utter madness of the partially Human face above the massive jaws. It stumbled forward to the end of the chains, the one binding its foot pulled tight against the iron spike driven into the limestone, the other pulling its wing painfully by the weight of the sprung trap.

Murra the Outcast said, "You will take... *nine* days to die." His voice was shocking, as sonorous as his breath was malodorous. Meese thought he might have frozen in terror if not for the beast's words. He was certain the horrid thing didn't know a number higher than nine. He grinned and pointed his finger at the beast. A thin beam of blue, flickering light struck the manticore in the face, for a split second drawing a zig-zag line as the beast lurched backward in pain. The beam scorched the wall as Murra threw himself back and forth against the chain. It would never hold if he got a few more feet to move. Meese adjusted his aim to target the area where the trapped leg connected to the body. The relatively motionless spot took the full force of the spell, opening a blackened hole in his hide.

Wellstone shouted, "Fire!" as she released an arrow. It struck true, while three javelins were launched by Carlin, Pel, and Voorsh, to varying success. No one had realized Murra might not bring his tail to bear instantly, but apparently, his instincts were to charge when his feet were on the ground. The volley of shafts, however, reminded him of his long-range abilities. He spun to the side, his weighted tail swinging round, and released a volley of his own. One spike stuck dead center in Pel's shield, while the other two went high, bouncing off the doorway or sailing through it. Meese thought the manticore might be too close to aim effectively, but turning gave him the room he needed to throw his weight against the chain. His paw was torn bloody, but the iron spike ripped free of the rock. Murra was suddenly six feet closer before the second chain pulled taught, stretching his wing back awkwardly.

Nowen said, "Should I—"

"No," Gladlow said, "it won't work. Same again," and threw a sphere of mercury powder as Nowen sent his projectile of glowing red. The hornet caused the furred flesh to ripple where it impacted, but the sphere struck with an earsplitting crack and opened a wound in the manticore's flank. Murra's rage increased and his wing began to tear. Soon he would break loose no matter the damage, and Meese realized with horror, it would effectively remove his ability to fly away.

Gladlow seemed to realize the same thing as the next volley of javelins and arrows struck. He said, "Pull back," and with just a few steps, the doorway was blocked by a small mass of shields and spears with just enough space for one person in the middle. Just as their ranks closed three of the manticore's spikes drove right into their midst. None hit Meese, but before he could check anyone else, he heard, "Meese. Light it." He raised his hands and sent his ribbon of flame rolling outward, hitting the manticore low and lighting masses of dried grass and harvested fur. The room was instantly filled with acrid smoke swirling up the air shaft. Meese felt a breeze pushing at his back as the cool mine air was drawn into the room to feed the flames. Murra roared incoherently as his fur curled and smoked. He thrashed against the chain, finally tearing his wing loose, leaving a thin bone protruding from tattered membranes. He turned in rage to charge the group but was faced with the bristling spears, a burning room, and the glowing projectiles of white and red.

Gladlow shouted, "Hold until he charges us, we need him to get closer!" Meese assumed this was a lame attempt at a bluff, but it worked against a thing whose stupidity was only outstripped by its capacity for violence. Murra turned and leapt up into the airshaft and scrabbled out of view into the billowing smoke.

The group burst from the front gate in a swirl of white smoke and panicked miners. The sun had long since set, but the few torches and fires of the mining camp illuminated the beast as he leapt down from his ledge. He had no doubt been attempting an attack, but his damaged wing spun him around and he landed hard and painfully. He had taken a moment to remove the trap from his leg before diving at his enemies. Despite the singed fur and the utter indignity of his landing, Murra was unencumbered and ready for battle.

"It was a clever trap for such... not clever things," he intoned as he stalked forward, but his damaged paw dragged on the ground limply.

Carlin shouted, "The poison finally worked!"

Meese shouted back, "Is that it?"

He thought Carlin shrugged, but they were scattering to flank the beast and provide several targets. This was the part of the plan Meese didn't like, from a plan filled to bursting with unlikeable things. The mages paired off with warriors in the expectation Murra would feel strongly about them and hesitate. Meese stood in front of Carlin, Gladlow with Wellstone, Nowen with Voorsh. Pel stood alone, boar-spear at the ready. Murra would have to choose and they each had their orders to act accordingly. Meese was betting he would go for Pel. They all hoped he would go for Pel. It was an obvious trap, but was Murra too stupid to realize it was obvious on purpose? Or was he even stupider and didn't see a trap at all? Murra was operating on an entirely different level. He charged Gladlow. Meese performed his spell as he wondered about the beast's thought process. Was he attacking the leader, in the hopes of crushing their morale and sending them into confusion? Maybe Gladlow smelled more musky? Meese would definitely be bringing that up. As Meese sprayed his jet of fire across the monster's body, he guessed the truth. Murra's final strategy was to attack the tallest.

Murra's charge was only hampered slightly by running on three legs, and as he reared back to slash and bite, his poisoned leg didn't respond at all. Gladlow triggered his shield just in time as the jaws snapped forward and one paw raked across it. Wellstone timed her attack perfectly, dancing around Gladlow to sink her slim blade into the monster's eye as he lunged. Voorsh landed on his back, driving the twin bronze spikes of her buckler into his shoulder and dropping her copper war club down on the base of his skull. Carlin's javelin and Pel's spear sunk into opposite sides. Gladlow pitched a double-sized sphere of purple liquid into Murra's face as he launched himself upwards, wings flapping. He screamed as the poison splashed his eyes and mouth. His broken wing did little to keep him aloft, and he folded them before losing control, dropping a few yards away.

Nowen asked, "Now?"

Everyone screamed, "Yes, now!" and the bleeding, burning manticore fell forward, asleep.

Gladlow said, "Ready yourselves." He took his spear as Pel drew her sword. Most others prepared javelins. Meese looked around, embarrassed that he hadn't planned for this part when the roar of a hundred voices rose behind them. Meese raised his hand to wave just before the miners, Hobs, and Goblins, ran forward with hammers and chisels to set upon the manticore.

"They sort of stole the stage, huh?" He lowered his hand and backed away with the others. When the miners stood back, the beast was a bloody mess and so were they. The two groups stood looking at each other, and Gladlow suddenly raised his fist in the air and screamed something in Hob. There was no reaction for a heartbeat, then a Goblin shouted, "Yay!" and the crowd descended into back pats and friendly shoves. Meese noticed each group stayed to themselves, though. The Goblins were careful to stay clear of the Hobs.

Gladlow said, "I told them Dugg is giving them tomorrow off." He snapped his fingers at Meese and made the give-me motion. Meese sighed and dropped a silver in his hand. Gladlow called out to a Goblin, Meese thought it might be the one who shouted first. He got suspicious looks and the little fellows started to scatter. He flashed the silver at that particular one and lured him near.

"You speak common?"

"Better than you speak Gukk, sky-pockets." The Goblin had a snarky fearlessness that branded her as a female of the species even more certainly than the higher voice and not terribly unpretty eyes.

"Get word to Dugg and the silver's yours." He then turned his back to her.

"Half now." She tried to look tough and found some success.

Gladlow said over his shoulder, "I'll ask a Hob," but looked at Meese and flicked his head toward the Goblin.

Meese sighed and tossed a copper. She snatched it out of the air, and he said, "The silver goes to whoever brings your boss."

Gladlow asked him, "Can you do anything about the fire?"

Meese looked up at the smoke billowing up from the ledge above. "It's burning like a furnace. It can't go for long..."

"It's also cooking whatever valuables might be stashed."

Meese cursed and thrust his hat into his friend's chest. "I'll smell like burnt hair for a week."

. . . .

Wellstone stood by the entrance, trying to breathe shallowly. As much as Meese complained, he put out the fires quickly. Air from the mine shaft kept the smoke billowing up the chimney tunnel, so he was able to get close. He took a breath and held it, stepping into the doorway. He made his hand flat, with his thumb cocked oddly, and made a patting motion every few seconds. Each time, a small area of flames would go out. He managed it a dozen times before exiting for a breath. He gave one delicate cough and sat down on a broken limestone block near the others.

Meese said, "The fire's out, but that means more smoke. Couple of hours maybe."

Wellstone offered her water flask and sat on the ground, leaning on the same block. It took more than a couple of hours, it was nearly dawn before they could enter without choking. Mostly. They dragged the charred skins, greasy with burned fat, into one great pile. They had found absolutely nothing for the first hour, but Wellstone realized the stone slabs the manticore slept on were the obvious place. It took everyone to shift the huge blocks to reveal a large hollow filled with seastone ore, various trinkets, and coins. They bagged the semi-valuables by the time that little Goblin poked her head in.

"Dugg's here. Pay me." She held out her hand suspiciously.

Gladlow looked around obnoxiously and shrugged.

"He's in the camp. I swear." She clenched her fists and stomped out. A little while later Dugg walked in, the Goblin girl looking smug. She caught her coin and disappeared.

Dugg said, "I'd have come sooner if I knew you paid so well."

Meese said, "Congratulations on your freed mining operation."

"I saw the carcass. What did you lot do to him?"

"Little of this, little of that."

"He looks like he was in a rock slide. What's this I hear about the miners killing him?"

Gladlow jumped in with, "We thought it would be good for your reputation. Sure, you hired outside help, but we just softened him up for your mining crew."

"Nice. And the day off?"

"The mine was filled with smoke. Day off today, clean up tomorrow, and double shifts until the *Frenzy* returns."

Dugg said, "A sound plan, but we have a small problem..."

Gladlow said, "No. I think you'll find you have a small problem. Good luck."

"Listen, I'll honor the bargain. Of course, I will. You have nothing to worry about. I just can't put any extra miners on shift unless I can find more food."

"You knew that from the beginning, didn't you?"

Dugg puffed up in offense. "I planned to get it from emergency stores, but I was denied before I even asked. I was just casually told by the storehouse keeper that it's all being locked down until Captain Lenogg returns."

Wellstone asked, "So, someone in Ningolohk is keeping track of what's going on here?"

"That I already knew. Not sure how they figured out my plans for the mine though."

Pel asked, "So, how much do you need?"

Dugg said, "Well, I have the fishing boats out all day and night, but we can't go far because of the damn eels. I'm told we'll be set up for more shifts in a week. It's not as bad as it sounds. It only takes one extra meal to work a miner, they still get their daily rations from home."

Pel asked, "Well, if you switched to double tomorrow, how long until you run out of food?"

"Maybe four days."

Voorsh asked, "How many days if you eat the manticore?"

Everyone looked at her in mild shock.

Gladlow said, "Hobs are too superstitious to eat something that could speak."

Dugg said weakly, "It's not superstition, it's disgust."

"Though, I've heard Humans have been known to eat them... and Goblins will eat absolutely any meat."

Pel said, "Put the Goblins on manticore rations and feed the Hobs on regular. Will they mind?"

Dugg looked impressed. "The Goblins will love it. The Hobs will tolerate it."

"Is that enough to be caught up?"

"Another manticore would do it."

Gladlow said, "Damn it. You can set some Hobs up to tend the Gnoll's trapline, but that won't help right away."

Carlin took Voorsh aside, but not far enough to keep anyone from hearing. She asked, "Sweetie, would your people trade with the Hobgoblins?"

Dugg started to protest, but Gladlow waved him down.

Voorsh said, "Many would not like such a thing."

Dugg said, "I agree. I've had the same thought, but it will take a long time before we aren't seen as a threat."

Voorsh said, "No. We do not trade food. It is to be eaten by our people or shared with our friends. Uljar-Molik does not see you as a threat. You are like rats who get into the storehouse. We chase away the rats and build stronger boxes. Why would we give food to the rats?"

"We deserve that, but it's insulting..."

"It was not meant to be."

Meese said, "I have a question, Voorsh. Would Uljar-Molik make an exception for steel?"

Again, Dugg was shaking his head, but this time kept his mouth shut.

Voorsh said, "The... Hobs do not want us to have steel. They are careful not to allow it."

Meese said, "That's right. To them, Uljar-Molik is the enemy. Why would they give greater weapons to an enemy?"

Dugg said, "I'd be strung up by the ankles for giving weapons to the Lizards. I don't think I could get enough steel, anyway."

Carlin said, "Maybe it wouldn't have to be all steel. Some of the important people in the village wore seastone. It's obviously valuable to them. Voorsh, just for discussion, what would it take to get a manticore worth of meat from your people?"

"Your question is very confusing Carlin, but I understand." She stared into space for a moment while everyone held their breath. "The metal from the armory and one hundred pounds of seastone."

Dugg's eyes almost popped out. "For meat? That's robbery!"

Voorsh asked, "You make jokes to me of robbery?"

"Right. Poor choice of words. Forgive me. The weapons I can spare. They were supposed to be distributed long ago, but the armor..." He shook his head. "I can offer fifty pounds of raw seastone and the weapons."

Voorsh said, "The weapons, the weight of armor in raw metal, and two hundred pounds of seastone."

"This can't be happening. Weapons, fifty pounds of iron anchor, and one hundred of seastone."

"Yes, but the seastone will be one and one half hundred. You will give us one of the armors that appears as scales."

Dugg spit in his hand and held it out to her. She stared for a moment as the tension built. Then she leaned over and also spit in his hand. She said, "The barter is complete."

Chapter Four Excerpt, Traveler's Luck book two: Poison Harbor

Gladlow looked around at the deserted streets. He found the nearest guard-tower and saw no one in it. "Damnit." They started to jog up the middle of the road, keeping as much distance from the dark alleyways as possible.

Meese said, "Our plans didn't cover this..."

"We expected something. Let's get our backs to the water—"

Hooded figures swarmed from four alleys, black cloaks, and swords the only distinguishing features. Gladlow pointed as he ran toward the group on the front left, they were the closest and would be the least spread out by the time he reached them. At a full run, Gladlow released the percussion spell into the crowd with a window-rattling boom. Those that weren't knocked back fell unconscious a second later with the wave of Meese's hand. The three that made it through both spells were left with ringing ears and enough distance to fail at boxing the mages in. Gladlow and Meese ran into the open mouth of the alley, the three in close pursuit, and as many as thirty more soon after. They needed to get out of sight quickly or it would soon be too late. Gladlow burst out of the alley onto another street. It hadn't been his first choice of direction but they would correct that at the next alley. He said, "Burn 'em," and Meese loosed a jet of fire into the alley, setting the three black cloaks ablaze and sending the wearers rolling on the ground. Gladlow could see the mob entering the far end of the corridor as he and Meese ducked around the corner.

They were surrounded and cut off in the small intersection. Groups of three appeared at every exit, the mob splitting to block the streets. It was a supremely coordinated effort, and evidence of a massive conspiracy. These were armed Humans mobbing the deserted streets of the cove. Gladlow took a moment to consider the implications. It proved either a great deal of influence over the Hobs or a large outlay of monies. Just getting everyone the godsdamned matching cloaks was a huge undertaking.

About the Author

Eric Gibson is a multi-genre writer with a penchant for injecting humor into the darkest storylines. He strives to weave you better and better tales, so if you'd like to leave a review on your favorite site, remember that stars are great but words are even better. Even a simple "I loved it" or "Not for me" makes all the difference. Thanks so much for reading.

Read more at https://www.thrillingspree.com.

9 798223 734789